ACTI♡N

QUINN ANDERS♡N

RIPTIDE
PUBLISHING

I0636047

Riptide Publishing
PO Box 1537
Burnsville, NC 28714
www.riptidepublishing.com

This is a work of fiction. Names, characters, places, and incidents are either the product of the author's imagination or are used fictitiously. Any resemblance to actual persons living or dead, business establishments, events, or locales is entirely coincidental. All person(s) depicted on the cover are model(s) used for illustrative purposes only.

Action
Copyright © 2017 by Quinn Anderson

Cover art: L.C. Chase, lcchase.com/design.htm
Editor: May Peterson
Layout: L.C. Chase, lcchase.com/design.htm

All rights reserved. No part of this book may be reproduced or transmitted in any form or by any means, electronic or mechanical, including photocopying, recording, or by any information storage and retrieval system without the written permission of the publisher, and where permitted by law. Reviewers may quote brief passages in a review. To request permission and all other inquiries, contact Riptide Publishing at the mailing address above, at Riptidepublishing.com, or at marketing@riptidepublishing.com.

ISBN: 978-1-62649-573-9

First edition
June, 2017

Also available in ebook:
ISBN: 978-1-62649-572-2

ACTION

QUINN ANDERSON

For Teal:
"While it is always best to believe in oneself, a little help
from others can be a great blessing." — Uncle Iroh

TABLE
OF C♡NTENTS

CHAPTER

Pete drew a shuddering breath and moaned. "Oh God, that feels so good." He arched his back, biting his lip in what he hoped was an enticing way.

"*You* feel good," grunted the man above him. Antoine. Or at least that was his stage name. He was hovering over Pete, naked except for his underwear. A thin sheen of sweat glistened on his skin. He'd inserted one of his legs between Pete's, spreading his thighs.

Pete's gaze dipped once down his toned body before he looked squarely at him. "I want you so badly."

Antoine skimmed his lips along Pete's jaw. "I can't wait to fuck you."

"Cut!" snapped a voice to their left.

The production team groaned in unison. The light shining in Pete's face lowered, allowing him to see beyond it for the first time in twenty minutes. Not that it did him much good. The set was doused in murky shadow. A handful of amorphous figures scurried to adjust the equipment dotting the periphery.

Pete propped himself up on an elbow, making the faux leather sofa he was reclining on squeak, and sought out a familiar silhouette. "What is it this time, Colette?"

"It's not you, Jaden," Colette reassured. "Your costar keeps ruining my shots."

Just then, the light tech adjusted the umbrella lamp back toward them. Pete blinked red spots out of his eyes and squinted in Colette's general direction. Though he couldn't see her face, he was willing to bet she was wearing her trademark scowl.

"Hey," Antoine protested, twisting his body toward her. "I didn't do anything wrong." When he shifted, he unwittingly jammed his elbow into Pete's solar plexus.

Pete—or Jaden, as he was known on screen—winced but didn't complain. This was far from the most uncomfortable he'd been during a scene. In fact, between the hot lights and Antoine's considerable weight crushing him, he was grateful to still have feeling in his limbs. He wiggled his toes just to be sure.

"Oh really?" Colette said sourly. "Because I could have sworn you were whispering sweet nothings to Jaden just then."

"Uh, yeah, I was." Antoine's full lips tilted down. "You told us to talk dirty to each other."

"The key word there is *talk*, not whisper. You have to speak loudly enough for the mics to pick up what you're saying." She pointed to one of the fuzzy boom microphones hanging over their heads. "Every time you speak against his skin like that—hot as it looks on film—we can't see your pretty face anymore, and more importantly, we can't *hear* you. The sexiest dirty talk in the world is worthless if our viewers don't know what the hell you're saying."

"Oh. Whoops." Antoine grimaced.

Colette pinched the bridge of her nose. "Look, kid, I get that you're new, but I need your learning curve to be less of a gentle merge and more of a tire-squealing *Tokyo Drift*."

"Okay," he agreed, nodding. "I think I can do that."

"Can you? I'm beginning to have doubts. Your call time was eight this morning. What time is it now?"

His face blanked. He scrambled for his phone, which he'd tucked between the couch cushions the moment he'd gotten on set. Every time they had a break, he dove straight for it, leaving Pete to either watch him text or find ways to occupy himself. Pete had already had six cigarettes this morning as a result.

Antoine clicked a side button, and the screen came to life. "It's a little after eleven."

"Which means?"

"Which means . . . it's almost lunchtime?"

A world-weary sigh sounded from the darkness. If Pete were a more poetic person, it might have given him some existential anguish.

"It means," groused Colette, "that between sound checks, lighting checks, and the actual filming, we've been at this for over three hours. And you know what we've got to show for it? Jack with a side of shit. Unless of course you think our subscribers are going to pay to watch two shirtless dudes make out for ten minutes. Because for that, they could just as easily turn on HBO."

The shadowy figure that was Colette shifted, her arms moving like she was massaging her temples. "I know I told you not to be shy with the foreplay, but for fuck's sake, get to it. We still have a whole anal scene to go."

Pete wanted to put a pillow over his head and block them all out. He hated it when Colette was pissed off, even if it wasn't directed at him. He had to admit, though, she was right. Antoine kept screwing up every time they got remotely close to the "big moment." Pete was surprised his costar had managed to stay hard this whole time, considering how little they'd done. He'd have to ask him afterwards how he did it. Probably Viagra or TriMix or one of the other classics.

Colette's voice broke Pete from his thoughts. "We're going to take a break. When we come back, Antoine, you're going to get your shit together and perform like you mean it. Are we clear?"

Antoine nodded, but his eyes had already strayed to his phone.

Colette muttered something under her breath and then directed her attention at Pete. "A word, Jaden?"

It sounded like a question, but her tone said otherwise.

He began the process of extracting himself from beneath Antoine, which was easier said than done. Partially because Pete was all limbs and partially because Antoine wasn't much help. He rolled onto his side but otherwise didn't move, fingers flying over the screen of his phone.

"New boyfriend?" Pete asked as he extricated himself.

Antoine smiled without looking up. "Girlfriend, yeah. How'd you guess?"

"I was glued to my phone just like that not too long ago. Didn't end well, though. Here's hoping you and your girl have better luck."

When he was free, he stepped carefully over the cords crisscrossing the floor, bypassed the large, imposing cameras, and edged up to Colette. All he had on was a thin pair of boxers, but he wasn't hard, and the crew members were too occupied with their equipment to bother with him. He'd worn less in front of bigger crowds. Considering his profession, it wasn't like he could afford to be modest anyway.

Colette's attention was fixed on a nearby review screen, on which the camera feed was playing in real time. Even just fiddling with his phone, Antoine looked good. Fit. Muscular. Pete made a mental note to do some weightlifting the next time he was at the gym. He cleared his throat in case she hadn't heard him approach. "What's up?"

"Where's your head at?" Colette asked without preamble.

He folded his arms across his chest. "What do you mean? Was I not good?" He gave her a surreptitious once-over, trying to gauge if he was in for a scolding. He didn't know much about his boss, except that she'd been in the biz for decades, and she suffered exactly zero fools.

She was dressed casually in jeans and a pink sweater, and she'd twisted her blonde hair up into a cute, messy bun. Wearing street clothes was always a good idea at Murmur Inc. They had no dress code to speak of, and anyone who spent time on a porn set ran the risk of... Well, the term *splash zone* came to mind. Her demeanor matched her relaxed attire, thankfully. Maybe he'd be spared.

Colette answered, "You were fine. In fact, I'd almost call you convincing."

"Almost?"

She considered him. He fought a strong desire to shield himself with his hands. "When I said you weren't the issue, I was being generous. I've worked with you long enough to know when you're not giving it your all."

Damn. He'd thought he'd put on a pretty good show. "What do you mean? I moaned in all the right places, and—"

"Is it your costar?" she interrupted. "Not doing it for you?"

He glanced at Antoine. He was shorter than Pete but cut like marble, with gorgeous bone structure and legs that declared a love of jogging.

"No, he's attractive. I think we can both agree on that. I'm just used to a little more ... professional courtesy."

"Ah, so he's not flirting with you? I noticed you two weren't talking much. That's never a good sign."

"Pretty much, yeah. I mean, it's not like it's a requirement, but having sex with a complete stranger is easier if they at least pretend to like you. Helps to grease the wheels, so to speak."

Colette nodded. "I get it. I remember that from back in my day. So, is that all it is? You two don't have chemistry?"

"That must be it." Pete pretended to survey the set, hoping she'd lose interest.

It didn't work. "You know, this isn't exactly a new occurrence. You're normally one of my better actors, but you've seemed distracted in the past few films I've cast you in. Even when you hit it off with your costars, the energy is never quite right. Is there something else going on?"

"No." Pete unfolded his arms, hoping to look less defensive, but that left him with nothing to do with his hands. His fingers itched for a cigarette. He prayed he didn't look as maladroit as he felt. "What could be going on?"

"You tell me. Something with school? Or your mom?" She looked at him sidelong. "Maybe you've got a new boyfriend on your mind?"

At that, Pete burst out laughing.

Colette glowered. "Laugh all you want, but I've lost some of my best actors to love. It happens."

Pete wheezed. "Not to me. See, to have a boyfriend, I'd have to actually speak to a man without falling all over myself."

"You manage pretty well when you're on camera."

"That's different. That's Jaden talking."

Colette made a rude noise. "I don't have time to play counselor. I have a lot of bland footage to painstakingly edit until it looks like you and lover boy over there are doing more than flopping halfheartedly against each other. But, for the record, dating is seldom easy for people like us, introverted or not."

Pete couldn't help but quip, "'Us'? You haven't starred in a film in, what? Two decades?"

"I don't mean porn stars, Jaden." She swept her hand around the room in a broad gesture. "I mean the men, women, and variations thereupon of the adult entertainment industry. You think anyone at Murmur Inc. has an easy time with relationships? News flash: dating involves getting to know one another, and eventually people ask what you do for a living. Just picture it. 'Hi, I'm Joe, and I spend my days having phone sex with strangers.' Or better yet, 'My name's Kim, and I masturbate in front of a webcam for money.' That tends to cut first dates short."

"Well, you don't have to worry about me. My complete lack of allure has ensured I'm not going to steal someone's heart anytime soon."

Colette looked beseechingly heavenward. "Like I would let you star in so many of my films if you weren't attractive. You may not have the same appeal as Antoine the Chiseled, but lots of people are into the baby-faced, big-eyed twink thing you have going on. Plus, you're tall."

"Wow," Pete deadpanned. "That's exactly what a man likes to hear. I may not be built or conventionally attractive, but at least most porn sites have a category devoted to me."

"Last I checked, that was a good thing in this industry. But whatever. Wallow in insecurity if you want." She pulled a phone out of her pocket and checked it. "Take fifteen, and then we'll try again. Hydrate, do some stretching, and above all else, work out whatever it is that keeps pulling you from the moment. People don't want to watch you think. They want to watch you get off."

Pete shifted from foot to foot. He wondered how many years he'd have to work in the sex industry before the frankness stop fazing him. "Yes, boss."

"Good. See you in fifteen." With that, she strode off, her black pumps clicking on the tile. When she reached the door, she threw it open, revealing a scene that was almost shockingly incongruous with the studio.

The hustle and bustle of Murmur Inc. lay beyond the door. The soundproof filming booths made it easy to forget there was a whole office waiting outside. And, at any given time, it was packed with people engaged in a variety of tasks, from phone sex to actual office work.

Colette's exit drew the attention of a few nearby employees, but none of them took notice of Pete. A half-naked man wasn't exactly an unusual sight around these parts. Even if it were, the door slammed shut again too quickly for them to register his lackluster presence.

Pete hunted around for his clothes, intent on having his umpteenth cigarette. His pants were strewn on the floor where Antoine had unceremoniously tossed them. He yanked them on and stuck his hands in the front pocket. When his fingers closed around a crumpled pack of cigarettes, he breathed a sigh of relief. Next he located his shirt and the long-sleeved flannel he'd thrown over it. His shoes and socks were a bit more difficult, but he managed to tug them on without tumbling over.

"I'm going for a cig," he announced to no one in particular.

None of the crew members looked up from what they were doing, and Antoine seemed even more disinterested in him than before, if that were possible. It wasn't personal, he reminded himself, but it still stung. He slipped out the door before his sense of rejection could reach critical mass.

The office looked like any other: there were cubicles, harried interns buzzing around, and even a break room featuring free, mediocre coffee. What set it apart, however, was the line of soundproof booths running along the wall. The tinted glass was impossible to see through, but a few of the red Live lights were on—including the one next to the booth Pete had just vacated.

The way he heard it, Murmur Inc. had once been a recording studio, but it had gone out of business sometime between eight-tracks and CDs. Once Colette scooped it up, however, she'd transformed it into one of Los Angeles's top adult entertainment companies. It had started out just filming porn, but with the advent of the internet, evolution had been obligatory. Now, it dabbled in a bit of everything.

Pete headed for the exit on the left, dodging scantily clad nurses and men in bondage gear as he went. He slipped through a double door and into a poorly lit staircase. Two flights of stairs later, he hit the outside air, and crisp sunlight left him blinking for the third time in the past ten minutes. It was a clear day, and *freezing*, but he took a deep, savoring breath.

He scanned the parking lot, surprised to find it devoid of people. Pretty much everyone at Murmur Inc. smoked. He couldn't say if it was the sex part or the office part that did it. Both seemed equally likely. When he wanted a moment to himself, it was difficult to find. It seemed luck was on his side today.

He stuck a cigarette between his lips and lit it with a cheap, plastic lighter. He sucked down a lungful of smoke. Eyes closed, he luxuriated in the sweet, satisfying nicotine. He exhaled, took another puff, and hugged himself for warmth. LA had mild winters, but his skinny frame provided no insulation. The wind cut through him like he was made of tissue paper.

Still, the cold helped to clear his head. Colette was right. He wasn't in it today, and that needed to change yesterday. She hadn't harped on him about it yet—not really, anyway—but if his work continued to slip, she wouldn't hesitate. Desperate young actors were a dime a dozen. If she wanted to replace him, all she had to do was take a stroll down Hollywood Boulevard with a sign that read, *No Experience Necessary.*

Pete couldn't risk burning a bridge with one of the biggest porn producers on the West Coast. Whatever mental block he was undergoing, he needed to take a wrecking ball to it.

At least he knew what his problem was. Well, sort of. The immediate issue was he kept getting sucked into his own head. There were so many little things to worry about in front of the camera. Was he making a weird face? Was his hair messed up? Were his abs flexed? Were his limbs in the way? He could go on.

The idea that porn was considered "easy money" made him want to laugh and cry at the same time. In reality, it was ten percent sex and ninety percent stamina. A twelve-minute clip took hours to film. It was grueling, even for a seasoned actor like him.

But that wasn't all that was holding him back. He'd never admit it out loud—Colette would fire him on the spot—but in truth, his job just didn't excite him anymore. The idea seemed strange, even to him. What could possibly be a bigger rush than life as a porn star? That was what Pete had thought when he'd first started. He'd hoped porn would get him out of his shell, make him more adventurous . . . Maybe even get people to notice him.

And in the beginning, it had.

He came alive in front of the camera. He said and did things he never would in real life. Now, however, it was a year later, and he wasn't the new kid on the block anymore. A fresh batch of porn stars was always right around the corner: new faces willing to do more for less. Every day, Pete found himself less and less motivated. The regular sex was still nice, but gone was the shivery, almost guilty thrill he'd felt the day he'd stepped foot on his first set.

In short, he was restless.

It wasn't like he'd planned on doing this forever. Few people did. He knew some women who joked about making grandma porn someday, but they were the exception, not the rule. Porn wasn't most people's end game.

Regardless of Pete's future plans, he needed to get it together, or Colette would decide it was time for him to retire whether he was ready or not. He couldn't let that happen. Tuition wasn't cheap, and he had no intention of graduating with back-breaking debt like his classmates.

He took one more drag before tapping his cigarette out and tossing it in a nearby trash can. Then he squared his shoulders and whispered, "'Once more unto the breach.'"

Back inside, he stopped at a water fountain and gulped down a few much-needed mouthfuls before heading back into Booth Eight. Everyone was more or less where he'd left them, though Colette had returned. She was fiddling with one of the cameras, minutely adjusting a series of switches. She looked up when he approached. "Ah, Jaden. Right on time. Strip down to your skivvies, and be snappy about it. We need to get going."

Pete rushed to comply, shedding his clothes in half the time it had taken to put them on.

"All right," she said when he was once more standing in his underwear. "I want you two to really go at it. Show me some passion. Antoine, you need a minute?" She waved vaguely at his crotch.

Antoine fondled his considerable erection through his boxers and then gave her a thumbs-up. "I'm good."

Pete stared despite himself. He really needed to find out what Antoine used. As something of a professional bottom, Pete was seldom required to be hard, but still. It might come in handy.

"Jaden, you ready?"

He nodded and slid onto the couch. "Yeah."

"Then we'll pick back up with kissing. Don't linger too long on that, though. We have plenty of shots of you groping each other. I want cocks out and lube on in the next five minutes."

They both saluted, and this time, when she called action, they kissed with enthusiasm. It was sloppier than Pete liked, with too much tongue and not enough lip play, but he bet it looked good on camera. At the end of the day, that was all that mattered.

When Antoine reached for Pete's underwear, he moved to help, lifting his hips so they could slide easily off and join his pants on the floor. His exposed cock was soft, but Antoine didn't seem to care. He spent a moment palming Pete for good measure before moving on, sliding a hand between his ass cheeks. Pete, for his part, acted like every touch was ecstasy, letting out exaggerated moans at all the right times. Even he thought he sounded into it.

Antoine hands grew surer on Pete's body. Within seconds, he reached for the bottle of lube they'd stashed next to the couch ahead of time. He handed it to Pete so he could make a show of preparing himself, though that too had been done in advance. Pete slipped two lubed fingers easily in, and this time when he moaned, it was genuine.

Moments like this reminded him why he'd stuck around for as long as he had. He was being paid to masturbate while a sexy man got ready to fuck him senseless. He could think of worse gigs.

Antoine procured a condom from between the couch cushions and rolled it down his length. He lined himself up and waited for Pete to withdraw his fingers before pressing forward. There was no build up, no pause of anticipation before the big moment, just a blunt, stretching sensation that made the bright lights dim in comparison.

Pete breathed in and out, relaxing as much as he could. Antoine, to his credit, gave Pete plenty of time to adjust before he sunk home. They had to stop a few times to get direction from Colette—which meant freezing in place, mid-fucking, while she arranged their limbs the way she wanted, like flowers in a vase—but for the most part, the scene was going smoothly.

At one point, Antoine flipped him onto his stomach and started fucking him in earnest. When that happened, Pete lost himself in the simple pleasure skittering up his spine. He even managed to get off, though his orgasm was only superficially satisfying. He had a newfound appreciation for the phrase *scratching an itch*. And the scene didn't finish when Pete did. They both had to keep going until the director told them they could stop. And Colette was nothing if not thorough.

The four-hour mark passed with no indication that they were nearing the end. Pete's energy flagged in a big way. His back ached, his muscles screamed, and all he wanted was to take a nap. Alone. Without anyone touching him. But Antoine was going strong. His dick jamming repeatedly into Pete was enough of a reminder.

Mercifully, about ten minutes later, Colette announced, "We have enough now to piece something together. You can come whenever you're ready, Antoine. Make sure the camera can see the big finish."

Antoine laughed and made a point of sinking deeply into Pete. "I could do this all day."

Pete spasmed, more from overstimulation than from pain. Even if he wanted to feel good at this point, he wasn't sure he could. It was all beginning to be too much.

It wasn't the most honest move, but Pete knew what he had to do.

He angled his hips up, allowing Antoine to sink deeply into him, and then clenched his sphincter muscles.

Antoine swore behind him, and his most recent thrust quavered. "Jesus, you're tight. Stay just like that."

"Oh yes," Pete moaned, barely keeping himself from sounding bored. "Fuck me, please. I love your cock."

He kept his muscles taut, his body stretched out like a bowstring, and after a few more sumptuous groans, Antoine's rhythm faltered. Even if he weren't a sex worker, Pete would know what that meant. Sure enough, Antoine only managed to rock into him half a dozen more times before he pulled out with a cry. He massaged the base of his cock as the tip of the condom filled.

Pete twisted around and pretended to watch rapturously. They held their positions until Colette called, "Cut! Wrap it. Or unwrap it, in Antoine's case."

A chorus of laughter sounded from the crew, and with a signal from Colette, it was over. The crew members started breaking down the set before Pete had even moved into a sitting position.

Antoine got up on shaky legs and offered him a hand. Pete waved it off with a polite smile. Standing wasn't a viable option for him just yet. Antoine shrugged and headed for a trash can, likely to dispose of the condom.

Pete watched his bare ass as he walked away, and then threw an arm over his face, blocking out the light. He was exhausted, his bangs were matted to his brow with sweat, and he was sticky all over.

He was going to sleep well tonight.

"Jaden? Got a moment?"

Pete uncovered his eyes and lolled his head in the direction of the sound. Colette was standing next to the couch, eyeing it like she wanted to sit but had the good sense not to.

"Need something?" he asked, slurring slightly. He yawned, mouth wide open.

"You did good today. After our conversation, at least. It was nice of you to help Antoine."

"I didn't do anything special."

"Don't deny it. It's a particular talent of yours. Not only can you convince the audience that you're into it, but you can convince your costars as well. It makes them perform better. If it hadn't been for all that moaning and writhing you did, the whole film would have fallen flat."

"Thank you." He hesitated. "I don't deserve it, though. I was just doing my job."

"Sure you do. I wouldn't have said it otherwise. But as it turns out, your job is precisely what I wanted to talk to you about."

His heart somersaulted.

She snorted. "Jesus, calm down. I didn't think it was possible to go from sexpert to skittish rabbit in three seconds flat. I have a proposition for you. The role of a lifetime, assuming you don't screw it up."

He raised a brow. "Right now?"

"Course not. That'd be cruel." Her smile was angelic.

Phew. Thank God.

"It's tonight."

Pete's groan sounded like an elephant's death wail. Just the idea of filming again made his ass clamp up. "I'm sorry, but I don't think I can. I'm spent, in an imaginative variety of ways."

"Hear me out. I'm planning a new summer series."

"It's winter."

Her eye roll emphasized the prodigious length of her fake eyelashes. "Brilliant observation, but as you should damn well know by now, anything with a summer release date needs to be filmed in the winter. We have quality standards to maintain. You want our films to look cheap?"

"Perish the thought."

"Exactly. So, like I said, it's going to be a big summer blockbuster. I'm talking heavy promos, teaser trailers, multiple filming sessions, the whole shebang. I'm going to call it *Heat Wave*. Pretty sexy, right?"

"Sure," Pete agreed. "What does that have to do with me?"

"Don't be coy. Obviously I'm thinking of casting you in it. You fit right into my artistic vision."

Pete would have scowled if he'd had the energy. "Meaning I look the part. I'm guessing you need a twink type to play opposite some muscled bear."

"More or less." She shrugged. "Is that such a bad thing?"

"The whole big top with little bottom thing is *so* played."

"Which is why we're going to deviate from the script a bit. *Heat Wave* isn't just porn. It has a story."

"Oh?"

"Yeah. It's about a shy college student who blossoms over summer vacation with the help of an experienced lover. It's a classic coming-of-age story. With lots and lots of fucking. You'll love it."

"I dunno. Sounds pretty typical to me."

"Don't write it off so quickly. This role isn't like anything I've offered you before. There's actual acting involved, for one thing. And scripts and photoshoots. Clothed ones. You used to model, right?" She nudged him with her foot. "When was the last time you were in front of a camera without your cock out?"

"I can't recall." Pete's mind was shutting down in rebellion.

"Hey, focus." She snapped her fingers in front of his face just as his eyes started to drift shut. "Tell me you'll think about it. This is a huge opportunity. And, frankly, you're lucky I'm offering it to you, considering how off your game you've been."

Pete frowned. "Not to push my luck, but why *are* you?"

"Because you've made me a lot of money in the past, and we all have bad days. I see potential in you. If you give it your all, I think you'll do great."

Coming from Colette, that was high praise. "Is the role mine, then?"

"Do you really think I'd make it that easy for you? You'll have to audition, but if you and the lead have the right chemistry, it's steady work. And steady pay."

At that, Pete perked up. "How much are we talking?"

"More than you've made doing the odd anal scene here and there."

Pete wavered. In this industry, even the big names had no guarantees about where their next paycheck was coming from. Job security was worth more than gold. And if he said no, Colette would be certain to remember this the next time a big role was up for grabs. Still, he had to look after himself. He wouldn't be any good to anyone if he sexed himself ragged.

"Who's the lead?" he asked. "Or are you auditioning for that role too?"

"Oh no, we know exactly who your potential leading man is. He's something of a rising star. I've been dying to work with him, but he's a crossover."

"Ah. He does straight porn too?"

"*Did* straight porn. My understanding is he's crossed over for the last time."

"Really?" Pete rubbed his chin. "So, is he straight, or bi, or what?" He knew a lot of gay men who thought banging a straight guy was the ultimate fantasy, but Pete preferred partners who weren't likely to have an identity crisis in the middle of a shoot.

"No clue. He's probably like your new buddy, Antoine. Straight as a wicket, but he knows there's way more money in gay porn, so here he is. That's the kind of business acumen I admire in today's youth." She flashed a toothy grin. "Either way, he comes with a whole truckload of logistical complications, thanks to how the straight side of porn handles STIs. I had to wait for him to get tested and cleared before I could cast him in anything."

"Jesus. Call me old-fashioned, but I vastly prefer Murmur Inc.'s policy: condoms, condoms, condoms."

"Well, if you do well in your audition tonight, you can double bag it for all I care."

He started to cite something he'd read once in a pamphlet about how that was actually less safe, but then he realized she was joking. "This guy must be an amazing fuck if you're willing to go through all that just to work with him."

Colette gave him a stern look. "I know we're sex workers, but you don't have to be so *crude*."

He smiled sheepishly. "Sorry."

"I'm just fucking with you. It's nice to see you unclench. And you're right, by the way. He's extra effort, but he's worth it. If I have my way, he'll be a regular addition to our roster."

"Do I get to know his name?"

"No, I know you. You'll google him and make all sorts of assumptions. I want you to meet him and let first impressions speak for themselves. I have a feeling you two are going to hit it off. I'll text you the time and place of the audition. Say you'll be there?"

After a lengthy pause, Pete said, "I'll think about it."

"Wise decision." She patted him on the shoulder and then wiped her hand on her jeans. "I'll let you recuperate. Go shower or meditate or whatever it is you need to do. I'll see you later."

When she'd gone, Pete sagged back against the couch, not even caring that he was still naked. He felt like he'd just waged some sort of battle. And lost.

Antoine had disappeared—he'd probably scurried away before Colette could get him in her sights—but the production team was still packing up. Pete watched them idly while he mulled over Colette's proposal. He needed the money. He always needed the money. But could he really handle two shoots in one day? Colette had said it was just an audition. That usually meant sex, but not always. Maybe he wouldn't have to do much.

The internal debate must have overwhelmed Pete, because the next thing he knew, he was waking up. He looked around, bewildered by the unfamiliar couch he was on and the blank walls all around him. A moment later, he remembered where he was.

"Shit," he said to the empty room. Everyone else was gone. It wasn't unusual for porn stars to nap between sets, so probably no one had thought to wake him. Pushing himself onto shaky legs, he located his jeans and slid his phone out of his back pocket.

"*Shit*," he repeated when he saw the time. He'd been asleep for hours. Good thing he'd had the foresight to tell his mom he might be late for dinner.

His notifications alerted him to a new text he'd received. An address and a time flashed onto the screen. Colette's audition. He would love to pretend he'd forgotten, but he suspected even his unconscious self had been fretting about it.

The address looked like a residence at first glance. That wasn't surprising. Porn was often filmed at people's houses. From the zip code, Pete guessed it was in Pasadena. He could google it to be sure, but he estimated it'd take him twenty minutes to drive there.

He took stock of himself. He felt better than he had before his nap, but that wasn't saying much. The smell of sweat and sex oozed from his pores. He desperately needed a shower. And to brush his teeth. And to take care of a few other maintenance issues.

Fuck it. Colette can be as pissed as she wants. I'm done for the day.

He was about to send her a halfhearted excuse when his phone buzzed in his hand. Colette had texted him again. He frowned. It was a photo this time. Why would she . . . ?

He opened the message.

In case you need some inspiration, it read.

But Pete barely noticed the text.

The photo was of a young man, and the moment Pete laid eyes on him, he knew he was fucked.

CHAPTER 2

Forty-five minutes later, Pete lurched up to a swanky house on Del Mar Boulevard in his derelict sedan. He started to double-check the address only to realize he didn't need to. There was a conspicuous cluster of cars parked out front, including Colette's red Mustang. It was safe to say he'd found the right place.

He parked his clunker by the curb and stepped out, not bothering to lock the doors. If someone stole it, the joke would be on them. The fading sun cast the street in hazy orange light interspersed with deep shadows. Out here in the suburbs, there were no monstrous buildings to block the sky, and so he had an unimpeded view of the sun's golden crown as it dipped below the horizon. The cold seemed to make the colors more vibrant, the contrast more vivid. He would have appreciated the simple beauty of it if he were one iota less nervous.

Standing in the driveway, he smoothed his clothes and ran trembling fingers through his wet hair. He'd stopped off at home to shower, rushing to avoid being late. His shaggy brown hair was heavy with water, plastered to his angular face. He'd thrown on his favorite blue hoodie for luck without thinking. His red flannel shirt peeked out at the sleeves, clashing horribly with it. He probably looked like he'd tumbled out of a washing machine. Anxiety trailed a cold finger down his spine. Maybe he should blow off the audition after all.

The photo Colette had sent him flashed before his eyes. His feet began walking up the driveway of their own accord.

The house wasn't a mansion by any means, but it made Pete's place look like a roach motel. He approached the double front doors, trying to ignore his erratic pulse. When he knocked, one of them swung open on its own. He absently wondered if Hitchcock was directing this gig.

He stuck his head in and was met by the sound of distant voices. He entered a well-lit and pleasantly decorated foyer, sneakers squeaking on the polished hardwood floor. No one appeared to welcome him, so he followed the voices down a short hallway.

When he rounded the corner into a living room, it took everything he had not to visibly react. The room had cheerful, coral walls and modern décor. Gray throw pillows decorated two large white sofas, and a patterned rug covered the floor. The recessed lights had been dimmed, creating a relaxed and intimate atmosphere.

But Pete's attention was captivated by six young men lounging on the sofas: his competition, undoubtedly. They were all lanky and waifish like Pete, with fair complexions and boyish features. Only someone had swapped out his gawkiness and replaced it with model-like good looks. There wasn't an average one in the bunch.

Pete swallowed. Well, this was off to a fabulous start.

"Hi," he greeted the room, raising a stiff hand. "The door was open, so I just, um. Yeah."

Two of them glanced at him, but no one replied. His face burned. There wasn't room on either sofa for him to sit, so he lounged in the doorway. Or at least, he attempted to. As was often the case, he had no idea what to do with his hands. He started to shove them into his pockets, but then changed his mind and crossed his arms over his chest. A moment later, he decided that looked too hostile. He let them hang at his sides, wondering if it were physically possible for him to be more awkward.

Voices to the right drew his attention to an open doorway he hadn't noticed before. Through it was a formal dining room. Colette was seated at a marble-top table with a mountain of paperwork stacked in front of her. A middle-aged blonde woman was sitting next to her; they were deep in conversation.

Pete couldn't hear what they were saying, but he was willing to bet the woman was the owner. She kept glancing at the men in the living room with big, moony eyes. He'd seen that look before. Must've been her first time. She was probably signing a release form right now.

Before he could attempt to get Colette's attention, a man strolled into sight.

"Are you done yet?" the man drawled. "I wanna get this party started already."

Colette said something back, but Pete wasn't listening. He froze even as his body temperature spiked. Though he'd never seen the man before, Pete instantly recognized him.

Christ. His photo hadn't done him justice.

The man had a swimmer's build: tall and lean. Pete could tell because he was wearing nothing but an unbuttoned black coat and gray briefs. Despite standing half-naked in a room full of people, confidence oozed from him. Pete wanted to reach out and see if he could actually feel it radiating from him like heat.

But if he were going to reach for anything, it'd be the man's glossy brown hair. It had been swept up into soft peaks that begged him to grab a handful. Pete's fingers tingled at his sides with the urge to touch it. The man had no body hair to go with it—porn stars seldom did—but he did have a hint of stubble on his sharp jaw, no more than a shadow. Pete could vividly imagine how it would feel scraping against his throat.

The man bent over the table to look at one of the papers in front of Colette, unwittingly highlighting the curve of his back. Fuck, if Pete had that body—and those cheekbones, for that matter—he'd be confident too.

Pete was staring. He knew he was, but he couldn't stop. Part of him wanted to write Colette a thank-you note, but another, much more paranoid part wanted to ask if she somehow knew how much the man looked like *him*. Pete's very own Evil Ex-Boyfriend. His Moby with an emphasis on Dick. Most people had a "one that got away." Pete had a "one who hurt him so badly, he wished they'd never dated in the first place." He still didn't like to talk about what had gone down between them.

Though that certainly hadn't stopped him from showing up for the audition. He must be some sort of masochist. Here he was, dead tired and looking like a mess, and yet he'd dragged himself out to the 'burbs for . . . what? A chance to confirm with his own eyes that his ex had not, in fact, become a porn star? Because *that* would have been hilarious, and so fucking hypocritical—

He shook his head, slamming a mental door shut on that train of thought. Regardless of who he looked like, his possible new costar was a five-alarm hottie. That was enough to pique Pete's interest, even as his insides squirmed.

As if on cue, the man glanced up and locked eyes with him. Pete tried to look away—he really did—but was rooted to the spot. Maybe it was the light, but Pete swore he'd never seen eyes that dark before. Pupil and iris were indistinguishable from each other. While Pete stood there helplessly, the man's gaze slid once, oh so slowly, down his body, and when he looked back up again, his eyes *blazed*.

Pete had been right. He was definitely fucked. It was as though the phrase *tall, dark, and handsome* had just been personally demonstrated to him.

The man turned to Colette—Pete could expound about the length of his neck—and whispered something. Colette's head shot up, and she looked directly at Pete.

Well, I wonder who they're talking about.

The man left as quickly as he'd appeared, though not before Pete got an eyeful of his plump ass. Jesus. His underwear might as well have been painted on.

When he was gone, Pete dragged his eyes back to Colette. She was watching him, her pink lips curled up in amusement.

Busted.

Colette turned to the blonde woman and said something he couldn't hear. They stood up and made their way into the living room.

"Gentlemen," Colette announced, "thank you for your patience. Joyce and I have tied up the last few loose ends, so if you've all got your IDs and paperwork ready, the auditions can begin."

A cheer rose up from the potentials. Pete stayed quiet, however, ruminating. There was no guarantee he was going to get this part, but he suddenly wanted it very, very badly.

"Chris, Chaz," Colette continued, turning to two of the men, "you're up first. Darko is waiting for you in the bedroom."

Darko? Like the movie? That was an odd choice for a stage name. Kinda gothic-sounding. Though it was light-years more interesting than *Chaz*. Sometimes he wondered what his colleagues were thinking.

Colette beckoned toward the door that Darko—was that his first or last name?—had just used. Chris and Chaz scrambled to their feet and disappeared through it. Judging by their eagerness, they'd also seen something they liked.

When they were gone, Colette made a beeline for him. She was grinning in a way that made Pete want to fall back a step. Like a lioness who'd just spotted a limping antelope. "Glad you could make it, Jaden. I had a feeling you would."

"Well, that picture was hard to ignore," he admitted. "But I'm sure you knew that."

"I had an inkling. I take it you like my newest star?" She raised a suggestive brow.

Pete hoped the flush crawling up his neck wasn't visible. "He's pretty gorgeous. You said his name is Darko?"

"Kyle Darko, to be precise. He's relatively new, but I have high aspirations for him. And for you, for that matter. Somehow, you managed to make an impression already."

Pete's heart thudded in his chest. "What do you mean?"

"When he spoke to me just then, he expressed a desire to work with you."

Pete frowned. "That sounds . . . bland."

"His exact words were 'I'd hit that at Mach five.'"

Electricity crackled up Pete's spine. His voice was embarrassingly breathy as he asked, "Really?"

"Yeah. Assuming you don't blow your audition, I'd say your chances are good."

Excitement flooded into him unchecked. Colette had wanted him to get his old spark back, and it seemed Kyle had already lit a fire within him. If Kyle could make him feel all this with a look, Pete could only imagine what actually touching him would be like.

So far, so good, though when the audition rolled around, he'd have to curb himself. If he appeared too eager, he'd look like a newb, or worse, a creep. Besides, he'd worked with some of the hottest guys in the industry. This was nothing new.

He needed to remember what was really important here: a chance to secure a steady paycheck for a couple of weeks. Every other job he'd booked had consisted of him showing up, having sex, and then leaving. If Colette was serious about having multiple filming sessions, this was going to be the most involved role he'd ever landed.

"I'll do my absolute best," he said in what he hoped was a casual way. "This role is a great opportunity. I really hope I get it."

"Me too. We'll see what Darko says after he's finished with the others. Some of them have a lot more experience than you."

"Is he picking his costar? I thought you were."

"A little of column A, a little of column B. Obviously I value his opinion. The chemistry needs to be just right, so if he says a guy is out, he's out."

Pete whistled to cover the anxiety that pierced through him. "Wow, you must really want him to be so accommodating."

"You'll understand when you meet him. He has this... magnetism. Just you wait." She patted him on the shoulder. "Now, if you'll excuse me, I'm going to check on how my new star is getting along with Chris and Chaz. It's still anyone's game."

She sashayed away, leaving Pete with a strange, uncomfortable emotion churning within him. It was sort of like competitiveness, but more incorporeal than that. Whatever it was, it made him burn up inside.

A mental shake failed to dispel the sensation. Jesus. He needed a cigarette.

He poked his head into the dining room and spotted a sliding glass door leading out to a patio. Perfect.

Joyce was still standing nearby where Colette had left her. Pete waved to get her attention and then jabbed his thumb toward the door. "Do you mind if I smoke? I promise I won't leave any butts in your yard."

"Sure thing, honey," she chirped. "In fact, if you'll give me a minute to grab some wine, I'll join you."

"Oh, okay," Pete said, surprised. "I'll wait right here."

"Want a glass?"

"No, thanks. I don't drink on the job." *And I'm also not old enough.*

She pushed open a door on the other side of the room, revealing a sliver of a neat, modern kitchen. Pete waited with his hands in his pockets, fiddling with his lighter and cigs. He caught one of the other men studying him out of the corner of his eye, sizing up the competition no doubt. No one attempted to speak to him. He'd forgotten how catty some porn stars could be when a gig was up for grabs. Not that he had room to talk. He wasn't exactly organizing a group outing, and he was *definitely* coveting the role.

Joyce reappeared with a glass of white wine in one hand and a pack of fancy, organic cigarettes in the other. "Shall we?"

Pete slid open the door and gestured for her to go first. A burst of cold air blew his now-mostly-dry hair into his eyes, but he held his position.

"What a gentleman," she cooed as she moved past him. She was dressed stylishly in a black cocktail dress and had thrown a short white jacket over her shoulders. If Pete had seen her at Murmur Inc., he would have assumed she was there to film MILF porn. Perhaps renting her house out was a way of getting her feet wet. That, or Pete had been in the biz too long, and he was starting to see porn stars everywhere.

Joyce led the way across the deck toward a set of tasteful patio furniture facing a wooden railing. A spit of moonlight-drenched yard lay just beyond it, ending in a tall fence. It was a clear, crisp night, though not a single star was visible. They seldom were this close to the city.

Joyce took a seat on a sofa and then patted the cushion next to her. Pete fell gracelessly into the space, all limbs as per usual. She handed him a lighter without speaking.

He took it. "Thank you, Ms....?"

"Call me Joyce," she replied. "What's your name?"

"Jaden."

"That's a cute name for a cute boy."

He almost choked midpuff on his cigarette. He handed the lighter back to buy himself time to recover. "Thank you."

"If you don't mind my saying, you look a bit young for this."

"I get that a lot, but I'm twenty, I swear. Plenty old enough. And we get ID'd and screened and all that before filming starts."

She took a dainty drag on her cigarette and exhaled away from him. "That's good to know. Thanks for not taking that wine I offered you."

"No problem. Colette would have kicked me off set anyway if she'd caught me drinking."

"Very responsible. Tell me, Jaden, why is someone your age doing this instead of . . . well, just about anything else?"

Pete restrained the sour expression that wanted to crawl over his face. Joyce meant well, he reminded himself. They almost always did. But man, was he tired of getting asked that.

"I do other things," Pete droned, reciting from a script. "I'm a student, and I have a part-time job. Porn is something I do on the side to make ends meet. I've actually only been in thirty or so films in the year I've been performing."

Joyce grimaced. "Sounds like a lot to me."

"Trust me, it's not. I have costars who have been in hundreds." Granted, they were seasoned vets who put "porn star" on their taxes, but he didn't mention that.

"My questions aren't bothering you, are they?" Joyce asked.

"A little bit, yeah."

Joyce stared at him, and in a flash, Pete realized she hadn't expected him to say yes. He quickly amended, "Just a tiny, *tiny* bit. Barely noticeable."

That seemed to mollify her. "I'm not trying to pry, I swear. I'm just curious. I'd never met an actual porn star before today, and suddenly I have a living room full of them."

He grinned. "I thought as much. I pegged you as a first-timer when I walked in."

"That obvious?"

"To me, it is. I recognize first-time jitters when I see them. Nervousness and excitement and a little edge of guilt, right?"

"Spot on. How'd you know?"

"That feeling is what got me into porn, more or less."

Joyce laughed. "That sounds like a story I'd like to hear one day, when I'm not hosting the gay Olympics at my house." She studied him again, eyes bright with curiosity. "You said you're a student. What are you studying?"

"Computer Science."

"Where?"

"I can't tell you that, sorry. It's one of those privacy things. If it got out to my classmates that I'm a porn star, I could get harassed. In fact, I *would* get harassed."

"Ah. I'm guessing Jaden isn't your real name, then?"

"Not even close. No one uses their real name in this industry." *Which means I'll never know Darko's real name.* That was an oddly disappointing thought.

"Seems like there are a lot of rules. And here I thought I'd just have to wash my sheets after."

"That might not be as big of an issue as you'd think," Pete said. "Clean up, I mean. Condoms are common practice in gay porn."

"No offense, but I'll likely wash them anyway." She wiggled the fingers of her left hand, making a large diamond ring glint in the moonlight. "Is the money as good as they say?"

"Depends." He shrugged. "This is one industry in which women absolutely make more than men, so there's that. And you get paid more for doing the 'harder' stuff. Like group sex and double penetration and the like. A lot of guys end up doing gay porn as a result, regardless of their orientation. It pays way better."

"Oh, so the men in there might be straight? What about you?"

"They might be for all I know, but I pitch my tent firmly in the gay camp." He flinched. "I regret the way I chose to phrase that."

She laughed again. "Sorry again for bombarding you with questions. Ever since my divorce, I've been looking for a hobby. Right on cue, I met Colette at a party, and she suggested renting my house out. Before I knew it, here I was." She hesitated, pressing her lips together. It seemed like there was more she wanted to say but didn't know how to say it. He waited patiently while she gathered herself.

Eventually, she asked, "You said you've been doing this for a year?"

"Just about."

"Reflecting back on it, if someone came to you and asked if they should get into the porn industry—maybe just to try it out—what would you say? Would you tell them to go for it?"

He did her the courtesy of considering it before answering. "I like my job. It's not what I plan to do forever, and the work itself can be challenging, but there's never a dull moment." Taking one last drag on his cig, he crushed it out in the ashtray. "I suppose I should check to see if it's my turn yet."

"I'll check for you." Joyce stood up. "I need more wine anyway. Have another cigarette. I have plenty more questions."

Before Pete could protest, she disappeared inside. He wrapped his arms around himself and tried not to shiver. Good company or not, he wasn't certain how much longer he'd last out here. And he certainly didn't want to be frozen through when his turn rolled around.

Joyce had offered a welcome distraction, but now that he was alone, preperformance butterflies swarmed in his abdomen. He still didn't know if the audition was going to involve sex or not. Despite his exhaustive session earlier, he found himself hoping it did. He usually had to psych himself up for a scene, but in this case, he was ready to go. He wondered how much of his attraction to Kyle had to do with his ex, and if it was fucked up for him to be turned on anyway.

Despite the cold, he didn't want to go inside only to be ignored by the potentials. He couldn't just sit here, though. He climbed to his feet and paced the length of the small deck, hoping to get his blood flowing.

He'd walked the perimeter twice before the sliding glass door opened.

"That was fast." He spun around, smiling. "Is it my turn?"

His smile evaporated from his face. *Oh God yes.*

Kyle was standing at the other end of the patio, his head tilted to the side as he regarded Pete. The outside lights cast deep shadows beneath his chin and cheekbones. He was still shirtless—and pants-less, for that matter—but he'd tied the coat shut around his waist. Pete couldn't decide if he was happy about that or not. It certainly did wonders for his cognizance.

Because, *fuck*, Kyle was even better looking up close.

Instead of speaking, he gave Pete a thorough and unabashed once-over. Pete was suddenly much, much warmer.

"Hey," Kyle finally said. He took a step closer, grinning. Or was it smirking? "Sorry if I startled you. I meant to announce my presence, but . . ." he bit his lip, and when he met Pete's gaze, he was *definitely* smirking, "I couldn't resist the opportunity to get a good look at you."

Pete's brain promptly crashed. He heard the screech of an old dial-up connection in his head. He attempted to reboot, but the whole system started spitting off angry red sparks. He probably seemed like he was having some kind of fit. Smooth.

He managed to clear his throat. "It's Kyle, right? I'm Jaden."

"I know. I asked Colette. You can call me Darko if you want. Everyone does."

"I'll stick with Kyle if that's all right. I'm not manly enough to call people by their last names."

Kyle chuckled, and the sound brushed against Pete's skin. "You're cute. I like that."

Pete wasn't certain how to respond to that. Saying *thank you* didn't seem quite right, so he went with, "What are you doing out here?"

"Looking for you."

Pete started to ask why but stopped himself. Duh. Colette had sent him to say it was his turn. "Right. Sorry you had to come get me. Are you cold?"

Kyle tilted his head to the other side in a distinctly feline way. "No. I was just fooling around with those guys. Sharing body heat and all that. I'm actually still sweaty. See?" He pulled his collar aside and angled his torso toward the light. A few beads of sweat were running down his chest. His extremely well-formed, beautiful chest.

Pete had to swallow several times before he could speak. "Ah, I see. I guess round one went well?" His stomach sank.

"Not really." Kyle propped a hip against the railing a few feet down from Pete. His coat fell open. Twin cuts of muscle peeked out the top of his underwear. He had that beautiful V-shape going on. Pete salivated.

"Don't get me wrong," Kyle continued, "they both performed well, and I know from past experience that Chaz has the stamina of a stallion, but they're not quite what I'm looking for."

Pete wanted to focus on what Kyle was saying, but he was too busy staring. He scrutinized Kyle's face in what he hoped was a subtle way. The more he studied him, the less he saw the resemblance between him and his ex. There was something else about him that caught Pete's attention and squeezed. Something that made his blood sizzle. But what? Kyle was handsome, no question about it, but wouldn't stand out in a room full of male models, and Pete had just vacated one.

"R-right," he stammered, realizing he was taking too long to respond. "What are you looking for, if you don't mind my asking?" He told himself he just wanted inside information. Anything that might give him a better shot at landing the gig. The lie sounded weak even in his own head.

Kyle's grin was wicked. He stepped closer, leaving just a few inches between them. "That's what I'm trying to find out. Though when you walked in, I felt like I had a much better idea."

Pete forgot how to breathe. He knew what Kyle was doing, of course. Flirting with him. Building a rapport. Getting him all hot and bothered so he'd be ready to go when their session started. It was exactly what a good porn star did, what Pete had wanted Antoine to do earlier that day.

And God, was it ever working. It was enthralling . . . and a bit unsettling. He'd never felt anything like this, and he didn't know quite what to make of it.

Kyle reached out and fingered one of the drawstrings on Pete's hoodie. Christ, even his fingers were sexy: long and thick. Pete didn't dare think about the implications.

"I like that you didn't dress up for this," Kyle murmured. Pete had to lean forward to hear him, and the second he did, he wondered if Kyle had meant for him to. Now their faces were close. "All the other guys in there might have just walked off a runway. It's so . . . calculated." He wrapped his hand around the drawstring and pulled on it lightly. Then he met Pete's gaze. "You look like you just tumbled out of bed and are dying for someone to drag you back. Would you like that?"

Christ. *If this guy is straight, then I'm Cher.*

Pete scrambled for an answer. Something suave and sexy. What he ended up saying, however, was the truth. "I don't know."

He was turned on in a big way, yeah, but when he prodded at his feelings, he found hesitation buried under all the lust. He'd wanted to be flirted with, even considered it part of the job. A professional courtesy. But this . . . this was setting off alarm bells in his head. Maybe he just couldn't get past the resemblance thing. Or maybe it was how genuine Kyle's flirting seemed, as if he were actually into Pete.

That was the problem, he decided. There weren't any cameras on them out here. Kyle didn't need to put on airs, and the false intimacy of it was jarring. They were porn stars. If they ended up having sex, it would be because someone paid them to. There was no reason to make this feel so . . . right.

Kyle rolled with it. "I can help you make up your mind, if you like." He put his free hand on the railing at Pete's side. "I love a challenge."

Fuck. Kyle was good.

He should return the favor, Pete thought. Flirt back. Whether Kyle meant what he was saying or not, Pete still wanted this role, and it needed to seem like attraction between them was mutual. It wasn't just on Kyle to make this work.

Unfortunately, Pete couldn't seem to do more than stand upright and sputter. He couldn't tell if he was hot or freezing, and his thoughts were muddled with a mixture of arousal and bewilderment. Despite what he'd just thought, Kyle's flirting still seemed real, and his body thought it was real too.

"You're shaking," Kyle said.

Pete willed himself to hold still but couldn't control the tremble working through him. "Sorry." He couldn't think of what else to say.

"Is it from the cold?" Kyle asked, his voice deepening. "Or something else?"

Pete couldn't begin to answer that question, but Kyle didn't seem to want him to. He lifted a hand slowly, almost lazily, and brushed his fingers over Pete's cheek.

"You're plenty warm," he whispered. "Must be something else, then. Am I coming on too strong? I can back off."

"No," Pete answered immediately.

"Then what is it?" The dare in his tone was unmistakable.

If either one of them leaned forward, it would bring their faces together. And for one magnetic moment, it seemed Kyle was going to do precisely that. His eyes floated from Pete's eyes to his mouth. Then, with enough deliberation to make Pete ache, he licked his lips.

Please kiss me, Pete thought dizzily. *Please, please kiss me.*

And just like that, it was over.

Kyle stepped away.

Pete almost followed him. He stared uncomprehendingly at Kyle's back as he headed toward the door. "Um, wait. Where are you going?"

"Back in," Kyle said without turning around. "It's freezing out here. You should head home before you catch a cold."

"But, I— Um. What about—" Pete raised a hand only to drop it again. "What about my audition?"

Kyle stopped just as he reached the door. "That *was* your audition."

Without another word, he disappeared inside.

CHAPTER 3

No matter how many times Pete replayed his conversation with Kyle in his head, he still had no idea what to make of it. Or him, for that matter. In the three days since his "audition," Kyle had kept Pete up at night in more ways than one. He just couldn't figure him out. Not that he was a master at reading people, but he'd been in porn long enough to tell when someone was genuinely attracted to him and when they were just doing their job. But Kyle . . . Kyle showed elements of both, and it left Pete confused, uncertain, and really, really horny.

At this point, he would settle for knowing if he'd blown the audition or not. Kyle's early dismissal of him didn't bode well to say the least. So much for Pete's concerns that they'd be having sex that night. Kyle hadn't even deigned to do a lighting test with him. Pete seriously doubted he'd landed the gig without even getting in front of a camera.

He hadn't heard anything from Colette yet—which was par for the course, considering how much she had going on at any given time—and could only imagine what she thought about it. She'd seemed willing to let Kyle pick his costar, but would she really cast Pete without seeing for herself how they worked together? Maybe if Kyle sang his praises, but after his cold dismissal, Pete doubted he'd received a glowing review.

That was the one thing that puzzled him the most. Why had Kyle walked away from him like that? Maybe he'd sensed Pete's eagerness and been totally creeped out. There was a thin line between flirting with your coworkers and slobbering all over them, and Pete had gotten drool on it.

His face burned with embarrassment. God, what was he, an amateur? Getting all worked up over a kiss like that. He routinely had sex on camera. In front of an audience. For the whole world to see. A kiss should have been the equivalent of brushing hands with a stranger on the bus. And it wasn't even an actual kiss. It was an almost-kiss. A nearly-kiss. A hypothetical kiss that couldn't become a theoretical one until more data was gathered.

Shit. He was becoming more and more convinced he'd blown it. And to think he'd really believed he had a shot. Colette had seemed so certain that Kyle and he would hit it off, and if the other potentials were any indication, he was the right physical type. Of all the things he'd imagined could go wrong with his audition—and his brain had conjured up a lurid cornucopia of possibilities—he'd never imagined being too attracted to his costar would be one of them.

Maybe this was for the best. Kyle engendered all sorts of uncomfortable emotions in Pete, and if one encounter with him had thrown Pete this far off his game, there was no telling what weeks of filming would do. Even as Pete thought that, disappointment rattled in his lungs.

Somehow, this was all his ex's fault.

Pete heaved a sigh that made his mattress groan beneath him. He'd spent the better part of the past hour staring constellations into the popcorn on his ceiling. Not five minutes had gone by without his thoughts turning to Kyle.

"This is pathetic," he grumbled. "I'm pathetic."

He pushed himself up into a sitting position, intent on doing something with his day besides moping. Between work, school, and his other work, he rarely had a morning to himself.

His socked feet made soft sounds on the hardwood floor as he padded to the door. He passed plain, pine furniture, stacks of books, and old band posters on the way. His Programming Logic textbook was open on his desk next to empty coffee mugs and a well-worn copy of *Slaughterhouse-Five*. His room might have belonged to any college kid in the city, if it weren't for the manila envelope on his dresser containing a stack of bloodwork. His job didn't require him to get tested, but he did once a month anyway. Better safe than sorry.

He poked his head into the hallway and listened. The town house was silent except for the occasional muffled noise from their next-door neighbors. No one was home. He trundled down the stairs and into the microscopic kitchen, heading straight for the fridge. It was barren, as per usual, sporting only ketchup packets, milk, a Chinese take-out container, and a jar of wilted pickles in miasmic juice.

He grabbed the take-out container and opened it. Damn. White rice. He poked it with a finger. Nope, more like tiny white rocks. He tossed it into the trash, stomach gurgling. He really needed to learn how to cook.

As if on cue, the front door opened. His mom stumbled in, laden with grocery bags.

"Mom," Pete cheered. He rushed to help her. "You brought food!"

"Hello to you too." Mom dumped plastic bags onto the dining room table. The sunlight streaming through the windows underscored the laugh lines fanning out around her warm brown eyes. "Help me put these away, and I'll make you something. I swear, you get skinnier every time I look at you."

Pete sidestepped that last comment and hauled the bags into the kitchen. Their groceries primarily consisted of frozen and boxed dinners—Mom was about as skilled in the kitchen as he was—but she'd also bought eggs and bagged salad, which he stashed in the fridge. Unpacking took less than ten minutes.

When he'd finished, Mom ran a hand through hair the same shade of honey brown as Pete's, with some gray peppered in. "What would you like?"

"Don't go to any trouble." Pete shifted from foot to foot. "I'm sure you're ready for bed. I can make food myself." He glanced at the clock above the stove. It was nine in the morning, which meant Mom had gotten off the night shift at the hospital two hours ago. She'd probably gone straight to the store after. She must have known somehow that he'd be too busy sulking to do it. Guilt washed through him, icy and bracing.

"Nonsense," Mom reprimanded, shooing him out of the kitchen. "Even I can operate a microwave. What kind of mother would I be if I didn't shove nuclear garbage down my son's throat?"

Pete laughed. "I'll take that over the organic kale and acai crap Aunt Caren is always pushing on us." He took a seat on a barstool next to the counter and watched Mom wrestle a TV dinner out of its box. She was blinking too much, light eyelashes sweeping over her eyes.

"Are you tired?" He wanted to slap himself as soon as the words left his mouth. "Of course you are. Can't someone else take the night shift for once?"

"Eh, I don't mind. The differential pay makes it worth it. Gotta put my boy through college." She reached over and ruffled his hair.

"Mooom," Pete whined, attempting to flatten his unruly waves. "Is that necessary?"

"I'm your mother. Annoying you is my job, and I take it very seriously." She leaned against the counter while the microwave buzzed behind her. "Do you have class today?"

Pete shook his head.

"Work?"

"Not until tomorrow. They put me on the late shift."

"Well, now we have something in common."

"You mean besides our astonishing good looks?"

Mom snorted. "Much as I hate to say it, you got your looks from your father. Except for my luscious locks, of course. How is Dad, by the way? Have you heard from him recently?"

Pete shook his head. "The next time I can expect a call is in February, when my birthday rolls around. And I guarantee it won't be on the right day."

"Hmm. Well, at least he gave you those beautiful blue eyes. All he ever gave me was a headache."

"That's putting it mildly." Pete hesitated and then dropped his gaze to the counter. "I actually did hear from him recently. He had news."

"Oh?"

He fidgeted on his stool and peeked up for her reaction. "Melissa is pregnant."

Mom was peering at the counter, fingering one of the colorful tiles embedded in it, but at that her head whipped up. "What?"

The microwave dinged, and she jumped away like it had shocked her. She opened and closed her mouth before turning around and pressing the door button. She gingerly lifted the steaming container and plopped it in front of Pete along with a plastic fork she dug out of the drawer next to the sink.

He looked from her to the fork and back again. "He sent me an email about it, along with a photo. She's *huge*. I guess he didn't think to say something sooner. Should I not have told you?"

"No, no," she said, waving him off but not quite meeting his gaze. "I'm happy for your father. And his girlfriend." She paused. "How huge are we talking?"

"Oh, colossal. Seemed like she might pop."

She laughed. "Good for her, and for Dad. He gets another shot at raising a family, assuming he doesn't walk out on her too." She clamped her mouth shut and then tried again. "That's wonderful news. Are you excited? You won't be an only child anymore."

Pete shrugged. "I don't think it's hit me yet. For all I know, I might never meet the kid. Dad hasn't visited in years, and I don't have a burning desire to go to Ohio."

"I don't know, kiddo. I hear it's for lovers."

"That's Virginia."

Mom's brow puckered. "Is it?"

"Yeah. No clue why." Pete picked up the fork and twirled it between his long fingers. "What about you? Excited for him?"

She mirrored his shrug. "To be perfectly frank, I don't know what he's thinking having a child so late in life. We had enough trouble when you were born, and we were spring chickens. It's all fun and games until you're changing dirty diapers at three in the morning while an infant squalls in your ear."

Pete wrinkled his nose. "Was I that bad?"

"No, actually, you were pretty quiet. Some things never change. Though by God, when you got going, you could blow a house down."

Pete cut into the gravy-covered meat product in front of him. The bite he took was scalding on the edges and lukewarm in the center, but he choked it down without complaint. "You know, you could try dating yourself."

"I would, but I think the government frowns on that."

Pete huffed around another mouthful. "You know what I mean. If Dad can start a whole new family, the least you can do is have dinner with a few comely strangers."

"Your father didn't start a new family. You're still his child, and that's never going to change."

"Well, what else would you call it? New girlfriend. New house on the other side of the country. Now a new kid. Sounds like starting over to me."

"He's just making some additions."

"However you label it, the message is pretty clear. He doesn't need us. He's moved on." He tried to keep his tone light, but bitterness seeped through.

Mom moved to stand in front of him. "Dad and I tried to make it work. We really did, but sometimes all the effort in the world can't fix something that's just not meant to be. I don't think he was ready to be a father. God only knows I wasn't prepared for my twentysomething boyfriend to knock me up on my thirtieth birthday. But then, life seldom throws you curveballs when you're ready for them. I'm just happy the lack of a strong father figure didn't have any effect on you."

Pete had to bite his tongue to keep from laughing. A porn star with an absent father. Sometimes the jokes wrote themselves. "The least he could do is help us pay the bills around here. This used to be his house too until he up and left it."

"It doesn't work like that, unfortunately. The second you hit eighteen, the checks stopped coming. Besides, we get by just fine, don't we?" She ruffled his hair again, and this time he didn't protest. "Though I do wish you'd let me help you more with your tuition. If you did, you could quit your job and focus on finishing your degree. School should be your top priority right now."

Pete offered her a lopsided smile. "We've talked about this. I want to pay my own way. If you were covering all of my tuition, you couldn't save for retirement, and I'm not having that. You already let me live here for free. I can take care of the rest. Besides, LACC isn't an expensive school."

She sighed. "All right. But if it starts to be too much, you'll let me know, right? Honestly, I'm not sure how you're pulling it off. The college fund your father and I set up only paid for your first year. A part-time position at a coffee place shouldn't even cover your books."

"Oh, I manage," Pete said mildly. "Money always seems to turn up when I need it."

"You must have an angel watching over you. Speaking of which, are we on for church this Sunday?"

"Yeah, of course. And the Sunday after that, and the one after that." His phone buzzed in his pocket, prompting him to scarf down the rest of his food and climb to his feet. "I'm going to study. Promise me you'll get some sleep?"

She nodded, but she was already eyeing the dishes in the sink.

"Don't even think about it," he said. "I'll do those. Okay?"

"Okay."

Satisfied, he headed back upstairs to his room. The second the door was shut behind him, he pulled his phone out of his pocket. It was a text message. He almost hoped it was Sana, his manager, telling him she needed him to work today after all. Even brewing coffee would be better than brooding in his room.

He tapped on the text, and a second later nearly dropped his phone. It was from Colette. Clammy sweat sprang up on his palms.

Are you free to talk?

He tried not to take work calls at home, whenever possible. His mom had bat-like hearing when it came to things he'd rather she didn't know. He could leave, but he'd just told her he didn't have work or school today, and his fingers were itching to hit the Call button.

Sucking in a breath, he willed himself to remain calm. This was probably just a courtesy call. She needed to let everyone who auditioned know the results. It didn't necessarily mean anything.

Even as he thought that, his heartbeat tripled.

His fingers danced across the keyboard. *I'm free. Call whenever.*

He stared at the screen, tense with impatience. Ten excruciating seconds later, an incoming call popped up. He tapped the answer symbol and then held his phone to his ear. "Hello?"

"Jaden, it's Colette," she said needlessly. "How've you been?"

"Great. You?"

"Peachy. How are your classes? And your mom?"

He blinked. Colette only bothered with small talk when she was in an exceptionally good mood. Maybe she wasn't calling to reject him after all. "They're both fine. What's up? I've been waiting to hear from you."

"Yeah, sorry for taking so long. I meant to tell you the good news sooner, but Darko and I had some details to iron out."

Good news. The words hung in front of him, each letter ten feet tall and flashing neon colors. He fumbled behind him until his hand connected with his bed, and he sank onto it. He waited for her to continue, almost bursting out of his skin. When she didn't, he lowered his voice and prompted, "So, I got the part?" *I get to see Kyle again?*

"Well . . ."

The neon letters popped like bubbles. Oh God, that was embarrassing. She must've been calling about something else. He knew it wasn't technically a competition, but this sure felt like losing.

He swallowed. "Ah, I see. Thanks for letting me know. I'm sorry if I let you down. I know you really wanted me for this."

"No, you misunderstand. You got the part."

"Wait, seriously?" He glissaded right over her last words in his excitement. "Please tell me you're not just playing with my emotions."

"I never play around when it comes to my work," she intoned, but there was a smile in her voice. "Congratulations."

"Oh my God, *thank you.*" He almost couldn't believe it. He must have done something right after all.

"Don't thank me. You earned it."

"Did Kyle say anything about me?" he blurted out, caught up in giddiness. He slapped a hand over his mouth. Wow, way to sound like he was still in high school.

To his surprise, Colette answered seriously. "He said you did brilliantly and that the two of you have off-the-charts chemistry. I look forward to seeing it for myself."

Pete's breath wedged in his throat. It seemed the attraction wasn't just on his end. Kyle felt it too.

"Anything else?" He cleared his throat. "I mean, did he have any feedback for me? I'm always looking to improve."

"Yeah, I'm sure you are." She chuckled. "He said you were charming, in a guileless way. And cute. The connection was instant, according to him. He made a few other colorful comments that I won't repeat because I'm pretty sure the acts he described are illegal in the state of California. But, needless to say, he wants to work with you."

He flushed, but for once, it wasn't with embarrassment. A hot, tingling sensation slithered through him and settled between his legs. "That's . . . wow, great."

"If the feeling is mutual, I'm going to offer you the role. I'm guessing from your breathlessness that it is."

He almost choked on his own tongue in his haste to answer. "Yes, the feeling is mutual."

"Then congratulations, Jaden. You're the newest star of *Heat Wave*."

"Thank you so much," he gushed. "I won't let you down. I promise I'll—"

"There is one thing, however," she interrupted. "A contingency, so to speak."

His excitement dampened as if it had its own personal rain cloud. "All right. What is it?"

"Darko said . . . How shall I put this? He said he kept getting the urge to pin you down."

"That doesn't sound so bad." In fact, from the moment Pete had met him, he'd had a strong desire for Kyle to do exactly that.

"Down, boy. He meant it in an 'oh shit, this guy's gonna bolt' kind of way. He said you seemed a little jumpy and tense."

Pete started to deny it only to realize he couldn't. Kyle had thrown him from the moment he'd laid eyes on him, and rather than try to hide it, he'd pretty much told Kyle to his face. Shit. "If he felt that way, why'd he pick me?"

"He must've seen potential in you. Or maybe his dick was doing the talking. Who knows. The point is, you're his top choice, but we have a runner-up on standby just in case. Chaz, to be precise. I'm willing to give Kyle the benefit of the doubt when he says you're the one—mostly because I thought you were the right pick as well—but believe me, I'll replace you if I have to."

That should have sobered Pete, but he was too busy wrestling with an insane spike of jealousy at the idea of someone taking his role. "What do I have to do to prove myself? Whatever it takes, I'm there."

"I like how resolute you sound. So, here's the deal: we were originally going to start promoting *Heat Wave* with a photo shoot, but now we're going to jump right into filming and save the publicity stuff for later. We'll start with a promotional teaser, like a movie trailer. Nothing serious, just a five-minute thing to get you both acquainted with your characters and give the people something to anticipate. You won't even have to be naked for it. You and Darko will fool around a bit and see how you work together in front of a camera. If Darko is satisfied with your performance, the part is yours. Sound good?"

His heart didn't know if it wanted to race or skip. He should be devastated. Kyle liked him, but not enough to pick him outright. Somehow, that was worse than being rejected.

Instead of discouragement, however, determination bubbled up in him. He needed to prove himself. He *would* prove himself. And when he was finished, Kyle would be the one left thinking about it for days.

"When do we begin?"

CHAPTER 4

On a beautiful Saturday afternoon—a little over a week after his phone call with Colette—Pete walked onto the set of *Heat Wave*. Or, as he knew it, Joyce's house.

It looked different in the daytime: less palatial and marginally less intimidating. According to Colette, a decent chunk of the filming was going to take place there. If nothing else, at least he had familiar surroundings to fall back on, and a potential friend in Joyce.

When he pulled up, he spotted figures standing out front. He prayed none of them were Kyle as he parked next to the other cars. He wanted to portray confidence, and arriving in a vehicle that was more rust than machine was not a part of his vision.

Luckily, when he jogged up, he saw Colette and Joyce standing on the veranda next to a woman he didn't recognize. Kyle was nowhere in sight.

"Jaden," Colette greeted him. "You look chipper."

"Happy to be here," Pete said, slightly out of breath. He nodded to Joyce. "Nice to see you again."

"Likewise, handsome." She held out a bejeweled hand for him to shake.

He kissed her knuckles instead. "You look lovely." It was true. She was wearing cropped jean shorts and a flowery top that left an inch of her tan stomach showing.

"I had to dress up for my boys," she teased. "Although your boy dressed down for you. Wait till you see him."

Pete perked up. "Did he now?"

"You can go in if you want." Colette's pursed lips suggested she was fighting back a grin. "Kyle's doing a mini photo shoot for another project, but once that's finished, we'll get started." She turned to the other woman. "Won't we, Yolanda?"

Yolanda hefted a large camera bag onto her shoulder with ease. "Ready when you are."

"Excellent." Colette looked back at Pete. "We still have a few technical details to go over. You remember your way around, right?"

"Yeah."

"Good. Go get a feel for the set. We'll be right behind you."

Pete hurried toward the house, fighting the desire to break into a jog. He let himself in the front door just like before. He couldn't tell if he was more or less nervous this time around. On one hand, he knew where he was going and what he'd find when he got there. On the other, if he bombed this, Colette would lose all faith in him, he'd be humiliated in front of Kyle, and he'd jeopardize a starring role in a major production.

So, really, no pressure.

The sound of shutter clicks led him once more in the direction of the living room. He took a deep breath and focused on putting one foot in front of the other. He'd gotten this role on his own merit, he reminded himself. This was his chance to show both Colette and Kyle that they'd chosen the right man.

When he'd woken up that morning, he'd stretched, practiced sexy faces in his bathroom mirror, and even masturbated, something he seldom did before a gig. He was loose, limber, and prepared. And above all else, he had something to prove.

He could do this.

He rounded the corner before the living room and skidded to a comical stop.

Kyle was lounging on the sofa, completely and gloriously naked, while a photographer fluttered around him, snapping photos. Pete froze, eyes wide open. *Christ. He's . . . beautiful.*

Oh God, he couldn't do this.

Though Pete tried to stop them, his eyes snapped right between Kyle's legs. Not naked, Pete realized, both relieved and profoundly disappointed. Kyle was wearing the *tiniest* pair of underwear in the entire world. The black fabric—no more than a strip of cloth, really—was slung low on his hips, and he had one thumb hooked in the waistband, tugging it down even lower. He was shirtless and possibly oiled; his skin gleamed in the sunlight pouring through the windows. From his messy hair to his curled toes, he looked *delicious*.

Pete's face turned atomically red. He looked away and ordered himself to calm down. What was wrong with him lately? Granted, walking onto porn sets was always a little awkward, and he didn't think he'd ever get completely used to seeing strangers naked—or having sex with them for that matter—but this was ridiculous. He was a professional. It was time to start acting like one.

Steeling himself, he looked back at Kyle. He was precisely where Pete had left him, supine on the sofa like a sunbathing jungle cat. Only now, he was watching Pete.

Pete's mouth went dry, but he didn't look away. As if sensing his determination, Kyle's lips twitched up at the corners. He lifted a hand to his hair, flexing his biceps. His fingers ran carefully through his mussed locks, and then he dragged them down his chest. Arching his back into his own touch, he smirked at Pete, and the message was as clear as if he'd spoken aloud: *I'm pretending it's you touching me right now.*

Pete's cock twitched in his jeans. The photographer was snapping a photo a second, but Kyle wasn't paying the slightest bit of attention to him. He smiled lazily at Pete and quirked an eyebrow, as if daring him to do something about it.

Pete knew a challenge when he saw one, and was determined to win this particular exchange. He let his eyes drift down Kyle's body, drinking in the sight of him. Out of his periphery, he could see Kyle tracking the path of his gaze. He made a point of lingering between his legs, sizing up the considerable bulge that lay there. Then he locked eyes with Kyle and slowly licked his lips.

The strangled noise that escaped from Kyle made the whole standoff worth it, in Pete's opinion.

Colette appeared at his side. "Having fun?"

His attention didn't waver from Kyle. "You could say that."

"As entertaining as it is watching you two, we should get started. Ready?"

Pete's whole body screamed *yes* in response. "Ready."

"Good." Colette signaled to the photographer, making a cutting motion by her neck. He retreated, and Yolanda set up in the vacated space. Colette directed her attention to Kyle next, pointing toward the dining room. "Get dressed. Your clothes are in the bedroom."

Kyle slid to his feet and exited in the direction Colette had indicated. He didn't so much as glance at Pete as he slipped through the doorway and disappeared.

Pete frowned after him. What was with all the mixed signals? Hot and cold didn't come close. More like nuclear and Siberia.

"Jaden," Colette said, breaking him from his reverie, "we have wardrobe for you to choose from if you want, but I think what you're wearing now is perfect."

Pete looked down at himself. He'd removed his jacket at the door, leaving him in jeans that had obviously not come pre-ripped and a plain blue T-shirt. He wasn't exactly what he'd call camera-ready. "You don't think I should dress up a bit?"

"Just trust me on this," Colette said. "You have that whole boy-next-door thing going on, mostly because you are one. It's perfect for this scene. You got my script, right?"

"Yeah, and I liked it. Short and sweet, just like porn ought to be. Though if I may toot your horn, I thought it sounded like a real movie. Except for all the raunchy sex, of course."

She smirked. "You've clearly never seen a Jess Franco film, but good. You understand your character?"

"Well, yeah." Pete ran a hand through his hair and winced when it caught on a tangle. "I kind of *am* my character: a young, gay college student who's shy and inexperienced with love. I don't foresee myself having any issues portraying that. I'm a little confused, though."

"About what?"

"Why not have me play someone more . . . I don't know. Cool. Sexy. Like Kyle. I get the whole opposites-attract shtick, and that can be really hot, but I don't think people are going to want to watch someone like me."

She waved dismissively. "Have some confidence, kid. Don't forget, this isn't just porn. We're filming a real movie here, with real characters. Our audience is going to identify with you *because* you're a regular guy. Plus, the backbone of this film is the way the leading males play off of each other. I haven't seen you two together yet, but Darko assures me you have the right dynamic. That, more than any amount of acting or wardrobe or writing, is what's going to make this film sizzle."

"If you say so." Pete couldn't keep insecurity from bleeding into his tone. "I just don't want to screw this up. I'm used to being Jaden on screen. I'm not sure how to be me."

"Just relax and let things flow. I'm sure you're going to be amazing."

"I appreciate your faith in me, even if I don't understand it."

Colette looked at him askance. "Tell me something: do you think Darko is attractive?"

Pete shrugged. "Yeah, he's hot. Obviously. The Pope probably thinks he's attractive."

"Is he just hot, or is it more than that? Do you feel something when you look at him?"

Pete really didn't want to answer that, but Colette was watching him expectantly. He nodded, not trusting himself to speak.

"Then believe me when I say the battle is already won. Relax and let your natural chemistry do its thing. You're a decent actor, but in this case, I think being yourself will do the trick."

Coming from Colette, that was a ringing endorsement. "Thank you. I'll give it my all."

"Promise?" said a deep voice behind him.

Pete spun around. Kyle had returned and was standing a few feet away from them, his hands tucked casually into snug black pants. He had on a navy-blue button-down shirt, and the sleeves were rolled up to his elbows. For the first time, Pete noticed twin black tattoos on his inner forearms. Dots? No. Constellations? Maybe. Whatever they were, they emphasized his arms in a way that was almost superfluous. As if anyone needed a reason to look at them.

"Speak of the devil," Colette said. "Jaden, you remember Darko, I presume?"

"Vividly."

Pete didn't realize he was staring until Kyle asked, "See something you like?"

"Um," was Pete's articulate response. He wasn't certain how to answer that. Agreeing seemed uncomfortable, but not agreeing would be a lie too egregious for Pete to utter. He found himself wondering if Kyle was wearing his own clothes or something from wardrobe. He couldn't possibly have great style too. That just wouldn't be fair.

"I'll take that as a yes." Kyle laughed, smoky and soft. The sound zinged up Pete's spine. He hid his reaction as best he could. If he was going to prove to Kyle that he deserved this role, he needed to be Jaden, not Pete. That meant being confident. Bold. Seductive.

Channeling his inner porn star, he cocked his head to the side and looked Kyle up and down, making no secret about it. "So far, so good, but I haven't seen it all yet." He gave himself a mental high five for pulling that off.

Unfortunately, it seemed his small victory was short-lived. Kyle was just getting warmed up.

"You shouldn't say things like that." His tone had just a hint of danger. It made Pete's cock throb. "I told you before, I *love* a challenge."

"Can you two wait for the camera, please?" Colette interrupted. She sounded more amused than annoyed, but Pete jerked back like he'd been caught doing something wrong.

"Sorry," he mumbled.

"I'm not," Kyle chirped.

Colette rolled her eyes. "Just go stand on your marks, please. Porn stars, I swear. Can't keep it in their pants for two seconds."

Pete scurried over to the first of two duct tape X's on the living room floor. They began the scene standing, but eventually they were going to end up on the sofa. Just thinking about it made his pants tight. Flirting was one thing, but soon he'd get to see if his chemistry with Kyle was as potent in action. He'd get to touch him. Kiss him. Taste him. He hoped he'd be able to keep it together. Kyle seemed like the sort of guy he could totally lose himself in. The idea was exhilarating. And utterly terrifying.

He ran lines in his head while Colette and Yolanda fiddled with their equipment. There was a camera set up on a tripod opposite the couch. Wires and cords snaked from it to a pair of TV monitors on the dining room table. Next to them was an open laptop attached to even more cords. Pete was willing to bet that would act as Colette's makeshift viewing station while Yolanda operated the camera. They could check the footage in real time and make adjustments. And catch every little mistake Pete made as it happened.

Again, no pressure.

Kyle wandered over, taking his mark a few feet away from him. Thank God Colette had written an innocuous start to the scene. If they were standing any closer to each other, Pete might have to check his blood pressure.

Colette hovered by the monitors. Yolanda stood behind the tripod and angled it square at them. The photographer stood at the ready, his camera poised. Everyone was in place. Even Joyce had found a seat at the table from which to watch the spectacle.

The moment of truth had arrived, and Pete was a cocktail of anticipation, apprehension, and arousal. He tried not to look at Kyle, but it was like his head was magnetized. Eventually, he gave up and stole a peek. Kyle was watching him, of course.

"Nervous?" Kyle asked, grinning like he already knew the answer.

"No," Pete lied. "You?"

"Nah. I've been looking forward to this." He studied the rug beneath their feet, and for the first time, a crack appeared in his confident exterior. "Have you?"

"Hmm?"

"Been looking forward to this?"

If Pete were to answer honestly, he'd sound like a newb, so he went with a professional response: "Of course. This is a great opportunity." His inner voice mocked him from the back of his mind: *A great opportunity to have sex with a guy you can't stop thinking about.*

"Ah, so is that your only reason?" Kyle seemed disappointed. "All work and no play?"

"What other reason could I have?"

"Oh, I don't know." His grin was back. "I can think of a few outside motivations."

"If you gentlemen are finished chatting," Colette interjected, "we're going to start filming. This is meant to be candid, so act like we're catching you in the middle of a casual conversation. A private moment between friends. Stay in character, act as natural as possible, and above all else, make it hot. We're all looking forward to seeing you in action. Aren't we?"

The crew members—including Joyce—cheered.

"Lights?" Colette asked.

The photographer checked his flash and gave her a thumbs-up.

"Camera?"

Yolanda touched a button at the top of her machine, and a red light blinked on.

She turned to Pete and Kyle. "Action!"

Pete took a breath. Now came the hard part: easing into the scene. Porn stars weren't known for being the best actors, and while Pete considered himself better than most, he usually needed some time to warm up. He also had no idea how good Kyle was, and that was going to play a big role in how smoothly this went.

He exhaled slowly and focused on getting into character. Colette had said to just be himself, and so he concentrated on what he was feeling right now. Tension, that was for sure. Anticipation. Excitement. Pete did his best to convey all of these emotions at once. He angled his chin down, seeming to look up at Kyle even though he was a few inches taller, and shoved his hands into his pockets.

"Well, this is it," he said with a nervous titter. "My house. Or rather, my parents' house, technically. What do you think?"

Kyle looked around and whistled. "It's nice. Much nicer than my digs. You said your folks are out of town, right?"

"Yeah, for a whole month. They're in France or something. Eating stinky cheese and drinking too much wine. They go every year when school lets out. I joke that they do it so they won't have to see me over summer break."

Kyle laughed, and the tension left Pete's shoulders. So far, so good. He resisted the urge to peek at Colette and gauge her reaction. If something was wrong, she'd stop them. Still, he ran through a mental checklist of things that could be off: everything from the angle of his head to his foot placement. Maybe he should—

Kyle interrupted his train of thought. "Your parents must trust you a lot to leave you alone in the house for so long."

Pete furrowed his brow. "What do you mean?"

"Dude, have you never seen a single high school movie? When your parents go out of town, you throw a massive party. You're practically obligated to. Let loose. Get wild. You know?"

Pete glanced down at the floor and then looked back up at Kyle through lowered eyelashes. "Um, not really. Even if I wanted to throw a party, I doubt anyone would show up. I don't have a whole lot of friends. Besides you, obviously."

Kyle leaned closer to him, seemingly unconsciously, and a thrill shot down his spine. "You act so differently around me, I keep forgetting you're the silent, brooding type. You know what they say about the quiet ones, right?"

His gaze slid over Pete's face, lingering on his lips. Then, his pupils noticeably dilated. Pete sucked in a breath. That wasn't acting. There was no faking a response like that. It was instinctive and primal and sexy as hell.

He almost leaned closer, but with extreme force of will, he stopped himself. They still had some dialogue to get through before they reached the part in the script where they could touch each other. But God, Kyle was tempting. Pete had never struggled to pace himself this hard before. The tension between them was palpable. He wanted to tear the script to confetti and lean in already.

But he couldn't. Colette was the one who signed his checks. Her words rang in his head: *"I'll replace you if I have to."* He had to do things her way.

Pete eased back on his heels, putting some distance between them in a subtle way. "I'm sure I have no idea what you mean. And for the record, I plan to use my vacation time to study, maybe get a part-time job."

Kyle groaned. "Please tell me you're joking."

"Um. No? I'm being serious."

"And that, my friend, is exactly your problem."

Pete was curious to see how Kyle would play the next few lines. He did his part, feigning confusion. "What is?"

"You're way too serious. It can't be healthy for someone your age to be so uptight." Kyle rolled a shoulder as if to emphasize his point. "I mean, studying over summer break? Getting a job? Come on. You need to relax. Unwind a little. It'll do you some good."

Pete had to admit, he was impressed. Kyle sounded natural, just like a concerned friend. It was totally at odds with the man who'd cornered him on Joyce's deck and seduced the breath from his lungs. He might have some acting verve after all.

Pete squared his body toward him. "And how do you propose I 'unwind'?"

One corner of Kyle's mouth rose. "You could get one of those deep-tissue massages. Or get some soothing tea." He slid a hand onto Pete's shoulder. "Or get laid."

Pete thought he was prepared for the touch, but when Kyle's warmth soaked through his shirt, goose bumps popped up all down his arm. He couldn't tell if he wanted to pull away or drench his entire body in the sensation. His instincts reacted for him, making him jerk like he'd been shocked.

Kyle retracted his hand and gave him a strange look. "Little jumpy there, Jaden?"

The use of his stage name brought Pete back to reality.

"Sorry," he mumbled. "I didn't mean to— Um. Never mind. What was I saying?" Promptly, all of his lines fell out of his head. Shit. What was he supposed to do next? He couldn't remember with Kyle's dark eyes watching him so intently.

He started to back away, but Kyle's fingers closed around his wrist.

"You're doing that thing again," Kyle said, his voice suddenly rough.

Pete swallowed. "What thing?"

"Making me want to pin you down."

Fuck. Please.

Pete's heart went into overdrive. Kyle wasn't going by the script anymore, and Pete sure as hell couldn't correct him. The most articulate thought in his head right now was, *Oh fuck yes*, and that wasn't going to win him a Pulitzer anytime soon.

He managed to remember his next line. "Why, Kyle, are you trying to seduce me?"

Kyle didn't miss a beat. "I thought I'd made that clear by now."

Damn. Good answer. Pete bit his lip.

That ended up being the wrong move, because Kyle's eyes zeroed in on the feature. "I can't seem to resist that mouth of yours."

Pete's brain went offline again. He could practically smell the hormones in the air. Suddenly, he no longer cared about the script. "Then don't."

"You mean that?"

This was it. Pete's chance to prove himself. "I'm not going to bolt, if that's what you think."

Kyle's eyes flicked toward the camera and back again. "Why would I think that?"

Continuity be damned. Pete went in for the kill. "I'm not going anywhere. So if you want me, I'm right here."

Kyle stared at him for a moment. Then he exhaled raggedly and lifted his chin. "Prove it."

Pete closed his eyes, intent on kissing him. Before he could, he felt a hand on his shoulder. Kyle shoved him, and the back of his calves hit the sofa. Pete fell onto it in a sprawl of limbs. He started to push himself up again, but Kyle kneeled between his thighs, freezing him in place.

All the oxygen in Pete's lungs left him as Kyle leaned on his hands, one on either side of Pete's shoulders. It would have been funny how easily he could make Pete feel caged in if it weren't so *hot*. He wasn't crawling over him yet, but the threat was evident in the curve of his full lips.

"Are you nervous now?" he asked.

"Yes." There was no point in denying it.

"Want me to stop?"

Pete shuddered and exhaled, "*No.*"

Kyle closed the distance between their bodies. Pete expected Kyle to kiss him—wanted so badly for him to—but he didn't. Instead, he propped himself up on one forearm and rucked Pete's shirt up with his free hand. For a moment, he just stared at the exposed skin. Pete tried not to squirm beneath the intensity of his gaze. Then Kyle whistled, and his hot breath tickled Pete's skin, making him flex.

"So you do have abs," he murmured. "They were hiding. I was wondering if you would. Been thinking about it more than I'd like to admit." He traced a finger around one of the muscles jutting faintly beneath Pete's skin.

Pete didn't say anything—*couldn't* say anything, if he were honest with himself. His entire world had narrowed to that single finger on his bare skin. It seemed like Kyle was touching all of him and none of him at once, and definitely not the parts Pete wanted him to touch.

After he was finished with the first muscle, he traced around the others, making Pete squirm. Pete never would have suspected Kyle was the sort to take it slow. He'd expected to get overpowered by the force of nature that was Kyle, to get overwhelmed, to get . . . well, to get fucked.

Instead, Kyle just touched him: stroked his skin, trailed fingers down his chest, even thumbed the hollows created by his hip bones. There was nothing inherently sexual about it, but it was one of the most sensual things Pete had ever experienced. All while he touched, Kyle moved their bodies slowly together, not thrusting so much as rolling like ocean waves lapping against the shore.

Pete could hear himself panting. The air itself seemed to be filled with Kyle, his scent or his pheromones or something. He couldn't think clearly enough to decide.

Kyle skimmed his lips along Pete's collarbone, and at the first scrape of stubble against Pete's neck—just the way he'd imagined it when they first met—Pete threw his head back and moaned with abandon. He couldn't fight it, couldn't hold back, just had to *feel*.

"Jaden," Kyle said, breath hot and damp against his jaw, "I'm going to kiss you now."

"Please," Pete pleaded. "Can you— I just— I want—"

Kyle shushed him with his mouth, brushing their lips briefly together. Pete tried to press harder against him, but Kyle stilled him with a hand in his hair.

"Just let me," he said, voice ragged. "Will you let me?"

Pete nodded, going boneless beneath him. He was already struggling to breathe, but when Kyle kissed first one corner of his mouth and then the other, the entire concept of oxygen flew out of his brain. He wanted to beg, wanted to plead with him to end his agony, but he couldn't form the words. Instead, he took a fistful of Kyle's shirt, needing the grip to anchor him to the earth.

Kyle shivered—Pete felt it up the entire length of his body— and then finally, *finally* pressed their mouths together. The first touch was everything Pete wanted and not enough at the same time. Kyle surprised him yet again by not immediately trying to shove his tongue down Pete's throat. He kissed just the way Pete liked: slow and deliberate and savoring.

Pete held on to Kyle's shoulders for dear life, comforted by his weight on top of him even as it locked him in place. Somewhere between the first flash of tongue and Kyle's teeth nipping his bottom lip, Pete forgot himself. This was what drowning must feel like.

At some point, he must have genuinely forgotten to breathe, because his lungs burned. He tore his face away and drew a ragged breath. When he looked back, Kyle was staring at him, expression caught somewhere between wonder and disbelief.

"Fuck." Kyle sounded wrecked. "You taste good."

"Cut!"

That word was supposed to mean something to Pete, but he ignored it. He slid his hands into Kyle's hair and urged him closer. Kyle's eyes darted back down to his lips, and for a captivating moment, it seemed like he was going to kiss Pete again.

"I said cut!"

Kyle jolted away from him. Pete almost whined in protest. He swung his head in the direction of the noise. It took him a moment to process what he saw, and then it all came rushing back. Colette. *Heat Wave*. Shit.

"Jesus, you two." Colette was standing next to the camera with her arms crossed. "I know I said act natural, but you still need to follow my directions."

"Sorry," Kyle rasped.

Pete studied him. His lips were spit-shiny, and his hair was wild. He didn't meet Pete's gaze as he moved backward into a kneeling position. Pete, on the other hand, couldn't seem to take his eyes off him.

"Did we fuck something up?" Kyle asked.

"Quite the contrary," Colette said. "That's a wrap."

At that, Pete finally glanced her way. "Really? You don't want us to do another take?" He couldn't keep the disappointment from his tone.

"Nope, I feel confident we have everything we need. Though I could have done without the deviations from my script." A gloating smile crawled over Colette's face. "I knew it. I *so* called that."

"What?" Pete asked.

"Your chemistry." She motioned between them. "The tension between you is tangible. Even when you finally kissed, it just got stronger. The second I met you, Darko, I knew you were the right choice to inspire Jaden. Hopefully it'll work the other way too."

Pete considered Kyle, attempting to gauge his reaction. His attention was directed at the floor, shoulders rigid. Pete frowned and pushed himself up onto his elbows. Had he done something wrong?

"So, what's the verdict, Darko?" Colette continued, seemingly oblivious. "I know I said I'd leave it up to you, but if I get a vote, I'd say Jaden's definitely in."

"Yeah." Kyle's voice still sounded rough, though now Pete couldn't tell if it was from desire or something else. "I can work with this."

He wished Kyle would acknowledge him. Anxiety clawed at his insides.

"Then we're all set." Colette gave Yolanda a signal, and she switched off her camera. "The next step is to work out the filming schedule. We have a photo shoot to do and scripts to go over and—"

"Would you mind sending me whatever I need when you're finished?" Kyle interrupted. "I'm not so great with the planning. I'm more of an action kind of guy."

Colette frowned. "I suppose, but you should really be present for this. *Heat Wave* is your project too."

"Just tell me when to show up, and I'll be there." Kyle climbed off the sofa. "Do you need me for anything else?"

Pete looked nervously between Kyle and Colette. There was no rule saying a porn star had to stick around once filming was done, but most did in case the director wanted to go over something or get in a quick interview. Maybe that wasn't Kyle's modus operandi, though. Pete had worked with people who needed to jet as soon as the scene wrapped. Usually people who had kids to get back to or spouses who didn't know what they did during the day.

That last thought made Pete stop short. Kyle had a whole life outside of this room. He could have a boyfriend. Or a wife, for all Pete knew. A family. The idea made his chest constrict for reasons he didn't want to entertain.

From the bewildered and somewhat irritated expression on Colette's face, however, it seemed like Kyle didn't usually run off so fast. "All right, you can go. I'll call you later." She said it like it was a threat.

Kyle didn't seem the slightest bit fazed as he strolled out of the living room, through the dining room, and out of sight.

Pete stared after him, wondering why he'd gone that direction instead of heading for the front door. Kyle had made it seem like he was itching to leave, and yet. Something else had to be going on.

Before he could think about it too much, Colette said, "Great work today, Jaden. You really connected with the scene."

"Thank you," he said, eyes still trained on the door Kyle had disappeared through. He swung his legs over the side of the sofa. "So, the role is definitely mine?"

"You heard Darko. He wants to work with you."

"Excellent. When do we start?"

There was a noticeable pause. Pete glanced at her. She was frowning, but it was different from how she'd looked at Kyle. Less annoyed and more troubled.

"What?" he asked. "Something wrong?"

"Not yet," Colette said. "But there could be."

"Hmm?"

"Tell me, what was different about today? What got you out of your head?"

"Kyle, obviously," Pete answered. "You said it yourself: we work well together."

"Yeah, but *that* was something else. I've never seen you show such passion on screen. I've seen a lot of porn in my life, and I can attest that it's possible to be sexual without being even remotely intimate. What you and Darko just pulled off was the opposite of that."

Pete couldn't tell if he was being scolded or not. "What are you getting at? I thought you said we did good."

"You did. Just . . . be careful."

Pete squinted at her. "Huh?"

"I just don't want— You and Darko seem—" She stopped with a huff. "Like I said, be careful. Okay?"

Pete wasn't certain what he was agreeing to, but he replied, "Yeah, okay."

Colette sighed. "Let's wrap this up. If you don't mind sticking around for a minute, I need to consult with Yolanda for her availability."

Pete nodded. "I'll be here."

As soon as Colette walked away, Joyce rushed over, a big smile on her face. "Jaden! You were so great! Totally hot."

Pete started to reply, but Joyce threw herself onto the sofa and engulfed him in a perfumed hug.

"Wow, okay," he half choked. "Did not expect that."

"I'm officially your biggest fan." She pulled away. "I wasn't sure how I'd feel about it at first. You know, because of the *gay* thing." She whispered the word, which almost made Pete laugh, considering the circumstances. "But that was hot! I'm starting to understand what Colette was getting at when she said this kind of porn is for women too."

"I'm glad you enjoyed it," Pete said. "That's a good thing, since you'll be seeing a lot of me and Kyle."

Joyce laughed. "Yeah, if he doesn't climb out my bedroom window and disappear."

Pete jerked away from her. "What? Why would he do that?"

"Because of whatever spooked him," she said, as though the answer were obvious. "I don't know what you did to the guy—and frankly, I don't know what you *could* have done. We were watching you the whole time—but if I were you, I wouldn't do it again."

"Wait, what? What are you talking about?"

"I suppose you couldn't see his face," Joyce said thoughtfully, tapping her chin with a manicured nail. "When Colette called cut and he pulled away, it was written all over him."

Pete's throat tightened. He managed to croak, "What was?"

"Well, I'm no expert, but if you ask me, it was terror."

CHAPTER

Two days later, Pete was still reeling from Joyce's revelation. It threw some light on Kyle's hasty departure, but that was the only illuminating thing about it.

Even work couldn't distract him. He'd spent the better part of his shift at the Globe, a coffee shop near his campus, replaying their kiss in his head. He couldn't seem to pinpoint what he'd done wrong. Kyle had seemed to enjoy it. Was he simply that good of an actor? It was a possibility. They were both there for the same reason, after all: because Colette was paying them to be.

That was a sobering thought. Had Kyle even *wanted* to kiss him? Pete had gone back and forth on this before, wondering if Kyle was as attracted to him as he seemed. Colette had confirmed it, but now he was back to doubting it.

Pete felt silly for dwelling on it, but he couldn't help himself. No matter how many times he ordered himself to focus on the gig, he kept getting drawn in by the mystery that was Kyle. That raised an uncomfortable question. What exactly did Pete want from his mercurial costar? Sex? Obviously. Something more? God, he hoped not. He'd thought he was too smart to confuse lust with love. It was the ultimate rookie mistake and not one Pete had ever been in danger of making. But then, he'd never experienced such magnetic attraction to another person before.

Pete sighed to himself. He'd gone into the shoot determined to prove himself to Kyle. Instead, he was agonizing over him yet again. He should have known he'd never be able to pull something like that off. Leave it to him to botch a seduction so badly he sent the other guy running.

Colette had certainly gotten her wish. Her leading men had chemistry, the kind that led to nuclear fallout and fire raining from the sky. Pete imagined sirens wailing in the distance. *Breaking News: Man Dies From Embarrassment After Making Ass of Himself in Front of Hot Coworker. More at eleven.*

Sometimes, Pete envied people with a nine-to-five. If they met someone they liked, they went on a date. When Pete met someone he liked, he banged them for money while a director told him to mind his angles.

It was remiss of him to let his attraction to Kyle override his common sense. He'd forgotten what porn was: business with a side of pleasure. No more thinking with his dick, he swore to himself.

The only thing left to do was wait and see how Kyle acted around him next time. Just thinking about it sent apprehension spiderwebbing through him.

"So, who is he?"

Pete—who had been staring at a fascinating stretch of empty space for the past five minutes—startled at the question. Sana had appeared next to him behind the counter.

"Sorry, what?" He smoothed the black apron tied over his clothes, even though it wasn't wrinkled. Guilt pierced him. He was slacking, and it was obvious. He picked up the washcloth he'd abandoned on the counter and went back to wiping up stray coffee grounds.

Sana's strained expression suggested she was holding in laughter. "I said, 'Who is he?' You've been making moony faces at the wall all morning. If you're going to be useless as an employee, you might as well provide some entertainment."

Managers weren't required to wear an apron—none of the employees were, really, despite what the handbook said—but Sana had thrown one over her yellow, ankle-length dress anyway. It was the only thing about her that wasn't colorful, from her patterned hijab to her personality. She also had on five-inch orange stilettos that looked like they could double as weapons. Despite being nearly as tall as Pete and on her feet all day, Sana lived in heels.

Pete arranged his features into what he hoped was an innocent expression. "I don't know what you mean."

"Sure you do. You've been wiping that same spot of counter for so long it's gone from dirty to clean and back again. And your other hand seems to have developed a mind of its own." She pointed to it, and only then did Pete realize he was still smoothing his apron. "That's a sure sign something's going on."

"Yikes. Am I that transparent?"

"Yup." She laced her long fingers together and rested her chin on them, elbows on the counter. "So spill."

Pete faltered. One of the reoccurring issues he'd encountered while leading a double life was that when people asked for details, he couldn't often provide them. He could only imagine how she'd react to the truth: *Well, you see, Sana, I'm distracted because I just had the best kiss of my life while filming this gay porno.*

Instead, he said, "It's nothing serious. I'm, um, worried about my class later."

"Isn't it a little early for that? I thought spring semester just started a couple of weeks ago."

"It's never too early to start worrying about midterms." He gave a beatific smile.

Sana quirked a thick, perfectly shaped eyebrow at him. "You are such a liar, but whatever. I just thought I'd ask, since you've scalded yourself with the milk steamer three times today."

Pete grimaced. That wasn't all he'd done. On top of the milk incidents, he'd given away seven dollars' worth of incorrect change and had spent half his shifts staring into space. It was a miracle it had taken Sana this long to say something to him.

"I'm sorry," Pete said sincerely. "I know I'm screwing up. I'll do better."

"Fair enough." Sana shrugged. "Just let me know if something's wrong, okay?"

"Okay."

Just then, a middle-aged woman approached them, nose in the air. She set a cup of coffee primly down on the counter and stared at them expectantly.

Pete took a step back, not because of the woman's venomous aura, but because of the twinkle in Sana's brown eyes. He knew what was coming next.

"May I help you, ma'am?" Sana asked, voice as sweet as spun sugar.

"You got my order wrong." Her vitriolic expression and tart, puckered mouth suggested she thought this was a personal attack.

"We're so sorry, ma'am," Sana said. "If you tell us what your drink was, we'll make you a new one right away."

"It's a little late for that," the woman sneered. "I can't take time out of my day to wait for *two* drinks. I have things to do. I wanted you to make it right the first time."

"We're so sorry again, ma'am," Sana repeated. "How about we refund your money?"

"That doesn't help me either. The service here is completely unacceptable." She paused for breath. Sana leaned forward eagerly just as Pete prayed the woman wouldn't say what he thought she was going to—

"Go get your manager," the woman sneered. "I'd like to speak to him."

Pete ducked behind the espresso machine and peeked over the top like a meerkat. As he watched, Sana rested her palms on the counter. The woman fell back, eyes fixed on Sana's face. Pete could guess what she saw there: pure, malicious glee.

"As it just so happens, ma'am," Sana replied, smile sharp as broken glass, "I *am* the manager."

Several people had looked up from their laptops to watch the exchange. Pete tried to edge farther out of view, an ambitious move for someone his height.

The woman looked flummoxed but recovered quickly. "Then I must say you're doing a terrible job. Your staff are incompetent, and don't get me started on the décor." She waved at the overlapping bumper stickers covering the espresso machine, which bore such catchy slogans as *Have you hugged a queer today?* and *Fuck the Patriarchy.* Then she pointed to the rainbow flag undulating by the entrance. "And I can only assume you have no idea what that flag means, or you wouldn't dare hang it outside a business. *Children* might see it."

"This is an independent coffee shop, ma'am. We do what we want." Sana was apparently no longer bothering to sound polite. "And we're LGBT-friendly, among other things. If you have an issue with that, we invite you to stop patronizing us."

The woman opened and closed her mouth several times. "That's it, I want to talk to whoever's above you!"

"That would be the owner, and he's the one who put the flag up. I'd fetch him for you, but he's currently on vacation with his husband."

Having apparently reached her limit on consumer fury, the woman whirled around and stomped out.

Sana called after her: "If you like that, you should hear our bathroom policy!"

Pete waited until the door had shut behind her before inching out from behind his makeshift shield. "I don't know how you do that."

"Do what?"

"Tell off customers like that. I feel queasy just watching."

"It's all about attitude, my friend. If theirs is shitty, they get shit back. Besides, Mr. Hamm legitimately told me I'm allowed to kick out anyone who doesn't fit the 'values' of our establishment. It's one of the many things I enjoy about this job."

"Well, I could never do it."

"And *that* is why you should be grateful to have such a wonderful manager." Sana batted her long eyelashes at him.

"More like a bloodthirsty she-demon," he rejoined.

"That is the single highest compliment anyone has ever paid me. Though, for the record, in my culture, I'd be a jinni. Get it right. Or, better yet, get back to work. If you're not going to be helpful here, Joshua could probably use a hand in the back."

Pete scurried off to do as she said, wondering how he'd ended up with two such similar bosses in such different industries. He ducked through the swinging door next to the line of sinks and found himself in the stockroom. It wasn't as big as the main room, but without the squishy couches, abstract artwork, and the eclectic odds and ends stuck everywhere, it was far less cramped.

As promised, Joshua was opening boxes and tallying their contents on a clipboard. He looked up when Pete entered. "Hey, flamer."

"Don't call me that," Pete answered without inflection. He was so used to Joshua's jabs, they barely fazed him anymore.

"Oooh," Joshua cooed, "a declarative statement. That's a huge step for you. Next you'll mouth off to Sana or—gasp!—say a bad word."

"Fuck off," Pete said cheerfully. "How's that for a bad word?"

Joshua pretended to fan himself. "Why I never! Much as I would *love* to trade blows with you, we have a lot of inventory to get through. Grab that box over there and start counting."

Pete did as he was told, even though Joshua and he had the same rank. He didn't mind, as long as something actually needed to be done. However, those times when Joshua ordered him to stack syrup bottles in the shape of bowling pins and play Stockroom Strike with him, he was far less willing to acquiesce.

They worked together in silence for several minutes. Before long, Pete fell into a rhythm: open a box, count cups and boxes of tea, and scratch numbers onto his inventory log. Wash, rinse, repeat. The monotony of it drowned out thought. For the first time in a week, he went fifteen whole minutes without thinking about Kyle.

Damn. In his head, the counter reset to zero.

"So, what's going on with you?" Joshua asked casually.

Pete didn't look up from the box he was prying open. "Why do you ask?"

"I'm just making conversation."

Pete's skepticism must have shown on his face, because Joshua dropped the casual act. "You looked like you were a hundred miles away just then. And to see a robot like you actually make a facial expression means something must have gone down." He paused. "Not that I care."

"Oh, of course not," Pete deadpanned.

"So, what is it? Boy troubles?"

"Why do people keep assuming it's a boy?"

"Because we're all praying it is," Joshua teased. "I've never met someone wound as tight as you. You need to get some action, stat."

Pete smiled serenely. "Ah, yes, that must be it. I'm suffering from a dearth of sexual activity."

Chances were he got laid more often than Joshua did. Not that Joshua was unattractive—blond, green eyes, nice face—and he certainly talked about his ventures at the local gay clubs often enough. He seldom mentioned hookups, though, either because it wasn't work appropriate (unlikely), or because he couldn't keep his mouth shut long enough for anyone to go home with him. Pete had gotten over his initial workplace crush on him by the end of his first day.

He managed to dodge the rest of Joshua's invasive questions until his shift ended a little after two in the afternoon. He gathered his belongings, waved good-bye to Sana, and then headed for LACC's campus. It was a twenty-minute walk to class when the weather was nice. At this time of year, Pete made it in fifteen.

When he arrived at CO SCI 104—Mathematics for Programmers—class was just about to start. The computer lab was filled to the brim, as per usual. Generally, the afternoon lectures were jam-packed, whereas the morning ones were populated solely by Pete and a handful of other nerds who never got invited to parties.

One such student waved at him from the back row. Pete hurried to grab the computer next to him before anyone else could pounce.

"Hey, Raj," he said when he was close enough.

"Yo," Raj said back, grinning. "Want to play *Minecraft* with me?"

"I would, but I actually have to take notes today. I hear the midterm is going to have us all praying."

Raj stuck his tongue out at him and turned back to his computer, where he already had the game booted up. He was the only friend Pete had managed to make in the Computer Science Department, and that was only because Raj had sat next to him one day and struck up a conversation. It was nice having someone to discuss programming with. Even his own mother's eyes glassed over when he started talking binary.

He threw his bag down next to his seat and settled in. Thankfully, his computer was already on, so when Professor Whiton appeared at the front of the class, he was ready to go. Whiton wasted no time getting into the day's topic: probability theory. She fired off notes almost faster than he could type, barely pausing for breath. She only let up to take questions. Pete was proud to say he had none.

He opened up an internet browser and googled their homework portal while she fielded a question about discrete integers Pete remembered from last semester. He logged in and then clicked the Recent Assignments tab. He almost cheered out loud when he saw no new entries. Thank God. He had big plans for the weekend, and having to study was not part of them.

His thoughts strayed to what Colette had told him at the end of the last shoot. Filming would take place over the course of the next several weeks. She'd more or less ordered Pete to drop his other projects and concentrate solely on *Heat Wave*. He'd agreed, failing to mention that he had absolutely nothing else lined up anyway.

Colette was willing to work around his schedule, to a certain extent, but she'd made it clear he'd be scheduled on weekends once she confirmed dates. That worked out great, as far as school was concerned. He only had class Monday through Thursday anyway. His job, however, was another story. He might be able to pull it off, since he usually worked Friday nights, and porn was more of a day gig, but there were no guarantees. If something came up, he'd have to hope Sana was feeling generous. Of his two bosses, she seemed less likely to murder him if he asked for a day off.

Pete sighed to himself. He prayed his schedule would work itself out. Not because he thought Sana would mind, but because he didn't want to feel like he was letting her down, or worse, hiding something from her. Which, of course, he was.

He checked back into the lecture to see if they'd moved on to anything new. Whiton was giving an in-depth answer to a basic question about data compression. Nope. A glance to Raj revealed he was engrossed in his game. Pete wondered why Raj had even bothered to show up.

Opening a new browser tab, he logged on to Facebook. He hardly ever posted anything—for a variety of reasons—but it was better than fretting about Kyle for the umpteenth time. He scrolled through his newsfeed, which featured memes, political tirades, and pictures of food. The usual.

He stopped when he saw a status from his mom talking about how she'd tried to make risotto and had blackened their best (and only) saucepan. He shook his head and typed a comment begging her to cook only when the fire department was on standby. She responded within seconds, flooding him with laughing emojis. Sometimes he regretted teaching her to text.

Pete scrolled for another few minutes, one ear cocked toward the professor, before boredom overtook him again. He opened a third tab and stared at the blank search bar, wondering what he should do next.

An idea popped into his head, and he found himself typing before he could think it through. He entered *Kyle Darko* into the search bar. The results took all of two seconds to pop up, and when they did, he was grateful he was sitting in the back. He quickly turned on SafeSearch, and the graphic images disappeared again, leaving links to a variety of porn websites. The school's firewall would block them if he tried to click on them, but he could still read their metadata.

Pete skimmed their titles: Hot Str8 Boyz, eXXXotica.com, GurlsNGays, and more. It looked like a good mix of both straight and gay sites. So, Kyle was a true crossover, then. Emphasis on *was* if what Colette had told him was true. Pete tried not to speculate about other people's sexual orientations, but at least one mystery about Kyle had been solved: he liked men. All question of him being gay for pay had been obliterated from Pete's brain the moment their lips had touched. Kyle might be faking his interest in Pete, but his interest in men was sincere.

Clearing his throat, he clicked the next button. Another page of results loaded. He wasn't certain what he was looking for. Maybe a personal website or a wiki page. If Kyle was new to porn, though, he might not have his own site yet. Pete had opted for a blog, which he hadn't posted on in weeks. At least it was free.

He made it through another page without finding anything more interesting than a brief interview Kyle had done for a local skin mag. It consisted of two questions: what were Kyle's favorite scenes to film, and what did Kyle find most sexy? Much as Pete was loath to admit it, he'd hastened to read the answer to the latter. Kyle was most attracted to confidence. Figured.

Maybe he should give up. Hmm. He decided to try his luck at one more page. He perked up when it loaded. The first result was a Facebook page for Kyle Darko. Pete's heart spasmed against his ribs.

He clicked the link and jiggled his leg with impatience as he waited for it to load.

When it did, he almost didn't know how to react. He spent a long minute staring blankly at the profile. It wasn't a fan page, like he'd expected, but a public profile. With friends and wall posts and pictures and everything. It looked as though Kyle actually used it.

Pete stared, mind whirring. Did Kyle have friends who knew he was a porn star? It couldn't be. He clicked on the About Me section. Links to the same websites Pete had seen earlier popped up, in addition to an online portfolio. Beneath that, there was a space for a bio, in which was written: "Lover by Trade. Porn Star by Name. Check out my work if you want to see what all the fuss is about."

Well, that clinched it. This page was definitely run by Kyle. That sounded just like him.

Pete scrolled through his wall. He told himself that he was just confirming what he already knew, but that was a lie. In truth, he couldn't pass up an opportunity to learn more about him. This was the first real insight he'd gotten into his mysterious costar.

Kyle wasn't from California like Pete was. He was originally from Miami, which actually made sense. His in-your-face attitude was much more East Coast than West Coast. And he had tons of friends. Tons. His wall was covered in page after page of posts inviting him to drinks or proclaiming what fun they'd had with him at such-and-such event. There were plenty of posts from guys too, saying how hot he was and entreating him to work with them. That part made Pete kind of proud. Out of all these potential partners, Kyle had chosen him.

He checked out Kyle's family information next, though he didn't expect to find anything. Kyle might have friends on his page, but surely he wasn't out to his *parents*.

To his immense surprise, there were five people listed as his siblings, including a woman named Vivian who looked so much like him there was no question she was his sister.

Pete spent a minute processing this information. Kyle had siblings, and they knew he was in porn. Christ. He couldn't even fathom that. To a lesser extent, he was also surprised to learn Kyle wasn't an only child. He'd sort of pegged him as one.

As that thought resonated in his head, he finally realized how creepy he was being. Stalking his coworker on social media. It was a public page, but still, he was months deep into his profile. No one with a mere passing interest in him would be looking at his beach photos from this past summer.

Pete closed the tab, mentally berating himself even as he was grateful he finally knew *something* about Kyle. As if he needed fuel to feed this weird fixation he was developing. Why was he spending time on a dude who blew so hot and cold, he reminded Pete of the broken AC in his car? He needed to get a grip. Especially considering he had no idea what things would be like the next time they saw each other.

Admit it, said a traitorous voice in the back of his head, *you like Kyle. And as much as you keep denying it, you think he likes you too.*

In his head, Pete jabbed the Escape key, shutting that line of thinking down. The last thing he needed was a crush on a coworker. Office romances were just as messy in porn as they were everywhere else. Sometimes even more so, in a literal sense.

And there was still the small matter of how much Kyle looked like Pete's ex. That added a whole double layer of weird to the situation. Pete had done his best to push that fact out of his brain, but now he had to wonder if some part of him didn't think Kyle was a second chance at making things work with *him*.

He put his face in his hands. God, why did this have to be so *complicated*?

Mercifully, Whiton interrupted his thoughts by announcing when their first exam would be and where they could find the study guide for it. Pete looked at his notes. He had a grand total of three paragraphs typed. Damn.

CHAPTER  6

Pete was lying on his bed, staring at his ceiling—as was his default brooding position these days—when his phone rang next to him. He turned his head to look at it, and upon seeing Colette's name, rocketed up into a sitting position.

For a full ring, he watched it, apprehension creeping through him like mist over the surface of a lake. She could be calling to schedule their next filming session, or to ask what the hell he'd done to Kyle. Either way, at least the waiting game was over.

He snatched his phone up before it could ring again. "Hey. What's up?"

"Morning, sunshine," Colette said.

So far, so good.

He switched ears. "Good morning."

"You sound awful. Rough night?"

"Kind of. I didn't sleep well." He felt a little better already, though. If she were calling to fire him from the project, she wouldn't be so jovial. She'd told him once that turnover was expensive.

"Hopefully my news will cheer you up. Remember when I said I'd call when Yolanda and I had the schedule worked out?"

"Of course." He leaned forward with anticipation even though she couldn't see him.

"Well, my little starlet, the time has come. We've got the next session all planned out."

He pumped a fist silently in the air. "When are we filming?"

"That's part one of why I called. We're *not* filming."

"Why not?"

"I promised you some modeling work, didn't I? It's promo pic time."

"Ah. I see." That was pretty standard. "What do you need from me? Head shots? I have work in an hour, but I can stop by the office tomorrow and see the photographer."

"Actually, that's part two. Since you and Darko play so well off each other, we want to do a joint photo shoot."

His relief morphed into shoulder-hunching tension. "Joint as in me and Kyle? Together? At the same time?"

"That is what the word 'joint' generally means, yes. Problem?"

"No," he blurted out. "No problem. It's just, I've never modeled with a partner before."

"Then it'll be good experience. And since I promised there wouldn't be any nudity, you can even use these shots in your mainstream portfolio. Assuming, of course, that the agencies you're looking at don't mind some homoerotic subtext. From my understanding of the fashion industry, they don't."

He laughed, despite the airplane-sized butterflies zooming around in his stomach. "I do need to update my portfolio."

"Perfect. Oh, and FYI, the photo shoot is going to be beach themed. We'll provide wardrobe, so you don't need to bring anything special. Just be ready to make love to the camera this Friday, eight in the morning, at the office. After the show you and Darko gave last time, I'm looking forward to a truly sizzling performance."

Gulp. "I'll do my best."

"Got any questions for me before I let you go?"

He hesitated, words rolling around on his tongue. If he were smart, he'd leave it alone, but nothing he'd done lately could be categorized as smart. "Not about the photo shoot, no."

"Something else on your mind?"

If Kyle were upset, he might have confided in Colette. She'd give it to Pete straight if he'd done something wrong, and then he could make sure he never did it again. Pete couldn't pass up an opportunity to hear the truth. "I was just wondering . . . did Kyle say anything to you after we filmed the teaser? About me?"

There was a pregnant pause. "You mean about your performance, or what?"

"I don't know. Anything." He winced. He had the vocal equivalent of a bad poker face.

"He had to leave right after we wrapped, so I didn't get to talk to him then. But when I called him earlier to tell him we were doing a photo shoot, he sounded excited."

Pete exhaled slowly. Joyce must have been mistaken, which meant Pete had been tormenting himself for no reason. He was too relieved to mind. Just to be sure, he asked, "He didn't seem freaked out or anything?"

"Why would he be freaked out?"

"No reason, I guess. He just ran off so quickly after filming ended . . . I wanted to make sure everything was okay, and it sounds like it is. Forget I said anything."

Colette was silent for a long moment. "You know, this isn't the first time you've asked me about Darko. You don't normally mention your costars to me. Why the sudden interest?"

"I'm not interested," Pete lied. "I was just looking for feedback."

Colette paused yet again, and cold sweat sprang up on Pete's brow.

"Look, Jaden, I'm going to be frank with you—"

Uh-oh. Now he'd done it.

"—I think you're losing sight of why you're here. We're making a movie, and as much as I want you and Darko to get along, this is a *job*, not high school. There's no place for all this he-said-she-said bullshit on my set. Things need to be kept professional at all times. Understood?"

Pete had to take a deep breath before his throat loosened enough for him to say, "Yes."

"Are you sure? Darko said you were the right choice for this, and I thought you were as well, but the way you've been acting lately doesn't instill faith in me. I need to know that you're committed to *Heat Wave* before we proceed. If you don't think you can handle a project of this magnitude, there's still ample time to replace you."

Pete's veins filled with ice. "I'm fully committed, I swear. I want this role. I'll do whatever it takes to make it work."

"Will you? You've always been quiet, and more than a little insecure, but those are internal problems. I've never seen you let someone else throw you off your game. If you can promise me right now you'll get it together, I'll believe you."

Pete swallowed thickly. To his surprise, his answer came out smooth and even. "I'll get it together, Colette. I swear. It won't happen again."

"Good. Keep that in mind when you show up to the photo shoot. Bring your A game, and don't you dare be late."

She hung up without saying good-bye.

He stared at his phone until the screen dimmed, stomach acid bubbling. Shit. Colette was right. He'd gotten so tangled up in his attraction to Kyle, he'd forgotten how much was riding on this. It was more than just money. It was his future with Murmur Inc. Colette clearly suspected his interest in Kyle wasn't strictly professional. And why wouldn't she? Kyle was gorgeous, and Pete was nipping at his heels like a lovesick puppy.

He shook his head. He'd taken two steps forward only to take one back. Porn was supposed to help his confidence, not crush it. Right now, it felt like he was doing everything wrong.

But not anymore. He was going to keep his promise to Colette, no matter what it took.

He made himself get out of bed and take a shower. He stood under the spray until the pelletized water stung his skin, thinking about nothing and everything all at once. Flashes of memories came to him: bright lights, salty sweat, and his reflection in Kyle's deep brown eyes. He imagined rinsing the thoughts off, letting them swirl down the drain.

His fingers were pruned by the time he got out of the shower. He put on clean clothes, brushed his teeth, and combed his hair. Afterward, he felt marginally better. At least, better enough to not call out of work.

The drive to the Globe was uneventful. Pushing open the glass double doors, he was comforted by the familiar smell of roasted beans. At least one thing in his life hadn't changed. Sana was in her usual spot behind the counter, teenagers were lounging on the squishy couches, and Joshua was skulking by the refrigerator.

After greeting Sana, Pete busied himself washing dishes: mismatched mugs, blenders, spoons, anything he could get his hands on. For the first hour of his shift, he actually managed to get his mind off things. When the second hour rolled around, however, there was a lull, and he had to hunt for ways to pass the time.

He filled the jugs at the milk station to the brim. Then he removed all the sugar packets from the trays and put them back in so they were facing the same way. He even married the little jars of spices that they kept up at the counter. After finishing, he looked around for his next task. All the customers had drinks and most were on laptops or smartphones, oblivious to him. Sana was flipping through an art magazine, and Joshua was rearranging the alphabetic magnets on the refrigerator to say various rude phrases.

There was nothing left to do. At least, nothing work related. There was one thing he could always do: give himself a fresh bout of cancer. He pulled his cigs out of his pocket, waved at Sana to get her attention, and then held them up. She nodded and went back to reading her magazine.

It was universally understood that if employees wanted to smoke, they needed to do so away from the storefront, which faced a major intersection and had a fair amount of foot traffic. Pete removed his apron and slipped out the side door, which led onto a smaller street. It was still fairly busy—it was impossible to avoid pedestrians in LA—but he was shielded from the view of the cars. He moved a good ten feet away from the door before lighting up.

There weren't many people walking around, as close as it was to dinnertime, but he made certain to exhale away from anyone who came near. The last thing he needed was some health nut getting on his case. LA was crawling with them, and he'd been lectured more times than he could count.

As if on cue, someone stopped a few feet away from him. "Hey."

Pete didn't look up. He made room for the person to pass and dragged on his cigarette.

The person didn't give up, however. In his periphery, they stepped closer. He tensed, preparing for a rant, but all the person did was repeat, "Hey."

Wait. He knew that voice. His head jerked to the side.

Sure enough, Kyle was standing next to him, looking abnormally normal in jeans and a black hoodie. He even had a pair of lime-green headphones around his neck from which the faint sound of music emanated. Pete stared at him. Had his brain conjured up Kyle? If only he'd spent the day thinking about piles of money.

"Um, hi," he eventually said back.

"How are you?"

Pete knew he should respond, but he was too busy staring at Kyle. As accustomed as he was to seeing Kyle in just his underwear, his street clothes were a beguiling treat. Kyle's dark hair was devoid of gel today and had been ruffled by the brisk wind. He hadn't shaved, and one of his shoelaces was untied. He should have looked like a mess, but somehow, it suited him. If anyone could make unkempt into a fashion statement, it was Kyle.

Pete's newfound resolve to keep things professional flew out of his head, along with his ability to form sentences.

"Are you all right?" Kyle asked after a full ten seconds of silence passed. "I know you're not the most talkative person, but this is a bit much."

"Oh, sorry," Pete mumbled. "You took me by surprise."

"Yeah, same here." He slid his hands into his pockets, rocking back on his heels.

"Did you follow me here?" Pete blurted out. As soon as the words left him, he wanted to smack himself. Kyle had just said he hadn't expected to see him. Still, people didn't simply run into each other in a city of nearly four million.

"No," Kyle said carefully. "It's just a coincidence. I wasn't even supposed to be on this side of town today, but my sister wanted to have lunch. I saw you standing here, so I thought I'd say hi." He stepped away like he was going to walk past him. "I can go, if you want."

"No, don't," Pete scrambled to say. "Sorry, I didn't mean to act all paranoid. It's just, um, a really big coincidence."

Well, clearly his worries that things might be awkward were completely unfounded. He sighed and threw his cigarette to the ground, stamping it out.

To his surprise, Kyle grinned. "Yeah, us meeting like this is pretty implausible. One might even call it fate." He waggled his eyebrows.

An unintended laugh burst from Pete. "I guess so."

Kyle's characteristic smirk slid onto his face. "Happy to see me?"

"Yeah, I am." It was true. He felt like a cloud had been hanging over him for days, but now that Kyle was here, it dissipated. "I was worried about you."

He winced. He hadn't meant to be quite that honest.

"Ah, let me guess: because of my disappearing act the last time we were together?" Kyle rubbed the back of his neck. He almost looked chagrinned. "Sorry about that. After our shoot, I . . . well, I needed to do some thinking."

"Thinking? About what?"

"I realized something, and it spooked me. I had to wrap my head around it."

Pete ran his tongue over his dry lips. "What'd you realize?"

"Am I holding you up from something?" Kyle asked. "Are you meeting someone? I don't want to keep you."

"No, I'm not meeting anyone. You are, though. Don't you need to find your sister?"

"Nah, I have some time. I'm chronically early to things. Being late makes me antsy."

Pete blinked. "I never would have guessed."

"Really? Why?" Kyle cocked his head in the feline way Pete had come to associate with him. Initially, he'd thought the motion was affected, just another seduction technique, but it seemed it was a genuine mannerism of his.

"I dunno." Pete shrugged. "You just don't seem like the sort of person who gets anxious."

"How do you know what sort of person I am?" Kyle watched him intently.

Pete held up his hands. "Whoa, man, sorry. I didn't mean it like that."

But Kyle was smirking again. "It's okay. I'm just teasing you." His eyes darted briefly down Pete and back up again. "You make me want to do that. I don't know why."

Goddamn. One little look, and Kyle could send him reeling.

"So, you have some time," Pete reiterated, not knowing where his sentence was going to end up. He struggled with what he wanted to say versus his ability to say it, and ultimately said nothing.

Luckily, Kyle had no such reservations. "Do you want to . . . I don't know." He glanced up at the sign hanging above the door to the Globe. "Get coffee? Or something? I can't stay for long, but it's a start."

A start to what? Pete had no idea, but he sure as hell wanted to find out. "Yeah, I'd like that." In a flash, Pete remembered where he was and what he was doing. "Shit. I can't."

Thank God he'd taken his apron off. There was nothing to indicate he worked here. He wasn't quite ready to reveal his cliché day job just yet. Or possibly ever.

Kyle blinked at him. "If this is your way of playing hard to get, I must say, it's working."

"No, no." Pete waved his hands. "It's not that. I just forgot I have work later." *And by later, I mean right now.*

"You're filming later?"

"No. I work, um, somewhere else. I have a day job." Pete mentally rolled his eyes at himself. He sounded about as genuine as the bags the street hawkers sold in Koreatown.

"Ah," Kyle said. "I guess it can't be helped, then. Shame."

"I'm sorry, Kyle." He looked down at the sidewalk. "I really am."

For a moment, Kyle didn't respond. Then he said, "You should call me Evan."

Pete nudged a pebble with his shoe and tried for a joke. "Is that like a kink of yours or something? Most guys ask me to call them daddy."

"No, it's my real name."

A record skipped in Pete's head. Slowly, he raised his head and choked out, "What?"

"Evan. My name is Evan."

Pete stared at him, eyes wide. A thousand questions flooded into his brain so quickly he couldn't articulate any of them. Instead, he repeated, *"What?"*

Kyle—Evan shrugged in what Pete assumed was an attempt at casualness, but it came across as defensive. "We're going to be working together for the next month, so we might as well get to know one another. You know, before we get to know each other in the biblical sense."

Pete would have laughed under normal circumstances, but he was still too shocked. Atomic bombs were going off in his chest. "But you can't . . . I mean, you shouldn't . . . You can't . . . tell me your name."

"I'm pretty sure I just did." His voice was confident, but he wasn't quite looking Pete in the eye. "It's really not that serious. Darko is my actual last name, and everyone calls me that. Well, except you."

"It's not the same. A first or last name by itself doesn't mean anything." Pete touched an exasperated hand to his brow. "I can't believe you just did that. We barely know each other. Do you tell everyone you work with? Because that's really not safe."

"You're the first person I've told, besides Colette obviously. Though for the record, lots of people in my personal life know I'm in porn. I'm not gonna lose any friends or whatever if they find out."

Pete had a flashbulb memory of when he'd googled *Kyle Darko* and found his Facebook with a whole slew of siblings listed. Before he could think it through, he blurted out, "I researched you the other day."

Evan smiled. "Really now? Why?"

"I was curious. I wanted to know more about you." Apparently, it was honesty hour.

"Interesting." He looked inexplicably pleased. "What'd you find?"

"A bunch of porn, of course, and your website, and uh, your Facebook."

"I see. Learn anything good?"

"Yeah, I did." He ran distracted fingers through his hair. "Are you out to your family?"

"They know I like men."

"I mean the other out. Porn star out."

"Yes." Evan studied him. "Does that surprise you?"

"Of course it does." He wiped a hand down his mouth. "I can't even *fathom* that."

"Can't you?" Evan cocked his head to the side. "So, you'd never come out, then?"

"Of course not!"

"But someone you know could stumble upon your videos at any time. Nothing on the internet ever goes away. You're not worried about that at all?"

"No," Pete said, sounding more confident than he felt. "It's a calculated risk, and I'm pretty good at math. There's way too much porn out there for anyone to accidentally stumble upon anything, and I haven't been in enough films to ping on anyone's radar." By the end of his diatribe, he could no longer tell if he was saying it for Evan's benefit or his own.

"It only takes one," Evan countered. "That's why I elected to skip the whole secret-identity shtick and let it all hang out. Literally."

A frisson slithered down Pete's spine, but it wasn't the usual excitement he felt around Evan. It was more like shards of ice mixed with a generous dose of panic. He couldn't even *think* about being out without stirring up memories he'd just as soon bury. "I'm not trying to lecture you, but you should keep Kyle and Evan separate. Do you realize what the wrong person can do with your real name? They could sell it to a tabloid or leak it to the internet. You just placed a lot of trust in me."

"Was that a mistake?" Evan asked, a hard glint in his dark eyes.

"No, of course not." Pete tried to look sincere, but he was willing to bet he just looked queasy. "I won't tell anyone. I promise." He almost added, *After what I went through, I would never*, but that would raise questions he had no desire to answer.

"Good. I didn't think you would."

"I have to ask, though . . . You don't expect me to tell you my real name, do you? Because I'm not comfortable with that."

"No," Evan said, somewhat sharply. "I didn't tell you so you'd return the favor. I told you because I wanted to. Is that so hard for you to imagine?"

"Sorry." Pete took a step back. "I didn't mean it like that. I'm surprised, is all. You keep throwing me for a loop, and it makes me babble."

"It's okay." His words and his tone didn't quite match. "I suppose I should get going." Evan started to walk past him.

With a burst of confidence Pete hadn't known he had, he grabbed Evan's arm. "Wait. There's still one thing I need to know."

"What's that?"

"Why me? Of all people to tell, why pick a guy you just met? It can't just be because we're going to work together, or you would have told your previous costars. Tell me the real reason."

Evan's eyes drifted down Pete's arm to where Pete's fingers were gripping his biceps. "I knew you had some fight in you."

Pete released him and stepped back. "Sorry. I just— I don't think I can take any more of this back and forth."

Evan faced him, and Pete suddenly became aware of how closely they were standing. "Back and forth?"

"Yeah," Pete continued despite himself. "I keep trying to figure you out, but it's impossible. You're hot one second and cold the next, and . . . I can't spend another night thinking about you, wondering if I've screwed things up. It's torture."

Evan blinked slowly at him, his thick black eyelashes casting long shadows on his cheeks. Then he smiled. "You've discovered my evil plan. I want you to spend all your time thinking about me."

Pete frowned. "Very funny."

"Who says I'm joking? And for the record, there's no cold here." He winked. "I'm always hot."

With that, he sidestepped Pete and sauntered away. Before he was out of earshot, he called over his shoulder, "See you Friday. I'm looking forward to our photo shoot."

Pete watched him shrink into the distance for an indeterminate amount of time. It wasn't until he vanished that the earth released its death grip on him. He stepped back until his shoulders hit brick.

Kyle had raised as many questions as he'd answered, though one thing was now crystal clear: keeping things professional was going to be a lot harder than Pete had thought.

He headed back inside and found Sana still at the counter, only now she had three empty espresso cups in front of her.

"Oh God," Pete groaned, "you didn't."

"I did!" Sana exclaimed, sticking a long finger in the air. She appeared somewhat deranged, as she always did when she binged on caffeine. "Who was that guy, by the way?"

Pete nearly dropped his apron halfway through putting it back on. "What guy?"

"The one you were talking to outside. I could just barely see you through the window. Was he bothering you?" She rubbed her hands together eagerly. "Was he giving you shit for smoking? If he's still out there, I'm happy to—"

"He was no one," Pete interrupted. "Just some guy."

Sana pouted. "Are you sure? Seemed like you were discussing something serious."

Pete turned away, hiding his face. "It was nothing, I swear. Don't worry about it. And for the sake of the general public, no more espresso for you."

CHAPTER 7

The day of the photo shoot, Pete rose shortly before dawn. Normally, he'd hit snooze at least five times and roll out of bed only when absolutely necessary, but not today. He was too excited. Miraculously, he'd gotten a decent night's sleep, helped by his earlier conversation with Ky—Evan. When the sun broke over the horizon, he was ready. Jittery, but ready.

He took his time going through his morning hygiene routine. Colette had said the photo shoot would be sex-free, but that didn't mean he and Evan wouldn't be getting up close and personal. He took a long shower, shaved his sparse facial hair, and cleaned his mouth so thoroughly he might be able to skip his next dental appointment. His clothing, however, he paid little mind to, since they were going to dress him anyway. He pulled on whatever was clean, threw a hoodie over that for warmth, and tiptoed past the sound of his mom's gentle snoring. The front door whispered shut behind him.

The drive to Murmur Inc. was uneventful, which was fortunate, considering how preoccupied he was with thoughts of seeing Evan. He shook his head and reminded himself that as soon as he stepped on set, he would have to call him Kyle again. Shit, that was going to get confusing. If he accidentally called him by his real name, it would be disastrous. Colette would skin him for one thing. She took the privacy of her employees more seriously than she took her business, and *that* was saying something.

Plus, as much as Evan had tried to act casual about it, it was clear he hadn't revealed his name lightly. Pete still didn't know quite what to make of that. It was a bombshell, for sure. And it had come at the worst possible time.

It was like Evan somehow *knew* that Pete had decided to back off, and had found a way to ensnare him yet again. Between having sex with strangers and doing it in front of more strangers, there weren't a lot of ways to create intimacy on porn sets. Evan had found a major one. Pete was now plagued by a simple question: why? Why had Evan told him? It hadn't escaped Pete's notice that Evan had dodged the question before. Whatever his reason, it seemed he was keeping it to himself for now.

Pete could speculate all day and never figure out what was going on in Evan's head. For now, his goal was to make it through this photo shoot alive. He needed to play it cool, which was unfortunate, considering he was . . . well, himself.

It's going to be okay, he reassured himself as he turned into Murmur Inc.'s parking lot. He'd done dozens of photo shoots before. This one wasn't going to be any different, even with Evan there, watching his every move. It was no big deal.

His blood pressure didn't believe him.

He parked his car and entered the building from the side door. He tried to psych himself up as he took the stairs two at a time, but he felt less like the sex god he was supposed to be and more like his character: a socially awkward, inexperienced college kid. Colette really did have a knack for casting. He was, however, less nervous than he'd been for the previous two shoots. That was a trend he fervently hoped would continue.

When he reached the third floor, he ducked past rows of cubicles where the phone sex operators were already busy at work. He scurried over to Booth Four. Colette had told him to expect a big production, but nothing could have prepared him for what he saw when he pushed open the door. His jaw nearly dropped as he surveyed the transformed interior of the recording booth.

Three things stood out to him in vivid detail. First, Colette was sitting in an old-school director's chair, a red scarf wrapped around her head and a pair of dark sunglasses balanced on her nose. She looked like she belonged on the set of one of the seventies' Golden Age masterpieces, like *Deep Throat* or *The Devil in Miss Jones*. Second, the room was crammed with people, from light techs to set directors to interns bringing coffee to the aforementioned. And third, the set itself was *gorgeous*.

It was like someone had taken a slice of California beach and transplanted it into Murmur Inc. The bright lights overhead perfectly simulated sunshine on a clear day, right down to the heat radiating from them. White sand had been smoothed across the breadth of the floor, which was dotted with palm trees in planters. The backdrop had been painted in cerulean and azure, imitating the ocean and sky.

Pete almost thought he could taste salt on the air. He was positive that with the right filters, the scene would look exceptional on film. He spent a moment simply standing there, drinking in the energy from the crowd. There was nothing quite like walking onto a buzzing set.

Colette spotted him and waved. He jogged her way, grateful for once that he was so skinny. He weaved through the throng with ease.

She was sitting in front of a dozen monitors, all connected to a frankly stunning array of wires. The majority of them showed the set from different angles, but the last three showed editing software.

"Jaden, darling," Colette greeted him in an affected old-Hollywood accent. "Marvelous of you to join us."

"Looks like you've found your own role," Pete joked. "Mademoiselle Director, your set is enchanting. You're taking summer to a new level."

"Just a little something to get you in the mood. And believe me, you will be soon enough."

Before he could ask what she meant, Colette pointed a turquoise nail at a monitor on the far right. "Check it out. It's raw, but you can have a sneak peek."

Pete walked around and peered over her shoulder. On the screen was a paused frame of video featuring Evan and him in Joyce's living room. "Is this the teaser? You're already working on it?"

"Yup. We're still cleaning it at the moment. There's a lot of editing to be done, but I expect it to be a hit. The camera loves you both." She tapped a button on a keyboard. The clip played, and though there was no sound, Pete recognized the exact point at which it began. Evan had just grabbed his arm and said he wanted to pin him down. Watching it from an outside perspective was almost as hot as being there. The intensity in Evan's body language was enough to give him chills.

He watched in silence as their figures interacted on screen. He had to admit, they looked good together. Their appearances were so different, they balanced each other. If he were one to wax poetic, he'd call it night and day. And there was definitely something powerful between them, something incendiary.

Instead of being eclipsed by Evan, Pete's performance had been improved by him. He could tell that for once, he wasn't overthinking things. He was just reacting, and the reactions Evan coaxed out of him were both genuine and visceral. He willed himself not to get hard while watching his own film. That would take masturbation to a whole new level.

"What do you think?" Colette asked.

"It's very, um, stimulating," he said. "Kyle and I make a good team."

"That's putting it mildly. There was a point where I thought I could toast a marshmallow just by sticking it between you guys. I almost had to hose Joyce off afterwards. Speaking of which, let's talk wardrobe."

"Was there a segue in there somewhere? Because if so, I missed it."

"You'll understand soon enough." She pointed to a table where several sets of beach gear had been laid out. "Go over there and change into the suit we picked for you. When you're finished, we'll turn you over to the set designers."

"So they can do what, exactly?"

"They're going to add verisimilitude."

Pete blinked at her.

"They're going to douse you with water and sand."

He wrinkled his nose. "Seriously? Hasn't anyone ever told you that sand gets *everywhere*?"

"Yup, it's nature's glitter. Can't be helped, though. You and Darko need to look like you're actually at the beach. And that means you'll need to be wet." Her face was a picture of innocence. "It's for the sake of authenticity, I assure you."

Pete glowered. "More like for your perverse enjoyment."

"Oh, not just my enjoyment, young grasshopper. I invite you to examine exhibit A." She indicated something over Pete's shoulder.

He turned to look and almost drooled. Evan was standing on the other side of the set, wearing form-fitting black swim trunks.

They looked like they'd been designed with him in mind. A handful of people were emptying water bottles over his head. The liquid sluiced down his bare chest, and when he shook his head, droplets flew like diamonds from his hair. He looked like he was in a shampoo commercial. A lewd one.

"So," Colette asked casually, "what do you think of my idea?"

"Murf." Pete cleared his throat. "Um, I mean, yeah. Nice one. Though I have to say, Kyle being hot is starting to get redundant."

Colette laughed and hooked her thumb over her shoulder. "Don your costume, and be quick about it. We haven't got all morning."

He did as instructed, praying he wasn't going to have to wear something embarrassing. It would be just like Colette to put him in a speedo, or a tiny thong like the one Evan had worn before the teaser. Although, the memory of that was almost enough to waylay his anxiety.

To his immense relief, when he approached the wardrobe people, he was handed a standard pair of light-blue swim trunks. They weren't even form-fitting like Evan's. They must have realized he couldn't pull something like that off. Small miracles.

He started to yank his shirt over his head, but something stayed his hand. Had Evan noticed he was here yet? He peeked toward the set. Evan was not-so-subtly watching him, of course, while the designers brushed sand onto his chest and abs. Pete had never envied them more.

He fingered the hem of his shirt. Evan had already seen him in various states of undress. There was no reason to feel self-conscious. Hell, anytime Evan wanted to see him naked, all he had to do was google him. So, why was Pete so nervous?

He turned his back to hide his face, and removed his shirt. Next, he shimmied out of his jeans but kept his underwear on before pulling the swimsuit up his slim hips. He forced himself to move at a normal pace, neither hurrying nor drawing it out.

When he finished, he steeled himself and whirled around. Evan had abandoned any pretense that he wasn't staring. His eyes were lowered, and Pete could guess what part of his anatomy they'd been focused on moments before. They slid slowly up, and when they reached Pete's eyes, they were black with desire. Pete had to look away before his cock took notice.

"Jaden," Colette called, "are you ready?"

"Yeah." His voice was embarrassingly uneven. "I am."

"Go stand by those trees so we can take some test shots." She pointed to an area that was thankfully several yards from Evan.

Pete took his place. Photographers swarmed him. He closed his eyes and fell into the familiarity of his role, letting quiet Pete melt away to be replaced with Jaden, who luxuriated in this sort of attention. He posed, and the photographers snapped dozens of shots of him from every angle before Colette called them off. She indicated for Pete to join her by the monitors once more.

"Look." She pointed to a screen on the left.

Pete made a soft, surprised noise. Whoever had chosen his costume had done a fantastic job. The particular shade of blue made his eyes stand out and injected some color into his skin. He looked like he actually set foot on a beach every once in a while, and that was an accomplishment in and of itself.

"Good?" Colette asked.

"Yeah," Pete said. "Ready when you are."

"Then by all means, go join your leading man."

Pete jogged toward where Evan was already in position, sand sliding pleasantly between his toes. The heat from the overhead lights warmed his exposed skin, and the din from the crowd faded away with every step he took toward Evan. He could almost pretend he was really relaxing at the beach. Though his haywire hormones weren't about to let him forget where he was and what he was about to do.

"Hey," he said when he reached Evan's side.

"Hey," Evan said back, smiling.

Pete stared at the ground to avoid staring at Evan. The set designers had done their work well. Water beaded on his bare chest like jewels, and every now and then a single drop would slide down his abdomen, making Pete yearn to follow its path with a finger, or better yet, his tongue.

Luckily or unluckily, a set designer chose that moment to dump a bottle of water over Pete's head. He stifled a yelp; the water was freezing compared to the warm, body-packed studio. He heard giggling from his right and turned just in time to get splashed in the face. While he sputtered and wiped water from his eyes, the giggles turned into full-blown laughter.

"This isn't funny," he groused.

"It really is," Evan said.

The crew retreated a moment later, leaving them in relative privacy.

"Be honest," Pete said under his breath. "How do I look?"

Evan raised a hand and brushed a thumb over his cheekbone, wiping away a droplet. Then he threaded his fingers through his hair, sweeping it gently back. "Sexy."

Colette approached them, sliding her dark sunglasses on top of her head. "Thanks for fixing Jaden's hair, Darko. He looked like a drowned rat."

Pete glared at him and muttered, "Liar."

Evan grinned impishly. "I meant it, though."

"All right, gentlemen," Colette announced. "Let's begin. There's no script today, but try to keep your characters in mind when selecting your poses. You're two friends who have recently become more. The idea is for you to act like you're falling in love before our very eyes."

Her words made something strange happen inside of Pete. It was like his guts quivered, not necessarily in a bad way. Out of his periphery, he saw Evan watching him. Pete didn't dare meet his gaze.

Colette continued obliviously. "Keep the atmosphere light and playful, like a real day at the beach, but I want to see some serious passion. Got it?" She looked at Pete.

"Yes." He was surprised by how confident he sounded.

Evan slung an arm around Pete's shoulders. "We got this."

"Good. On that note, hold that pose." She snapped at a nearby photographer, who started clicking away. "Jaden, relax. You look like Darko's arm is burning you."

It was. Just that little bit of skin-on-skin contact seared him. Pete had wondered if some of the tension between them might have abated after their kiss, but it seemed Evan still affected him as strongly as ever. What would happen when they finally had sex? Would it scratch Pete's ferocious itch? Or would it make him an addict? He really didn't want to speculate about which seemed more likely.

He couldn't think about it right now anyway. Everyone was watching him expectantly, waiting for him to put on a show. He breathed until his muscles relaxed. Then he slid an arm around

Evan's waist, and they grinned at each other like best buddies. The photographer instructed them to make minor adjustments—move a hand up, angle a leg differently, stand closer or farther apart—and then she snapped away.

Pete tried to keep his character in mind, but his brain was inundated with a hundred niggling thoughts. Colette had instructed them to fall in love on film, and Pete had no idea how to portray that. He'd never been in love; lust was his territory, at least professionally. Any deeper emotion than that was uncharted and potentially full of monsters. Best to steer clear. But if Colette said that's what they had to do . . .

Evan nudged him. "Hey."

Pete startled, almost breaking the pose the photographer had just maneuvered him into. "What?"

"What just happened?"

Pete blinked. "What do you mean?"

"Your energy vanished. What was going through your head?"

The photographer cut in. "Quit the chatter. Your mouths are blurry in half my shots."

They both fell silent, but Pete could still feel Evan's attention on him.

"Well?" Evan asked under his breath a moment later. "What was it?"

"The photographer said not to talk."

"So? Scared she's gonna tell the teacher on us?"

Pete snorted. "You must be new if you haven't learned a healthy fear of Colette yet."

"Just keep your voice down and she won't even notice."

Pete huffed. There was no getting out of this conversation. Out of the corner of his mouth, he whispered, "What gave you the impression I was thinking about something?"

"Don't bullshit me," Evan murmured back. "I can tell when you're overthinking it. Mostly because you start to suck."

"No need to sugarcoat it," Pete muttered.

"I didn't hear a denial, though." Evan swung around to Pete's other side. He looped an arm around him and then pointed at something down the "beach." Pete shielded his eyes from the light and pretended to look, and the photographer snapped a few photos of them like that before instructing them to switch it up again.

"Admit it, you were thinking about something," Evan continued, voice no louder than a rustle.

"You're . . . annoyingly perceptive," Pete responded.

"Which is a fancy way of saying I'm right."

"What do you care?" Pete asked, more than a little defensive.

"I care because if you're still thinking, then I'm not doing my job."

It was becoming a struggle to keep talking quietly when he wanted to demand that Evan explain himself. "And your job is?"

"To get you out of your head." Evan grabbed his shoulder and spun Pete around to face him. Evan's expression was devilish. "To knock you off-balance so you stop thinking and start feeling. It's beautiful when you do."

"That's good," Colette called from the sidelines. "I like how you amped up the intensity, Darko. Even the talking—which is so not subtle, by the way—kinda looks like a confession. I actually don't hate it. Keep going. It's time to spice things up." She signaled to two men, and suddenly there were three photographers instead of one.

Pete started to get back into position, but Evan pushed him again, literally keeping him on his toes. It must have looked like they were just horsing around, because no one said anything.

"Do you know what I told Colette when I first met you?" Evan's voice was no more than a low vibration.

Pete swallowed. "No."

"I told her I wanted to fuck the thinking out of you. I meant it. I love the moment when you get so turned on, your whole brain shuts down."

The air was suddenly charged, like little bolts of lightning were striking between their bodies.

Pete protested weakly, "My brain does not shut down."

"Don't even try to deny it." Evan smirked, stepping closer. "I've memorized your tells."

"Very nice!" Colette called again. She'd moved to stand with the photographers and was watching them with laser-like focus.

Pete blinked at them like a deer, overcome by a sudden bout of jitters. Evan grabbed his face and turned it toward him. His fingers were warm and insistent on his jaw.

"Don't look at them. Look at me. What story are we telling here?"

"Colette said—"

"Forget what she said. We're the ones who have to convey the message with our bodies." One of his hands slid down Pete's side, and the sound of shutter clicks filled the air. "We're supposed to be friends who are slowly falling in love right now. How do we want to show that?" His hand moved back up to Pete's waist, stroking the bare skin reverently.

Pete was having trouble breathing. "I don't know."

"Why don't you know?"

He blurted out, "Because I can't think with you touching me."

Evan's grin widened. "Good."

He moved into Pete's space, his hand still roving over Pete's body. He dragged the back of his fingers up Pete's stomach and then ghosted a thumb over a nipple.

Pete's heartbeat spiked. His attention narrowed until it encompassed nothing but the feel of Evan touching his skin and the heat pouring from Evan's body.

He started to say something—he had no idea what—but Evan leaned forward until their lips were a hair's breadth apart. It shouldn't have been as hot as it was, considering they'd had a make-out session of epic proportions a week before, but Pete could feel Evan's breath brushing against his mouth. Evan's eyes seemed to have some kind of proximity effect. They got more intense the closer he was to them. Pete was dizzy with want within ten seconds.

"Christ, you are so sexy," Evan breathed. He sounded as wrecked as Pete felt. "You have the most beautiful eyes. Crystal clear, like ice. Sometimes I can't sleep at night thinking about them."

Pete forced a laugh, unsure of how else to react, and joked, "That's quite a line. If I didn't know any better, I'd think you really were falling in love with me."

Evan paused, then continued as if Pete hadn't spoken. "You have the best reactions. They're so intense and honest; it's irresistible. I love drawing them out of you, turning your brain off and filling your head with nothing but me." He raked his fingernails lightly down Pete's chest.

"Kyle," Pete gasped. He tried to say more but couldn't. Everywhere Evan touched him lit up like fireworks.

"Like right now, I can tell you're right on that edge. If I can touch you just right, make you feel good, you'll give in to it." He drew a shallow breath. "Tell me what you want."

Pete made a small, pitiful noise and inaudibly mouthed, *Evan.*

There was a loaded pause.

Pete sucked in a breath. He might have just crossed a major line. He searched Evan's face for a reaction: unease, betrayal, maybe even anger. As he watched, Evan's eyebrows shot up, and his eyes darkened.

Pete started to stammer an apology, but then Evan shoved him none too gently. His back hit one of the palm trees, thankfully not hard enough to send them toppling over. He had just enough time to regain his balance before Evan was on him.

Evan forced their bodies together, pressing his mouth hotly to Pete's ear as he demanded, "Say it again."

Pete shuddered from head to toe and whispered, "Evan."

"Oh fuck." Evan kissed him with such brutality, his lips bruised. Distantly, he heard Colette shout something that sounded suspiciously like encouragement, as if they needed any.

Evan kissed him like he needed him to breathe, which was funny, because that was the one thing Pete couldn't seem to do. The bark of the tree scraped his back, and he was hot, much too hot, but all he could focus on was the torturous, hard friction of Evan's mouth against his. The first sweep of tongue left him weak, and when he parted his lips to let Evan slide into him, he had to grab Evan's shoulders for support.

Evan shifted up, pushing him harder back like he couldn't get close enough. Pete matched the movement without thinking, rocking his hips forward. He hissed at the contact. He hadn't realized how impossibly hard he was until his cock met Evan's lower belly. Evan moaned against his mouth and pivoted until Evan's erection nestled insistently against his thigh.

Pete groaned and tightened his grip on Evan's shoulders. That seemed to spur Evan on, because he rocked them together, and they gasped in unison. It wasn't nearly enough. Their pesky swimsuits were in the way, and they were just barely dragging against each other, the fabric harsh and their bodies too slippery from water and sweat, but it felt *amazing.* Pete needed more.

Just as Pete thought he was going to burst out of his skin, Evan slid a hand down and thumbed the waistband of his swimsuit. Pete's whole body seized up as he waited for him to continue. His thoughts were a silent mantra of *Fuck, fuck, fuck, please.*

Evan's fingers dipped below the elastic, caressing his lower belly. "Do you want me to touch you?"

"Yes," Pete said, barely able to push enough air out of his lungs to form the words. "Evan, please."

Evan's hand dipped into Pete's swimsuit, and—

"Cut!"

Evan tore his mouth away and growled, actually *growled.* "Are you fucking kidding me?"

"Oooh, touchy." Colette grinned like the Cheshire cat. "Sorry to break up the fun, boys, but we said we were going to keep this shoot clothed. If I'd let you go any longer, someone would have ended up pregnant."

The crew laughed. Pete's face flamed. He felt like he'd been caught in flagrante, which made zero sense, considering he was being paid to be here.

Like you wouldn't do this for free.

Well. His thoughts were back online, and they had a lot to say.

He edged away, distancing himself from Evan. It was no easy task. Evan was still holding him tightly, and when Pete shifted, he flexed his grip as if to stop him. A second later, however, he dropped his hands, and Pete was able to put some much-needed space between them.

"Are we finished?" Pete was lightheaded and uncomfortably hard. If they did another take, chances were he'd come in his swimsuit— and it was very much his swimsuit now. He doubted wardrobe would want it back after this.

"I can probably make what we have work," Colette answered. "But I'd rather do another round just to be sure."

Shit. "Do we have to?" He hated how whiny he sounded.

"I thought you wanted things to add to your portfolio? Unless you think you can use one of the shots of Darko shoving his tongue down your throat."

He sighed. She was right. "Can I get some water before we try again?"

"Sure. Do what you need to do." She clapped her hands. "Take five, people. Then we'll resume. Darko, great work. Your acting gets better every day."

Evan answered too quietly for anyone but Pete to hear. "It's not acting."

Pete didn't look at him, scared of what he might see if he did. He got off set as quickly as he could without breaking into a run. A refreshments table had been set up along one of the walls. It was covered in sandwiches, coffee, and bottles of water.

He made a beeline for the latter and sucked half of one down in a few gulps. He spent a moment breathing deeply, willing himself to calm down. It was no use. He was still hard. He adjusted his clothing in the front, hoping that would help, but even the brush of fabric against him was too much.

Fuck. He'd known keeping things professional wasn't exactly an option anymore, but they had crossed a major line today. The shoot had in no way called for sex, or even for them to kiss each other, and yet Pete hadn't been able to hold back. He couldn't hide behind Colette's orders or *Heat Wave* this time. He'd kissed Evan because he wanted to.

Evan had a way of crawling under his skin and touching all his most tender places. It made him feel vulnerable and euphoric at the same time. And it scared the shit out of him.

He needed to face facts. This wasn't a typical will-they-won't-they scenario. In a few weeks, they were going to have sex. And it would be public, not just to Colette, or Yolanda, or the people in the studio, but to everyone with an internet connection. Forever. Permanent. Jaden and Kyle's first time, immortalized forever on the silver screen. The sooner he stopped romanticizing this, the better.

"Get it together, Griflow," he muttered to himself.

"'Griflow'?"

Pete glanced to his left. Evan was standing next to him.

"H-hey," Pete stammered. "I didn't see you there." *Shit. That was my real last name. Quick, distract him.* "How are you?"

"I think you know the answer to that." Evan's smile was pure sin.

Arousal twanged in Pete's lower belly from that alone. God, he really had it bad for him.

"You ran off fast." Evan's tone wasn't accusatory, but there was a sharp edge to it that raised goose bumps all over Pete's body. Evan was only a foot or so away, but he was scrutinizing him with laser-like intensity, as if he were trying to read fine print scrawled on Pete's face.

"I was, um, thirsty." Pete took a swig as if to prove his point.

"I'm surprised you can think about anything besides that hard-on you're sporting."

Pete choked on his water. There was no sense in denying it. Evan had felt the truth for himself, could probably see it now.

He cleared his throat. "It's a hazard of the job, you know? It happens."

"Yeah, it does," Evan agreed. "I know that for a fact." He tucked a thumb into his waistband, letting his hand rest right next to his groin. Even if he weren't wearing a tight swimsuit, his erection would have been obvious.

Pete stared at the fat outline of Evan's cock for far longer than he should have, his brain moving sluggishly. Knowing Evan was turned on when they were working was one thing, but seeing it when there weren't any cameras to act as a buffer was different. Real. Raw. He didn't trust himself to speak without giving away just how badly he *wanted*.

Evan's voice took on the deep, rumbling quality of distant thunder. "It seems we both have the same problem. Why don't we do something about it?"

Goddamn. Pete didn't need a road map to figure out where this conversation was headed. Just thinking about it made his mouth water.

"What do you want to do?" Pete asked, needing to hear the answer out loud.

Evan reached out and cupped Pete's erection. "You."

Pete gasped and pressed into the touch. Evan obliged him, palming him through the damp material. Christ, it felt so good to be touched by him. All the frottage in the world couldn't compare to the feeling of Evan's deft fingers finally, *finally* on him.

Evan's pupils were so wide, his irises had disappeared. "Do you want me?"

Pete stared at him for a moment before looking nervously around them. "We have to get back to work."

"That wasn't a no."

It sure as fuck wasn't, but Pete needed to say the closest thing to it that he could manage. "We shouldn't."

"But you want to." Evan slipped his hand into Pete's clothing. Pete trembled, tense and needy, as Evan's hand trailed down through his pubic hair, stopping just before where he really wanted it. "You don't shave?"

"No," Pete said weakly. "Don't want to look any younger than I already do."

Evan licked his lips. "That's weirdly hot. You have so little body hair, except where it counts." His eyes burned. "I want to see it. Let me."

Oh fuck. One more look like that, and Pete wasn't going to be able to remember why he thought this was a bad idea. "We can't just fuck in a room full of people. Even on a porn set, that's frowned upon."

"I don't mean here. You could meet me in the men's room, or we could go somewhere."

"The shoot isn't finished yet."

"Fuck the shoot. Come with me."

Jesus, did that ever sound appealing. Pete could just picture it, getting shoved into one of the bathroom stalls and having Evan pin him against the wall, fingers and lips everywhere. He wondered if he'd go slow, draw it out, like he did the first time they kissed, or if he'd simply yank Pete's trunks down, wrap a hand—or God, a mouth—around him, and give him the relief he ached for.

A fresh wave of arousal surged through him at the thought. Evan still had his hand in Pete's pants, and Pete actually felt himself harden beneath his touch.

Evan must have felt it too, because he glanced down and whistled. "Well, someone likes the sound of that." When he looked back up, his expression was curiously soft. "Come with me?" He removed his hand and reached for Pete's, taking it in a loose grip.

Pete sucked in a breath at the strange intimacy of the gesture. Every fiber of his being was screaming at him to say yes, but a voice in the back of his head nagged at him. He'd never handed out a freebie in his life. It'd be one thing if Evan were a hot guy picking him up at a bar, but he wasn't. He was a colleague. They had to work together for the next several weeks. This could ruin their working relationship.

It could have bigger consequences than that too. If Evan told people that Pete had fucked him recreationally, he might start getting jobs for all the wrong reasons. But was that really what Evan was trying to do? Score a free ride out of him? Pete didn't want to believe it, and Evan seemed genuine enough, but Pete had been burned by a pretty face before . . . one that looked painfully like Evan's.

He couldn't do it. There was too much riding on this. Fucking Evan on the side was asking for trouble, especially while he was still so uncertain about what he wanted from him. He couldn't risk this job and a mountain of potential sore feelings for a quick fuck.

His resolve solidified even as his dick begged him to reconsider. But what really drove the nail home was Colette's voice echoing in the back of his head: *There's still ample time to replace you.*

"I'm sorry," Pete said genuinely. He pulled his hand from Evan's grasp. "I don't work for free."

Evan stared at him blankly for ten full seconds, and then his eyes shuttered like doors had slammed behind them. "Ah. I see." He took a step back, and Pete felt every inch of the distance between them as if it were being yanked from his sinew. "You'd think after the first few times you turned me down, I'd have gotten the message. This really is just a job to you."

The disappointment in his voice cut Pete to the quick. Baffled, he asked, "Is it supposed to be something else?"

Evan looked miserable. "No. But I'd hoped so."

Oh fuck. What had he done?

"I mean," Pete fumbled, "it's not *entirely* a job to me."

"You don't have to lie. I'm a big boy. I can handle rejection."

"I'm not lying." Pete sighed. "Look, I'm obviously attracted to you. *Really* attracted to you. But I don't want to risk this—" he waved between them "—because we're both horny. Okay?" He hated how uncertain he sounded, like he was asking for permission. Was it even possible to be this bad at human interaction?

To his complete shock, a small smile crept over Evan's face. "What do you think this—" he mimicked Pete's waving motion "—is?"

Pete stared at his feet. "I don't know. I've never . . ." He stopped short.

Evan's voice was gentle and probing. "What?"

"I've never *felt* something like this before," he admitted. "Colette keeps calling it chemistry. I don't know if that's the right word for it, though."

"If you knew what it was," Evan asked, "would you want to pursue it?"

"I don't know." Pete raised his water bottle to his lips just to have something to do.

Evan studied his face with keen eyes. "I wish I could read you better."

Pete nearly spat out the sip he'd just taken. "*What*? Half the time I feel like you're reading my goddamn mind."

"That's just body language. When you're not acting, you're reserved to the point of being indecipherable, and it's intimidating."

"Me. Intimidating. That's a new one."

"It's true. Why are you holding yourself back?"

Pete had no desire to answer that question, but he also didn't want to lie, so he settled for a different truth. "Colette's threatened to remove me from the project."

"What?" Evan looked shocked. "Why?"

Pete shrugged. "Probably because I have a tendency to mix business with pleasure when it comes to you. She thinks I'm not dedicated enough to *Heat Wave*, that I have other things on my mind. I promised her I'd get my shit together. If I don't, I'll lose this job."

Evan was silent for a long moment. Eventually, he asked, "So, as long as *Heat Wave* isn't jeopardized, we can do what we want, right? Colette won't take you off the project?"

"I guess. That's not really the point, though."

"Do you have your phone on you?"

"Um." Pete glanced at the wardrobe station, where he'd deposited his clothes. "No, it's in my jeans."

"Go get it."

Pete hesitated. "Why?"

"Because we're going to start small."

Pete didn't think he'd ever had so much trouble following the path of a conversation. "I'm confused."

"Just go get your phone." Evan shooed him away.

Pete did as he was told. His erection had somewhat subsided, but every step made fabric brush against it. By the time he made it there and back, he was twitchy with overstimulation.

"Here," he said without preamble, handing his phone to Evan. He hugged his chest and closed his eyes, willing his dick to chill out. He suspected it would if he could just get away from Evan long enough.

He heard the sound of fingers tapping on a screen. After a few seconds, Evan gave the phone back. "All yours."

Pete took it wordlessly. There was no need to ask what Evan had done to it. That much was obvious. "Want me to call so you'll have my number too?"

Evan smirked. "If you'd be so kind."

Pete found the name *Evan Darko* under his recent contacts and tapped the Call button. As it rang, he studied Evan. "I'm not complaining, but I don't understand how this is going to keep me from getting fired."

"It's not," Evan said. "In fact, it's probably a terrible idea. But I can't stay away any longer either, and I promise I will do everything I can to keep you on this project. I think we can have our cake and hopefully eat it off of each other." He tilted his head and flashed an impish smile. "I'm in if you are."

Pete only had a vague idea of what he was agreeing to, but he didn't hesitate to say, "I'm in."

CHAPTER

W ithin twenty-four hours, Evan sent Pete what felt like a hundred texts.

The first few times his phone went off, he ignored it, assuming it was his mom. Sometimes when she was bored at work, she scrolled through the emojis on her phone and sent him the ones she thought he'd like. He didn't have the heart to tell her he'd seen them all already.

When the notifications kept coming, however, he snatched his phone off the nightstand, praying there hadn't been some kind of emergency. But no, all the texts were from Evan. Pete was accustomed to getting a trickle of texts a week, primarily from Sana. Now, a full day later, he had dozens, and they showed no sign of stopping.

It took him a while to get into the habit of checking his phone, but now he found himself reaching for it every few minutes, getting excited if there was a new notification, or putting it away disheartened if there wasn't. But Evan rarely disappointed him.

Most of what he sent consisted of song recs, goofy selfies, and photos of his food. But he also fired off questions like he was about to take an All Things Pete quiz. He asked everything from his favorite color—blue, very exciting—to what movies he'd want with him if he were trapped on a desert island that was somehow outfitted with Blu-ray. They even got into a heated argument about whether or not the eagles from the *Lord of the Rings* could have flown the Fellowship to Mordor, which nearly ended in blood.

Pete had never had this much fun.

And he was well on his way to being able to ace his own Evan quiz. From his texts, Pete discovered that Evan played baseball on a local amateur team, loved Indian food, and that the tattoos on his arms were in fact constellations. He sent Pete a shot of a telescope set up near a large window, along with the message, *Mapping the Rho Ophiuchi nebula complex.* It seemed he was an amateur astronomer.

As many subjects as they covered, there was one question Pete still hadn't gotten the answer to: what did all of this mean? It was obvious to him by now that Evan liked him. He wouldn't waste so much time and effort on someone he didn't like. But *how* did he like him? Did he just want to hook up, or did he want something more?

Which in turn begged the question: did Pete want him to want more?

All this uncertainty was starting to make his brain hurt. And considering his tentative position with Colette, it would probably be better if he didn't ask.

The relentless flood of texts continued until the next night, when Pete was lying in bed, decidedly not sleeping. He was watching light striate across his ceiling as cars drove by, fruitlessly willing himself to close his eyes. His phone was charging on the nightstand, or at least, it was until it buzzed. *Another text*, he thought. But it kept on buzzing.

He sat straight up in bed and stared at it. No one ever called him. He actively discouraged people from doing so. Talking on the phone was just another way for him to bumble through social interactions. He snatched it up anyway and glanced at the screen, mind already jumping to the only person he'd spoken to all day.

Sure enough, Evan was calling him. This late at night, what could he possibly want?

Oh God. Considering what he'd proposed the last time they'd been together, there was a chance he was calling for phone sex. Pete had tried his hand at doing that professionally before he became a porn star. Needless to say, it wasn't his specialty.

He had one ring left until it went to voice mail. If he was going to answer, he needed to do it now. It took him a fraction of a second to decide.

Heart racing, he hit the Answer button and held the phone to his ear. "Hello?"

"Hey, it's Evan."

Pete smiled. "Yeah, I know. You programmed yourself into my phone, remember?"

"Smart-ass. I was being polite." There was a strange crunching sound, like maybe Evan had taken a bite of something. A second later, he mumbled, "Did I call too late?"

Pete stifled a yawn. "No. I couldn't sleep anyway."

"How was your day?"

Pete frowned. This was suspiciously normal so far.

"It was good," he answered slowly. "Are you eating something?"

"Yeah, popcorn. I'm watching a movie."

Hmm, maybe he's not calling for sex, then. "Which one?"

"*The Adventures of Buckaroo Banzai Across the 8th Dimension.*"

Pete blinked. "Bless you."

"Never seen it?"

"Never even heard of it."

"It's great. Something of a cult classic. Have you ever heard the phrase 'No matter where you go, there you are'?"

Pete thought about it for a minute. That actually sounded familiar. "I think I've seen that somewhere before."

"Probably tattooed on a hipster. It's a popular quote. I don't think the movie came up with it, but it made it famous. It's one of those universal truths that speaks to people."

Pete frowned. "I guess I'm not deep enough. I don't get it."

"Don't take it literally. And it helps if you hear it in the context of the film."

"Ah. Maybe I'll rent it or something."

"We'll watch it together."

Pete's heart skipped a beat. As he struggled to think of a response, Evan laughed his smoky-sexy laugh, the one that made Pete's insides turn molten.

"What's so funny?" he asked.

"Oh, nothing. I just keep forgetting who I'm dealing with. Sometimes I think I can actually hear gears turning in your head."

"Sorry."

"Don't be. I'm just teasing you." There was a beat of silence. "Like right now, I swear I can hear you frowning. What's on your mind?"

"It's just . . . Did you really call to ask how my day was?"

"What were you expecting?" Evan's tone dripped with suggestion.

Pete turned bright red. "Nothing! This is just so normal, it's almost abnormal. I wasn't expecting it."

"Good. I like to keep you on your toes." Another crunch. "There was something I wanted to talk about, though. I've been thinking about what you told me, about Colette threatening to fire you. What exactly did she say?"

"I don't remember verbatim. She said something like if I can't handle a project like *Heat Wave* she can find a replacement."

"I thought that might be the case. Do you think she meant it?"

"Of course. Colette doesn't make empty threats."

"I'm not so sure."

"Why?"

"This project is her baby. If she'd really believed you were a danger to it, she would have fired you earlier. Before it was too late."

"'Too late'?"

"Think about it: all the promo materials for *Heat Wave* are finished. And sometime in the next week, we're going to film part one. If she were to replace you, she'd have to reshoot *everything*. At some point, that'll become too expensive for her to do."

Pete's eyes widened. "That . . . is a really good point. I didn't even think about that."

"Yeah, and you know how Colette loves to mind her bottom line. Although, truthfully, I don't think replacing you was ever on her agenda."

"Then why threaten me?"

There was a rustling sound, like Evan was changing positions. "I think she was just trying to scare you. Maybe even protect you."

Pete didn't bother to hide the disbelief in his tone. "Protect me? From what?"

"Haven't the faintest."

Something in Evan's tone nagged at Pete. He suspected Evan knew exactly what it was but didn't want to say. "It sounds like you put a lot of thought into this. Any particular reason?"

"I felt guilty for giving you my number even though your job was allegedly on the line. And I was worried her threat would scare you into keeping your distance from me. But if it turns out Colette's bluffing, we can keep doing what we're doing. Everyone wins."

Pete almost couldn't draw enough breath to ask, "What are we doing?"

There was an interminable pause.

"Have a drink with me."

"Uh." Pete glanced at the clock on his nightstand. It was already midnight. "Right now?"

Another low laugh. "No, I know better than to meet up with you now. Going out this late can only lead to bad decisions. Enjoyable ones, but bad nonetheless. I meant tomorrow, or the next time you're free. What's your favorite bar?"

Pete was grateful they weren't having this conversation in person, or he'd probably swallow his tongue. "I don't have one."

"Okay. We'll go to my favorite bar."

"I can't." Pete squirmed. "I'm not twenty-one."

Evan groaned. "I should have known. No one as twitchy as you has access to alcohol."

"I'm not twitchy," he protested. "And it's not like it's permanent. I have to age eventually."

Evan laughed. "That's true. My bad for assuming. You look young, but you're so serious, I figured you just have a baby face. How old are you?"

"Twenty."

"So close and yet so far. When's your birthday?"

"February sixth."

"That's not long from now." There was another rustling sound. "Let me buy you your first beer."

Pete's pulse flickered. "It wouldn't be my first. I've definitely consumed alcohol in the past."

"Oh, have you, good sir?" Evan said, affecting a snooty accent. "Then perhaps I'll afford you your first opportunity to consume *legal* alcohol."

Pete huffed. "I don't sound like that."

"You kinda do. Why?"

"Why what?"

"What's with the vocab? Are you super smart or something?"

"Not really. I consider myself average in just about every way. I read a lot, though. Sometimes I catch myself talking like how people do in books."

"You're definitely not."

"Huh?"

"Average. That's not how I would describe you at all."

Pete fiddled with a strand of his hair, uncomfortable and pleased at the same time. "If you don't mind my asking, how old are you?"

"Twenty-three."

"*What*? How are you only three years older than me?"

"Are you saying I look old?"

"No! It's just, you were *acting* as if— I mean, you do look older, but not like—"

Evan was laughing again, too hard to speak, apparently. He giggled for a solid minute while Pete made indignant noises.

When Evan finally had himself under control, he said, "I'm sorry. I really am. You're just so *easy*. And for the record, three years is a long time."

"Is not," Pete retorted just to be difficult.

"Uh-huh. Since you can't get a beer with me, want to do something else?"

"Like what?"

"Get coffee? Tea? What sorts of beverages do you prefer to consume?" He did the snooty voice again, and this time Pete laughed.

"At this point, I think coffee runs in my veins."

"Then meet me for one. Tomorrow. How about that place I saw you outside of before?"

Shit. He couldn't bring a boy to the Globe. Sana would have questions, Joshua would never let him hear the end of it, and Evan would know about his not-so-glamorous side job.

He blurted out the first excuse that came to mind. "I can't tomorrow. I have class."

Silence.

"You have class on Sundays?"

Fuck. What a dumb lie to get caught in. Why didn't he just suggest a different coffee place? There was a Starbucks on every corner, for Christ's sake. He couldn't very well say that now, but he couldn't keep up with the lie either. He ended up struggling with his own tongue for an agonizing stretch.

Mercifully, Evan broke the silence. "I didn't know you were a student."

Pete leaped at the chance to change the subject. "Yeah, full-time. Hence, Colette keeps scheduling us to shoot on weekends."

"What are you studying?"

"Computer Science."

"Not planning on being a world-famous porn star, then?"

Pete snorted. "Not anytime soon. I'll probably get a job as a database admin, or if I'm lucky, a programmer. They make great money, and I love to code. It's like reading, only with numbers."

There was a smile in Evan's voice as he said, "You are just full of surprises."

His tone made Pete's chest twinge with an indecipherable emotion. He suddenly wanted to ask Evan if their coffee date was . . . well, a *date*. The words tingled on the tip of Pete's tongue, but he held them back. He didn't want to shatter whatever tentative thing they had going on. And that was a scary realization. He'd only been talking to Evan outside of work for a couple of days, and he already felt like he'd miss him if they stopped. What was he going to do when *Heat Wave* wrapped and they no longer had a regularly scheduled excuse to see each other?

"I'm going to go to sleep," Evan said, breaking Pete from his thoughts. "Have a good night."

"Wait," Pete said. "We never decided about coffee."

"Ah. So, that wasn't your subtle way of telling me you're not interested after all?"

Pete struggled to fill his lungs. "Interested in what?"

"Me," Evan said simply.

He wanted to beg him to elaborate, but he'd pushed his luck too far in this conversation already. "No, I just got my days mixed up and thought tomorrow was Monday. Though I genuinely do have plans for tomorrow." Church with his mom counted as plans, right?

"When are you free, then?"

"I have work and class during most of the week, but I'm off Friday, assuming Colette doesn't need us."

"She probably will. Not that I'm complaining. I've been enjoying my work a lot lately."

Pete smiled. "Me too."

"So, we'll try for Friday?"

"Yeah. I'd like that."

There was a sound on the other end of the line like Evan had cleared his throat. "All right, I really am going to bed. It was nice talking to you."

"You too."

"Night."

"Night."

Pete hit the End Call button and then flopped onto his back. Well . . . that wasn't what he'd expected. He rolled onto his side and repeated the entire conversation in his head until he fell asleep.

When he woke up the next morning, he didn't remember dreaming, and yet he somehow knew Evan had been in his thoughts all night. Naturally, the first thing he did was reach for his phone. Sure enough, he had a text.

You're cute when you're sleepy.

Pete's heart went from just-woke-up to just-ran-a-marathon in three seconds flat. Well, that answered one question. He was definitely going to become an addict.

Sunday rolled into Monday. Pete felt like all he did with his free time was sleep and text Evan. On his walk to class, he almost collided with another pedestrian when he attempted to walk and type at the same time.

If he ever saw Antoine again, he resolved to apologize for judging him for being glued to his phone. He officially had no room to talk.

His Programming Logic class was taught by Professor Mejia, an elderly but robust man who talked often about his experiences working with computers the size of offices back in the sixties. He was a lot less focused than Professor Whiton, and he had a tendency to go off on unrelated tangents, which meant Pete spent most of his lectures daydreaming. On normal days, that wasn't a problem, but today he could have used a distraction, if only to take his mind off Evan for a moment.

He walked into the lecture hall twenty minutes before class was set to start and scanned the room. Only a handful of students had arrived, and Raj wasn't among them. Pete grabbed two seats in the back and pulled his laptop out of his bag. He fired it up and opened his notes.

He managed to study them for five whole minutes before he gave up and opened Facebook. He was on Kyle Darko's page before he even had a chance to think about it. There were a dozen new walls posts, including one from his sister thanking him for lunch.

Man, he really was out to his family. The idea still made Pete uncomfortable. He remembered high school, how fast rumors had spread and what had happened to the people they'd been about. College was a bit better, but he wasn't going to start introducing himself as Pete Griflow, adult entertainer, anytime soon. Evan was seriously brave. But then, he was a fit, handsome man with what appeared to be a large support network. That could make anyone brave.

Pete was about to close the window when he spotted a status update amidst all the posts. His heart skipped as he checked the time stamp on it: 12:32 a.m. the previous night. That was around when they got off the phone.

It said: *History is a-made at night.*

Pete raised a brow at that. Was he referencing their talk, or something else? He pulled Google up in his browser and pasted the status into the search bar. The movie Evan had mentioned from the night before popped up in the results. Why had he chosen that particular quote?

Right on cue, his phone vibrated.

How's class?

Pete typed a quick response. *It hasn't started yet. So far so good.*

"Hey."

Pete yelped and dropped his phone. Half of the now-full classroom turned to look at him. He ducked his head down as Raj plopped into the seat next to him.

"Sorry," Raj said, sounding anything but. "Why so serious, Heath?"

"No reason." Pete snatched up his phone just as it buzzed again.

You forgot your thruster.

He shook his head. Must be another movie reference. Evan had said they'd watch it together, but if he sent any more cryptic messages, Pete would have to download it.

Raj peered over his shoulder. "Who are you talking to?"

"No one." Pete set the phone down on the far corner of his desk and turned back to his notes. He pretended to type until Raj shrugged and pulled out his own laptop.

Professor Mejia walked in a few minutes later and began the lecture, offering Pete a welcome respite from his own thoughts. He and Raj sank into comfortable silence until Pete's phone buzzed again, vibrating loudly on the desk. He grabbed it, heart pounding.

"Someone's popular," Raj joked. "Is it a"—he leaned closer and whispered—"boy?"

"No," Pete squeaked.

The disbelief was so plain on Raj's face that Pete abandoned the pretense. "Yes. Well, sort of. He's a boy, but I don't know if he's a *boy*."

"Somehow, that made sense." Raj waited until Professor Mejia had turned his back before saying in an undertone, "Tell me about him."

"There's not much to tell." Pete matched his volume. "We met a few weeks ago."

"Where?"

Heat crept up his neck. "Um, at my job." It wasn't a lie.

Raj smirked. "And they say making coffee won't get you anywhere in life. Has he declared his intentions toward you?"

"Not in so many words."

Raj paused long enough to jot down a quick note before turning back to Pete. "But he got your phone number? Isn't that a pretty clear sign that he likes you?"

"It's kinda more complicated than that."

"Did he ask you out on a date?"

Pete started to say no, but then he remembered their conversation last night. Evan had invited him to both drinks and coffee. Ostensibly, they were going to meet up on Friday. It could be just as friends, but even Pete wasn't insecure enough to think Evan's interest in him stopped there.

"I don't know," he answered honestly.

"Not for nothing, buddy, but how can you not know if you were asked out?"

"I just don't know what his intentions are, to use your word. He's invited me to things, but he's never explicitly said they were a date."

"People don't usually declare, 'This is a date' when asking people out, but I'll give you the benefit of the doubt. We're not sure how the boy feels. What about you? Do you want to date him? You think he's attractive and all that?"

Pete turned red at warp speed. "Dude, you're straight. Are you sure you wanna hear about this?"

"Don't you play the Bro Card with me," Raj reprimanded him. "I may be straight, but I'll have you know I have a healthy appreciation for the male form. That, and I'm dying to know who could have captured the elusive Pete's attention."

Pete huffed. "Fine. Yeah, I'm attracted to him. Ridiculously so. But that could very well be fucked up."

"Why?"

"He looks a lot like Christopher. Or, at least, I thought so at first."

"Uh-oh. Wasn't he the Roxie Richter to your Ramona Flowers?"

"Yup. He fucked me up pretty badly. And if I can allow myself a moment of pettiness, this guy I'm kinda flirting with is a hotter version of him."

Raj whistled lowly. "Jackpot."

"Not jackpot. It totally freaked me out at first. I'm over it now, but it still makes me wonder if the attraction I feel is a hundred percent for him and not for my ex."

"Damn, son," Raj said soberly. "That's some *Maury* shit right there."

Pete shoved him.

Laughing under his breath, Raj said, "Sorry. For the record, I think you're reading way too much into this. You said you're over it, right?"

"Yeah. Now that I've gotten to know him, I realize they're nothing alike."

"Then you're in the clear."

Professor Mejia glanced their way. They fell silent until he turned around to write something on the board.

"I dunno," Pete said. "Part of me thinks it's a bad omen. Christopher burned me. Like, tossed me onto a pyre and then pissed on the ashes."

"I remember that. You were a mess for weeks. You never told me what happened between you guys, though. Just that he dumped you in spectacular fashion."

Pete pretended to type something to cover the flash of pain that he was certain was visible on his face. "I don't want to get into it. We just weren't compatible."

The truth was a bit more complicated than that. A memory came unbidden to the forefront of Pete's mind.

"You're disgusting. I can't believe I ever let you—"

He slammed a wall between himself and the memory, blocking it out. He swore under his breath. Nearly a year had passed, and he still had trouble thinking about it.

"Well, fuck that guy," Raj said, unwittingly echoing Pete's train of thought. "Don't let him ruin your future relationships. He's not worth it. You know that girl I dated last summer?"

Pete furrowed his brow in thought. "Sandra?"

"The other one."

"Andrea?"

"The other one."

". . . Megan?"

"Yes, that's the one. Well, she was really good friends with Jess."

Pete stifled laughter with his hand. "The *other* girl you dated?"

"Exactly. And see, Jess and I didn't end well, so Megan could have totally held a grudge against me. Done the whole 'sisters before misters' thing or whatever. But she didn't. She gave me a chance, and we dated for like six whole weeks as a result."

"You do realize that's not anything like my situation, right?"

"Sure it is. The overarching theme is the same: don't let other people prevent you from pursuing someone you like. Yeah?"

Pete nodded. "Yeah, I guess. That's not the only thing holding me back, though."

Raj leaned closer, pretending to copy something from Pete's notes, and whispered, "Oh?"

"We're . . . really different."

"Say it ain't so!"

"You don't understand. He has this . . . charm, I guess. This magnetism and the personality to back it up. I've never even met any of his friends, but I'm willing to bet people flock to him. Honestly, if he reminds me of anyone anymore it's my dad. No one was surprised when he fell in love with someone else. Women were always throwing themselves at him."

"When I ask this next question, please imagine it's Oprah speaking. Do you think your early relationship with your father is shaping your relationships with men now?"

Pete shoved him again.

Raj looked unrepentant. "But for real, you think this guy might be a player?"

Pete thought about all the posts he'd seen on Evan's Facebook, all the messages from guys, and all the invitations to work with him. Evan had no shortage of options, but that didn't mean he acted on them. "I don't know. I don't want to jump to conclusions. I guess I just don't understand why he'd choose to date me of all people. He could have *anyone*. Someone more confident. Less neurotic. More fun."

"Hey now," Raj protested, "no one's more fun than you."

Pete shot him a wry look.

"Okay, so you might not be the *most* exciting person, but life isn't all about wild parties and having the Best Night Ever every time."

"That so does not make me feel better."

"Look, you're great, okay? You're smart, and you're down-to-earth, and you're a loving friend. Also, as someone who has hung out with you and your mom, I know you're a hell of a son. Even if it's not this guy, someone out there thinks those are the absolute best qualities a person can have, and they are gonna fall so stupidly in love with you. I swear it."

Pete looked down at his desk and smiled. "Thanks, man. That's sweet of you to say."

"What are friends for?" Raj clapped him on the back, wincing when he hit his shoulder blade. "Ouch. Eat a sandwich."

"Won't help any." He shrugged. "I can eat my face off and never gain an ounce."

"I hate you," Raj said emphatically.

"Don't. My diet is shit. Skinny doesn't automatically mean healthy."

"Speaking of food, your birthday is rolling around soon, right?"

"Yeah. Three more weeks."

"Are we getting dinner? Celebrating? It's the big two-one, right? You must be planning something."

Pete started to say no, but then his conversation with Evan flashed into his mind.

"Have a drink with me."

Was Evan serious about taking him for his first legal beer? If Evan would be there, suddenly celebrating didn't sound so bad.

Pete struggled to keep his tone casual. "I think I might get drinks with the boy. He wants to take me to his favorite bar." He glanced at Raj for his reaction.

He was staring wide-eyed at him like he'd just announced he intended to join a nunnery.

Pete frowned. "What?"

"Dude . . . are you in *love*?"

"What?" Pete only barely managed to keep his voice down. "Why would you ask that?"

"Because *you*, the most introverted person I know, are talking about celebrating a birthday with a guy you just met. I can't even get you to go to a bar with *me*."

Pete sniffed. "That's because I'm not old enough."

"Bullshit. Plenty of the bars around campus are lax about checking IDs. You don't go because you hate crowds, loud music, and drunk people. And now you're voluntarily subjecting yourself to all three. Must be love."

"It is not!"

Raj ignored him. "So, is this an invite-only thing, or can I come too? I want to meet this guy who has you all head over heels."

"I am *not* head over heels. And no, you can't come. I don't want you scaring him off."

"Oh, come on," Raj whined. "It's your birthday! I promise I'll behave." He batted his inky eyelashes.

Pete started to relent—he was a sucker for Raj's puppy eyes—but then he remembered one very important detail: he'd met Evan through sex work. For anyone else, introducing a coworker to your friends was innocuous. But for him, it was an invitation for disaster.

Someone was bound to ask what Evan did for a living, and Evan was *out*. He'd probably just tell them. Jesus.

"Sorry," Pete said, "but it'll be a date sort of thing, so I can't have my friends there. He already knows I'm awkward. If I bring you, it'll seem like I need reinforcements." The lie rolled smoothly off his tongue. It was unnerving.

Raj shrugged and turned back toward the front of the lecture hall. "I get it. I'm not trying to cramp your style. We should still do something, though. Maybe the day after or whatever."

I don't deserve such good friends.

"Yeah, we should." He looked guiltily down at his keyboard as Professor Mejia finished one anecdote about his hometown of Granada only to start another. Pete resolved to suck it up and go out with Raj sometime. If he couldn't handle celebrating his birthday with his closest friend, how was he going to handle getting drinks with Evan?

Poorly, said a snide mental voice.

Class ended a half hour later. Pete said good-bye to Raj, but not before he promised him they would do something soon. Maybe even go to a club. The offer perked Raj up like a frat boy who'd just heard a keg being tapped. It assuaged Pete's guilt a little.

He went home, and after a quick conversation with his mom about how his day went (fine) and what he wanted for dinner (mac and cheese), he retreated to his room. He'd just thrown his bag onto his bed and unpacked his laptop when his phone dinged. He had it in his hand so fast, his brain lagged behind the movement, leaving him staring blankly at it.

"I need to get out more," he muttered to himself before turning on the home screen. Another text from Evan.

Can I call you?

If Pete were a more demonstrative person, he might have clicked his heels together with delight. He texted back: *Absolutely.*

Not five seconds later, the call popped up. He let it ring twice before he answered it, not to be coy, but to relish the anticipation.

"Hello?"

"Hey. Did you get Colette's email?"

He frowned. "Not gonna ask how my day was?"

"Right, sorry." Evan sounded frazzled. "How was your day?"

"It was good." Pete sat on his bed and settled against the pillows. "Is something wrong?"

"No." There was a telling pause. "Not exactly. I was just wondering if you saw the new filming schedule Colette emailed to us."

"I did not. Did she send it to our personal emails, or—"

"No, to our Murmur Inc. accounts."

"Oh, I haven't checked mine today. Can you tell me what it said?"

"We're filming again soon."

"What day?"

"Friday."

"Ah." His stomach sank. "The day of our coffee date. We could go beforehand?"

"No, she's got us booked for first thing. We'd have to go at like five in the morning, and then be at the shoot immediately after. Seems kinda silly."

Anxiety sucker punched Pete in the gut. He hadn't realized how much he'd wanted to hang out with Evan outside of work until the opportunity was ripped from him. It had felt right, somehow. Like it was something they needed to do before . . . He sighed. "I guess it can't be helped. Did she say what we were going to be doing?"

"She said we're ready to start filming for real."

Pete's stomach lurched. "Right. So, you and I are going to—"

"Have sex."

They both fell silent. Seconds dragged on, feeling like claws into Pete's skin as they passed.

When the quiet became deafening, he forced himself to say, "We knew we were going to from the start."

"Yeah. And not to be weird, but . . . I want to."

Pete didn't understand how his body could get so hot and so cold at the same time. "Me too. It just feels really—"

"Soon." Evan made an exasperated sound. "It's not, though. If we'd been booked together in any other movie, we would have fucked already. There wouldn't have been any photo shoots or filming sessions or anything. One and done. Never to see each other again."

"Yeah." He wet his lips. "But we weren't."

Evan didn't respond.

"Did she say for certain we'd be having sex this week?"

"Not penetrative, no. She wants to film us doing other stuff first." He hesitated. "She wants me to get you off. My character is more experienced than yours, after all. I'm supposed to show you the ropes. It'll probably be a handjob or something."

"That sounds, um, good." He meant it. Just listening to Evan mention sex was enough to turn him on. But he was still struggling to articulate whatever it was twisting his stomach into curlicues.

He wanted this. He wanted *Evan*, but they'd just started to get to know one another, and suddenly, the fact that they were going to have sex was all too real. Sleeping with strangers on camera was one thing. Evan wasn't a stranger anymore.

Pete had just opened his mouth when Evan beat him to it. "I wish we had more time."

Pete closed his eyes. "Me too."

Evan sighed. "I have to go. I'll see you in a few days."

He hung up before Pete could say another word.

CHAPTER 9

Friday came all too quickly, and Pete found himself back at Joyce's house on a brisk, overcast morning. According to Colette, *Heat Wave* was going to pick up more or less where it had left off. Same setting, same story, same handful of people gathered together in the living room. Only now, everything felt different.

When Pete walked in, Yolanda was setting up her camera, Colette was bent over her laptop, and Joyce waved at him from her seat at the kitchen table. Everyone was in their place.

Including Evan. He was standing on his mark by the windows, bathed in early-morning sunlight. Set against a backdrop of aluminum sky and silhouetted in silver, his dark features were even more striking than usual.

Pete took his place next to him without asking Colette. "Hey." He tried not to fidget. It was hard to know how he was supposed to act. Despite the hesitations he'd expressed during their last phone conversation, he was still excited to be here. To be with Evan. But judging by the serious look on Evan's face, the feeling might not be mutual.

"Hey," Evan said back. "How are you feeling?"

"Tired. I don't think I slept all week." He had the dark circles under his eyes to prove it.

"Me neither. I was thinking about you."

Pete slid his hands into his pockets. "Same."

"I feel like I should say something."

"Like what?"

"That's the thing." Evan shook his head. "I have no idea. 'No hard feelings' keeps coming to mind, but that's not right. I just— I don't want you to think . . ." He raised his hand only to drop it, letting it hang limply at his side. "I don't know. Just feels weird, I guess."

Guilt stabbed Pete right between the ribs. He didn't know what he'd expected when he walked on set, but he'd thought he could at least count on Evan to be his usual devil-may-care self. His seriousness was ramping up Pete's already-heightened anxiety.

He tried to shrug it off. "You don't have to say anything. We've both done this before, right? It's no big deal."

Evan sighed. "Yeah. Right."

Pete gave him a sidelong look. "You, um, seem off."

"I feel off."

"Want to talk about it?"

"There's nothing to say, to be honest."

Pete stared down at his feet. "Is it wrong that I'm excited to be here?"

Evan finally turned toward him. "Of course not. Why would you think that?"

"Because you seem so miserable. I don't want to enjoy this if you're not enjoying it with me."

"I'm not miserable, I promise. I'm being a brat. Throwing a tantrum because I didn't get my way. Ignore me."

"I can't." Pete steeled himself. There was something he needed to say, something he'd been rehearsing in his head all week. He cleared his throat and did his best to appear casual. "You know you can leave, right?"

Evan looked sharply at him. "What are you talking about?"

"You can even blame it on me, if you want. I know you have bills to pay, same as everyone else, but you don't have to do anything you don't want to do. We don't have to film today, or ever."

He watched the dust motes swirling in the sunlight streaming through the windows to avoid making eye contact with Evan. A moment later, something warm brushed his elbow. Evan's hand.

When Pete glanced up, Evan's face was close to him. "What on earth made you think I want to quit?"

"I dunno. You said yourself it feels like it's too soon, and you're obviously not thrilled to be here."

Evan stared at him. "Wow, you really don't get it, do you?"

"I guess not. Explain it to me?"

"I'm not upset because I'm here. I'm *thrilled* to be here with you. I wouldn't do you the disrespect of having sex with you if I didn't want to. I'm sulking because we didn't get to hang out this morning, but I'll get over it."

Pete studied his face. He looked sincere, and Pete desperately wanted to believe him. "You'd tell me if your consent was anything less than enthusiastic, right?"

"Of course."

"Then we're going to do this?"

Evan's eyes blazed. "We are, and it's going to be a hell of a ride."

Pete took a half step toward him, but before he could reach out for him like he wanted, Colette clapped her hands. "All right, gentlemen, let's begin."

Pete almost cursed out loud. She had the *worst* timing.

She held up a blue folder. "I have a copy of the script here if either of you need to look over it."

"I'm good," Pete said. "I read it like a hundred times."

Evan raised his hand like he was in school. "What are we doing about the rain?"

"Good question. We'll have to edit the footage to show that this is a new day, but for the most part we're still going to pick up where we left off. Your characters just had their first kiss. They've acknowledged that they're attracted to each other, and they're about to explore what that attraction means."

Pete held back an undignified giggle. The parallels between the script and real life were uncanny.

She continued. "The scene is going to begin on the sofa."

Evan started toward the one beneath the window.

"No, not that one." She pointed to its twin, which was placed against the adjacent wall. "Sit over there. The light from the windows is washing you both out. Jaden, I'm excited to see what you do with your character's emotions here. I want to see uncertainty from you, but also intrigue. And Darko, you're looking to portray confidence. Your friend here is new to all the pleasures out there, and you want to help him discover them."

Evan smirked, and his old, cocky self shined through. "In other words, I'm like his gay sex tutor."

"If that's how you want to think of it, sure. Sound good?"

Evan caught Pete's eye. "Sounds hot."

Pete felt a bone-deep thrum of arousal. He couldn't agree more.

"Anyone need to warm up before we begin? Stretch? Drink some water? Do some vocal exercises?"

They shook their heads.

"Good. Get into position, and we'll begin."

Pete took a seat on the couch, taking stock of himself as he went. He felt the familiar side effects of Evan's nearness: quickened pulse, shallow breathing, and his blood threatening to fly south for the winter. But he also felt comfortable. And *eager*. No matter the questions he had about the nature of their relationship, he wanted Evan. And he was about to have him.

Evan flopped next to him and wasted no time throwing an arm around the back of the sofa. It felt so natural, Pete didn't even question what to do. He leaned back until Evan's arm rested against his shoulder blades. Something tickled his skin, prompting him to glance to the right. Evan was brushing his thumb along his arm where his sleeve ended.

God. It was ridiculous what such a small touch could do to Pete. He could only imagine what it was going to be like when they were finally naked together. The thought alone made him shiver, and Evan pressed minutely closer.

"Ready?" Colette asked them.

Evan looked at Pete.

Pete nodded.

"Yeah," Evan said, "we're ready."

Colette signaled to Yolanda, who flipped a switch on the side of her camera. The red recording light blinked.

Colette took a seat in front of her laptop and called, "Action!"

Pete envisioned pulling his character on like he'd pull on a glove. It was both easy and difficult, considering his character was so much like himself. He was accustomed to being Jaden on screen, not Pete. He hadn't thought it was possible for porn to make him feel any more exposed.

He peeked to his left, obviously enough that the camera would pick up on it. Evan was watching him, of course. His face was a mosaic of emotion. There were hints of uncertainty, but for the most part, he was tense, like he was waiting for Pete to give him some kind of signal. He looked like a man who had no idea how to proceed. It was convincing.

The first line of dialogue was his. Show time.

"So," he began. "That happened."

"Yeah," Evan agreed. "I think our friendship might be in jeopardy."

Pete laughed. "I'll be honest, I'm not sure how to act around you now."

Evan smiled. "Me neither. And to think, I'd just convinced myself I could live with being only friends . . ." He quickly shut his mouth, like he'd said something he hadn't meant to.

Pete leaned closer. "What was that?"

"Nothing." Evan turned his face away, and when he looked back, his expression was neutral. "Do you regret kissing me?"

Pete didn't even need to act this next bit. It was true.

"No. I could never regret you."

"Cut!"

He jumped and looked at Colette. "What's wrong?"

"What's with you two?" she asked in lieu of an answer.

"What do you mean?"

"You feel . . . different. Not necessarily in a bad way. I just feel like I'm watching you have a conversation."

"Isn't that the point?"

"No, I mean, where's the tension? The anxiety? Your chemistry is still there, but it doesn't feel quite how it used to. Jaden, you in particular seem different. Much less jumpy than before."

Well, that was easy enough to explain, though Pete had no intention of saying anything. They'd gotten to know each other. They were comfortable now. He hadn't expected Colette to pick up on it. He prayed that was all she picked up on.

He asked, "What do you want us to do differently?"

"I'm not sure exactly. It's not like it's *bad*. I'm just used to you guys having this twitchy sort of energy around each other." She cocked her head thoughtfully. "This might actually be for the best. Jaden, no offense, but before there were times when I thought you were going to piss yourself. Having you be more relaxed will help the audience relax.

Just try to ramp up the energy a bit. This isn't a long scene, so if the sexual tension isn't built right, it'll seem forced."

"Not enough sexual tension," Evan paraphrased. "I never thought I'd hear that. Whatcha think, Jaden? Can we do better?" He slid a hand onto Pete's thigh.

Pete gulped. "I think we got this."

They reset their positions, and this time, when Colette called action, Pete channeled the emotions Evan had made him feel when they'd first met. Back when he'd known him as Kyle, a man with a bewildering amount of sex appeal and a predilection for leaving him wanting more. The memory alone gave him goose bumps.

He shifted a bit toward Evan, making it look like he was solely focused on him. Which, honestly, he was. Evan's body language had changed as well. Both arms were on the back of the couch now, and he'd spread his legs a bit. He looked more confident, commanding. More in control. Pete had to admit: it was hot.

"So," he said, lacing his tone with nerves, "*that* happened."

They went through the dialogue again, and this time, their attitudes were completely different. When they reached the part where Evan asked if Pete regretted it, it sounded more like a tease, like he already knew the answer and was daring him to deny it.

Pete paused, nibbling on his lower lip. "I could never regret you."

Right on cue, Evan's eyes swept to Pete's mouth. "Good." His voice was all darkness and sin. "Kissing is the tip of the iceberg, you know. There's so much more we could do."

Pete looked down. "I dunno. I've never, um, you know . . . with a man."

"I could show you. Teach you."

Pete let out a shaky laugh. "Is that what you want?"

"Oh, I *want*."

Evan slid his fingers into Pete's hair, grabbing a handful. He used it to tug him closer, and Pete didn't hesitate to follow his lead. They kissed slowly, deeply, and then feverishly. Pete melted into it. Evan's lips were every bit as wonderful as he remembered: soft and firm and insistent against his. The best part was the flash of stubble he felt whenever Evan shifted to get a new angle. It scraped his skin in the most delicious way.

Pete expected Evan to push him onto his back at some point, but instead he inched closer until Evan's chest was pressed to his side, one hand in Pete's hair while the other rested on his chest. Pete didn't care what positions they were in. He'd flip upside down like a bat if Evan wanted.

Pete could spend all afternoon kissing him, but Evan clearly had other plans. The hand on Pete's chest moved to one of his nipples and rubbed it through his shirt. Pete jolted at the sensation, cock thickening, and belatedly remembered to moan for the benefit of the camera. He'd have to do a better job of remembering it was there, that there were other people around. He wanted to forget, to dissolve into Evan and just *feel*.

Evan moved his lips to Pete's neck. "Do you like that?" He thumbed Pete's nipple again, harder.

"Yes," Pete rasped.

He nibbled on his earlobe and then whispered, "What about that?"

There was no way the microphones had picked that up. Pete couldn't respond without confusing the audience. Colette would call cut, and they'd have to start over. Not that he would mind that.

Pete moaned again for lack of anything better to do.

Evan laughed, soft and breathy against his ear, and murmured, "I know they can't hear me. I don't want them to. Answer the question."

Pete nuzzled his face into Evan's neck—out of view—and mouthed, "I don't mind it, but ears aren't really my thing." He put a hand over the one Evan had in his hair and guided it down. "But I am sensitive here." He pressed down on Evan's fingers until the nails scraped the nape of his neck. A quiet, pleasured noise escaped from him. To his ear, it sounded completely different from the ones he affected for the camera. He glanced at Evan for his reaction.

Evan was watching him with wide, wondrous eyes. "Christ, what am I going to do with you?" He freed the hand from Pete's nape, slid it down his chest and stomach, and dipped between his legs. "At least I know what to do with this."

Pete hissed and arched into the touch. His cock, which had been plenty interested in what they were doing before, filled with blood so quickly it left him dizzy. "Oh God, don't stop."

"Wasn't planning on it." Evan palmed him expertly through his jeans. He lowered his voice. "You feel so perfect in my hand. Just the right size, and so *warm*."

Pete threw his head back, partially out of enjoyment and partially to hide his mouth as he asked, "Why are you whispering? Colette would want you to speak up."

There was a beat of silence. Then, Evan said, "I want some parts of this to be just between us."

An unfathomable emotion grabbed Pete's heart and squeezed.

One-handed, Evan expertly popped open the button fastening Pete's pants and slid the zipper down.

"Fuck," Pete said, dazed. "That was hot."

Evan snickered. "Just you wait." He slipped his hand into Pete's underwear.

Pete was far from camera-shy, but it dawned on him that Evan was about to see his dick for the first time. He tensed up, preparing to contain a bout of self-consciousness, but then Evan's hot fist circled around him, and his bones turned to jelly.

At that point, Yolanda took her camera off the tripod and moved closer with Colette and a hand-held microphone on her heels. Undoubtedly, they were trying to capture all the embarrassing little noises Pete was making. He tried to control them, make them less needy and more sexy, but with Evan's hand wrapped around his cock, there was no stopping the soul-searing moan that resonated from deep within him.

He shuddered from head to foot, and Evan cursed in his ear, fingers tightening around him, which only made Pete moan more. It was like a feedback loop, one that was quickly threatening to overwhelm Pete. He already felt like he was about to—

"Cut!"

Pete made a frustrated noise as Evan's hand withdrew from his pants. Shit, he'd never gotten that close that quickly before. They hadn't even done that much.

"What's wrong now?" Evan asked.

"Nothing to do with you two, don't worry," Colette answered. She surveyed the windows. "The sun went behind a cloud, and we need to wait for the light to come back. Just hang tight."

Easy for you to say. Pete looked around, blinking as the room came back into focus. It had definitely darkened. He hadn't even noticed. But then, it was hard to think about anything other than Evan's hand resting on his thigh. It was tempting to angle his hips toward it, but they had to hold their positions. Both for easier editing and because they couldn't very well keep getting off when the camera wasn't rolling.

Get it together, Griflow. He leaned his head back, staring at the ceiling. They still had a lot of filming to get through.

"Hey."

Reluctantly, he returned his head to its upright position. "Hmm?"

Evan gave his shoulder a gentle rub. "All right?"

"Yeah. It's just, um, hard, for lack of a better term. To stay in place." He squirmed against Evan. "I didn't want you to stop touching me."

Evan let out a tight breath. "The feeling is mutual."

Just then, the room brightened again. Pete's eyes stung a bit as they adjusted.

"We're good to go," Colette called. "Start back up where you left off. Jaden, you seemed close just then. Were you?"

He felt more than saw Evan watching him. "Yeah, sorry. I got carried away. I've got it under control."

"It's okay. Just try to hold off for another ten minutes or so. We need to get some varied shots of you." She turned to Yolanda and started discussing angles.

He took a deep breath and flexed his toes to distract himself from the dull ache in his groin.

Out of his periphery, Evan's grin was unmistakable. "Did you really almost come?"

Pete huffed. "Wipe that look off your face. It happens to the best of us."

Evan's grin only grew. "I'm not complaining. I'm taking it as a compliment."

Colette shot them a stern look. "Save it, gentlemen. If you can behave, we might finish by lunchtime, pardon my word choice." She glanced at Yolanda, who nodded, and then called, "Action!"

Evan's hand was back between Pete's legs before he could even blink. "Oh *fuck*."

"That's it," Evan said, pulling him out of his underwear, "tell me how it feels." He formed a loose fist around Pete's dick but didn't stroke yet. Pete tensed, body taut with need. Being touched by him without any real satisfaction was *torture*.

"Kyle, please, do something," he pleaded. "I need it."

Evan laughed. "Listen to you. First time with a guy, and you're already making demands. I hoped you'd be one of the needy ones, the ones who once they have a taste, they can't get enough."

He gave Pete's cock a slow stroke from root to tip. Pete grabbed his shoulder, holding on for dear life. Pete made the mistake of looking at Evan's face. He was staring at Pete's cock, watching the head peek in and out of the circle he'd made with his fist. He looked rapturous.

I wish I could taste you, Evan mouthed, face tilted away from the camera. Audibly, he said, "You make me so hot. How does it feel?"

"Good," Pete responded. "Can you tighten your fingers a little, and— Ah!"

His hips bucked of their own volition. It was like Evan had read his mind. Just as he reached the base of Pete's dick, he gave him a soft squeeze, and pleasure crackled up Pete's spine. Fuck. He *really* wasn't going to last long.

"I love the sounds you make," Evan said, watching him. Pete almost wanted to look away, his gaze was so intense. "I can't decide which I want more: to tease you until you're whimpering, or fuck you fast and hard, make you come undone so I know what that sounds like too. What do you want?"

"Kyle, I want, ah," Pete babbled, trying and failing to express the jumble of half thoughts in his head. "Just, please, can you—"

Evan buried his face in Pete's neck and breathed in deeply. His hand started moving faster, stroking Pete in earnest. No matter how hard he tried to control himself, Pete kept getting louder and louder. He pressed a hand to his mouth, but there was no smothering his moans.

"Don't," Evan ordered. "I want to hear you. Move your hand."

Pete wrenched it away but replaced it with Evan's mouth, kissing him sloppily. It was all he could manage right now, clouded as he was by desire. Something was coiling low in his belly, getting ready to spring. He bucked his hips shallowly in time with Evan's thrusts.

"Kyle," he whimpered, pressing his sweaty brow against his cheek. "I'm close."

"What do you need?"

Pete had no idea how to communicate it. He couldn't think straight with Evan's hand working him. He exhaled raggedly. "More. I need more."

Evan let go of him, and Pete almost sobbed. But then Evan scooted a little away and got into a sitting position: feet on the floor, legs spread. He snaked his arms under Pete, lifted him easily, and deposited him in the space between his legs. He wrapped his arms around Pete and pulled him back against him until shoulder blades hit solid chest.

Before Pete could settle, Evan yanked his jeans and underwear down to his knees. Then his hand mercifully returned to Pete's cock. Pete gasped and canted his hips up into it, desperate for more.

Evan's voice was at his ear. "You're so hot I can't stand it."

Pete could only imagine how obscene he looked, cock jutting straight out from his body, thighs spread wide—or as wide as they could go with his pants still on—and splayed against Evan's chest while Evan pumped him and whispered filthy things in his ear.

"Oh God. Oh fuck." He couldn't hold back anymore. He rolled his hips, trying to somehow milk more out of Evan's fist.

Evan let out a startled moan. Curious, Pete repeated the motion, and that was when he felt it. Evan's dick was pressed against his ass, right in the cleft. When Pete moved his hips, he rubbed against it. He thrust into Evan's hand one way and against his erection the other.

Evan tightened his grip. "Fuck, that's good. Do that again."

Pete was almost too turned on to take orders, but he complied, fucking Evan's fist and rubbing against his cock in two simple motions. Feeling Evan's dick nestled against him added a whole new level of sexiness to what they were doing. He couldn't stop thinking about how close they were to having sex, just a few layers of fabric and a couple of inches between them. Maintaining any semblance of rhythm was impossible. It was graceless and awkward and *perfect*.

Evan seemed to think so as well. He made a guttural sound that reverberated through his chest and into Pete's. "Fuck, I can't. So good." His grip loosened, and his strokes became sloppy and quick.

Pleasure buzzed in Pete's veins, desperate to break the surface. He just needed—

He laid his head on Evan's shoulder and looked blearily at him for inspiration. Evan was watching Colette, communicating something with his eyes. She gave him a thumbs-up, and his pace doubled. Through a haze of arousal, Pete understood: Evan had asked for permission to make him come. Thank God. He could feel his balls drawing up in preparation for orgasm, and his every sense was narrowing to that one spot deep between his legs that was about to release. He was *so* close. He just needed something to push him over the edge.

Evan must have read it in his body, because he snaked the other hand between his legs. Pete expected him to massage his balls, but he passed right by them.

It took Pete a second to realize where he was headed. *Oh shit.*

With surprising delicacy, Evan pressed his thumb pad against Pete's hole. Pete sucked in a breath that somehow managed to be a sob.

Evan—his voice no louder than a plucked cello string—asked, "Can I?"

Pete only had enough cognizance left for a single word: "*Yes.*"

Evan cursed, a hot puff of breath against Pete's sweaty neck, and pressed into him. He might have intended to finger him. Pete would never find out. At the first harsh burn of penetration, he came so hard he saw stars.

His orgasm felt as if it were being wrung from his very soul. The sound he made as it washed thickly over him was somewhere between a gasp and a choked cry.

"Fuck, I can't, I can't—" he whimpered.

"I've got you," Evan said, kissing the side of his face. "I've got you."

Evan held him through it, whispering soothing things into his hair. Pete was too fucked out to listen, but he picked up on some key phrases: *gorgeous* and *perfect* and *so good.*

When he was spent, he sagged back against Evan. Evan mouthed his jawline, not kissing in the traditional sense of the word, but the sentiment was there.

They held their positions until Colette called, "Cut."

"Thank Christ," Pete slurred. He was still cradled between Evan's legs. He gathered his strength and looked at him. "Want me to move?"

"Don't you dare," Evan murmured, nosing his cheek.

"Good, because I don't think I can." Pete's head lolled back onto his shoulder. "You might just have to deal with me lying against you for the rest of your life." He was sweaty, his shirt was sticking to him, and his stomach was covered in his own semen. He should be scrambling to clean up. Instead, he felt like he could fall asleep right where he was.

He shifted again, unthinking, and Evan gasped.

"What...?" Pete started to ask, but then he felt it. Evan's erection pressed against the small of his back. Oh. Of course. Evan hadn't gotten off. Pete had forgotten in the wake of his own pleasure. Wow, he felt like an ass.

"Um, Colette," he asked. "Are we doing another take?"

"Nope. That's all for today, gents. Nice work, both of you. We got some great shots. Jaden, you in particular were mesmerizing, though Darko was no slouch either."

Pete was oddly disappointed. It didn't seem fair for only one of them to get off. "Since we're already here, why don't we keep filming? Kyle should get off too."

"Not in the script," Colette said without looking at him. She was already bent over her laptop. "Our run time is maxed as it is with everything I have planned." She paused, a thoughtful slant to her mouth. "Though I suppose we could get some bonus footage for the DVD release. Darko, what are your thoughts?"

Evan shrugged. "I don't mind either way."

"Hmm. Let's wrap, then. I need to get back to the office."

Pete watched miserably as Colette and Yolanda conferred over the dining room table. He caught Joyce's eye, but even she only offered a thumbs-up.

This felt wrong, no matter what Evan said. Pete couldn't leave him hanging. Not after the frankly phenomenal orgasm he'd just had.

Maybe that was how Evan had felt after their photo shoot, when he'd wanted to get off with Pete. Why had he been so against that idea? Probably because he hadn't had sex in a nonprofessional capacity in . . . fuck. *Months.*

Pete knew what he wanted to say, but he couldn't have this conversation while he was still draped in Evan's lap, ass flush against his cock. He pushed himself up and over, half-flopping to the side in an uncoordinated mess. His muscles weren't ready to cooperate just yet. He forced himself into a sitting position and arranged his limbs into what he thought was a vaguely human shape.

"Um," he began, awkward as a company Christmas party, "do you want some help with that?" He made a vague gesture at nothing.

Evan chuckled. "With what exactly?"

Pete exhaled. Evan would make him say it, the bastard. "Do you want me to get you off?" A wave of shyness descended on him, which was ridiculous, considering he's just had his dick expertly stroked by the same man he was propositioning.

"I thought you don't work for free?"

"I knew that was going to come back to haunt me," Pete grumbled, face burning. "That was before, you know? I feel like I know you better now, and, um . . . I feel rude. And since you got me off, it's only fair?"

As soon as the words were out of his mouth, he wanted to smack himself. *It's only fair.* Nice one, Pete. Way to make it sound like it's your turn to do the dishes.

He was just calculating how quickly he could get to a bridge and fling himself off it, when Evan laughed.

"Don't worry about it. Our time will come." He sounded so certain, as if he were stating a fact. "Besides, I don't think Joyce would appreciate us sneaking off to have sex in one of her bedrooms. I'm willing to wait for when we can do it right."

Despite having just come, Pete's body warmed. He ducked his head down and asked quietly, "Any idea when that might be?"

"I already made my move. It's your turn." His grin was positively evil.

Pete swallowed. "So, about that drink."

CHAPTER  10

"Please?" Pete pleaded. "Pleeease? I'll get down on my knees if you want."

"Don't beg," Sana scolded without looking up from the register. "It's demeaning. I have half a mind to deny your request just for that."

"But it's my birthday," he wailed. "You can't turn a man down on his birthday."

"No, it's a few weeks *before* your birthday, which means crushing your dreams is still perfectly acceptable." She closed the drawer and faced him, arms folded across her chest. "Why do you want tomorrow off anyway? Isn't it a little early to be celebrating?"

"It's a preliminary celebration," he said. "A warmup. You only turn twenty-one once, and I want to do it properly."

"But you can't even drink yet. What's the point?"

"There are plenty of ways to have fun without alcohol, as you well know."

Sana rolled her eyes. "I guess. Still seems kind of silly." She walked toward the baked goods display, heels clicking on the linoleum floor, and opened the back panel. "You young people confound me."

He snorted. "You're not even thirty yet. You talk like you're ancient."

She pulled a roll of cellophane out of a cabinet and started wrapping up various artisan breads and cakes. "You'll understand when you're my age. Speaking of which, if you're going to take a day off, why use it to go clubbing? You hate clubbing. Everyone with half a brain hates clubbing."

"I don't *hate* it," he lied. "I've never really been, except for a few regrettable forays when I was a freshman. My goal for the next year is to get out more. Be more adventurous. I've lived here my whole life, and I feel like I've never been anywhere. Do you want to stand between me and broadened horizons?"

"I suppose not." She pointed at the front door. "Did you lock that?"

"Yeah."

"And you turned off the Open sign?"

"Yup."

"Then why the *fuck*," she snarled, "are customers lined up outside?"

He turned to look. Sure enough, some cantankerous-looking men in dress shirts and slacks were standing outside the front entrance. They knocked on the glass impatiently.

"We're closed!" Sana shouted. "Come back tomorrow."

The men muttered something rude and trudged away.

Pete, who had sequestered himself behind the espresso machine, peeked around the corner. "Are they gone?"

"Yup. Good riddance."

"I love having you for a manager, even if you do scare me shitless half the time."

"People need to learn: hours of operation are not polite suggestions."

"How much of LA do you reckon you've scared off at this point?"

"That was a lovely attempt to derail the conversation, but I'm not fooled. Back to the subject at hand: what's with you being Mr. Social all of a sudden? I've never known you to willingly subject yourself to crowds."

He pretended to hunt through a drawer for something so he wouldn't have to look at her. "I'm social. Just, you know, selectively. And I want to make a big deal out of my birthday this year. I'm allowed."

Her tone said she wasn't buying what he was selling. "All right, fine. You can have tomorrow off. But you owe me big time. Why didn't you ask me earlier?"

Because I hadn't asked Evan out yet. "It was a last-minute thing. I just found out this morning. I'm really sorry."

"Well, Saturday is our busiest night, so you have to find someone to cover your shift. Don't bother asking Joshua. He's off that night too, and trying to get him to cover a shift is like trying to get an imam to do shots during Ramadan."

Pete snorted. "I already asked Morgan, and she said yes."

"Then I guess that's that." She looked at him sidelong. "If you're really trying to turn over a new leaf, I think it's working. You seem different lately."

Pete glanced down at himself. "Do I?"

"Yeah. I can't quite put my finger on it, but you're—" she flicked a hand vaguely at him "—more confident, maybe? Or happier? I'm not sure. I've noticed you talking to customers more. Smiling. Laughing. I'm curious to know if this change came from within or if someone inspired it."

He was grateful his face was downturned, because it flamed. "What makes you think there's someone?"

"All the times I've caught you staring off into space with a big, goofy grin on your face, for one thing."

Damn. It was funny that Evan thought him inscrutable, because when it came to his feelings for him, Pete felt like an open book.

He opened his mouth, not even sure what he was going to say, but Sana cut him off. "For the record, even if your recent change in attitude wasn't totally self-motivated, I'm still proud of you for getting out of your comfort zone."

Pete smiled, touched. "Thank you." He couldn't help but tease, "Going soft on me?"

"Not a chance. Take the trash out."

He laughed. "Yes, ma'am. When I'm finished, can I leave for the night?"

"Yeah, I'll close up."

Pete dragged their trash and recycling out to the bins behind the shop and, after saying one final good-bye to Sana, made the walk home in silence. His thoughts, however, were far from quiet.

He still couldn't believe he'd actually asked Evan out that morning. To a club nonetheless. A *gay* club. Where there would be music and dancing and hot, sweaty men, all of whom would undoubtedly flock to Evan. Pete was actually kind of looking forward to that part. It was satisfying, in a caveman sort of way, to think that half the guys at the club would probably trade a kidney to be in Pete's shoes. Would wearing an *I'm With Him* shirt be too much? Probably.

He'd have to thank Raj the next time he saw him for the inspiration. Raj was the one who'd suggested he celebrate. It was such a convenient excuse too. *Hey, my birthday is coming up. Why don't we do something?*

Now if only he hadn't blurted out the name of the first gay club that had popped into his head. Why hadn't he named a bookstore or a restaurant or somewhere they'd actually be able to hear each other? Then again, Evan seemed like the sort of person who would thrive in dim light, surrounded by warm bodies, gyrating to a pulsating beat.

Pete wiped drool from his mouth. Maybe he hadn't made such a bad choice after all.

In a little less than twenty-four hours, he'd find out. In fact, he hoped he was about to find out a lot more than that. This would be the first time they'd hung out outside of work. That was the real litmus test.

Pete was sure it would go well, considering how much talking they'd done already, but there was still a lot he didn't know about Evan. Before this went any further—whatever this was—he needed to figure out if they were even compatible. Evan could have totally different values from him. He could belong to a cult. He could listen to Nickelback.

As if on cue, Pete's phone went off just as he got to his front door. He stood on the darkened stoop beneath a parenthesis of moon and read the text Evan had sent him.

Venus is in retrograde.

His fingers trembled from the cold as he typed, *What does that mean?*

No clue. My brother keeps saying that and winking. It's terrible.

The winking?

No, the fact that a member of my own family is into astrology.

Pete chuckled.

The front door wrenched open. "Pete?"

He shrieked and dropped his phone. "Jesus Christ, Mom." He scooped it off the ground and, after checking to make sure the screen hadn't cracked, slid it into his pocket. "What the hell?"

"Language," she scolded, stepping back to let him into the house.

He gravitated toward the warmth seeping out of the doorway. Mom pulled her fluffy bathrobe tighter around her and took a seat at the dining room table. Papers were spread out all over it. They looked like bills at a cursory glance. There was also a cup of tea next to a plate with some half-eaten chicken nuggets and ketchup on it.

"What are you doing up this late?" Pete asked.

"Thanks to how my schedule has been, it's morning for me. Sorry for scaring you. I heard someone walk up to the door and laugh. I figured it was either you or a deranged serial killer."

He frowned. "So, you decided to open the door?"

"I was fairly certain it was you." She glanced at him. His face must have been something to behold, because she giggled. "I'm not saying it was the *best* plan. Want some tea?"

"After working in a coffee shop all day? Definitely not. I was planning on crashing." He shifted his weight onto his heels. "Unless you want some company? Or some help with those?" He pointed at the bills.

"No sense in both of us crying over them." She ruffled his hair. "Get some rest."

"Okay." His phone was burning a hole in his pocket. He raced up the stairs to his room and flew out of his work clothes. He pulled on a shirt and some pajama bottoms and flopped into bed.

He hadn't expected to talk to Evan that much today, since they'd seen each other this morning and were going to see each other again tomorrow, but their conversation hadn't tapered off at all. He sent him a text: *How was your day?*

After clicking off his lamp, he held the glowing screen in front of his face until a response appeared.

It was great. Tomorrow will be even better.

Another text popped up right after that one. *There's something I've been wanting to ask you. I was going to save it for tomorrow, but I feel like when I see you, I'll lose my nerve.*

He couldn't even imagine a nerveless Evan. Must be something serious. He stared at the message for what felt like eons before typing, *What is it?*

A response came instantly, suggesting that Evan had already typed it out. *Would you ever consider coming out?*

He frowned. *I came out when I was sixteen. Neither of my parents were surprised.*

I mean coming out as a porn star.

Uh-oh. Where had that come from?

Pete instantly knew his answer: no way in hell. Just like he'd told Evan when they were outside the Globe, he'd only gotten into porn because he was certain no one would ever find out. He knew in his heart that there was nothing wrong with what he did, but he'd attended church every Sunday of his life. A lot of puritanical bullshit had been instilled in him from birth, and no matter how he tried to root it out, it was buried deep. If it weren't for the support of his parents, he might not even be openly gay.

Heart galloping, he replied, *I could never do that, no. I'm not like you.* He was tempted to add something like, *And I know from experience that it doesn't always go as smoothly as it did in your case,* but he held back. He wasn't quite ready to talk about that just yet. Instead, he typed, *Does that disappoint you?*

He hit Send before he could change his mind. His phone was silent for six torturous minutes. Then it vibrated.

No. That's one of many reasons why I can't stop thinking about you.

His whole body tingled. It was the same feeling he got when he missed a stair or slipped but managed to catch himself. It gathered in the soles of his feet and then spread into the rest of him, making the fine hairs on his arms stand up. The sensation of falling was so strong, he wondered what he was falling into.

He left Evan's last text unanswered and went to bed. The next morning, he rose early despite several attempts to sleep in. With no class and no work to help while away the time, he was forced to resort to household chores and homework. Mom was thrilled, which was its own reward, but nothing could hold his attention. He spent fifteen minutes scrubbing the same plate only to abandon it in favor of cleaning their unused stove.

It didn't help that the sun set early in the winter, making it seem later than it was. The final few hours before his "date" dragged on for a localized eternity. He enlisted Mom's help in selecting his outfit for the night. He told her he was going to meet up with friends, but from the twinkle in her brown eyes, he could tell she didn't believe him.

After digging through his entire closet and discarding absolutely everything that even resembled a hoodie, they settled on a white, long-sleeve shirt with a blue sweater pulled over it and black pants. It wasn't original, and it was far from traditional club attire, but when Pete checked out his reflection, he thought he looked pretty good.

Hopefully Evan would too.

After saying good-bye to Mom and promising not to stay out too late, he made the drive into town. The club was located near L.A. Live, one of the newer nightlife hotspots. He was miraculously able to find street parking within walking distance. He had to pay an exorbitant amount for it, but the prices would only get worse the closer he got to the clubs.

He stepped out into the cold night and made his way down Figueroa Street. Eight blocks later, a building with a neon-green sign reading *Twist* came into view. A paltry handful of people were waiting outside. It was only a little after nine, and nightlife in LA both started late and ended early. Until the after-parties began, of course.

He scanned the faces outside the club. None of them belonged to Evan. It occurred to him that if he wanted to call this whole thing off, now was his last chance.

Breathe, he commanded himself, as anticipation smacked into him with the force of a tidal wave. He was just hanging out with a coworker. No big deal. Evan wasn't going to bite him. Well, actually . . .

His phone hummed. Too late to back out now. He pulled it out and scanned the short message.

Boo.

His brow scrunched. What?

Strong arms wrapped around him from behind. "Gotcha."

Pete yelped and pried himself free.

Evan burst out laughing. "Oh my God, your face."

"Holy shit, Evan." He couldn't decide if he was more startled, pissed, or pleased to see him.

"I like it when you use my real name."

Twin spots of heat bloomed in Pete's cheeks. "I know you do." He'd experienced that firsthand. But it would take more than a little flirting to assuage him. "Why'd you sneak up on me?"

"I thought it'd be funny." He smirked. "It was."

"Whatever," Pete grumbled. People were starting to line up in earnest. He gestured at the club. "Let's go inside."

They headed for the end of the line, which now had about a dozen people in it. Evan shocked him by taking his hand. He almost stopped dead in his tracks, but after a precarious wobble he kept moving, praying his hand wasn't clammy.

He must have tensed or something, because Evan said, "Way too easy."

Pete regarded him. "What is?"

"Getting a reaction out of you. Or at least, it is now that I know what to look for." He squeezed his hand. "You're freezing. We should hurry."

The line moved mercifully quickly. To Pete's immense embarrassment, when it was their turn, the bouncer spent at least thirty extra seconds examining his ID. Even after it passed, he made a point of drawing giant black X's on the back of his hands with marker. Evan had the decency not to comment, though his lips kept twitching like he was fighting a smile. Pete wanted to liquesce and seep into the ground.

They entered through the metal and glass front doors. Pete was thankful and disappointed to discover clubs had not changed at all since he turned eighteen. There were flashing lights, pop music, and clusters of people at the bar. The dance floor was largely unpopulated, but it wouldn't remain that way for long. Once the crowd had some liquid courage in it, people would turn out in droves. Pete prayed he would be spared that particular torture.

They made a stop at the coat check and then stood between the bar and the dance floor. Pete looked to Evan. "What would you like to do?"

Instead of answering, Evan pressed his fingers into the small of Pete's back, guiding him toward the bar. Pete wet his suddenly dry lips and allowed himself to be led.

They slid into a space between a group of glittery drag queens and some hipsters.

"You want anything?" Evan asked.

Pete fingered the X on the back of one of his hands. "Water."

"Excellent choice."

A bartender appeared as if summoned by his decision. Evan leaned over the bar and ordered something Pete couldn't hear. He used the opportunity to examine him. His clothing selection for the evening was similar to what Pete had seen him wear in the past: dark, well-fitting jeans and a button-down shirt that suited him so well it seemed tailored.

That pretty much confirmed it. Evan had fashion sense. Pete cursed the injustice of it. It was like he'd won some sort of gene pool lottery, whereas Pete had been given a consolation toaster.

As he stared unabashedly, something pinged in the back of Pete's mind. He squinted at the jacket. It was hard to tell in the dim light, but he thought it might be the same one he'd worn the night of the audition. The same night Evan had cornered him on Joyce's deck in his underwear.

Gulp.

Evan turned around suddenly. Pete averted his gaze, but it was too late. There was no way Evan hadn't seen him staring.

Instead of teasing him, Evan pressed a cold glass into his hand. "Here. Cheers."

Pete dutifully clinked his glass against Evan's. It was water, as promised, but he couldn't tell what was in Evan's. Something dark. A rum and Coke? He'd pegged Evan as the sort to either drink beer or fruity cocktails with little umbrellas in them. Pete could picture both.

Evan answered his unasked question. "It's Coke."

"Just Coke? You're not drinking?"

"Nah, it wouldn't be fair." Evan brushed a thumb over the back of Pete's hand. "Besides, I want to be clearheaded for this."

"For clubbing?"

"Something like that." Evan took a swig of his drink and surveyed the room. "Let's find somewhere quiet."

"I don't think that's possible."

Evan laughed and grabbed his hand, dragging him over to a smattering of tables on the other side of the room. They were far enough from the DJ that the bass wasn't quite so overwhelming, though it still throbbed like a communal heartbeat in the air.

There was what appeared to be a lesbian couple at one of the tables, but they were engrossed in their own conversation. It was as close to privacy as they could get without ducking into one of the darkened corners. Pete could only imagine what went down in there. He set his drink down and took a seat. Evan did the same, and their knees brushed under the table.

Pete racked his brain for something to say, which should have been an easy task, considering there was still so much he wanted to know about Evan. All throughout the day he thought of things, but now that they were together, his mind was blank. He blamed the insistent press of Evan's leg against his.

He decided to start simple, raising his voice over the music. "Have you been here before?"

"I have, but it's been a while. Clubbing was never really my scene." He looked at Pete askance. "I wouldn't have thought it was yours either. I was surprised when you said you wanted to come here."

Pete grinned. "What do you mean? I'm obviously a total club rat."

"Could have fooled me. I took you for the type to have a few friends over on the weekends and drink craft beer."

"That's probably what I'll do on my actual birthday. I haven't decided yet." He fiddled with the glass in his hand and cleared his throat. "If I end up doing a birthday thing, would you like to come?"

"Depends. Would I be your date?"

Pete choked on his own saliva. He tried not so sound as flustered as he said, "Um, yeah, I guess. If that's, uh, what you want."

"Maybe." Evan's grin was wicked. "We should probably see how tonight goes before we start planning date number two."

Pete felt like all the blood in his body had broken loose and was sloshing aimlessly in him. "That would make this date number one, wouldn't it?"

"And you tried to tell me you're not smart." He rubbed Pete's shoulder. "It's a date if you want it to be."

He swallowed. "I probably wouldn't have called it that if you hadn't said something."

"Why not?"

"Wouldn't have had the nerve. I was only able to ask you out because I had my birthday as an excuse. Dates are big, scary things that I suck at."

Evan cocked his head to the side. "What about me? Am I a big, scary thing?"

Pete wet his lips. "You used to be. Not so much anymore."

"Then we've made progress." Evan reached across the table and placed his hand on top of Pete's. "You don't need an excuse to spend time with me, and you don't have to invite me to places you don't enjoy because you feel like you should. At this point, I'd jump at the chance to put a jigsaw puzzle together with you."

Pete's heart mimicked the heavy rhythm of the music. "How do you see through me so easily?"

Evan leaned forward, his eyes intent on Pete's face. "I'm looking very, *very* closely."

Pete had to try twice before he could speak loudly enough to be heard. "I'm glad you told me to make a move, though I'm kind of surprised you didn't beat me to the punch. Why didn't you ask me?"

"What's it matter?"

"Because you probably wouldn't have dillydallied so much."

Evan snorted. "'Dillydallied'? Really? I bet that's the first time in recorded history that someone has said 'dillydallied' at a club. Sure you don't want to go with a safer word? Like 'shilly-shallied'?"

Pete flushed. "Very funny."

A roguish smile curved Evan's lips. "Sorry, I can't help it. The urge to tease you is overwhelming."

"You've told me that before."

"It's as true now as it was then. But to answer your question, I enjoy a good chase, but not for wild geese."

"What?"

"Dance with me." Evan stood up, holding his hand out to Pete.

Pete blinked at it, still reeling from the sudden change in topic. When he recovered, he racked his brain for an excuse. He was still struggling when something suddenly glommed onto him from behind. The thing knocked him forward, rattling the table. If Pete had to guess, he'd wager it was a human-sized octopus.

"Hey, flamer," cooed a familiar voice in his ear.

"Oh God, no," Pete ground out. He jerked around in his seat, praying he was having some sort of hallucination.

But no, Joshua was standing next to him. He stepped back, an evil grin on his face. His blond hair had been gelled into spikes, and he was decked out in proverbial club clothes: skinny jeans and a slashed shirt with black mesh peeking through.

"Oh God," Pete repeated. "Please make it go away."

Joshua pouted. "Nice to see you too."

"What are you *doing* here?"

"I come here all the time. The real question is, what are *you* doing here. Did you lose a bet or something?"

Pete whined like a wounded animal. How could he forget that Joshua was a club rat? And how did everyone who'd ever met him know he didn't like clubs? This was a disaster.

"Everything all right?" Evan piped up.

Joshua glanced at Evan and then did a double-take. He looked him up and down, eyes widening with each pass. "Holy shit. Is *he* with *you*?"

"He is," Evan answered, peering curiously at Joshua. "Who are you?"

Joshua clapped Pete on the back. "I'm Joshua. Flamer and I work together."

Evan squinted at Pete. "Flamer?"

"Yeah, that's what he calls me. He thinks it's okay because he's gay, but really it's just uncomfortable." *Although, I'm grateful for once that he never uses my name, or my secret identity wouldn't be so secret anymore.*

"It's just a joke," Joshua said, eyes still glued to Evan.

Evan, however, was watching Pete. "When he says you *work* together, does he mean . . ."

Oh shit. Pete could see right where Evan's brain had gone, and considering Joshua was an attractive gay man, it wasn't a difficult leap. Pete started to deny it—just the thought of sleeping with Joshua made him queasy—but he stopped short. He couldn't very well say, *Oh no, he's not in porn*, in front of Joshua. And he couldn't say, *He works at my other job*, either, or Joshua would want to know what his *other* other job was. Fuck.

Luckily, Joshua came to his unwitting rescue. "Ever heard of a coffee shop called the Globe?"

Evan's eyes widened. It was funny that they'd just talked about jigsaw puzzles, because Pete could practically see him fitting pieces together in his mind. "As a matter of fact, I've been there."

"That's where we work. If you ever want to drop by, I'd be happy to serve you." He batted long, pale eyelashes.

Pete couldn't tell if he wanted to face-palm or throw up.

"I'd love to," Evan cooed back.

Pete sucked in a breath. Oh God. What if Evan thought Joshua was hot?

Suddenly, Evan grabbed Pete by the hand and yanked him to his feet. "Now that I know *he* works there, I'm sure I'll be by all the time. It was nice meeting you. If you'll excuse us, we have some dancing to do."

And with that, Evan strode off, dragging Pete with him and leaving a pouting Joshua behind with their abandoned drinks. They weaved through the crowd until they were on the far side of the dance floor, out of sight of the tables.

Evan stopped and faced him without releasing his hand. "Charming friend you have there."

Pete prayed his hand wasn't sweating in Evan's grip like a cold drink on a summer day. "He's not my friend. He's just a coworker."

"Yeah, I got that. You work at that coffee place I saw you in front of?"

"Um, yeah." He shuffled his feet. "It's my day job."

"So, when I saw you outside that one time, and you said you had to go to work, you were being literal?"

"Mm-hmm."

"Why didn't you tell me? I could have come back when you were on break."

Pete was conspicuously silent.

"Did you . . . not want me to know you worked there?"

"Um, sort of."

Evan frowned. "Why? Did you think I was going to march inside and shout 'Hey, everyone, this guy's a porn star'?"

"No," Pete said quickly. "Nothing like that. I just— Look, this is really embarrassing. I—I didn't tell you because I didn't want you to think I'm"—he made an awkward gesticulation toward himself—"exactly what I am. A boring college student with a boring job and a boring life. It's not very sexy, you know?"

Evan snorted. "You could be covered in coffee grounds and still be sexy, believe me. Out of curiosity, though, why have a second job at all? I bet that place doesn't pay you in a week what porn does in an hour."

"You're right, but I live with my mom, and if I showed up with a bunch of money and no explanation for how I got it, she'd ask questions. I had to have a part-time job."

"You could just tell her the truth."

"I could also set myself on fire, but I have no intention of doing that either. I seriously, *seriously* doubt she'd be okay with it. Besides, I'd keep my day job regardless. It's a steady paycheck I can rely on when no one books me for a month at a time. I'm not a rising star like you are. I'm not always in demand."

Evan's expression was impish. "Sounds like that job is your secret identity. You're working as a reporter for the *Daily Planet* so no one figures out you're actually Superman."

"Well, when you put it like that. Thanks for taking this so well. I shouldn't have kept it from you."

"I understand," Evan said, light and airy. "Everyone wants to look cool in front of their crush."

"I do not!" Pete squawked, which in no way helped his case. "You're not— I never— I'm not—"

Evan attempted to smother his laughter with a hand and was only partially successful. "I feel like a teenager."

Pete frowned. "Because I never got over my awkward phase?"

"No, because you seem so delightfully *new* to this. If I weren't certain someone had to have fallen for you by now, I'd think you'd never dated before."

"You're not that far off. I've only had two serious relationships, and one of them didn't end well." He shifted his weight uncomfortably.

"Not to bring up past lovers while on a," he swallowed, "date, or anything. I think that's one of those things you're not supposed to do."

Evan shrugged. "You have a past. So does everyone. I want to learn more about you, including the not-so-happy parts."

Pete fiddled with one of his cuffs so he'd have an excuse to look down. "Really?"

Evan touched Pete's chin and lifted it. "Yeah, and for the record, you're not the only one with baggage. I have some horror stories of my own, if you'd care to hear them."

"Another time," Pete said. "I'd rather our first date was just about us."

Evan grinned wolfishly. "Then how about that dance?"

"I don't dance. If you think I'm awkward under normal circumstances..."

"I'm willing to bet you've just never had a good partner." Evan laid a hand gently on his hip and used it to draw him nearer. Pete's breathing hitched. "Come on, you invited me to a club. Did you honestly think I wouldn't rope you into a dance at some point?"

He guided Pete into a swaying motion that matched the slow tempo of the current song. Pete slid his arms over Evan's shoulders. Their faces were so close, Evan could probably hear how rapidly Pete was breathing.

Evan smiled. "See? It's not so bad."

"Only because I'm dancing with you," Pete said. "Though I like that you get me out of my shell." They were revolving in place. He could hear the dull murmur of voices around them, but he kept his eyes on Evan. If he focused, the rest of the club melted away, leaving them alone on the dance floor.

Suddenly, the music shifted to a more upbeat tempo. Their dance fell out of sync. Pete dropped his arms and started to move away.

Evan pulled him back. "Ready to learn another move?"

"I think I'm still getting the hang of this whole 'swaying' thing."

"We can stop if you want." He put a hand on Pete's waist. "But I think you'll enjoy this next one."

Pete sucked in a breath against a sudden wave of arousal. It really wasn't fair what Evan could do to him with a simple look.

"Yeah, okay," he murmured. "Show me."

Pete had no idea how Evan heard him, but judging by the wicked curve to his lips, he understood. He slotted their hips together, one of his thighs insinuated between Pete's legs. Then he gripped Pete's waist. "Move against me like this." He rolled his hips in a way that was nothing short of obscene.

Pete went from awkward to weak with arousal in a flash. He imitated the movement clumsily, praying his fledgling erection wasn't too obvious.

"It's more like this." Evan slid his hands down to the small of Pete's back and bodily showed him how to move. Within seconds their dance devolved into grinding. It was all Pete could do to hold on and try not to get embarrassingly hard. But with Evan pressed to him, warm and solid and insistent, it was a labor of Herculean proportions.

Evan's mouth found Pete's ear. "You asked me out because you wanted to get to know me, right?"

Pete exhaled shakily. "Right."

"This, in my opinion, is the best way to get to know someone."

Pete struggled to think as desire rolled through him like smoke, blotting out all other thought. "By humping them?"

Evan chuckled, the sound a deep vibration that mingled with the bass. "No, by dancing with them."

"What can you learn from that?"

"Oh, you'd be surprised." He brushed their cheeks together. "You, for example, have this whole quiet, shy thing going on, yet you have no problem with this very public display of affection we're committing right now."

Pete suddenly remembered they were in a room full of people. He looked around, and made eye contact with a few people who were watching them. Most of the attention was directed at Evan, but Pete saw one guy who was *definitely* looking at him.

"What does that tell you about me?" he asked, even though he had an inkling of where Evan was going with this.

Evan lifted a hand to his face, cupping it and sweeping a thumb over one of his cheekbones. "I think you're not as shy as you pretend to be. If you were, you couldn't be in our line of work. I bet if I got you turned on enough, I could take you into one of those dark nooks and do whatever I wanted to you."

"Evan," Pete whimpered, "I'm already turned on."

Evan groaned and brushed his lips along Pete's jaw. "I almost wish you hadn't told me that. You're so very tempting, Jaden."

Pete frowned. He wasn't sure why, but his stage name sounded jarring all of a sudden.

"What is it?" Evan asked, apparently sensing his tension. "Is something wrong?"

"Yeah, actually." Pete knew what he had to do. His purpose in asking Evan out tonight was to find out who he really was, but he couldn't do that if he wasn't being himself. It wasn't fair to either of them. He craned his neck down until his lips were hovering right by Evan's ear, and whispered, "Pete."

Evan twitched, and Pete suspected his breath had tickled him. "Peat? Like that stuff they use for fuel in Scotland?"

"Technically yes, but I mean *I'm* Pete."

Evan almost smacked their heads together. "What?"

"That's my real name. Pete Griflow." Pete shrugged to hide the healthy dose of panic washing through him. Had Evan felt this way when he'd told him? Scared and nervous and utterly *exhilarated*? "Glamorous, I know."

In lieu of an answer, Evan grabbed two fistfuls of his sweater and walked him backward off the dance floor. He didn't stop until Pete's back hit a wall next to a support beam. There was virtually no cover. Half the room could see them if they looked over, but Evan didn't seem to care.

"Pete," Evan said.

"Don't wear it out," Pete joked nervously.

"I didn't think— It's been so long since I told you." His eyes were skittering along Pete's features, from his hair to his mouth to his chest and up again, as if he were seeing him for the first time. "I was starting to think you were never going to—" He stopped and shook his head. "Which would have been fine, of course, it's your name."

"I would have told you eventually no matter what."

Evan nodded. "I'd hoped you would. I'm sorry. I'm babbling. I'm just *really* happy to meet you, Pete."

Pete put his hands over Evan's. "It was about time we graduated to being on a first-name basis."

"That's putting it lightly." Evan let out a breath and pressed closer. "Knowing your real name is weirdly hot. I can't even explain it. It's like this naughty little secret we share."

"We have a few of those now."

"Pete." It was clear from his tone that he wasn't addressing him, more like listening to the sound. "Just to warn you, I might say your name until it loses all meaning."

"I felt the same way when you told me yours. I couldn't get it out of my head. I kept repeating it over and over. Evan."

He shuddered. "Fuck, it's ridiculous how much that turns me on. I can just imagine you doing it too. And it's extra hot because everyone else calls me Darko."

"Darko is sexy, though."

"I like Pete. It's not the most exciting secret identity, but it suits you."

"Oh, thanks," he teased. "Because I'm not exciting?"

"Believe me, you're the most exciting man I know." He rocked his hips against him like he'd done out on the dance floor. Pete gasped. Even through denim it was obvious how hard he was.

"So, Pete," Evan said, skimming his lips along Pete's jaw, "where do we go from here?"

The energy between them shifted in an instant, escalating like a spark bursting into a flame. Pete had wanted Evan before, but now he *hungered* for him. It was like the part of him that had been holding back this whole time had finally given in, and all the lust he felt for Evan had broken free.

"Evan, I want you."

Evan kissed his neck, openmouthed and hot. "Tell me what you want me to do."

A shiver spilled down Pete's spine, and his cock swelled, straining against his pants. He drew a deep breath that somehow made him feel like he had less air than before. "*Kiss me.*"

Evan obeyed like he'd been waiting to hear those words his whole life.

It was a harsh kiss, needy and desperate, and Pete couldn't get enough. He slid his fingers into Evan's hair and tugged, trying to pull him closer even as their mouths sealed together. He felt a flash of teeth against his bottom lip—just enough to make him whimper—and then Evan ran his tongue over the flesh he'd just abused.

Pete didn't know if it was possible to faint from being too turned on, but there was a chance he was about to find out.

"Do you know why I wasn't drinking tonight?" Evan sucked on a mouthful of his skin, pulling off with a wet, popping noise.

"Fuck, ah, *Evan*," was all Pete could say in response.

"It's because I thought this might happen. Hell, I wanted it to. And I wanted to feel every part of it with complete clarity. But more importantly—" he licked the section of skin that Pete suspected he'd just left a hickey on "—I wanted *you* to know I was sober."

Pete could barely put words together well enough to ask, "Why?"

Evan took Pete's face in both of his hands and spoke against his mouth, his lips sliding over him like velvet. "You don't know how maddening it's been, trying to get you to realize how much I like you. I thought I was painfully obvious. I even outright propositioned you, but still you seemed to think I didn't mean it. Well, not tonight. There are no cameras here, Pete, no scripts, no Colette ordering me to kiss you, and I haven't had a drop to drink. Everything I'm doing right now is because I want to." He drew a ragged breath. "I want this. I want *you*. Please tell me I can have you."

Pete could scarcely speak. He stared at him, wide-eyed. He'd known for a while now that Evan liked him, but Evan had just demonstrated that he *understood* him. His weird insecurities and neuroses and all the back and forth that had been clouding his head ever since they'd first met. And that . . . *that* was shockingly hot.

He looked Evan square in the eye. "I'm yours."

Evan made a sound in the back of his throat that was like a moan collided with a growl. Then he pressed their lips so hard together, it actually rocked Pete back against the wall. Evan kissed him breathless. He kissed with a vengeance, but also like they had all the time in the world to discover every way their mouths could fit together.

Pete kissed him back to the best of his ability, but it wasn't enough. Now that he'd given in, he needed *more*. The things they'd done so far were just an aperitif, a flirtation that merely whet his appetite.

He trailed his hands slowly down the side of Evan's face to his chest, and then finally to his stomach, giving him time to move away if he wanted to. Instead, Evan canted into the touch, like he wanted to accelerate Pete's inevitable journey south.

Pete reached the waistband of his jeans and dipped his fingers into them, stroking all the skin he could reach. Evan gasped against his mouth, making his lips tingle. Pete panted for breath. He pulled back, resting his sweaty brow against Evan's, and panted for a second. His hot breaths mixed with Evan's. He was tense with the anticipation of knowing where this was headed, and Evan felt the same against him.

There was so much he wanted, so much to taste and touch and explore, but he couldn't overthink this. Swallowing, Pete pulled one hand out of Evan's pants and traced the outline of his erection though his jeans. Evan quivered like a plucked string and moaned so throatily, Pete swore he felt it in his bones.

Distantly, Pete realized he'd never seen Evan's cock. That needed to be rectified *immediately*.

Pete fumbled with his fly, fingers shaking too hard to make any real progress. Evan made a pathetic noise and rested his head on Pete's shoulder like he lacked the strength to support it.

"Is this okay?" Pete mumbled, bleary with lust. "Can I touch you?"

Evan didn't even hesitate. "Yes, Pete. *Please.*"

Confidence surged into him. Fuck, it was intoxicating to be the one reducing Evan to a puddle for once. His fingers steadied, and he popped the button open. Just as his fingers touched the zipper, a bright light flashed in his face. He threw a hand up to shield his eyes, blinking away a stinging red afterimage.

"What the fuck?" It was Evan's voice.

"You two, out," barked a man.

Pete peered over Evan's shoulder. A burly man holding a flashlight was standing nearby, wearing a black shirt with the word *security* written across it in block, white letters. Shit. A bouncer.

"What's your problem?" Evan asked.

"You are. You can't fuck in the club. If you wanna get it on, get a room." He stepped back and waved toward the exit with his flashlight. "Out."

Shit.

Evan took Pete's hand. "I was just thinking I could use some fresh air."

He tugged Pete toward the exit. To Pete's horror, the bouncer followed after, shining his light on them the whole way as if to prevent them from slipping back into the crowd. Pete kept his head down until they were back outside in the frigid night air.

There was hardly anyone on the streets, meaning everyone had likely found their party for the night. Pete pulled his phone out of his pocket. It was 11:46 p.m. It felt like they'd been in there for years, but it had only been three hours.

Pete sneaked a peek at Evan. He had his hands in his pockets and was looking up at the stars with a sly smile on his face. He seemed inexplicably pleased.

Pete apologized anyway. "Sorry about that. I guess I got carried away."

"Don't worry about it. Of all the reasons to get kicked out of a club, we picked the best one." He glanced at Pete. "Did you drive here?"

It was a simple question, but it made Pete's heart skip. "Yeah."

"Where's your car?"

Pete nodded to the right. "About five minutes that way." *Is he going to ask me for a ride home? Or to come back to his place?*

As if reading his thoughts, Evan took a step toward him. "That's a shame. I wanted to offer to drive you home. Maybe I can make it up to you some other way." He took Pete's hand—already icy from the wind—and brought it to his lips. "If I were a true gentleman, I'd at least walk you to your car."

"At least," Pete agreed.

"It would give me a chance to say good night to you properly."

Pete felt a renewed surge of arousal. He leaned unthinkingly toward Evan. "And what does a proper good night from Evan Darko entail?"

Evan grinned his trademark devilish grin and brought their lips a hair's breadth apart. Pete could almost feel the unspoken invitation burning against his skin.

Please, Pete thought desperately, *please, God, invite me back to your place.*

And then Evan did the worst thing imaginable. He stepped away. "Drive safe. I'll talk to you soon, Pete."

Evan turned on his heel and walked away.

CHAPTER  11

Pete made the drive home in a stupor. It was a good thing he'd lived in LA his whole life, because if he'd been called upon to name what streets he took, he wouldn't be able to. He was on autopilot, the core of his brain devoted to replaying his date with Evan in technicolor detail.

Had he done something wrong at some point? Evan had said that he'd been trying to make Pete realize he liked him from the start—a dizzying revelation in and of itself—and Pete had practically thrown himself at him. If Evan had wanted him, he could have had him. So *why* weren't they together right now? Honestly, he should give up on trying to figure Evan out. It seemed their telepathy only went one way.

Pete muttered under his breath, "Totally unfair."

With a start, he realized he was going fifteen miles over the speed limit. He took his leaden foot off the gas and watched the speedometer inch down to the appropriate number. Great, now he felt like he was crawling home. Not that it mattered. It wasn't like anyone was waiting for him.

He exhaled heavily. As far as first dates went, it could have been worse. Pete hadn't totally embarrassed himself on the dance floor, and Joshua hadn't outed him before he'd had a chance to tell Evan his name for himself. That was something. And if Evan didn't want to sleep with him, that was his call.

He just wished he knew why Evan had left so quickly, because he was willing to bet he'd missed something. Pete was no expert on the man, but he had gleaned one thing in the past few weeks: Evan was a drama queen. This wasn't the first time he'd flounced off into the night, leaving Pete to puzzle over his motivations. Something was up, and Pete wanted to know what it was before he tortured himself all over again.

After pulling into the driveway and killing the engine, he stayed in his seat for a moment, debating. Should he call Evan? Just to make sure he hadn't pissed him off? Or would Evan want some space? They'd seen a lot of each other lately, and it was after midnight.

Pete couldn't decide. He had the animal instincts of a newborn kitten. After a solid minute, the cold drove him inside.

Mom was still up when he plodded through the front door. She was sitting on the well-worn couch in the living room. The glow from the TV illuminated her profile. She looked at him when he entered and offered him a smile.

He attempted to smile back, but it must have been more of a rictus, because she asked, "Everything all right, kiddo?"

"Uh, yeah." He sounded about as genuine as Ebenezer Scrooge at a charity event.

She gave him the sort of knowing look only a mother could produce, one designed to make duplicitous children spill their guts.

It worked. "The night didn't go quite how I planned."

"Ah. You didn't have a good time?"

"No, I did. I just . . ." He stopped and made a frustrated gesture, as if that explained everything.

Miraculously, Mom seemed to understand.

"You're home kind of early," she said. "Did your friends want to leave? Or did something happen?"

Pete hesitated. Was he ready to tell her about Evan? Close as they were, he tried to spare her the traumatic details of his sex life—and not just the obvious ones. Then again, she had more relationship experience than anyone he knew, even Raj. She might have some invaluable insight.

You don't have to give her Evan's life story. Keep it simple. Vague.

"Nothing happened, per se. That's sort of the problem. I'm having boy trouble."

Mom pumped a fist in the air. "I knew it. My mom senses were tingling. You were spending far too much time brooding, even for you."

"Thank you for that," he grumbled.

"Sorry, honey." Mom waved at the spot next to her on the couch. "Better tell me all about him."

He flopped down and sighed. "His name is Evan. He's, um, a friend, but I think we're about to become something more. Maybe." He shook his head. "We haven't discussed anything serious, but it's pretty clear we're into each other. We just can't seem to *get* there."

Mom looked like she was trying not to smile. It reminded him of Evan, as most things did these days. "What's holding you back? Did your date not go well?"

"That's the thing. It went great, right up until the end." He fell silent. How was he going to explain what was wrong without saying Evan didn't want to sleep with him? The answer was surprisingly easy: he wasn't.

She cocked her head. "Did he kiss you?"

"Mooom," Pete whined, face turning red. In his head, a voice answered, *Yeah, and I was ready to do a lot more than that.*

"I'm not trying to embarrass you, I promise. Well, maybe a little." She chuckled. "Call me old-fashioned, but that's my litmus test for if a date went well. The proverbial Good Night Kiss."

That gave him an idea. "Actually, that's the problem. He *didn't* kiss me, and I really thought he was going to." A kissing-is-sex metaphor. It was hardly original, but at least Bram Stoker would be proud of him. "Any idea why he didn't?"

"Lots of reasons. He didn't feel like it. Or he didn't think the moment was right. Or he was nervous or scared or not in the mood. A good-night kiss is a sign that a date went well, but it's not obligatory." She eyed him. "Do we need to have the consent talk again?"

"I've had it with myself plenty of times tonight, trust me. I'm just worried that I did something wrong, you know?"

"What makes you think that?"

"Well, I'm me, for one thing." He shrugged. "I always think I've done something wrong. And also, you'd understand if you knew Evan. If ending the date with a kiss had been his plan, he would have done it."

"Did you make it clear you wanted him to? Consent works both ways, you know."

"I was forthright about it. At least, I think so."

"That doesn't mean much," she teased. "But on a serious note, I wouldn't fret. It was only one date. I'm certain you'll have another shot at a first kiss. And maybe after that there can be a first-time-meeting-Mom." She nudged him with her elbow.

His lips twitched up. "Of course."

"I know moms are supposed to say things like this, but keep in mind, if this boy doesn't work out, it's not the end of the world. You'll meet someone else."

"People keep telling me that. I'm not sure if it makes me feel better or worse."

She laughed. "That's because it's true. You're only twenty. You have so, so much time. More than you even know. Time to get your heart broken and to break some hearts in turn and to learn to be alone only to meet the perfect guy the next day. Trust me, I know. It'll all work out, and when you look back on it, a first-date kiss will be one little step in a whole journey."

"Thanks, Mom."

She was right, although in this particular situation, there *wasn't* time. *Heat Wave* wasn't going to last forever. What would happen when they moved on to other projects? Got new costars and started having sex with them? They might miss their only chance to figure out if what they had was *real* or just one of Colette's scripts come to life.

He'd thought spending time together outside of work would help, but he was as confused as ever. They were trapped in this weird in-between area—no longer strangers, but definitely not boyfriends—that made his feet itch for solid ground.

Mom broke him from his thoughts by patting him on the back. "Well, you certainly can't do anything about it tonight. Sleep on it. Things will seem clearer in the morning."

"Yeah, okay." He snorted. "I'll just go to bed and definitely not lie awake thinking about it."

She ruffled his hair. "Men. Am I right?"

"Yup."

"Love you."

"Love you too. Night."

He trotted upstairs and stood motionless in the middle of his room. His eyes traced over his furniture without really seeing it. His bed was normally his favorite place in the whole house, but right now it seemed utterly unappealing. Probably because he was so abuzz with thoughts of Evan, he wasn't going to sleep anytime soon. The digital clock by his bed read, *12:26 a.m.* That gave him a solid seven hours to dwell before the sun rose. Better get started.

He emptied his pockets, setting his keys, wallet, and phone on his dresser. He checked the latter out of habit and froze. He had a text from Evan. How had he not felt his phone vibrate? It was practically one of his vital signs these days.

He selected the text. Two seemingly innocuous words appeared on the screen: *Still awake?*

Pete's heart leaped into his throat. He typed back, *Yes.*

Seconds passed in silence. Then, *Can I call you?*

If it meant hearing Evan's voice, Pete would talk about the mating call of the platypus right now.

He didn't bother replying. Instead, he found Evan's name in his contacts list and hit the Call button. His heart tapped out a rough staccato rhythm against his ribs as it rang once, twice, three times.

On the fourth ring, the line clicked. "Hello?"

"Hey." His voice cracked. Off to a good start. He cleared his throat. "I got your text." He winced. It was like there was a record for unnecessary remarks he was trying to break.

Evan laughed. "I figured as much. Were you sleeping?"

"No. You?"

"Not even close."

Pete attempted to say something smooth. "So, what's up? Miss me already?"

"More than I can say."

Pete's heart was suddenly too big for his chest. "Were you calling to make sure I got home all right?" *Please say no*, he prayed. *Say you want to talk things over. Or to explain yourself.*

"Actually, no, I wanted to explain myself."

Pete mouthed, *Thank you*, to the ceiling. "Explain what?"

"I'm sure you can guess my general train of thought."

"Tell me anyway."

"I was thinking about you. About us. A slew of dirty thoughts, of course." He chuckled, but his tone didn't quite live up to the joke.

Pete wet his lips. "Go on."

"I could have asked you to come home with me tonight. You would have said yes." It wasn't a question.

Pete didn't bother affirming what they both already knew. "It's okay that you didn't. I understand."

"I don't think you do." There was a shifting sound. Pete pictured Evan leaning forward with anticipation. "Pete, I wanted to ask you to come home with me. I wanted to so badly."

Words were burning on Pete's tongue: *Then why didn't you?* But he swallowed them. It didn't seem like Evan was finished speaking.

"There's something I need to ask you," Evan continued. "I already know the answer, but I want to hear you say it."

"Okay."

"Do you like me? As more than just a costar or someone you want to have sex with?"

Pete didn't hesitate. "I do."

Evan exhaled. "Well then. Do you have anything you want to say?"

Pete felt the same energy between them that he'd felt earlier tonight. Potential, yearning to become kinetic. It was like Evan was waiting for something. Some kind of signal. But Pete had no idea what—

It occurred to Pete that he'd been exceptionally dense.

Evan had been trying to bring them closer from the start. He'd told Pete his real name before a first date had even been on the agenda, and during filming, he always made sure there was something just between them, something the cameras couldn't see. But Pete had been an uncertain mess from the start. Evan was probably looking for Pete to meet him halfway or, more accurately, to take a single step forward after Evan had already chased him down the street.

Well, if it was a move he wanted, Pete was about to make one.

He switched his phone to his other ear. "Evan, there's something I need to tell you. Something I've known for a while without actually knowing it, if that makes sense."

"It does, in a weird way. Tell me."

"I feel like we did this whole thing out of order. Running before walking. Fucking before holding hands, you know? Not that our relationship was ever going to be traditional, but . . . there's one thing I want to do the right way."

"What's that?"

Heart pounding, Pete said, "I don't want the first time I have sex with you to be in front of a camera. I don't want an audience. I want it to be just you and me."

The silence that descended between them was magnetic. Pete actually took a half step forward, as if that would bring him closer to Evan.

Evan exhaled sharply, and then, in a voice that was as raw and vulnerable as an exposed nerve, he said, "My place?"

Pete looked at his clock again. "Tonight?"

"Right now."

All the air left Pete's lungs at once. The reality of Evan's words soaked into him like warm sunlight. This was really going to happen. He'd have to sneak past his mom to get out, something he'd never done even in his formative years. But as the logistics spun out in his head, he realized there was nothing he wouldn't do to get to Evan.

"Text me your address." He had no idea where Evan lived, but he was willing to bet he'd make it there in record time.

"Okay. I'll be waiting."

"Not for long."

They hung up, and within seconds, Evan sent him directions to his apartment in Glendale. Pete could be there in less than twenty minutes. A frisson of excitement spread through him. And to think, Mom had told him to sleep on it. The very idea of going to any bed but Evan's was unthinkable.

Still in his club clothes, he snatched his keys off the dresser and dashed downstairs, already rehearsing the excuse he'd give Mom. There was an emergency. A big one. No time to explain.

To his relief, however, he found her asleep in front of the TV. She must've been exhausted. He paused long enough to drape an old quilt over her before he crept out the front door and locked it behind him.

The drive was agony. It took everything he had not to speed like earlier. He could just imagine what he'd say if he got pulled over: *Officer, I'm so sorry I was speeding, but I have a good reason. I'm about to have wild sex with a guy I really like.* That might not go over so well.

Gradually, the industrial city center melted into the greener, residential areas. Boutiques morphed into shopping plazas, bars became grocery stores, and office buildings transformed into manicured parks.

Focused as he was on his destination, he didn't realize how nervous he was until he pulled into a parking lot next to a row of brick buildings. A stone sign out front read, *Ocean Villas.* He stepped out of his car and spent a second just staring at the neat buildings. Evan was waiting for him behind one of the white doors. What would it be like to finally be with him? What sort of lover was he when he wasn't performing for a camera? Pete's mouth watered at the prospect of finding out.

He found the correct building and raced up a black metal staircase to the second floor. He passed three doors before he came upon the one he wanted: number 1226. His pulse thundered in his ears as he raised his hand to knock. His knuckles rapping against the wood were barely audible.

It must have been loud enough, though, because he hadn't even lowered his hand yet when the door opened. Evan stood on the threshold in what Pete could only assume were his pajamas: an old T-shirt and soft-looking gray sweatpants. His hair was sticking up in places, like he'd run his fingers through it one too many times. They stared at each other. Tension sprang up between them so thickly, it crept into Pete's lungs with every breath.

"You came," Evan said, eyes wide.

"Nothing could have kept me away."

Evan sucked in a breath and then wordlessly stepped back, making room for Pete to enter. Pete almost stumbled in his haste to follow after him.

When he was inside, Evan closed the door. Pete took in the small apartment in a sweep. They were standing in a living room with gray walls, tile floors, and large windows. The furniture was simple and modern, and there were black-and-white photos of the city on the walls. It both suited Evan and didn't. Pete couldn't quite put his finger on it. It was like looking at a catalog picture of a typical young man's living room. It lacked Evan's ineluctable personality.

Stop analyzing his wall art and make a move, he scolded himself. He turned to face Evan.

Evan looked more handsome than Pete had ever seen, even more so than when he was on set with stylists and makeup artists and hand-picked costumes. He looked like *himself*, not his character. And there was something powerfully erotic about that.

Evan was watching him, clearly sizing him up. Pete swallowed and tried to think of something to say, something about how long he'd wanted this, how much it meant to him. Words buzzed in his head, but he couldn't get them to form a sentence. Then Evan took a step forward, cupped his chin, and kissed him.

Pete's thoughts muted as if someone had pressed a button. It was more than that, though. Time stood still. Pete could scarcely breathe from the electric intensity of Evan's touch. It felt like a first kiss, and in a way it was: their first kiss that was just for them, without anyone else around. No audience, no acting, no pressure. Pete drew a ragged breath and almost sobbed when Evan tilted his head, finding the perfect angle. When Evan's tongue laved his bottom lip, Pete swore he'd never experienced anything so profound.

He tried to give back as good as he got, but he couldn't focus. His lips were operating on autopilot, he was so caught up in letting himself *feel*. He must've been doing a fair enough job, though, because he could hear Evan breathing hard, could feel the rise and fall of his chest against him.

Through the haze of arousal blanketing his thoughts, Pete was able to determine one thing: he wanted more.

Acting on instinct, he grabbed Evan's biceps and walked him back. Three steps later, Evan's shoulder blades connected with the door. Pete cherished the surprised look on his face for a moment before he pounced. Evan was hot and solid against him, sinew and muscle. He got as close to him as he could, pressing their bodies flush, wanting to feel every inch of him.

"Fuck," Evan mumbled against his mouth, "that was really hot."

Pete kissed Evan like he needed his mouth to breathe. Even with their height difference, their bodies seemed to line up just right. Evan suddenly bucked his hips, and his erection rubbed against Pete's.

Holy shit. Pete's vision blurred. He must not have been the only one, because Evan moaned and started shuffling them farther into the apartment.

They stumbled a few times—especially Pete, who was toeing his shoes off as they went—but they managed to make it to the sofa. Evan gripped his shoulders like he intended to maneuver him onto it, but Pete beat him to it. He grabbed a handful of Evan's shirt and dragged him down on top of him.

Evan's weight felt phenomenal. So comforting and yet so incredibly arousing. Pete wrapped his arms around him and buried his face in Evan's neck, breathing in Evan's salt-and-soap smell.

Evan dragged his lips down Pete's throat, and the scrape of his stubble was exactly as Pete had imagined. It set his nerves on fire.

"I almost can't believe I finally have you here." Evan kissed the hollow of his throat. "Everything you do feels so good. Even just being under me is," he shivered, "fuck."

Pete tried to respond, but Evan's hand found its way into his shirt, and his words caught in his throat. He gasped out, "Oh God, yes. Can you move just a little—" Pete shifted one of his legs out from under Evan until his knees were on either side of him. Evan sank into the space between his thighs, and they both groaned.

"That's perfect." Evan rolled his hips, and their clothed erections came together. He repeated the motion, and dragged his blunt fingernails down Pete's stomach. The dual sensations left Pete speechless.

Evan nipped at his throat. "You like that?"

"Evan, more," he ground out, squirming under his fingers.

"That wasn't a yes." Evan reached for his jeans. "Say it."

Pete had to force himself to keep still when all he wanted was to arch up into his touch. "Yes, Evan, it feels so good." Evan's fingers were almost where he wanted them. He canted his hips up, desperate for friction.

"You're so eager." Evan kissed him again, a sweet slide of lips. "We have all night. I plan to take my time with you."

Pete gasped as Evan unzipped his jeans, fingers brushing against his cock through the material. Belatedly, Pete wished he'd thought to put on something sexier than plain, white boxers. Something like what Evan had worn when—

"You're thinking again," was all the warning he got before Evan shucked his pants down to his thighs like a magician yanking a tablecloth out from beneath a dinner setting.

"Oh God." Arousal throbbed deeply between Pete's legs. He scrambled to push his boxers down too, freeing his erection. It bobbed up, ruddy with blood even though Pete would swear all his blood was in his face right now.

Evan made no secret of looking at him, eyes raking up and down from his face to his cock to his spread thighs and back up again. Pete could only imagine the picture he presented: splayed out on the sofa, panting, and bleary with arousal.

Evan didn't give him a chance to feel self-conscious, however. He kissed down his body, starting at his neck and ending at his waist. Once there, he swirled his tongue around his bellybutton, nibbled on his hip bones, and stroked the insides of his legs. In short, he did everything but what Pete wanted him to do.

Just when Pete thought he couldn't take the teasing anymore, Evan pushed himself up into a kneeling position, one leg on either side of Pete's, and dug into his front pocket. He extracted a condom and held it up. The wrapper gleamed dimly in the light.

Pete got infinitesimally harder at the sight of it alone. God, it felt like he'd been waiting to get fucked by Evan for *years*. He suspected this was going to redefine what sex meant to him.

The need to give back reared its head again, but the second Pete reached for Evan's sweatpants, he pushed his hands away. Evan tore the condom wrapper open, shifted down Pete's body, and rolled the condom onto him like a pro. Which, point in fact, he was. He gave Pete a leisurely, loose-fisted stroke. Pete's brain short-circuited. His head fell back against the sofa even as his hips arced off it, chasing the touch.

"Please don't think I'm complaining," Pete panted, "but I really wasn't expecting to be the one wearing the condom tonight."

"Shh," Evan said. "Let me take care of you."

Pete started to ask what Evan's plan was, but the words never even made it out of his throat. Evan scooted down his body, locked eyes with him, and gripped the base of his cock. Without looking away, he swirled his tongue once around the head before taking Pete into his mouth.

That alone was exquisite, but when Evan sank down until his nose was buried in Pete's pubic hair, Pete's whole body convulsed. He gripped Evan's shoulders for dear life. Evan's mouth felt heavenly: burning hot with just the right amount of suction. It wasn't quite what Pete wanted, though. Evan should get off too.

"Wait," he attempted. "If we change positions, I'll—"

Evan swallowed around him in answer. Pete's eyes shuttered closed against his will, and his grip on Evan's shoulders tightened. Evan was apparently the king of deep-throating, because he took all of Pete in like it was nothing. He sunk down to the root and pulled back again without hesitation. Pete stared at the mesmerizing sight, slack mouthed and vibrating with need.

Evan popped off long enough to say, "Relax. This is just to take the edge off. I have plans for our first time, and if you're bursting to get off, I might not be able to do it the way I want to." He licked a long stripe up Pete's cock. "And I want to do it thoroughly."

Pete swore his dick got even harder just listening to him. He closed his eyes and leaned back, relaxing into the sofa. Evan sunk down on him again, all swirling tongue and perfect friction.

"Christ," Pete murmured, more to himself than to Evan. "You're so good at this." He forced his eyes open, needing to see what was happening to believe it. Evan's lips were already dark pink and shiny with saliva. He wrapped them around the head of his dick and suckled at it in a way that made Pete's thoughts turn to gibberish.

Pete slipped a shaking hand into Evan's hair, not pressing, just feeling the soft, fine strands. It was like the touch opened up another circuit of connection between them, and suddenly everything felt more intense. Evan held the base of his cock steady as he took him in again and again. There wasn't even a hint of teeth, just delicious, mind-numbing pleasure.

Pete felt a familiar twinge low in his belly as Evan's free hand dipped down to fondle his balls. The combination of sensations was already becoming too much.

"Evan," he whispered, "I'm close." He didn't usually come so fast. It was a little embarrassing, but he guessed when it came to receiving oral, stamina didn't matter. Instead of making him back off, that seemed to spur Evan on. He redoubled his efforts, taking Pete's cock deeply into his mouth and sucking until his cheeks hollowed. When Evan rolled the heel of his hand against Pete's balls, Pete came undone.

He tightened his fingers in Evan's hair and tried to shout a warning, but then he was coming. His eyes slammed shut and his whole body went rigid as sharp pleasure lanced through him. Evan kept sucking, milking his orgasm. Just when he reached the brink of overstimulation, Evan pulled off. Pete deflated into the sofa and spent a minute breathing heavily.

When he could form a coherent thought again, he scrubbed a hand over his face. "Christ, Evan. That was . . . *wow*."

Evan looked so pleased with himself, Pete couldn't help but quip, "Joke's on you. Now I'm going to sleep for a week."

"Oh no you don't." Evan climbed to his feet and reached down for Pete. "I have an entire catalog of sexual acts I want to do with you. We're going to get through at least some of them tonight."

The idea made Pete's mouth water. "I'd like that." He wobbled on unsteady feet and grabbed Evan for support. He happened to glance down, and his eyes snapped to Evan's groin. The sweatpants did nothing to hide his erection, tenting the soft material in the front. Evan had to be hard to the point of pain.

Pete grinned. "Want some help with that?"

Evan palmed himself and shuddered. Even though Pete had just come, his cock twitched in response. "I'm all right for now. Sometimes riding the edge for a while makes it better in the long run."

"We'll find out soon enough." Pete ran his tongue over his bottom lip.

Evan smirked. "C'mon. We need to relocate before the real fun can begin."

"Why?"

"Because I live with—"

Something brushed against Pete's foot. He yelped and jumped away, heart pounding.

"—two furry assholes." Evan gestured at the foot of the couch. "That's Scout."

Pete almost clapped a hand over his mouth. A striped tabby with two tails and a lumpy, misshapen body had appeared out of the shadows and was staring expectantly at him with big, green eyes. Pete was just debating making a run for it when a lump split off and took the form of a second, almost identical cat.

"And that's Sentry," Evan concluded. "They're twin sisters."

"Oh thank God," Pete said, wiping a hand across his mouth. "I thought you lived near a nuclear power plant or something."

"Actually, your theory could be right. They're both little monsters, which is why we need to relocate. They have issues with personal boundaries."

"So, if we'd kept having sex out here . . . ?"

". . . One of us would have gotten pounced on. Or worse, scratched somewhere unfortunate."

"The perils of cat ownership." Pete started to pull his jeans up, then he remembered the now-used condom. "Um. Where should I—"

Without a word, Evan pulled the condom carefully off of him. He disappeared through a doorway on the left that Pete hadn't noticed in his pre-orgasm haze. He returned a moment later. "Kitchen's that way, by the way."

"You threw that in your *kitchen* trash?"

"I'm a porn star. Believe me when I say my garbage collectors have seen worse."

Pete grinned. "Fair enough. So, your room?"

"My room."

Evan took his hand and led him through the living room and down a short hallway. He opened a single door at the end of it and flipped a light switch, illuminating a room with large windows and pale-green walls.

Whatever Pete had expected from Evan's room, this wasn't it. Comic book paraphernalia of all shapes and sizes dotted the shelves, the way books did in Pete's room. From the stacks of DVDs to the Catwoman posters on the wall, it was a marked difference from the style of the rest of the apartment.

He glanced at Evan and raised an eyebrow.

"Yeah, I know. It's like an eighteen-year-old's dorm room. I made an agreement with my mom. The rest of the place can pretend an adult lives here, but my room is mine."

"I like it." Pete looked around. "It suits you. I thought the living room was nice, but it wasn't as personal."

"There's a metaphor in there somewhere," Evan joked. "Something about what we display on the outside versus how we are on the inside. Fill in the blanks as you please."

Just then, Scout and Sentry appeared at the threshold, mewling. Evan firmly shut the door on them. Two sets of paws appeared under the door, but after a minute, they disappeared.

When he seemed satisfied, Evan walked over to the bed, which Pete was relieved to see was devoid of Spider-Man sheets, and sat down. He didn't motion for Pete to join him. Instead, he waved at his walls, as if to indicate that Pete should feel free to look around.

Pete relished the opportunity to take a peek at Evan's sanctum sanctorum. He started with the Catwoman posters, pointing to one featuring Halle Berry. "Big fan?"

"You could say that." He cocked his head to the side. "Do you know what Catwoman's real name is?"

"Uh." Pete thought about it. "No."

"Selina Kyle."

"You named yourself after her?"

"Yup. She was always my favorite."

"That explains so much," Pete murmured. Evan gave him a quizzical look, so he added, "I've thought since the moment I met you that you have feline mannerisms. Between your two pets and this, it makes sense. Why do you like her so much?"

"I'm a sucker for a well-written villain."

"I thought she was a good guy."

"She might have graduated to antihero in more recent portrayals, but classically speaking, she's always been bad."

Pete snorted and moved on. Evan didn't have a desk by his window like Pete did. Instead, he had a telescope that Pete recognized from the photos he'd texted to him. There was a black stool near it, upon which lay a leather-bound journal.

Pete pointed at it. "For recording alien sightings?"

"Of course not. I do what any sensible American would do and post my sightings on the internet."

"Can you even see anything out here?"

"We're far enough away from the city center that the light pollution isn't so bad. If it's really clear out, like it is tonight, I can see planets and the bigger stars." Evan got up and walked over to him. "Want to see?"

Just having Evan near him again made him see stars, but he nodded anyway.

"Don't touch it," Evan instructed, inching closer. "It's already pointing where I want it. Look through here. See if you can pick out the constellation."

Evan moved behind Pete, ostensibly to guide him. Evan wasn't touching him, but Pete swore he could feel him in the scant inches between them. Breathless, he peered through the eyepiece on the telescope. At first, the stretch of sky it was pointed at just looked like the regular swath of faint stars he was accustomed to, but after a moment, he was able to pick out a pattern. It was one he recognized.

"Your tattoo." Pete half turned and brushed a finger over Evan's forearm.

"Good eye," Evan said. "That was the first constellation I ever picked out when I got into astronomy."

"Which one is it?"

"It's Aquarius, the water bearer."

"I'm an Aquarius."

Evan's voice was suddenly deep. "I know. You told me your birthday's the sixth, right?"

Pete nodded. "Yeah. Funny coincidence."

Evan slanted his face toward him, and when he spoke next, his breath brushed Pete's cheek. "As it just so happens, I don't believe in coincidences."

Pete swallowed hard. "What's your other tattoo?"

"Perseus. I don't think we can see that one. It's not as bright."

"That's okay." Pete abandoned the telescope and slid his arms over Evan's shoulders. "I gotta hand it to you. Bringing a boy up to your room and showing him the stars? That's a good move."

"You saw through my clever seduction technique," Evan teased. "Guess that means we can't have sex now."

Pete huffed. "Mood killer."

"I think I can revive it." He licked a long line up Pete's neck that made his whole body tingle.

Pete made a small noise and pressed closer. Evan feathered kisses along his jawline. Evan's voice was soft and acutely vulnerable as he said, "I was so worried you weren't going to show up. That you'd change your mind. Every minute was agony."

"I couldn't get to you fast enough." Pete brushed their lips together. "This is your last chance, you know."

"For what?"

Pete ghosted his fingers down the side of Evan's face, lingering over the sharp cut of the cheekbone. "Last chance to decide you don't want this after all."

Evan breathed out a laugh. "I can't even say how badly I want this." And this time, when he kissed Pete, it was slow, like magma rolling down a hill.

CHAPTER  12

I t didn't stay slow.

The second Evan's lips touched his, all the urgency Pete had felt before came rushing back. His world narrowed to two things: how good it felt to touch Evan, and his burning, all-encompassing desire to get as close to him as possible. He didn't just want Evan. He *needed* him.

As Evan kissed him—deeply, desperately, purposefully—the outside world melted away. He knew eventually the sun would rise, time would march on, and he'd have to do things like go to work and class and be an adult, but none of that mattered right now. What mattered was he was in a room with a bed, with a man he wanted down to his marrow. As far as Pete was concerned, time had taken the night off.

Pete, Evan mouthed against his skin. There was no breath behind it, no actual words. He was letting him feel the shape of his own name on Evan's lips. He had both hands on Pete's waist and was holding him like Pete was the only thing tethering Evan to the earth. Pete leaned into the firm, possessive touch, urging him on.

But Evan clearly wasn't satisfied with just touching for long. He reached for the remainder of Pete's clothing. Pete had only partially refastened his jeans, and Evan quickly undid them and pushed them down. Pete was able to wriggle out of them with minimal effort. That left him with his shirt and sweater, both of which Evan was already inching up his abdomen.

"Oh no you don't," Pete murmured. "I'm always the first one to get naked. It's your turn." He fumbled with Evan's sweatpants.

Far from protesting, Evan watched Pete drag the soft fabric down over tight underwear that outlined his cock beautifully. Pete let the sweatpants drop, pooling at Evan's feet. Evan dutifully stepped out of them. His attention vacillated between Pete's face and his hands as if he couldn't decide which he was more enraptured by.

Pete thumbed the elastic waistband of his underwear. "Want these off?"

Evan whimpered in lieu of an answer.

Pete slid them down an inch at a time. "You shouldn't have gotten me off first. Now I'm going to tease you."

"Please don't," Evan begged. "I can't wait any longer."

"We'll see about that." As soon as Pete pushed the underwear down enough to free Evan's dick, he lost his resolve.

Evan's cock was precisely as he'd imagined it from all the times he'd felt it against him: not overly long, but thick and dark with blood. It rose straight out from carefully maintained pubic hair. The shape of it was what got him, though. It was perfect, like Evan should be used as the model upon which dicks were based. No wonder he'd become a porn star. Words kept popping into Pete's head: epitome, proverbial, quintessential. They bobbed around in the rising tide of lust that was sweeping through him.

Pete wrapped his hand around Evan's cock automatically, eager to feel its velvety heat. Evan pressed his lips together, visibly restraining himself.

"Don't do that," Pete said as he stroked him once, slowly, from base to tip. "Don't hold anything back."

"I won't," Evan panted. "I swear. Just don't stop."

Pete watched his foreskin slide over the head, and his mouth watered. "Fuck, you have the most beautiful cock I've ever seen."

Evan shivered and seemed to gather himself. "Considering our profession, that is a serious compliment." He nosed Pete's chin. "Bed?"

"Yes, please."

Evan led him to it by the hand and pushed him down onto the blue duvet. Then he sat astride Pete's hips and peeled his shirt off. Pete was momentarily speechless. Seeing Evan naked while posing for a photographer was very different from seeing him naked and flushed on top of him, breathing hard and looking at him with such want it seared his skin.

"Holy shit."

Pete hadn't intended to say that aloud.

Evan laughed. "My sentiments exactly." He yanked Pete's sweater and shirt over his head and tossed them carelessly behind him. He ran both hands down Pete's chest to his stomach. The touch was maddeningly light, the pads of Evan's fingers dancing down the outline of Pete's ribs. Pete tensed beneath it, unintentionally making the subtle outline of his abs pop out beneath his skin. Evan leaned down and kissed each and every one of them in turn.

At this point, Pete was so hard he couldn't see straight. He shifted his hips under Evan until their erections met. They moaned in unison.

"Eager?" Evan teased. "I got you off before so I could take my time with you. But it seems you're going to be gagging for it no matter what I do."

Pete bucked his hips again, desperate for whatever friction he could get. "Please, Evan, do something, anything. I can't take it."

Evan let out a taut breath. "On your stomach."

Pete scrambled to comply, flipping over. As soon as his back was turned, Evan's weight disappeared from the bed. Pete craned his neck to look behind him. Evan riffled in the top drawer of his nightstand for a second before extracting lube and condoms, which he tossed unceremoniously onto the bedspread. Pete tried not to stare. *Three* condoms? He swallowed thickly just as Evan's weight returned. Instead of straddling his hips again, Evan kneeled between his knees. There was the sound of a cap opening, a squirting noise, and then a brush of fingers at the small of his back. A warning.

"Ready?"

Anticipation curled in Pete's gut. "Yeah."

Evan breeched him slowly, too slowly: just one finger that was slippery with lube. Pete could take more than that. He said as much, but Evan's measured pace didn't change. Pete would have to be patient.

His erection was trapped between his stomach and the mattress. The urge to thrust against the sheets for some kind of relief was overwhelming. As if sensing his frustration, Evan shifted the finger inside of him, and pleasure bloomed in Pete's core. He swore under his breath, which unfortunately prompted Evan to stop his slow slide into him. "All right?"

"Yeah, sorry," he said automatically.

Evan laughed. "Don't be. I'm just making sure I'm not hurting you."

Something about his tone struck Pete as odd. "Is something wrong?" He twisted around again to look at him and was surprised to find Evan smiling from ear to ear.

"Not at all."

Pete gave him a look.

"It's nothing, I swear. I'm just ... really happy. Like, sunshine-and-rainbows happy. I love everything about this."

"I'm glad you're happy, but I promise I've put on much better shows than this."

"No, that's exactly why this is perfect. It's real, not the fake rock star sex that takes six hours and a team of editors to make." He kissed the nape of Pete's neck. "This is exactly how I wanted this. How I wanted you."

Pete smiled. "Then I suggest you get on with it." He pushed back against Evan's fingers. "I'm not delicate. If you don't hurry up, we'll never get there."

Evan doubled his pace, stretching him carefully. "How does that feel?"

Pete squirmed. It burned a little, but it was such a relief to have Evan in him, any part of him, he didn't care. "Good. Keep going."

Evan added a second finger, and Pete swore again. Between coming earlier and Evan's slow pace, he hadn't expected this to do that much for him, but it was. His erection hadn't flagged at all, even without direct stimulation.

"Still good?"

"Yeah. Maybe move a little to the— *Oh.*" Evan brushed his prostate, and Pete felt it thrum throughout his whole body. "Oh. Fuck. Do that again."

Lips kissed the center of his back, right between his shoulder blades. "Tell me what to do. Anything you want."

"More. Just give me *more.*"

Evan obeyed, working him open with increasing fervor. Pete tried not to be too demanding, but by the time Evan added a third finger, he was a panting mess. He wasn't even certain he was forming real words, outside of *yes* and *now* and *Evan*.

He must've communicated his desire well enough, because after a particularly guttural version of Evan's name, Evan murmured, "Damn," and removed his fingers.

Pete heard the distinct sound of a condom wrapper, but he didn't look over his shoulder. He closed his eyes and let the mystery of what Evan was doing send tingles up his spine. There was some rummaging and a squelching sound—lube? Lube. Pete could hear Evan slicking himself up, and boy, did that ever make his skin prickle.

Evan smoothed a hand down his back, wordlessly telling him what he was about to do. Even with the notice, he jumped when the head of Evan's cock nestled against his hole.

Evan paused. "Okay?"

"More than okay." Pete pressed back, and Evan's cock breached him just barely. Not enough. Not even close to enough.

"Oh fuck," Evan mumbled. He thrust forward, seemingly instinctively, and sunk in about an inch. "Fuck, Pete, stop wriggling."

"I can't." Pete pushed back again, and Evan had to grab his hips to stop him. "More, Evan. You won't break me, I swear."

He felt the tremor that worked its way through Evan. "Just hold on a little longer."

Pete made a frustrated noise that must have gotten through to Evan, because he thrust in again, deeper this time.

Pete couldn't have stopped the luxurious moan that poured from him if he'd tried. "Yes, fuck, just like that. More."

"You're insatiable." Evan pressed a kiss behind Pete's ear and whispered, "I love it."

Evan fucked into him in what seemed like the smallest of increments, but eventually a deep thrust brought Evan's hip bones into contact with his ass. Evan panted against his skin in hot, damp bursts, Evan's forehead resting on Pete's shoulder. Evan's hips twitched, and Pete felt the movement so deeply inside of him, he couldn't separate it from himself.

"Feel good?" Evan asked breathlessly.

"So good." Pete turned his head to try to kiss him, but the angle was all wrong. He settled for rocking his hips back, dragging another beautiful moan from Evan. As if by instinct, they started moving together. Pete rocking back, Evan thrusting into him, coming together in a way that made Pete's world tilt on its axis. He couldn't remember the last time he'd felt this connected to a sexual partner. And he didn't think he'd ever felt such intense reactions, such greedy need even now that he finally had Evan where he wanted him.

Just as he grew restless for more, Evan sped up the pace, thrusting deeply into him. Pete's cries drowned out even the creaking of the mattress. The angle wasn't quite right to stimulate his prostate every time, but it happened enough, and there was something so satisfying about being skin to skin with Evan. He could almost come from that alone. And it helped that his cock rubbed between his stomach and the soft sheets with every thrust.

"Fuck, Pete, you feel so good," Evan groaned from somewhere above him.

Evan rolled into him and then ground his hips, and Pete moaned wordlessly. Now *that* hit his prostate. Fuck. So many sensations at once, he couldn't see straight.

Evan grabbed his waist and flexed his fingers. "Can you come like this?"

Pete had never come untouched in his life, but if anyone could manage it, he'd put money on Evan. "Maybe."

Evan pulled out of him, and Pete almost sobbed at the loss. But then hands were on him, turning him onto his back. Too fucked out to care, Pete allowed Evan to arrange him how he wanted: shoulders on the bed, legs spread wide, right knee pressed to his chest.

Evan spent a moment just looking at him, eyes sweeping across his face, down his torso, and settling between his legs. Pete knew how he must look: open and pliant and vulnerable. But instead of feeling insecure, he just felt *good*.

Evan held the base of his cock and guided himself back into Pete. Pete's whine of need tapered off when Evan sunk home and then pressed closer, making Pete's toes curl.

Pete's head lolled to the side, but he kept his eyes cracked open just enough to see Evan's exquisite expressions. Evan clenched his eyes shut tight when he thrust in, like he had to brace himself against the intensity of it. It was mesmerizing and beautiful and achingly hot.

Taking a shaky breath, Evan seemed to gather himself. He wrapped a hand around Pete's cock and gave him a stroke that made him jolt.

"Oh God," Pete moaned. "More, just like—" Evan stroked him again just as he switched angles, and this time when he bottomed out, Pete's nerve endings lit up.

"*Evan, oh fuck!*" He grabbed Evan's shoulders and writhed beneath him, trying to chase the feeling. The dual sensations were stimulating him just right. It was almost too much. He was going to fly apart into a thousand pieces any second now.

Evan gripped his hip, holding him steady, and repeated the motion.

Pete whimpered. "Fuck, that's it. Just like that."

The last of Evan's reservation crumbled away. He fucked Pete brutally, his hand moving fluidly over Pete's cock.

Pete howled beneath him, seconds away from unraveling. "Evan— I'm so— I want— I'm—"

"—close," Evan finished. "Me too. Come, Pete. I want you to come all over my hand and your stomach. I'm right there with you."

"Yes," Pete said blearily, not even sure what was coming out of his mouth. "Can you . . . I need . . . closer."

Miraculously, Evan understood. He settled on top of Pete—chest to chest, skin to skin, as close as they could get—and pounded into him. Pete wrapped his arms around him and held on for dear life. Evan's thrusts were quick and deep, barely pulling out before pushing back in, and it was *perfect*. Pete almost couldn't breathe. Out of all the sex he'd had, all the elegant, award-worthy orgasms he'd put on for all and sundry, he'd never felt anything like this before.

It was cliché, but Pete swore his orgasm swept through him like a tidal wave. It seeped into every part of him, white-hot and shocking in its intensity. Evan whimpered blissfully as Pete came all over his hand, as if Pete's pleasure were somehow wired to his own. A moment later, he cried out, thrust hard into Pete, and froze, muscles locked in ecstasy.

A minute passed where neither of them moved. They just breathed together, loud and ragged, in a tangle of limbs. When his pulse stabilized, Pete forced his eyes open.

His sweat was already cooling on his chest, among other fluids. He tried to shift, but with Evan on top of him, he could barely move. He quickly abandoned the idea of going anywhere and smoothed a hand down Evan's back instead. Contentment soaked into him everywhere their skin touched.

It was only after a long, quiet moment that Evan stirred. He made a soft sound and lifted his head, bringing their lips together. It was more of a smear than a proper kiss, exhausted as they both were, but the sweetness of it left Pete weak.

A beat later, Evan pushed himself up into a kneeling position and pulled gently out of him. He removed the condom and, with astonishing accuracy, tossed it into a trash can next to the nightstand. Then he flopped down beside Pete and held out his arms.

Pete stared blankly at him.

"What, you've never cuddled before?" Evan slurred, eyes half-closed.

"Sorry," Pete mumbled. He tucked himself into Evan's embrace. "It's just, the last time I had sex without a room full of people was months ago. Cuddling isn't part of the after-filming procedure."

"If it's any consolation, I think you did great," Evan said, skimming his lips along Pete's nape.

Pete couldn't stop the pleased smile that spread across his face. "Really?"

"Oh yeah."

"Even without a director?"

Evan laughed. "It's funny. 'Regular' people want to be porn stars in bed, but porn stars just want to be people." He kissed his temple. "You were even better than I imagined, and I have imagined sex with you a *lot.*"

Pete snuggled closer. The steady, soothing rise and fall of Evan's breathing threatened to lull him to sleep, but he managed to keep his eyes open.

Evan planted a kiss on his temple. "You tired?"

Pete stifled a yawn. "A bit."

"Feel free to pass out."

"Ah." He drummed his fingers lightly against one of Evan's forearms. "I can stay the night, then?"

Evan gave him a squeeze. "Like I would let you go anywhere right now."

"If you want to stay up and talk for a while, I can do that."

"Nah, I know you're exhausted. But thanks for the effort."

Evan got out of bed long enough to flip off the light switch—affording Pete a phenomenal view of his bare ass as he walked away—and then turned down the sheets. Pete navigated under them, but instead of returning to Evan's embrace, he sidled up to his back and threw an arm over his waist.

Evan snorted. "You want to be the cuddler, instead of the cuddlee?"

"I'm taller," Pete murmured. "It's my birthright."

"Whatever. Night, Pete Griflow."

Pete's cheeks reddened for reasons he didn't entirely understand. "Good night, Evan Darko."

CHAPTER  13

That night, Pete slept the perfect, deep sleep of the truly satiated. When he woke up, there was no moment of disorientation. He blinked against the sunlight pouring through the window and knew exactly where he was: he was with Evan. Even if he hadn't known that, the limbs sandwiched between his and the smell of sweat and soap would have been enough to remind him.

Pete stretched, careful not to move too much. His joints popped, and his muscles burned. He felt pleasantly sore and utterly refreshed.

Evan stirred next to him, roused by Pete's movements, or as if he'd somehow heard his thoughts. One of his eyes cracked open. Pete had seen Evan during the day plenty of times, but never this close and in such ideal light. The morning sunlight hit his face at just the right slant, confirming something Pete had long suspected. His eyes were such a deep brown they were just a few shades lighter than his pupil. They were beautiful.

Evan's mouth twitched up. "Didn't anyone ever tell you it's rude to stare?"

"Sorry." A few weeks ago, Pete probably would have been embarrassed, but now, all he could do was smile. "Good morning."

"Morning." Evan kissed his forehead. "How'd you sleep?"

Pete stretched again, toes spilling over the end of the mattress. "You have to ask? I don't think I moved all night."

"Good point. If you had, I would have felt it." Evan snuggled up to his chest and breathed deeply.

Pete squirmed. "That tickles."

"Good."

They lay there for a moment in sleepy, sunny serenity before Evan shifted, propping himself up on an elbow. "Want some breakfast?"

"Not just yet. I want to stay in bed."

Evan grinned. "Well, if that's what's on your mind—"

Pete pushed him away, laughing. "I didn't mean it like that."

"All right." Evan settled back down. "Talk to me."

"Um . . . how 'bout that local sports team?"

"I hear they won the World Bowl Cup," Evan teased.

"All right, fine. What do you want to talk about?"

"You. Tell me about yourself."

Pete considered him. "What do you want to know?"

"Everything. How'd you get into porn? Where'd you grow up? What's your family like?"

"Easy enough. I was born and raised in the city. Never lived anywhere else. My parents are divorced, so it's just my mom and me. Feel free to make the obvious 'daddy issues' jokes."

"Wouldn't dream of it. It's not your fault he skipped out."

"As for porn, it just sort of happened to me." He shrugged. "I wanted to help my mom with bills, you know? Pay my own way."

Evan gave him a squeeze. "Very responsible."

"I started out modeling—all wholesome, catalog stuff—but then someone told me how much money I could make doing nude work. I resisted, at first, but models are a dime a dozen in LA, and eventually the job well dried up. One day, someone handed me Colette's business card, and the rest is history."

"She recruited you into porn?"

"No, actually. She started me off in phone sex. But I wasn't any good at it, and I wasn't making any money. Eventually, I decided to try out other avenues."

"Why'd you pick porn? You could have done cam work or nude modeling, like you said."

"I dunno, I guess I liked the idea of porn. You know, getting paid to have amazing, impossible sex. Getting to hang out on set with beautiful people. Having hundreds of fans who adore you and want you. It's . . . beguiling."

"I bet you have a lot of fans."

"Uh, no." Pete laughed. "I had a bit of a following when I first started, but it fizzled out. I didn't put much effort into it."

"Well, rest assured, you have a big fan right here."

Pete slid his fingers into Evan's messy hair, playing with it. "What about you? How'd you break into the biz? Colette gave me the impression you're kind of a big deal."

"Not yet, but I could be, given enough time."

"How long have you been doing this?"

He grinned. "Two months."

Pete blinked incredulously. "But that would mean . . ."

"I was still pretty green when I signed up for *Heat Wave*, yeah. I only had a dozen or so gigs under my belt."

Holy shit. He'd known Evan was new—Colette had called him a "rising star" after all—but he hadn't thought he was *that* new. Evan was a natural. He'd walked onto set like he was meant to be there, whereas Pete still stumbled half the time.

Pete worried his bottom lip. "There's something I want to ask, but I don't want to be invasive."

"Pete, we just had sex. It doesn't get more invasive than that."

"True. Is porn your only job? I haven't heard you mention another one or school or anything."

"It is, but I spend most of my time building my brand. Marketing. Networking. Interacting with fans on social media."

"That makes sense. Your Facebook was inundated with posts. Are you working on any other projects besides *Heat Wave*? You must be, since we only film once a week."

Evan looked at him askance. "Are you sure you want to know the answer to that?"

Pete nodded. "I'm not the jealous type, despite my many anxieties. Porn is a job. You have to work, same as me."

"So, just to clarify, now that we've slept together, you're not gonna ask me to quit?"

Pete glared at him. "That would be really hypocritical of me, wouldn't you say? I certainly don't intend to quit."

Evan held up his hands in a gesture of surrender. "I'm just making sure. I've heard horror stories from people who said their significant others expected them to quit once things got serious, as if you'd do that with any other job. But just so you know, I haven't taken on any new gigs since *Heat Wave*. My decision to cross over to gay porn left me in sort of a weird standing in the community. I need to build my reputation back up, and I think Colette's film is going to be a big help."

"Why did you cross over, if you don't mind my asking?"

"Because I'm gay," Evan said matter-of-factly. "I only did straight porn because I thought it would be the best way to get my name out there, but the money in gay porn is so much better, and it's more of a niche market. I decided to focus on cultivating a smaller but more dedicated fan base."

Pete regarded him, impressed. "I gotta admit, when I heard you were a crossover, I assumed you were at least bi. Was it hard having sex with women?"

Evan shrugged. "Straight guys do gay porn all the time. And how many of the women in *Lesbian Orgy VII: the Reckoning* do you think are actual lesbians? You're in porn; you should know this."

"I guess I'm not as involved as you are. I never would have thought you were so new. You sound like you really know the industry."

"Yeah. Remember when you said you found my Facebook?"

Pete nodded.

"Well, if you were to google me now, you'd find a lot more than that. Blogs and interviews and social media accounts. You name it. I could probably write a dissertation on porn at this point."

The passion in Evan's voice was mesmerizing. Just listening to him talk about it was enough to make Pete excited about his job. "If there were ever anyone who was born to be in porn, it's you."

"Funny you should say that." Evan nuzzled his cheek. "I got into porn because of my family."

"Oh?"

"I'm the youngest of five," Evan said innocently. "I had to distinguish myself somehow."

A surprised bark of laughter burst from Pete. He slapped a hand over his mouth, but it was too late.

"What was that?" Evan asked, giggling. Within seconds they were shaking together. Pete fell weakly onto Evan's chest and ended up resting his head there. Evan breathed laughter into his hair and kissed his brow.

When Pete could speak again, he said, "That's one way to stand out. You went straight from school to porn?"

"Not quite. I started out as a stripper and then graduated into porn. It was a natural progression for me."

Pete's brain stopped at *stripper* and supplied him with a vivid image of a shirtless Evan working a pole. Gulp.

Evan nudged him, smirking. "Still with us?"

"Sorry, I'm back now. How'd your parents react to the news?"

"It's not like I told them over Thanksgiving dinner or whatever. My parents weren't thrilled, but they knew I was going to do what I wanted."

"Hmm, all right, then. Next question: what's with all the comic book stuff?" He waved at Evan's room.

"What, you were never into superheroes?"

"Yeah, but mostly when I was younger."

"I guess I didn't grow out of it." He shrugged, which made Pete's body rise and fall with the motion. "I dunno. I always liked the idea of heroes and villains. Especially ones like Catwoman who sort of walk both lines. I said I was a sucker for a good villain, but I like good guys who play bad even more."

"That makes sense. We play with moral boundaries every day we go to work, right?"

"I actually don't think we do," Evan said. "If people wanna judge us and call us immoral for being in porn, that's on them. We wouldn't be able to produce it if it weren't in demand, right? So, if people want to shame porn stars, they should really shame the people who keep us in business."

Pete chewed on his lip. "That's not how it works, though. Not in reality."

"It should be. Then we wouldn't have to hide behind fake names."

He peeked at Evan. "That really bothers you, doesn't it?"

"Yes and no. I kinda like the idea of having a sexy secret identity, but I wish there weren't a need for it. I tried to stick as close to the truth as possible by using my real last name." He kissed the top of Pete's head. "And of course, when I realized I had feelings for you, I told you my name right away. I wanted you to know the real me."

Pete opened his mouth to stammer something sweet back, but then he stopped. "Wait . . . you told me your name right after we filmed the teaser. We'd met twice at that point."

Evan's eyes had gotten comically wide, and for once, Pete could read him like a book. His expression said it all: he hadn't meant to reveal that.

"Evan are you telling me you've had feelings for me since—"

"Oh wow," Evan exclaimed, "I just realized I am *starving*. How about I make you that breakfast I mentioned earlier?"

Pete gave him a sour look. "You're changing the subject."

"Obviously so, yes. Ready for food?"

He sighed. If Evan didn't want to talk about it, there was no forcing him. "There's one last thing I'm curious about."

"Shoot."

"Most people I know are in porn as a means to an end, but the way you talk makes it sound like you're doing it because you . . . I dunno, like it. You get what I mean?"

"Yup," Evan said. "And you're right, I enjoy my work. I mean, having sex for a living is the dream for some people, right?"

"Yeah, but it's more than that, isn't it? You like the industry itself. The business side of it."

He chuckled. "Very astute."

"So, you don't have any plans to quit? Get a 'regular' job, or whatever it is the squares call it?"

"I actually want to be a director someday."

"Like Colette?"

"Yup, she's my idol. The dream is to one day have my own company, just like her. The way I see it, it's one of the most stable industries you can work in: it's been around forever, it's not going anywhere, and as long as there are horny people in the world, there will always be demand."

Pete moved his mouth into a thoughtful moue. "I have to say, I've never thought of it like that before."

"Most people don't, even fellow sex workers like us. That's why I'm hoping I'm gonna go far." He nuzzled his chin. "If we keep talking about porn and horny people, I'm going to want a round two."

"Oh no," Pete deadpanned. "That would be horrible."

Evan kissed him. "Don't tempt me." He stretched and threw his arms around Pete. "What are your plans for today? Maybe we can go get breakfast."

Pete was momentarily distracted by his biceps but managed to answer. "What's today again?"

"Sunday."

"Sunday," Pete repeated. A second passed, and then he shot up in bed. "What time is it?"

Evan looked over Pete's shoulder at the nightstand. "Nine."

"Shit. I have to get home." He jumped to his feet and hunted for his scattered clothes.

Evan sat up, and the sheet they'd slept under slid down his chest to pool at his waist. Pete allowed himself a moment to salivate before hastily pulling on his clothing.

Evan swept his dark hair out of his eyes. "Got a hot date or something?"

"I go to church with my mom every Sunday." Pete's foot got caught in his jeans, and he had to pause to right it. "It starts in about an hour. No doubt, she's already awake and wondering where I am. I didn't tell her I was leaving last night." He looked around for his shoes, only to remember he'd taken them off in the other room.

The moment he opened the bedroom door, Scout and Sentry nosed their way in. Pete quickly retrieved his shoes, the tabbies' green eyes on him the whole time. Their names were starting to make sense to him. As soon as he returned, they made a beeline for the bed and hopped up with Evan, rubbing against him.

Evan petted them with both hands, but his eyes were on Pete. "You're religious?"

"Yeah, but I'm not an asshole about it, I swear." Pete sat down on the floor to pull on his socks, grateful for a reason to not look at him as he asked, "Is that a problem?"

"Not at all. It's more of a curiosity, for reasons I don't think I need to explain."

Pete laughed, climbing to his feet. "You'd be surprised. Sex workers have a prominent place in the Bible."

"I actually suspected you were religious," Evan said slowly, almost reluctantly.

Pete looked at him. "Why's that?"

"Well, you more or less called porn immoral a second ago. That's not an attitude I expected from someone who's been doing this for a while. And you're kinda conservative at times, like when you said you thought we were doing this backward, as if lots of people don't have sex before they date these days. Plus, you said you'd never come out to your family, which makes me think you're ashamed of what you do. Religion and shame sometimes go hand in hand, right?" He laughed, but it sounded forced.

Pete was quiet for a long moment, absorbing what Evan had said. When he spoke, he directed his words at the floor. "This whole me-not-coming-out thing. Is that going to be a point of contention between us?"

He saw Evan's head jerk up out of his peripheral vision. "Huh?"

"This is the fourth time you've brought it up. Seems like it really bothers you that I don't want to tell my mom I fuck guys on camera for a living."

"It bothered me at first, but I'm over it now."

"Are you sure? Because I hate confrontation, and if you don't tell me something's wrong, I'm not going to wrestle it out of you. I want everything to be okay."

"It is okay," Evan said, "for now. I don't know if it will be years from now, but that's a problem for Future Us, wouldn't you say?"

Pete hesitated. That was *so* not a resolution, but he couldn't have this conversation with Evan right now regardless. "Okay, but promise me if you start to be not okay, you'll tell me *immediately*."

"I promise."

Pete walked over and kneeled on the bed. He leaned on his hands, one on either side of Evan's hips, which brought their faces close together. He lingered there, soaking up the simple joy of being near him. "I had such a good time last night. And this morning. I'm gonna miss you."

Evan kissed him. It was soft and sweet, but Pete could feel his disappointment in the shape of his mouth. "You definitely have to go?"

Sentry rubbed against his arm as if entreating him. "Yeah, I'm sorry. My mom is probably worried. I shouldn't have left without leaving a note or texting her or something. Besides—" he kissed him again "—with all the sinning we did, I need church now more than ever."

Evan snorted. "Okay. Want me to show you out?"

"Nah, if you move that sheet, I'm not going to be able to leave."

"All the more reason, then."

Evan started to get up, but Pete pushed him back, laughing. "I'll see you soon."

"Okay." Evan settled against the pillows. "Don't worry about locking the door behind you. I'll get up and do it in a minute."

"All right. Bye."

"Bye."

Pete exited the apartment and made his way to the parking lot where his car was waiting for him. The whole ride back to his house, he couldn't stop smiling. By the time he pulled into the driveway, his cheeks hurt.

The thought of confronting Mom, however, diminished his mirth. He didn't have any texts or missed calls from her, but there was no way she'd missed his absence. He could only pray she hadn't discovered his empty bed until the morning. If she'd been up all night worrying, he would never forgive himself.

You're an asshole, he thought as he opened the front door. *If you come out of this alive, you are taking your mother to dinner.* He looked around, not sure what to expect.

To his surprise, Mom was sitting at the dining room table with a cup of coffee and a slice of burned toast. She'd pinned her hair up with pearl-studded clasps and was wearing a modest powder-blue dress. She had a magazine open in front of her, one of the cooking ones that she always swore would inspire her to become a master chef. There was nothing to suggest there was anything unusual about this Sunday.

"Morning," she said without looking up.

He stared at her for a moment before parroting, "Morning." He tossed his keys and wallet onto the counter on his way into the kitchen. He watched her out of the corner of his eye as he poured himself a cup of coffee, but she didn't look at him.

He sat down at the table next to her. She didn't so much as twitch. Oh God, she must be really pissed off.

"Sorry I left without saying good-bye last night." Better to get this over with. "You were asleep, and I didn't want to wake you."

"No need to apologize." She finally looked up. Instead of seeming angry, she was smiling. There was a knowing sparkle in her brown eyes. "Did you get that good-night kiss after all?"

He looked down at his feet and nodded. "How did you—"

"A mother has her ways. Go get dressed and meet me down here. We need to leave in ten minutes. You know how Pastor Beauchamp hates it when we're late."

And with that, she turned her attention back to her magazine, flipping one of its glossy pages.

Pete scurried away. It was a miracle she'd let him off that easily, and he didn't want to do anything to change her mind. They attended what Pete imagined was a lovely service, but in truth, he didn't hear a word of it. He was hyperaware of his phone in the front pocket of his khakis. He desperately wanted to text Evan, but if he so much as touched his phone during church, Mom would in no way exemplify the Christian ideals of forgiveness.

When they returned home, he raced up to his room under the pretense of changing out of his nice clothes. In truth, he planned to call Evan as soon as he'd finished.

Just as he pulled off his shirt, his phone buzzed. He bent over and snatched it out of his front pocket while his arms were still in the shirt holes, which led to quite a bit of cumbersome flailing.

He forced himself to finish removing his shirt before checking his notifications. Evan had texted him.

How was your morning?

He smiled and tapped out a reply. *Great. Yours?*

Terrible. Couldn't stop thinking about you. Still can't.

Pete's chest filled with a warm, light feeling. It felt like a strong breeze was all it would take to lift him right off the earth. *I've been thinking about you too.* He hesitated and then wrote, *I miss you.*

Evan's reply was instantaneous. *Come over?*

Pete's heart soared only to plummet back to the ground. *I can't. I have to work later to make up for taking yesterday off.*

He waited for a reply. None came.

A week ago, that would have freaked Pete out, but after the night they'd just spent together, he was positive Evan wasn't upset. Maybe disappointed, but not with Pete. With their situation. The same goofy grin from earlier came back to reclaim his face. He should have gotten to know Evan sooner. He'd spent weeks fretting for no reason.

Much as he wanted to linger on the thought of him, he had homework and studying to do before his shift. He spent the next few hours poring over his Programming Logic textbook and taking careful notes. By the time he left for work, he'd more or less forgotten his unanswered text to Evan.

When he walked into the Globe just after two in the afternoon, he was surprised to see the shop was empty. Sunday afternoons were seldom busy, but he could generally count on a handful of people to make the hours pass. He peered out the storefront windows, checking the weather. Thick, dark clouds blotted out a sky the color of sheet metal. Sometimes rain drove people in; sometimes it convinced them to stay in their warm homes. Today, it must have been the latter.

The shop seemed even emptier without Sana behind the counter. She'd normally give him a luminous greeting before ordering him to do something. Even that would have been welcome, because then he'd have something to *do*. Instead, Joshua perched in her customary place. He spotted Pete and did a horrible imitation of Sana in a high-pitched voice. "Why, *hello*, Pete. It's just us today."

"Once more unto the breach," Pete muttered to himself. He retrieved his apron from the back room, put it on, and busied himself washing mugs in the hopes that Joshua would take the hint and leave him alone.

He had no such luck.

Within seconds, something knocked his elbow. "Hey, flamer. Don't ignore me."

At least he was back to his usual voice. Though Pete was going to enjoy relaying his impression to Sana later. She was going to have *kittens*.

"For the last time," Pete stated evenly, "don't call me that."

"*Ooh*, that was downright assertive. Where'd this sudden burst of confidence come from? Your hot boyfriend?"

Pete started to say something acerbic but stopped short. Was Evan his boyfriend? His better judgment told him that one date and a steamy night together did not a boyfriend make. But maybe they were heading in that direction? An excited laugh bubbled up in his throat. He had to fight to keep it down.

A second later, he realized Joshua was staring at him.

"Um, he's not my boyfriend," he said in a monotone.

"Really? Then why do you have that dopey look on your face?"

"I do not. This is none of your business."

Joshua snickered. "Methinks the lady doth protest too much."

"That's not how the quote goes," he snapped, abandoning the mug he was washing.

"Right, because you're an expert in Charles Dickens."

"That was Shakespeare!"

Joshua had just opened his mouth, ostensibly to deliver a hot retort, when the bell above the front door rang.

Both of their heads swiveled in the direction of the sound.

Pete gasped, heart leaping into his throat.

Evan strolled through the door, looking like sex on legs in red jeans and a long-sleeved black shirt. He'd pushed the sleeves up to his elbows, and his tattoos peeked out beneath the cuffs.

Evan's eyes swept over the mostly empty room before landing on Pete. He flashed his trademark impish smile. "Surprise."

Pete's breathing hitched. Well, now he knew why Evan hadn't responded to his text.

"Hi," he said, for lack of anything more articulate.

"Speak of the devil." Joshua clapped his hands together. "We were just talking about you."

"All terrible things, I hope," Evan said, though his eyes never left Pete's face. "Happy to see me?"

Pete stared back wordlessly. He didn't have the necessary vocabulary to describe how happy he was. God, just being near him again was enough to excite him. He cleared his throat and willed himself to keep it together. "Of course."

Joshua looked between them, falling curiously silent. Pete finally tore his gaze away from Evan long enough to quirk a brow at him. If Joshua missed an opportunity to make a snide remark, it was cause for alarm.

A frown was weighing down the corners of Joshua's lips, but he remained silent.

"Something wrong?" Pete asked.

"No," Joshua answered slowly. "Your boyfriend just looks different in the light, I guess. At the club it was too dark for me to really see him."

Pete knew better than to ask what that was supposed to mean—it was probably something rude—so he walked around the counter and approached Evan. "Thanks for stopping by. I'm thrilled to see you."

"Oh, it's my pleasure, believe me." He looked around. "Is this place usually so quiet?"

"No, I think it's the threat of imminent rain that's keeping people away."

"I saw the rainbow flag out front. Is this place cool?" His tone was suspiciously casual.

"Yeah, we're LGBT-friendly, and just about every other kind of friendly too."

"Is that so?" Before Pete could react, Evan leaned up and kissed him. Pete turned violently red and looked at Joshua out of the corner of his eye. He was watching them, but instead of leering like Pete expected, his brow was furrowed. It was like he was trying to do long division in his head.

Now Pete was really concerned, almost too concerned to enjoy the kiss. Almost.

Evan pulled away and brushed a thumb over his cheek. "Want to give me a tour?"

"It'll have to wait for my break. There's a lot that needs to be done, and I just got here."

"Go ahead," Joshua said. "It's dead anyway."

Had Pete been a more expressive person, his mouth would have popped open. Joshua *never* let someone else go on break if he could go first. Pete hastened to take him up on the offer before he changed his mind.

"Follow me, sir," he said to Evan with a flourish of his arm. "We begin our tour in the Field of Squishy Armchairs."

He led him toward the main room. Before he could take more than a few steps, Evan sidled up to him, a sly grin plastered on his face. "Did I hear him call me your boyfriend?"

Pete nearly tripped over his own feet. He sputtered, "Uh. I didn't— He doesn't— That is to say—"

Evan covered his mouth to smother his laughter.

Pete huffed. "You're so mean."

"I tease because I care." He laced their fingers together.

Pete scanned the room. There was one customer hunched over a laptop at a corner table—so focused on his laptop, Pete had to wonder if it had winning Lotto numbers on the screen or something—but otherwise the Globe was devoid of life.

"As you can see," Pete intoned, "it's very exciting here. Positively bustling. From the pretentious abstract art on the walls to the chipped mugs, we're a real cultural hub. And don't get me started on the milk station." He gestured to it. "I could wax poetic about the intricacies of the nutmeg shakers."

Evan chuckled. "Fascinating. Lead on, tour guide."

Pete took him behind the counter—which he thought might be illegal, but no one said anything—and headed for the stockroom. That prompted a round of raucous hooting from Joshua that meant he was back to his old self. Pete scowled at him and told him to grow up, but the second the door closed behind them, Evan pinned him against the wall and kissed him breathless. That turned into a furious make-out session that almost convinced Pete he didn't need this job and should just walk out, taking Evan with him to the nearest bed.

Luckily, Evan pulled away before his hormones could completely circumvent his sense.

"We should stop." He put some space between them with obvious reluctance.

"I'd hate to give anyone a free show, or get you in trouble."

"Yeah, good call," Pete said, masking the tiny pang of disappointment he felt. He took Evan's hand and led him out of the room, purposefully not looking at him, lest he start blushing again. Joshua was busy helping a customer when they exited, so they were spared any further comment.

Pete looked around. "There's not much else to see, I'm afraid."

Evan pointed at a hallway near the entrance. "What's down there?"

"The bathrooms and a supply closet. Like I said, there isn't much to see."

Evan shoved his hands into his pockets and peered up at the ceiling, unwittingly emphasizing his long neck. Pete was overcome by a strange impulse to kiss his Adam's apple. He only resisted through sheer force of will.

"Do the bathrooms have to be opened with a key?" Evan asked.

"Yeah, but I have one right here." Pete pulled it out of the pocket of his apron. "You can use it if you need to."

"Why don't you show me how? I think I'd benefit from a personal demonstration, and—" his lips curled up suggestively "—it's a lot more private down there."

This was a bad idea. Pete understood that perfectly well, but Evan's smile went straight between his legs, and thanks to their earlier make-out session, he was more than a little horny.

"We shouldn't," he protested weakly.

Evan closed a hand around his wrist. "Come on."

Pete allowed himself to be led toward the hallway. He chanced a look in Joshua's direction. Blessedly, he was engrossed in making whatever drink the customer had ordered. Judging by the scowl on his face, it was a complicated one. He could never remember more than three ingredients at a time. He'd probably mess up and have to make it again, which would buy them some time.

If Pete were a good person, he would offer to help him.

Pete kept walking.

The blood that should have been powering his brain was trickling downward. They made it to the end of the hallway, which had three doors: the closet Pete had mentioned and two gender-neutral bathrooms. Pete unlocked one with trembling fingers. Evan placed a hand on his, steadying it, and as soon as the lock clicked, he swept them in. He shut the door behind them.

It was pitch-black inside, the only light coming from a thin crack at the base of the door. Pete couldn't see Evan, but he swore he could feel him, like his energy was crackling around Pete. The sound of his own labored breathing and his pulse thundering in his ears drowned out all other sound, so it came as a complete surprise when Evan pounced.

The first touch of lips was like a spark in the darkness. When Evan cupped Pete's face and stepped closer, eradicating the space between them, it grew to a flame. Pete hesitated for all of two seconds before he melted into it, kissing back with everything he had. He threw his arms over Evan's shoulders and pressed against him. He'd been half-hard since the stockroom, and now that they were alone, desire suffused his body.

Evan chuckled against his mouth. He pulled back with a smack of lips. "So eager. Where's the shy man who wouldn't have sex with me in a porn studio's bathroom?"

"Maybe you fucked him out of me last night," Pete said.

Evan made a low, rumbling sound, and Pete was once more reminded of a cat. "I was just planning to get you off, but if you keep talking like that, you'll be in for a repeat performance."

The arousal that surged through Pete was so potent his knees wavered from the force of it. Evan had both hands on his waist. His grip tightened when Pete falter, as if to help support him.

"Promise?" Pete breathed back.

Evan brought their lips together, not kissing, just touching, and mouthed, "You asked for it."

Pete expected to be kissed, but instead Evan flipped the light on. Pete blinked spots out of his eyes. Before he could recover, Evan shoved him against the sink—which made a worrisome creaking noise—and stepped between his spread legs. The possessiveness of the act sent a shiver up his spine.

Evan brought their faces close but didn't kiss him. Instead, he slid his arms around his waist and fumbled with something. Drunk as he was with arousal, it took Pete a moment to realize it was his apron tie. Evan unknotted it and slipped it above his head, tossing it aside. Then, he reached for the hem of his shirt.

Pete was just about to object—much as he loved being skin to skin with Evan, he couldn't very well strip in the bathroom—but Evan didn't pull his shirt off. He just shoved it up enough to get at his pants. At the feel of Evan's fingers on his fly, Pete finally realized what they were doing.

"We should get back out there," he panted. Despite what he'd said to Evan, he was not the guy who had sex in the bathroom at work.

"If that's what you want, sure," Evan said. "But I don't think it is. You're just saying that because you think you should. You want to be in here with me." He rubbed Pete through his jeans. Pete almost wasn't fast enough to stifle the moan that burst out of him. He rocked into the touch, pleasure skittering up his spine. Evan stroked him deftly through the thick material. If he hadn't been hard before, he certainly was now.

"Evan, we can't," Pete squeaked, even as he did nothing to stop him.

"We can. We may have only had sex once, officially, but I know what gets you off. It won't take more than five minutes, I promise."

Pete was so keyed up, he had no doubt. The last of his resistance fizzled out with a pathetic spluttering sound.

"Okay," he relented, "but *please* be quick."

Evan's smile was sinful. "I love it when you say please."

He sank to his knees, and *oh God* did that make Pete dizzy. Evan planted a light kiss on the front of his pants, where his dick was straining against the zipper holding it in. Pete gripped the sink behind him so hard his knuckles must be white. He wanted to beg Evan to hurry up, but his hormones threatened mutiny if he did anything to interrupt what was happening. Evan eyed his groin, licking his lips. Then he met Pete's gaze and mouthed the outline of his cock, hot and damp even through the denim.

Pete was so hard he couldn't see straight. Oh fuck, he'd thought he needed to worry about getting caught, but it seemed the real danger was coming in his pants. Evan had the button open and the zipper down before Pete could process the movements. Evan dipped his tongue through the opening. It had to be uncomfortable, licking Pete's dick through his underwear with metal teeth from the zipper in the way, but it looked hopelessly erotic, and Evan didn't complain. It wasn't even a direct touch, and Pete felt like he was going to burst.

A second later, Evan withdrew his tongue and rose to his feet. Pete whined, but then Evan spun him around. He used his torso to bend Pete over the sink, guiding Pete's hands to grip the edges of the porcelain bowl. Then he found Pete's gaze in the mirror. Pete didn't need him to speak to understand: he wanted Pete to watch what he did next.

Evan's hands ghosted down Pete's sides to where his jeans and underwear were hanging from his hips. He slid them down, taking care to move his boxers in such a way that his erection bobbed up, slapping his stomach. The visual was almost as hot as what they were actually doing. Dating a fellow porn star had some *serious* perks.

Evan stopped showing off and got serious a moment later. He pushed Pete's clothing down to his knees, seeming impatient to have it out of the way. Then he kicked the inside of one of Pete's shoes. It took Pete a moment to understand before he spread his legs as wide as his pants would accommodate.

He heard rather than saw Evan exhale. There was such raw desire in that sound alone, Pete shivered in response. Evan pressed himself against Pete's back, letting him feel his still-clothed erection, before fumbling with his belt buckle. And, oh fuck, just the clink of metal on metal made Pete's cock swell. He let his head loll between his shoulders; he hadn't the strength to support it any longer.

Not being able to easily see behind him added a new layer of sexiness to what they were doing. He had to picture all of Evan's movements in his head. He heard the *click click click* of his zipper being pulled down, followed by a rustle of fabric that had to be him shoving his pants out of the way. It was followed by a second of loaded silence. Pete imagined he was maneuvering his dick out of his underwear, too eager to deal with another article of clothing. By the time it was over, Pete's mouth was watering.

Evan pressed against him again, and his erection, hot and hard, settled between Pete's ass cheeks. He rocked his hips, breathing heavily. There wasn't any sort of lube to guide the way, but Pete loved every second of it: the heaviness of him, the closeness, the harsh friction of skin on skin.

"Jesus Christ," he muttered, flexing his fingers on the edge of the sink.

Evan slid a hand into his hair and grabbed a fistful, pulling his head back. He licked a wet stripe up his throat. "Don't forget, you have to be quiet."

"Oh, fuck you." It was all Pete could do to hold himself upright.

"Please do." Evan's mouth drifted up his neck to the skin behind his ears. He was still thrusting slowly, but his movements were getting more purposeful, more wanting.

Pete gasped, "Condom."

"Way ahead of you."

Evan released him and rummaged with something. Pete chanced a peek over his shoulder. What he saw was very close to what he'd imagined: Evan's jeans and underwear shoved down to the tops of his thighs, his cock jutting straight out of his trimmed hair. He'd just pulled a condom and a packet of lube out of his back pocket.

"You came prepared," Pete said, not sure if it was an accusation or a compliment.

"I was a Boy Scout." He winked, ripped open the wrapper, and slid the condom on. Then he opened the lube and coated the fingers on his left hand. Pete turned back around and braced himself. The first swipe of lubed fingers against his hole made him tense—not with pain, but anticipation—but he managed to relax by the time Evan pressed into him.

Pete's breath caught in his throat. "Fuck, Evan, that feels so good."

Evan shushed him. "If you can't keep it down, we're going to get caught."

Pete whimpered helplessly. Evan added another finger, and his whimper turned into a whine.

Evan laughed, a hot puff of breath against his damp skin.

"What?"

"Nothing. It's just, there was a part of me that thought you'd be quiet in bed. I thought all that moaning you did when we were filming was for the benefit of the camera." He nipped at his earlobe, making him gasp. "I'm *thrilled* to discover I was wrong."

Pete was too frustrated by the slow drag of Evan's fingers to tease him back. "Hurry up. We'll get caught anyway if you take too long."

"You're so demanding." It in no way sounded like a complaint. Evan withdrew his fingers, took himself in hand, and nudged the head of his cock against Pete's entrance. "You want me?"

Pete was gripping the sink so hard, he had to flex his fingers to get the blood flowing again. "You know I do. I always want you."

Evan pressed against him again, and this time, the head of his cock popped just barely into him. "I know, but I like to hear you say it. How badly do you want me?"

Pete made a strangled sound. "So badly."

Evan met Pete's eyes in the mirror. "Then take me." He slid fully into him in one liquid stroke.

It felt so good, Pete swore he saw God. "Evan, *fuck*, do that again."

Evan drew his hips back only to slide home again, rocking them both onto their toes. He didn't hold back, didn't slowly work his way in or give Pete time to adjust. Evan just gripped his hips and pushed him up farther on the sink, slamming home, making Pete's mouth fall open.

Evan pulled back, breathed, and snapped back in, playing with different rhythms and angles. He had a marked talent for finding the right combination to drive Pete wild. After a half dozen thrusts, Evan shifted a little, rocked into him, and sent pleasure crackling along Pete's nerve endings.

Pete knew it wasn't possible, but Evan actually felt bigger than he had the night before. Maybe it was the angle or the force with which he was thrusting into Pete, but Pete wanted to claw at the walls, he was so full of Evan's cock. He didn't realize how loudly he was moaning until Evan bit the back of his neck, startling him into silence.

"Pete," Evan murmured, licking the spot in apology, "you have *got* to be quiet."

"I can't," Pete whined. "You feel so good."

Evan shuddered and fucked deeply into him, hips to ass, chest to back, skin to skin. "Do you want someone to interrupt us?" His hand found its way to Pete's leaking cock.

Pete didn't even register that he'd spoken. The hand stroking him had just become the center of his universe. It was almost too intense. He tried to articulate what he needed, but his tongue slipped around the words, unable to form them.

He managed to focus long enough to find Evan's reflection in the mirror. "Please."

Somehow, Evan understood. He clamped a hand over Pete's mouth. Pete placed one of his on top of it, holding it firmly in place.

Now that Pete's mouth was covered, Evan slammed hard and deep into him. Pete bit down on his palm; it had to hurt, but Evan didn't say a word. His face was tortured as he fucked him, brow coated in sweat, eyes half closed, mouth open.

"Fuck, I'm almost . . . I'm so . . ."

Pete whimpered against his hand to indicate that he understood. He pushed back against the sink as Evan's thrusts grew increasingly forceful. The metal hinges and piping squeaked in protest, but mercifully held. It wouldn't matter how quiet Pete was if they burst a pipe. Even so, he wasn't even certain he was capable of caring right now. It felt like Evan was touching every part of him at once, reaching into his core and stoking a fire that was spreading through his veins.

From the look on Evan's face, he was experiencing something similar. He found Pete's reflection again and held his gaze. His expression was open and defenseless. He kissed a bead of sweat rolling down Pete's cheekbone and whispered brokenly, "I don't know how I'm ever going to get enough of you."

Pete wasn't sure when this had shifted from kinky to intimate, but it plucked something deep within him, and suddenly, he was right on the edge. There was a dizzying, fucked-out moment where Pete thought to himself that this was hands down the best sex he'd ever had, and he was having it shoved up against a sink in a coffee shop bathroom.

Evan was stroking him sloppily. If he managed to get a decent rhythm, Pete would come. Or if he hit his prostate in just the right way. Or, honestly, if a light breeze came along. He couldn't tell Evan this while his hand was covering his mouth, but he didn't need to. Evan would take care of him, make it good for him. He knew it.

Just then, Evan's pace faltered. He pulled out of him only to drive back in, making the sink Pete was gripping shudder on its foundation. He repeated the motion, and Pete was thrown a few inches forward from the force of it. Pleasure sizzled up his spine as he was filled to overflowing. He moved his free hand from the sink to the mirror, bracing himself. It rattled in its frame, but he hardly noticed.

"Pete, I'm gonna come," Evan said through gritted teeth. "Are you . . . ?"

It was too late. Evan cursed and thrust home one last time, as deep as he could go, before he stilled. He bit down hard on the junction between Pete's shoulder and neck, whimpering as he came. The blossom of pain made the pleasure all the more vivid, like a bright, burning star in the night sky.

Watching him pant and whimper through his orgasm did Pete in. A few sloppy pulls on his cock later, and he liquefied. Pete's orgasm ripped through him, overwhelming him. He bit down on the heel of Evan's hand in an attempt to stifle the moan that resonated in his chest. Even with the makeshift gag, he was positive someone had to have heard him. Pleasure that explosive and incendiary couldn't be contained.

Thankfully, his come mostly landed in the sink. If it had gotten on his clothes, he would have been in serious trouble.

Evan recovered faster than he did. He sucked in a breath. "Wow, that was amazing." He kissed the spot he'd bitten. "I hope I didn't hurt you."

Pete made a muffled noise.

"Oh, shit, sorry." He pulled his hand away from Pete's mouth, trails of saliva connecting it to Pete's bruised-red lips.

As they watched the strands snap, he was positive they were both thinking the same thing: *If there were a camera around, that would have been a perfect shot.*

"I'm fine," Pete answered. "Better than fine, actually." He fidgeted. "Though I'd like it if you'd please get out of me now."

Evan obeyed, pulling gently out and throwing the condom into the toilet with a wet *plop.*

"Dude, there's a trash can right there." Pete sighed. He flushed it. "Inconsiderate customers always throwing all sorts of weird shit in there." Despite his words, he could feel a smile stretching his face.

Evan chuckled and let his hand fall to his side. Pete snatched it up a second later. "I didn't break the skin, did I?"

"Nah, I'm fine." He smirked. "These are some battle scars I can be proud of."

"Me too." Pete kissed him.

Evan tucked himself back into his pants. "We should go. If they're not already missing you, they will soon."

"You're right." Pete scrambled to clean himself up and put his apron back on. He glanced at his reflection. His hair was a mess, his lips were dark, and he had a distinct just-fucked flush that nothing but time could get rid of.

He groaned. "Well, this ought to be fun."

Evan sidled up behind him and pulled him into a hug. "Was it worth it?"

Pete's stomach flopped strangely. Not in a bad way, exactly. He just felt sort of . . . light, but also nauseated. He didn't know how to describe it.

"Yeah," he said. "Worth it."

They exited the bathroom with Evan walking a few steps ahead. It wasn't much, but it was all they could really do to suggest they hadn't just left together.

When they rounded the corner to the main room, everything was pretty much as they'd left it: empty and quiet, though now Joshua was arguing with a customer about how much cinnamon constituted a "dash."

Joshua fell silent when they appeared, however. His eyes narrowed as he looked between them. Pete's face instantly burned. He must've heard them, or at least noticed their prolonged absence. He expected Joshua to make some sort of lewd remark, but for once, he didn't. His eyes did linger on Pete's neck, however. Fuck. He undoubtedly had a mark that was purpling by the second. He flipped his shirt collar up and tried to look innocent.

Evan touched his elbow. "I gotta get going."

"Okay." Pete kissed him.

Evan pulled him in for a deeper kiss that lingered on Pete's lips long after it ended. Evan turned like he was going to leave, and Pete's chest twanged strangely.

"Before you go," he blurted out, "I have a question."

Evan stopped a foot away. "Shoot."

"Were you really a Boy Scout?"

"I was. Does that surprise you?"

"No, I've come to expect such things from you."

"Then I'll have to try harder."

Pete took his hand and sighed. "I'll miss you."

Evan opened his mouth only to shut it again. It looked like he was debating with himself. Before Pete could ask if something was wrong, Evan turned back, kissed him, and said, "I'll miss you too." He waved good-bye, and when he did, Pete saw the faint marks from his own teeth still on Evan's palm.

That wasn't an image he was going to forget anytime soon. Something tugged strangely at his insides: that same light, dizzying feeling he'd been experiencing a lot lately. Before he could identify it, there was a voice at his elbow, "You two are not subtle at all."

Pete jumped. "Jesus, Joshua, you startled me."

He ignored Pete's comment. "What's up with you and mega hottie?"

Pete turned atomically red. "Uh, I was just showing him around, and—"

"That's not what I meant. Although, that was *also* not subtle."

Pete blinked. "Then what?"

Joshua sighed in a long-suffering way. "If you don't know, I'm certainly not going to tell you." He flounced away in the direction of the customer he'd abandoned. "Get back to work, lover boy."

Pete dutifully obeyed. He figured he owed Joshua some obeisance after the stunt he'd pulled. If it weren't for his sore muscles and pervading feeling of satisfaction, he wouldn't believe he'd actually done that. Or that Joshua had left him off so easy.

The rest of the day passed uneventfully. Pete drove home just as the sun was setting over the glittering, metallic cityscape. He said hi to his mom, scarfed down some dinner, and spent the next few hours reading before bed. As soon as he lay down, however, his head filled with thoughts of Evan. It made him smile even as he ordered himself to sleep.

He finally dozed off, and his dreams were as full of Evan as his thoughts. In them, he swore he could feel Evan's touch, hear his voice, see the radiance of his smile.

Just before dawn, he woke up, gasping and coated in sweat, and sat straight up in bed. His eyes landed on his window, where the parted curtains granted him a view of a handful of dying stars, the last ones to survive the burgeoning light of the sun.

He'd probably never be able to look at stars again without thinking about Evan: his warmth, his playful eyes, his laughter, and the way he made Pete feel like he could do anything, be anyone, the way he inspired and excited him, and—

"Fuck," he panted. "I'm in love."

CHAPTER

"Are you sure?" Raj leaned closer and squinted at him.

"Yup," Pete answered, "I'm sure."

"Are you *sure* you're sure?"

Pete made an exasperated noise. "Yes. I'm in love. Totally and completely in love with a guy who's not even my boyfriend. And you know how I know? Because that is precisely the sort of awkward mess I would get myself into."

Raj sat back in his desk and whistled. "Fuck, man. I almost can't believe it. The times, they are a'changing."

"Yeah, tell me about it." Pete waited for Professor Mejia to turn his back before he nudged Raj with an elbow. "I bet you regret ditching our Monday class now. You could have heard the juicy news a whole day sooner."

"Not for nothing, buddy, but that party was totally worth it. You should have come. Besides, we couldn't have talked during Whiton's class. I'm pretty sure I'm going to fail her midterm."

"We're all going to fail her midterm," Pete soothed.

"Not you, smarty-pants." Raj shoved him, prompting the professor to look their way. They fell silent and waited, stock-still, until he turned back to the board.

Pete paused long enough to jot down what Professor Mejia was saying about automated algorithms before leaning back toward Raj. "What do you think I should do?"

"Hell if I know, man. I'm still processing the fact that you have a lover."

"Can you *please* not call him that?"

"I'm just teasing you. It's my sacred bro duty. I was beginning to think I'd never get my shot. Not that I thought you were incapable of landing a boyfriend, or anything. It's just, from what you said the last time we spoke, I wasn't sure you and what's-his-face were gonna work out."

"Evan," Pete supplied.

"Right, Evan. Does this mean you're over all your misgivings about him? Because if so, that is some mighty fast turnaround."

Pete fiddled with the pen in his hand. When he spoke, his voice was quiet but certain. "Yeah, I'm over it. Looking back, I don't know how I ever thought he was like my dad. Or Christopher. He's nothing like them, and I was too jaded to see it." He paused, a smile tugging at his lips. "He sure didn't let me be that way for long, though. Every step of the way, he was breaking down my walls. Keeping me on my toes. Surprising me into being honest with myself. He's incredible. I don't know how I resisted for as long as I did."

Raj laughed. "Jesus, you really are in love. Which begs the question: what are you going to do about it?"

"I'm not sure." Pete looked at Raj thoughtfully, his eyes drifting to the silky black hair. Pete had always thought Raj had the most beautiful hair he'd ever seen, and that was still the case, but now Evan was a close second, what with his messy locks that were perfect for grabbing a handful.

Pete shook his head, dispelling the image before he could cause a public incident: "The thing is, I don't know what Evan wants."

"Don't you?" Raj gave him a sidelong look. "I've never even met the guy, and I'm willing to bet he's got it bad for you."

"Don't get me wrong, I'm sure he likes me, but that doesn't automatically mean we're going to have a committed relationship. We haven't even known each other for a full month. I couldn't tell you his favorite color." Although, as soon as the words left his mouth, Pete thought, *I bet it's green.*

Raj shrugged. "So, get to know him better."

"Well, of course. I want to know everything about him."

"Problem solved."

"But I also need to figure out when is the right time to have the 'I love you' conversation."

"Tell him now."

Pete gave him a sour look. "It's not that simple."

"Why not? You're working yourself into a froth when you should relax and let things happen. Love isn't complicated unless you make it that way."

Pete worried his bottom lip. "What if . . . what if he doesn't feel the same way, though?"

"Then he'll tell you. And it'll suck, and you'll probably be totally heartbroken."

"Thanks, Raj," Pete grumbled.

"But," Raj continued, "he'll appreciate that you were honest with him, and I seriously doubt he'll stop seeing you over it. If he doesn't feel the same way, he will soon. I know it's scary, but if you want your happily ever after, you gotta take some risks."

Pete eyed Raj suspiciously. "When did you get all wise?"

"I've always been wise, my Padawan." He stretched back in his seat and folded his arms behind his head. "But for real, I've been in and out of more relationships than you'll probably have in your life, and I've made a lot of mistakes. But time and time again one thing has held true: being honest is never a mistake."

"Huh." Pete fell silent.

Raj turned his attention to his laptop, ostensibly catching up on all the notes Professor Mejia had written. Pete could tell he was giving him a chance to gather his thoughts. The trouble was, his thoughts might as well have been a herd of cats for how easy they were to manage.

Finally, he said, "You're right."

Raj glanced at him, fingers poised over his keyboard. "I am?"

"Of course, though it's one of those easier-said-than-done situations. I swear, sometimes being me is so frustrating. I know I should tell him, but when I think about actually doing it, my stomach flips."

"You can do this. I know you can."

Pete racked his brain. "Maybe I should do something special? Like, take him out to dinner and then tell him?"

"That's a great idea," Raj said mildly. "As long as you're not just planning that so you can stall."

Pete grimaced. "Saw right through that, huh?"

"Yup. Though I do think it's a good idea to do something special. Sure beats blurting it out after you've just accidentally invited your ex to her little sister's bat mitzvah. Remind me to tell you that story some time. Anyway, are you doing anything for your birthday next weekend?"

"Damn, I'd nearly forgotten. I guess I should. Got any suggestions?"

"Throw a party. Invite everyone you know, namely me and Evan. That way I'll get to meet him."

Pete tapped his chin. "You know what? That actually sounds like a plan."

Raj's mouth dropped open. "Really? So, it's true. Love can change a man!"

Pete waited for the next time Professor Mejia wasn't looking and then smacked Raj on the shoulder. "Keep in mind, everyone I know consists of like five people, including my mom. But yeah, I think a party is the way to go. It'll give me a deadline. I'll have to tell him before then."

"Why?"

Pete laughed. "If he's going to meet all of you, I need to do something to lock him down first. And I can't tell him *at* the party. Just imagine me trying to proclaim my love in front of an audience."

"Oof, good point. Though I still think you'd manage. Love has a tendency to worm its way out of your heart and into your mouth no matter how hard you try to contain it."

"That was almost poetic."

"'Almost'? You insult me. So, if this hypothetical party did take place, when and where would it be?"

"Um." Pete thought about it. "My birthday is Monday, so I guess the Saturday after that? At my place?"

"Will your mom be cool with that?"

"Oh, she'll be thrilled. Any time she sees me interacting with other humans, it's like Christmas."

"Then it's settled." Raj reached across the aisle and clapped him on the back. "Text me later this week to let me know it's still on, and I'll be there. I'll bring booze and my scintillating personality.

And possibly a camera so I can take pictures as proof that our very own Pete Griflow actually threw a party."

"Very funny."

They spent the rest of the lecture trading banter under their breath and, occasionally, paying attention. By the time it let out, Pete felt much more confident about the whole situation. He studied in the library until just before two in the afternoon and then worked a shift at the Globe. While there, he invited Sana to his party, which served a double benefit: once he'd invited people, he couldn't back out.

No sooner had the invitation left his mouth, than she declared nothing in the world could keep her away. She launched into an in-depth discussion of drinking games and themes that Pete was thankfully not required to participate in. Her enthusiasm was contagious, however, and Pete allowed her to talk him into doing a nineties theme in honor of the decade of his birth.

"Now that you can drink legally, you'll have to rely on your old memories instead of forming new ones," she informed him.

"Looking forward to it," he replied. She rattled off a list of things she intended to bring: snap bracelets, gel pens, Pokémon cards, and more. If she remembered even half of them, it would be a better party than Pete could have hoped to throw on his own. By the end of his shift, he was in such a good mood, he might have invited Joshua had he been around.

When he got home, he found his mom sitting at the dining room table with a copy of *Gone with the Wind*. Like mother, like son.

"Hey, kiddo," she said when he walked through the door. She bookmarked her place and swiveled in her seat to face him. "You look chipper. What's up?"

"I have a favor to ask." He approached and gave her a kiss on the cheek. "Can I have a party next Saturday for my birthday?"

"Here?"

"Yeah."

She gave him a knowing look. "Why not at a restaurant? Or more appropriately, a bar?"

He shuffled his feet. "There's someone I want you to meet."

She pressed her lips together; the upturned corners told him it was with mirth, not displeasure. "Of course you can. Should I expect a raging house party? Maybe order a keg? Have paramedics on standby?"

"It'll just be me and a few others, I promise." He gave her a quick hug. "I'll clean the whole house beforehand and everything. And I'll owe you one."

"Not at all." She patted his cheek. "I'm excited to meet your friend. I like him already."

"I like him too." He excused himself up to his room. Once there, he pulled out his phone, took a deep breath, and sent the most important invitation of them all:

Want to come to a birthday party at my place?

He scrolled through his recent texts with Evan as he waited for a response. It mostly consisted of silly photos and random movie quotes (Evan's doing), but there were other messages interspersed that made Pete's heart flutter.

I miss you.
When can I see you again?
I was just thinking about you.
I miss you.
Send me a picture. I want to see your face.
I miss you so much.

His phone buzzed, prompting him to scroll back down to the most recent messages.

Absolutely. What should I bring? Myself, tied up with a bow?

Pete spent a solid minute lingering over that mental image before he replied. *I guess whatever movies you still have on VHS. It's 90s themed.*

He got ready for bed while he waited for Evan to text him back. He didn't have to wait long.

A themed party? You continue to surprise me.

Pete smiled at his phone. *Wasn't my idea, but you'll get to meet the mastermind there.*

One of your friends, I take it? Please don't say Joshua.
God no.
Good. Will your other friends be there?

Yup. All both of them. And my mom.

Sounds great. I'll be sure to wear something that'll leave an impression. Like bondage gear.

Pete laughed and set his phone on the nightstand. He climbed into bed and fell asleep so quickly he barely remembered lying down.

He woke up early the next morning to an email saying his class had been canceled. He spent another hour in bed, drifting in and out of consciousness. In his more lucid moments, he replayed his last encounter with Evan in his head, which prompted a morning masturbation session that left him with a burning need to see the subject of his fantasy. He had work that afternoon, but maybe they could hang out beforehand.

Grabbing his phone, he texted Evan. *Morning. When's the next time you're free? I want to see you.*

Evan had said his days were mostly filled with marketing and building his brand. Surely that meant he'd be free for a coffee date. Maybe even brunch or something else hideously domestic.

Pete trundled downstairs and made himself a cup of coffee so black it seemed to absorb the morning sunlight, which draped itself lazily over the counters. He listened to the house around him but heard nothing but the distant drone of traffic. Obviously his mom had been up at some point—who else could have made the coffee?—but she'd probably gone back to sleep.

He took his mug and tiptoed back upstairs as quietly as he could, nudging his door open with an elbow. He stood in front of the bookshelf by his desk. On the off chance that Evan couldn't hang out, he'd spend his morning reading. He scanned the worn titles on his shelves before selecting an old favorite: *The Castle of Otranto*. What it lacked in strong female characters it made up for in unintentional hilarity. Any book that started out with someone being crushed by a giant helmet was a winner in Pete's eyes.

He was just about to hop back into bed when he saw the notification light on his phone blink. He snatched it up. Evan had texted him back. Would that ever stop thrilling him? Undoubtedly not.

You're in luck. It seems we're going to see each other soon.

Pete frowned at his phone. Before he could put much thought into the message, another text appeared, this time from Colette. He almost smacked himself. Of course. She probably wanted to film this weekend. He'd almost forgotten about *Heat Wave* in the wake of his burgeoning relationship with Evan. They still had at least one more scene to film.

He tapped on Colette's message and scanned it. *Are you free today?*

That was a bit odd. Surely she wouldn't want to film during the week. They'd been filming predominantly on Fridays and Saturdays. Pete had expected that pattern to continue.

Depends. Why?

A rare location opportunity presented itself. Sorry for the short notice, but it's too good to pass up. Can you be ready in an hour? Say yes.

It was an order, not a question. Hmm. The text didn't say where the location was, but it must have been a big deal. Colette had made it clear from the start that this project was her baby, and thus far she hadn't rushed a single aspect of it. For her to do so now suggested they'd struck milieu gold.

Pete's immediate response was to say yes, anything to see Evan again, but he had work that afternoon. He couldn't very well ask for another day off so soon. Even Sana wouldn't be cool with that.

I have work at two. Will we be finished by then?

It took less than a minute for Colette to reply. *I can't make any promises, but with the way you and Darko have been knocking this out of the park, it's likely. But keep in mind, it's the final scene. We're going to keep filming until we get it right.*

Pete glanced at the clock next to his bed and debated with himself. It was nine now, which meant he had roughly four hours to get there and film the scene, and then another hour to get home, shower, and head to the Globe. If everything went smoothly, that was plenty of time. If it didn't, he would be late to work for the first time in his life. He had no idea how Sana would react, but if it was anything like how she reacted to customers who pissed her off, he'd rather not witness that.

But then, this was a chance to see Evan. It had only been a few days since he'd woken up next to him, and yet something inside of him—his bones, or maybe his soul—ached for him.

On a professional note, if the location was as noteworthy as Colette made it seem, people would notice it. They could be up for set design awards. That could mean huge exposure for Evan. It'd be great for his career.

Or your career, a voice in his head reminded him. *Remember, you're a porn star too. Or is Evan all you can think about now that you're in love?*

He shut the voice out and texted Colette back: *I'll be there.* He didn't wait for a response. He got ready as quickly as he could: showering, brushing his teeth, and throwing on whatever clean clothing he could find.

When he checked his phone again, Colette had texted him an address. His eyes nearly popped out of his skull. The filming location she'd given him was an LA landmark that Pete knew well: Griffith Park.

Holy shit. The park was home to all sorts of things. The zoo. The observatory. And perhaps most notably, the renowned Hollywood sign. Pete had a sudden, vivid vision of himself having sex with Evan in front of the giant letters. Talk about a big O.

He shook his head to dispel the image. There was no way in hell they'd get permission to film there. They were probably filming somewhere in the park itself.

A fire kindled in Pete's lower belly. Outdoor sex was a guilty pleasure of his. Not because he was especially into exhibitionism, but because it felt like doing something wrong. Breaking the rules. And the idea of having sex with Evan was exciting in any form. He was in for one hell of an afternoon.

As he made the short drive to the park, he reflected on what just about everyone who knew him had told him recently: Evan was having a marked influence on him. He was going to clubs and throwing parties and getting out of his comfort zone. An entire year of sex work hadn't managed to break him out of his shell, and Evan had done it in a couple of weeks.

Then again, he was also ignoring lectures and risking getting in trouble at work. The idea was a little unsettling, and yet he just couldn't convince himself to be concerned. He'd been good his whole life. It couldn't hurt to let loose a little.

Speaking of which, he wondered what would happen when he saw Evan again, now that he knew he loved him. God, he hoped he didn't just blurt it out or something.

This whole love thing was bewildering.

Before he knew it, he pulled up into a gravel parking lot on the south side of the park. He spotted Colette's red Mustang and parked next to it. Just as he'd suspected, they were nowhere near the Hollywood sign. He couldn't tell if he was relieved or disappointed.

He stepped out of the car and hugged himself for warmth. It was a clear, sunny day, but this early in the year it didn't start to warm up until the afternoon. He hoped they wouldn't have to completely strip down, though he wouldn't put it past Colette. He could already hear her in his head: *It's for authenticity. This is a* summer *production. If it were warm outside, you wouldn't have your clothes on.*

"Jaden, are you even listening to me?"

Colette's real voice invaded the imitation playing in his head. He startled; he hadn't even noticed her walk up. "Hey, sorry. I was just . . . um . . ."

"From the moony look on your face, I take it you haven't heard a word I said." She was standing with her hands on her hips at the edge of the parking lot. Yolanda was next to her, silent like a sentinel as always. "At least you're on time. We just finished setting up."

"Is Kyle here?"

"How did I know that would be the first question out of your mouth?" Colette about-faced and strode toward a nearby picnic area. "Yes, he's here. Follow me."

There were a handful of couples wandering around and a woman playing with her dog, so this definitely wasn't their filming location. Not unless Colette had ramped up *Heat Wave's* kink level without telling him.

Curiosity kindled in Pete as they turned toward a footpath slicing through the grass. The trees lining it were still green and loaded with leaves, thankfully, or they'd never be able to claim it was summer. A light frost from last night's chill coated the grass, but it was patchy and would melt within an hour.

They walked at a brisk pace for about ten minutes, heading straight into the trees. The path tapered off after a while, yet Colette seemed to know precisely where she was going. Eventually, Pete could no longer hear signs of life nearby, just the crunch of their shoes on the grass.

"You know," Pete said, "if you needed a good place to hide my body, there are plenty of dumpsters in town."

"Harr harr," Colette said over her shoulder. "We're almost there."

A few minutes later, they broke through a copse and came upon what would have been a clearing if it weren't for one beautiful, old tree in the center. It wasn't huge, but by LA standards, it was like something out of a high fantasy novel.

What really grabbed Pete's attention, however, was the fact that Kyle was standing beneath it.

He had a picnic basket on one arm, and there was a red, checkered blanket spread out beneath his bare feet. He turned at the sound of their approach, his dark hair ruffling in the breeze. He smiled at Pete, and his eyes crinkled at the corners. He looked like a full-page spread in a fashion magazine.

Pete thought his heart might stop. Had it not been for the recording equipment dispersed nearby, he could have pretended they were meeting up for their second date.

"Hey, gorgeous," Evan greeted him when he was close enough, his smile stretching broadly across his handsome face.

"Hi," Pete said, beaming. He wanted to reach out and touch him, kiss him, but he remembered Colette at the last second. He shoved his hands into his pockets to keep them from acting of their own volition. "Been waiting long?"

"Long enough. Wanna warm me up?"

"Please save it for the camera," Colette interrupted. "I feel like I've had to tell you guys that at least once per scene." She went to stand next to the main camera. "Jaden, you can probably guess what today's theme is."

"Yeah, the props were a dead giveaway. A picnic in the park. Why did we have to rush out here, though? You made it sound like it was now or never."

"That's because it is. We were given an extremely small window of opportunity to film. I know you don't care much for the business side of the industry, but for the record, you have *no* idea how hard it is to get a permit to film outdoors. Normally, the Entertainment Industry Development Corporation couldn't care less what we're filming, but since this is a public location, there are all sorts of obscenity laws we have to skate around. Basically, to get this permit, we had to jump through a hoop that was wrapped up tight in red tape and then set on fire."

"Well, that's visual," Pete said. "How'd you swing it?"

"I have my ways. The point is, filming had to happen today, and for a location like this—" she made a broad, sweeping gesture toward the picturesque tree nestled in the center of the sun-drenched clearing "—I was willing to make some concessions."

"Is this area ours for the afternoon, then?"

"We alerted park authorities that we're filming, and they've been instructed to keep people away from here. It's not a high-traffic area regardless. But if any tourists wander this way, they're going to get a hell of a show." She waved at the blanket. "We need to get started. Take your place at Darko's side while Yolanda and I check the mics. Hopefully the wind is feeling cooperative."

Pete did as he was told, approaching the blanket. He toed his shoes off, keeping his eyes down. Just being close to Evan flooded his mind with images: Evan behind him, dark eyes meeting his in the mirror, Evan's large hand pressed hard against his mouth . . .

He shivered and stepped onto the blanket. He hoped his thoughts weren't written all over his—

"You're thinking about the coffee shop, aren't you?" Evan asked.

Fuck. Denying it would have beggared belief. "How do you do that?"

"It's no skill on my part. Your face is like an instruction manual." He kept his voice low so only Pete could hear. "What part were you thinking about?"

He smiled sheepishly and reached out to brush his fingers against Evan's. "Your hand."

"I've replayed that memory in my head a few times myself." He stepped closer and brought his lips to Pete's ear. "Guess what I'm thinking right now."

Pete's heart thumped hard against his ribs. "Something lascivious, obviously."

"Oh, lascivious. Breaking out the SAT words this early in the morning, huh?"

Pete laughed and smoothed out a crease in the blanket with his socked toe. He had a feeling that if he looked Evan in the eye, he wouldn't be able to stop himself from telling him how he felt. He imagined swallowing the words, but they kept climbing back up.

"Hey, what's going on?" Evan asked, touching his arm.

"What do you mean?"

"You're acting all shy. It's adorable. Something up?"

"I'm just a little nervous about the shoot."

Get it together, Griflow. Romantic location or not, they were here to work. Now was not the time to make a love confession. And Colette might not be able to remove him from the project at this juncture, but if he professed his love for his costar in front of her, she would have something to say about it.

"Gentlemen."

Speak of the devil. Colette was standing near the perimeter of the blanket with an open laptop balanced on one arm. She was typing with her free hand. After a pause, she said, "Could you both please state your names at a normal volume?"

"Jaden Prime," Pete answered automatically.

"Kyle Darko," Evan echoed.

"Good," she said. "Now could one of you whisper something to the other?"

Evan craned his neck up to Pete's ear and murmured, "I dreamed about you last night. Your eyes and how you feel under me."

Pete sucked in a breath. *Don't tell him. Please don't tell him.*

"No good," Colette announced. "We couldn't hear that."

Evan's breath tickled his ear again. "Is it bad that I'm okay with that?"

"Now *that* we heard," Colette scolded. "Make your whispers more of a dull roar, and we should be fine. If you're too quiet, we'll be here all day."

"I have it on good authority that Jaden has no trouble being loud," Evan said with a suspiciously straight face.

Pete would have laughed, but he was hung up on *"We'll be here all day."* He turned to Evan. "I have work later today."

"Call out."

"I can't. My manager will eviscerate me."

Evan's wicked grin was back. "We'll just have to get it right the first time, then. Which begs the question," he called over to Colette, "what are we doing about your script? This location obviously wasn't planned on, so a lot of the dialogue won't work."

"I'm aware. You'll have to improvise a bit. Pretend this is a real date and just say what you'd normally say to each other."

If only she knew how easy that would be for them.

Colette charged on obliviously. "The good news is there isn't going to be a lot of dialogue regardless. This is more of an action scene, so to speak."

Pete swallowed. "What are we doing?"

She answered without looking up from her laptop. "Anal."

Pete's jeans were suddenly a size too small. He'd figured as much, but hearing it said so definitively was a special kind of turn-on.

"Darko is going to top, obviously," Colette continued. "Jaden, as the one with more experience, I expect you to be an active bottom."

"I think I can manage that." He was already salivating.

Evan was tense next to him. Pete nudged him with his elbow. "You okay?"

"Fuck yeah." His voice was deep and rough. "I just can't believe how much that turned me on. I'm a little light-headed."

Pete chuckled. "I know the feeling. You've been doing that to me for weeks now."

"Feel free to get revenge anytime you like."

"Would you both have a seat please?" Colette directed. "This scene is self-explanatory: you're on an afternoon date. You start flirting with each other, and things get heated. Keep the overall storyline in mind. This is an exciting time for your characters, right at the budding of a relationship. You shouldn't be able to keep your hands off each other."

Evan threw an arm over Pete's shoulder. "I don't know how Jaden and I will ever pull that off. We clearly can't stand each other." He gave her with a saucy wink.

Colette rolled her eyes. "It's tragic, really. You're so handsome when you're not speaking. Get into position, please."

They sat cross-legged in the center of the quilt. Pete started to arrange himself a respectable distance away, but then Evan wrapped an arm around him and guided him back until he was leaning against his chest.

"Can't resist a chance to make me the little spoon, huh?" Pete teased.

"Just playing my role as the top." He planted a kiss in Pete's hair. "Though there was a part of me that was hoping Colette would pull a twist ending and ask me to bottom."

All semblance of coherent thought in Pete's brain went flying out of his ears. He angled his neck until he could see Evan in his periphery. "You wanted to bottom?"

"Sure, why not?"

At Pete's flabbergasted expression, he added, "I can't expect to top for the rest of our lives, can I? Of course we'll switch things up."

For the rest of our lives. Pete's entire system crashed. No signal. Motherboard fried. Please insert recovery disk.

"Everyone ready?" Colette announced.

"Ready," Evan said.

Yolanda gave a thumbs-up from her spot behind her camera.

Pete muttered something vaguely akin to, "Yarth."

That was apparently all Colette needed because she crouched down next to a mic stand, laptop balanced on her knees, and called, "Action!"

Pete settled in Evan's arms, head resting on his chest. He looked up at the sunlight filtering through the leaves of the trees and said exactly what he was thinking. "This is nice."

"Yeah," Evan said. Pete couldn't see him clearly, but he felt the contented sigh he let out against his neck. "I love lazy days like this, especially if I get to spend them with you."

Pete tilted his head to the side and smiled. "Me too."

"It's so quiet out here. It's hard to believe we're still in the city."

"Yeah," Pete agreed, relaxing again. "We haven't seen another person in hours. It's like we're in our own little world." He threaded his fingers with Evan's.

"That's good," Colette called to them. "You two seem very cozy. If I didn't know better, I'd think you were a real couple."

Gulp. Pete tensed up, but Evan ran a soothing hand down his arm. "It is pretty private out here. You know what that means?"

Pete raised an eyebrow. "What?"

"No one can hear you scream." Suddenly, Evan started tickling him.

Pete screeched and scrambled away, but Evan's strong arms wrapped around him, hauling him back. His fingers wormed their way into his shirt. Pete thrashed in his grip, but Evan's hold was impossible to break. Somehow, he ended up on his back with Evan holding him down, yelling, "Say uncle! Say uncle!"

"What are you, my older brother?" Pete groused, pushing at Evan's chest. It was useless. The man was carved from marble.

Evan grabbed his wrists and pinned them to the blanket. "I hope not, or else this would be really awkward."

Pete panted for breath, grateful to be trapped if it meant he wasn't being tickled any longer. Evan was breathing hard too, gazing down at him. It occurred to Pete that they were in a very compromising position: Evan on top of him, straddling his hips, their faces close, and their breath hot between them.

The mood shifted from playful to suggestive in a flash. There was an electric moment where neither of them said anything. Then Evan shifted on top of him.

"Jaden," Evan said, "I want to kiss you."

"Please do," Pete panted.

The kiss started gentle—just a warm brush of lips that banished the morning chill—but it quickly became downright filthy: tongues and teeth clashing, and little noises escaping from Pete whenever their mouths parted.

Evan released his wrist and trailed a hand down his stomach, heading slowly toward Pete's swelling cock.

Pete broke the kiss. "What are you doing?"

"I would think that was obvious."

"We can't," Pete gasped. "Anyone could walk by. We could get caught."

Evan nibbled on his neck. "I know. That's what makes it so hot." His hand slid between Pete's legs and cupped him.

Pete arched into the touch. "That feels good."

Evan laughed breathily. "I thought you wanted me to stop"

Pete tried to think past the flood of arousal infusing his whole body. "Kyle, I . . . I want . . ."

"You're already hard." Evan's fingers working him through his jeans. "But say the word, and I'll stop. Is that what you want?"

Pete huffed. "No. But we have to be quick, okay?"

"I make no promises."

They fumbled with each other's clothing, going for speed instead of grace. Pete pushed his jeans and underwear down to his thighs but otherwise left them on. The cold bit into his skin. Thankfully, Colette didn't direct him to disrobe completely.

"Do you have a . . ." Pete trailed off. He feigned running an agitated hand through his hair.

Evan picked up on his bait. "A condom?"

"Yeah." He bit his lip, playing shy for the camera.

Evan dug one out of his back pocket and held it up off-center. It looked weird from where Pete was, but the camera angle would make it look like he was showing Pete while simultaneously giving the audience a good look.

"On your knees," Evan ordered, pupils wide.

Pete wordlessly obeyed. Evan made a show of sliding lubed fingers into him and remarking about how tight he was.

It would have been business as usual, except for the fact that Evan knew exactly how Pete liked to be touched. He sunk two fingers into him with just the right amount of force, working him open, and when he curled them unerringly toward his prostate, Pete couldn't stop the broken moan that burst from his lips.

"Fuck, Kyle," he gasped, gripping the blanket under them in both fists, "do that again."

Evan smoothed a hand down his clothed back and seemed about to do just that when Colette signaled to them.

They held their positions. She approached.

"Nice work," she said, walking around them and studying their angles, "but I want you to ramp up the tension. Right now this feels . . . comfortable. Like it isn't the first time you've had sex."

Evan made a noise that sounded suspiciously like a snort. Pete glanced at Colette, praying she hadn't noticed.

If she had, she ignored it. She walked back over to Yolanda. "Try it again. This time, let's see some first-fuck jitters."

Finally, something Pete excelled at.

"Action!"

Pete made a small keening noise and pressed back against Evan's fingers. "Ah! Kyle."

"Shh," Evan said. This time, when he ran his hand down Pete's back, the gesture felt more soothing than possessive. "Easy, easy. Don't hurt yourself."

"I can't help it," Pete whined. He tried to push back again, but Evan stopped him by grabbing his hips. "I want you so badly."

"You can have me," Evan said, "but you have to hang on for a minute longer while I get you ready."

Pete shivered. "All right, but please hurry."

"Well, since you asked nicely."

Evan fingered him until he was a squirming, shaking mess. By the end of it, Pete could no longer tell if his moans were real or fake. He was freezing and hot at the same time, numb and oversensitive. It was all he could do to make sure he was facing the camera and had a relaxed, pleasured expression on his face. He wanted to jump on Evan and ride him until he came all over his chest, shouting Evan's name, but that wouldn't fit Colette's "vision."

"You ready to take my cock?" Evan asked loudly. He leaned down, chest to Pete's back and whispered, "Everything feel okay?"

"Yes," Pete said to both. "Fuck yes."

Evan pulled his fingers out of him. "I can't wait to be inside of you."

"Please fuck me," Pete begged. "I'll die if you don't." He wasn't just talking dirty. He was *drowning* in desire, unsteady with need. He felt physically empty without Evan inside of him.

Evan took mercy on him and got into position. He nudged Pete's knees apart and pressed gently on the small of his back until Pete arched it just right. Then Evan guided himself into Pete.

The first stroke in made Pete's brain cut to radio silence. He groaned, closing his eyes so he could fully absorb the sensation. He heard shuffling and knew without looking that Colette and

Yolanda had moved closer to capture his reaction. Evan thrust into him again, harder this time, and Pete threw his head back.

"Christ, you feel so good," Evan said. He put a hand on Pete's shoulder and used it as leverage to rock harder into him. Pete lost the strength to hold himself up and collapsed onto the blanket. Evan followed him down, draping his whole body on top of Pete's, never losing his rhythm for a second even as he changed from thrusting to grinding inside of him.

Pete was already close. It was embarrassing how little stamina he had lately. And by lately, he meant ever since he'd started having sex with Evan.

He wrapped a hand around himself and managed to pump once before Evan reached under him and smacked his hand away.

"I think you were holding out on me before," Evan purred in his ear, too quietly for the microphones to pick up. "I think if I fuck you just right, you can come untouched."

Pete's whole body trembled. Evan fucked him so hard his eyes crossed, quick thrusts designed to stimulate his prostate. Pete held on for dear life, digging his fingers into the grass beneath the blanket.

"Oh God, Kyle," Pete cried out. "I'm close."

"Already?" Evan teased. He shoved himself deeply into Pete and held himself there until Pete keened. "I could fuck you all day."

"Fuck, please let me touch myself. I want to come."

Instead of answering, Evan shifted to a different angle, one that made Pete's vision blur. Every stroke in made pleasure shoot into him, raw and overpowering. The tension between his legs was building to an apex. He wanted to cry, it felt so good. He wanted to scream. He wanted to *come*.

Evan buried his face in Pete's hair and breathed in. "You're incredible. I can't get enough." He reached a hand around Pete's chest and found a nipple, rolling it between his fingers. It wasn't the touch Pete wanted, but it was like his desperation had opened new channels in his brain. The stimulation of that area connected to his groin in a way he'd never felt before, and within seconds, he was coming. He didn't remember opening his mouth, but he could hear his moans echoing in the clearing, exquisite and tortured.

Evan slowed his thrusts, presumably to avoid overstimulating Pete while his postorgasm sensitivity was at its peak. Regardless, Pete almost asked him to pull out. He was so oversensitive, just having him still inside made his nerves light up. But they needed the shot, and overstimulated or not, he loved being connected to Evan.

When he'd recovered enough to push himself up on his elbows, Colette got their attention again.

"That was hot," she said, "but *way* too kinky for a first time. Like, bordering on orgasm denial. That would have been great if we were filming a second or third time, but we need to start vanilla and then build to the harder stuff."

"What should we do?" Pete asked blearily. *Please say "Stop filming and take a nap in the grass."*

"We'll focus on Darko's orgasm and either cut yours or transpose it so it looks like you came second. This time around, make it more intimate. In fact, get on your back, Jaden."

Pete flopped over, all too happy to not have to support his torso anymore. Evan kneeled between his legs and looked to Colette. She gave him a thumbs-up.

Pete lifted his head enough to see Evan. He'd removed his shirt, revealing carved musculature and roseate nipples. His pants were around his knees. One hand was holding the base of his plump cock. Even through the condom, Pete could see the rubicund, blood-filled color of it. Pete had never asked him before if he used drugs to stay hard. Knowing Evan, probably not.

The whole atmosphere of the shoot felt different now that they were facing each other. Evan studied him, and he stared back, trying to convey everything he was feeling with his eyes. Their intimacy felt more vivid now, more intense. Pete wasn't even cold anymore, nestled as he was in this private, silent exchange between them.

Evan leaned down and kissed his chest. "Was that too much earlier?"

"Not at all." Pete let a sloppy grin plop onto his face. "It was great. I've never come like that before."

Evan kissed him, wet and sugary. The kiss distracted Pete as Evan eased into him, rolling his hips in gradual, fluid movements. Pete sighed with every thrust. He relaxed, enjoying the ride even if it gave him no physical pleasure. Just being close to Evan like this was comforting. He was tired and sore, but there was no part of him that wanted this closeness to end. It was hard to remember he was working, hard to be Jaden fucking Kyle and not Pete having sex with Evan.

Evan pumped three times into him and then, surprisingly, pulled out. Pete expected him to change angles and push back in, but instead he squeezed the base of his cock and shuddered.

"What's the hold up?" Colette called.

"Sorry," he panted. "I'm too close. I need a minute."

She frowned. "Really? Normally we have to bring in eight naked guys, hang up posters of John Boyega, and make a sacrifice to the heathen gods to get you to blow your load. What gives?"

Evan wordlessly looked at Pete.

Pete swallowed as understanding washed through him. His spent cock twitched even though there was no way he was getting hard again anytime soon.

"Sorry," Evan said to Colette, eyes still on Pete. "It's just, uh, sometimes a scene gets to you, you know?"

"Well, get it together," Colette commanded. "If we walk away from this without some decent footage, I'm going to be pissed. You don't know what I had to do to get this location."

"I'll hold it in, I swear."

They resumed filming, and though Evan put on a good show, he had to stop a few more times and breathe before he could perform. By the time Colette signaled that they had enough footage, he was dripping with sweat despite the cold and had a look on his face that Pete could only call agonized.

Evan came the *second* Colette told him he could, though saying he unraveled would be more accurate. He fell boneless on top of Pete, almost sobbing as his orgasm racked him. Pete held him through it, stroking his quivering, sweat-soaked back.

After, he raised up on his elbows and smeared his lips against Pete's. "Fuck, I can't . . . I don't think I've *ever* . . ." He gave up and kissed Pete again. "That was amazing. You're amazing."

"Pleasure's all mine. Though there is one thing."

"What?"

"You're crushing me." He wriggled under Evan, showcasing how very trapped he was by Evan's more muscular frame.

Evan laughed and pushed himself off. "Sorry. I'll try to roll to the side the next time I have an orgasm that alters my world view."

Pete reached for his hand. "It's okay."

"That's a wrap, boys," Colette interrupted. "Nice work. At least, toward the end."

Oh shit. Pete had almost forgotten about her. "Thanks, Colette. Need anything else from us?"

"No," she said, but she had a strange look on her face, somewhere between displeasure and curiosity. She opened her mouth as if to say something more, but instead she grumbled, "Porn stars," as if that were a complete sentence in and of itself.

Pete blinked. "Huh?"

"I might have expected this from Darko, but not from you, Jaden."

Pete sat up. "Expected what?"

"Oh, nothing." She snapped her laptop closed as if shutting the door on the conversation. "You'll have to hurry if you want to have time to shower before work. Unless you want to show up smelling like sex and the great outdoors."

Pete rifled in his pocket for his phone and checked the time. Shit.

"I have to go," he said to Evan.

"Can I come with you?" Evan waggled his eyebrows.

"No," he said firmly. "I don't trust you to keep your hands to yourself."

Evan pouted. "Fine." His expression transformed into a grin. "You can make it up to me."

"How?"

"Stand up." Evan got up, hooked his hands under Pete's armpits, and hauled him to his feet.

Pete made an embarrassing squealing noise. "Evan, what the hell?"

"Get dressed and follow me." He turned to Colette and shouted, "We'll be right back."

She waved him off, too deep in conversation with Yolanda to even glance their way.

Pete had just pulled his pants up to his hips when Evan grabbed his hand and tugged him to the other side of the tree. Out of view of their makeshift picnic, he pulled out his phone and held it up. "Smile."

"What?" Pete covered his face with his hands. "No way!"

"Come on," Evan whined. "We don't have any pictures together."

"Evan, we've done entire photo shoots."

"Yeah, but those are work photos. I don't want some stuffy professional shot. I want something natural."

Pete made a rude noise. "You know some couples pay a lot of money to have professional photos taken of them."

Evan looked triumphant. "Some *couples*, huh?"

Pete opened and closed his mouth. He wisely decided not to comment further. "I don't want to take a photo when I'm all disheveled and sweaty and sexed-out."

"But that's precisely how I like you." Evan kissed him, and Pete's already weak knees threatened to collapse. "Please? For me?"

One glimpse of Evan's beseeching smile, and Pete folded like a house of cards. "All right. Fine."

Evan tapped his camera app and faced it toward them. It was a pretty shot with the sunny clearing and vibrant green grass in the background. Pete smoothed his ruffled hair and smiled. Evan planted a kiss on his cheek and, without peeking, tapped the camera button.

The shutter clicked, and the image froze on the screen. Evan brought it closer so they could see. Maybe Pete was drunk on hormones, but he was actually a little touched. They looked great: flushed and healthy and strangely in tune with one another.

"You like it?" Evan asked. "Because I love it."

Pete's lungs throbbed. He wondered if it were possible to be so content it actually hurt.

"Yeah," he agreed. "It's *perfect*."

CHAPTER  15

"I know your secret."

Pete didn't look up from the register. "Go away, Joshua." He finished counting the quarters and moved on to the dimes. *Ten, twenty, thirty, forty . . .*

"Maybe you didn't hear me. I said I know your secret."

Fuck. Pete lost count. He dropped the coins back into their slot with a clatter and then glared at Joshua. "Do you mind? I can't start my shift until I finish counting the register." Some corner of his brain had absorbed Joshua's words, but it had shuttled them off to a "deal with later" pile. He had a laundry list of things on his mind: midterms were in less than a month, Sana had a million tasks for him, and he hadn't had a chance to see Evan in nearly four days. He wasn't in the mood for Joshua's shit.

Joshua pouted at his dismissal. Pete probably wasn't giving him the reaction he was shooting for. Good. Maybe he'd take the hint and go away.

Pete scooped the dimes out of the tray again and started over. *Ten, twenty, thirty—*

Joshua leaned closer, an elbow on the counter, and shoved his phone in Pete's face. "Check out what I found."

Pete saw a flash of bare, muscular chest and yelped, shoving the phone away with his free hand. "Dude, is that porn?"

"Yup," Joshua chirped.

"What the fuck?" Pete stared at him. "That's weird even for you. And I'm pretty sure that violates like a dozen sexual harassment laws." He turned back to the register, mumbling rude comments under his breath, and did his best to block Joshua out.

"Hey, I'm trying to do you a favor. You and your boyfriend's sex tape got leaked."

Now *that* Pete heard. He dropped the dimes again, this time on accident. Most of them landed in the tray, but a few rolled across the counter and fell to the tile floor with a metallic *ping*.

He whirled to face Joshua. "What?"

Joshua smirked. "I thought that might get your attention." He held out his phone again. "This is you and him, right?"

Pete was almost too afraid to look. A degree at a time, his eyes drifted down to Joshua's phone. His browser was pulled up and displayed some sort of LGBTQ porn site, judging by the fact that it was dripping with rainbows and dicks. The colorful genitals weren't what caught Pete's attention, however. There was a banner ad for *Heat Wave* flashing on the sidebar, featuring a photo of Evan and him on a makeshift beach that Pete recognized all too well.

"Why, Pete," Joshua said, fluttering his eyelashes, "I never would have guessed."

The pleased expression on his face was totally at odds with the nuclear apocalypse that was going off inside of Pete right now. His brain retrieved what Joshua had said before and replayed it at a thunderous volume: *"I know your secret."*

Pete's body grew cold from head to toe, and he was willing to bet all the blood had drained out of his face. He stared forward but somehow didn't see Joshua at all. His attention floated around the Globe, which had taken on the surreal quality of a dream while somehow looking the same. Sunlight spilled across the gray tile floor, customers dotted the mismatched furniture, and Sana was chatting with someone near the milk station, wearing a fetching electric-blue headscarf. It was so normal, but *off* at the same time. Probably because of the paradigm shift occurring in Pete's brain.

Pete stared at him, silent as death. He opened his mouth only to close it again. What could he possibly say?

Joshua must've gotten sick of waiting for him, because he nudged him with an elbow and said, "What are the odds, right?"

For once, Pete couldn't agree more. Of all the ads in all the world, Joshua had to see his. Hadn't he heard of ad blockers?

Oblivious to his internal apocalypse, Joshua said, "I mean, who would have thought you have an evil twin in porn."

Pete snapped out of his horror and stammered, "W-what?"

Joshua continued like he hadn't heard him. "I can't believe how much the guy on the right looks just like you. He's even got your freaky huge eyes. And the other guy's a dead ringer for your hot boyfriend. What a coincidence, right?"

Oh fuck. In an instant, Pete understood. Joshua didn't know it was him. The ad was tiny and pixelated; of course he couldn't tell for sure it was him. Pete could still salvage this. If he could just wipe the shock off his face, if he could just *think* fast enough. But panic made him sluggish, and his facial muscles refused to cooperate with the orders he mentally screamed at them.

Joshua glanced up at him, and in an instant, Pete knew it was too late.

His panic was written all over his face; he could feel it. Because the moment Joshua looked at him, his eyes widened.

"Oh my God," Joshua breathed. "Is . . . is it *you*?"

He glanced between his phone and Pete so quickly, Pete thought his head might fly off his neck.

Joshua sucked in a breath and started to shout, "Holy sh—"

Pete clapped a hand onto his shoulder, hard. Several people had turned to eye them, including Sana. A fresh wave of panic flooded into Pete.

"Back room," he hissed. Apparently, fear made him strong, because Pete hauled Joshua off like he weighed nothing, yanking him through the swinging door behind the counter.

Joshua stumbled but caught himself. He whirled around and stared at Pete with giant green eyes.

Pete stared back, and it occurred to him that now that he had Joshua here, he had no idea what to say to him. Pete was no closer to forming actual sentences. Joshua might as well have punched him in the stomach. He grabbed the counter for support. Black spots danced around the edges of his vision. For a terrifying moment, he thought he might actually faint.

Judging by Joshua's face, his silence didn't just speak volumes. It spoke whole libraries. "Is it true? Is this really you?" He held the phone up like an accusation.

Pete didn't respond. His vision tilted, and the contents of the inventory room appeared to slide around like they were going to be dumped out of frame.

"God, it's true," Joshua breathed. "I can't believe it. I was just trying to rile you up, or tease you, or . . . I don't even know. I can't believe you're a—" He cut himself off.

That, for some reason, shook Pete from his stupor. "Say it."

Joshua looked blankly at him.

"*Joshua,*" Pete said pointedly.

"Fine!" Joshua turned beet red and averted his gaze. "You're a porn star!"

Pete was unprepared for the physical reaction that came with hearing someone say it out loud. He'd asked Joshua for it, but now he wanted to flinch away, as if the words were a physical blow.

"This I gotta see." Joshua moved his thumb to tap the screen.

"You can't click on it!" Pete screeched. He reached out and snatched Joshua's phone from his hand. The very idea of Joshua watching his teaser was even more disturbing than what was currently going on.

"Hey, give that back." Joshua reached for it, but Pete smacked his hand away. Joshua rubbed the back of it, glaring at him resentfully. "Don't be mad at me. I really didn't think it was you. This is your fault."

In so many ways. "Sorry." The word tumbled out of him on autopilot.

Joshua looked everywhere but at him. "I seriously didn't know. I thought I'd tease you about your porn double and you'd turn red and yell at me. I thought it'd be *funny*. And I definitely wasn't expecting you to go all Terminator on me. I didn't think you had it in you." He eyed him up and down. "There's a lot I didn't think you had in you."

Pete managed to say, "I guess you don't know me as well as you think you do."

It was a miracle he could speak at all, considering his veins had frozen over. A horror movie was playing out in his head, one where Joshua burst out of the inventory room and announced that Pete was a porn star to the entirety of the Globe, which was suddenly populated by Pete's mom, professors, friends, pastor, entire high school class, and essentially everyone he'd ever met.

He had to stop that from happening. He had no idea how, but he had to do something.

While he was still stricken, gears were apparently turning in Joshua's head.

"Wait a minute," Joshua said, eyes growing large again. "If that was really you, does that mean the other guy was your boyfriend? You're *both* in porn?"

"Will you keep your voice down?" Pete hissed.

"That explains it! I *knew* I'd seen him somewhere before. I kept trying to figure out where I knew him from. Now that I think about it, I've seen his . . . um, work." Joshua wet his lips, and for the first time in Pete's life, he wanted to hit something.

Oblivious to him, Joshua was already staring off into space, a look of perturbed realization creeping over him. "Oh God, I can just imagine it. Porn star boyfriends. Doing dishes in nothing but yellow gloves. Having sex-toy centerpieces in the living room. Going off to work every day together all, 'Honey, what are we filming today?' 'Well, dear, we're having another orgy with the Smiths!' And it would all be so . . . domestic."

Pete would have facepalmed if he'd had one iota more of his wits about him.

Finally, Joshua seemed to sense his discomfort. "Are you all right?"

"No," he answered honestly. "I'm really not."

Joshua shifted from foot to foot. "I wouldn't have recognized you if you hadn't freaked out. You look different with, um, clothes on." He turned vaguely green.

"Yes, I'm painfully aware of that." Pete's panic was starting to transform into anger.

Joshua's eyes had gotten funny-big again, like a cartoon owl. "I don't know what to say."

That last sentence hurtled Pete back into reality. Oh God. What *was* Joshua going to say?

His heart actually skipped a beat. If Joshua told Sana, he could lose his job. They couldn't expressly fire him for being a sex worker, but they could easily find another reason to justify terminating him.

Even if Sana stuck up for him—and he had no idea if she would—it wasn't her shop. She could be overruled. Or worse, she could agree. He could lose a friend.

Pete's knees nearly buckled. This was the living hell he'd imagined a hundred times, the vague threat that had loomed over him ever since the first day he'd walked into Murmur Inc., the one he'd feared but had never truly believed would come to pass. He had no idea how to feel. Embarrassed? Betrayed? Did he even have a right to be upset? He'd put himself on the internet for all the world to see. It seemed ridiculous now to think that no one would ever find it.

"Hey," Joshua prompted, "do you—"

"What are you going to do?" Pete interrupted.

At that, Joshua looked confused. "Uh, nothing?"

Pete stared at him. "What do you mean *nothing*? You're not going to tell Sana?"

"Honestly? I haven't thought that far ahead. I'm still wrapping my head around the fact that *you*, of all people . . ." He shook his head. "Are you sure you don't have a doppelgänger or something? Because I saw you with my own eyes, and even I think that would be more plausible." Josh hesitated. "If you did have, you know, an evil twin or something, I'd believe you."

Pete appreciated the out Joshua was handing him, but it was too late now. "No, I don't have a twin."

"Ah. I'm guessing your boyfriend doesn't either."

"He's not my—" Pete cut himself off, making a shoving motion with his hands as if he could push the words away. "Oh, forget it. No, he doesn't either."

They lapsed into awkward silence.

Pete scrutinized Joshua out of the corner of his eye. This was the sincerest he'd ever seen Joshua act. Gone were the usual theatrics and his obnoxious attitude. In fact, he looked as embarrassed as Pete felt.

"So," Pete said slowly, "if you're really not going to tell anyone, what are you going to do? There's no way you're just going to let me off the hook."

Joshua shrugged. He seemed almost bashful. "I dunno. I might blackmail you a little."

"*Blackmail me?*" Pete hissed.

"I said a little! I'm not a criminal mastermind, okay? I'll probably just make you take the trash out for me or something."

Pete wanted to laugh, but he was too shocked. Joshua was treating this like a fun prank opportunity. Pete had expected judgment from him, or revulsion, or shame, but he was mostly just staring at Pete like he was seeing him for the first time.

Pete needed to make it clear how serious this was. There was a chance he could convince Joshua not to say anything, but not if Joshua thought this whole thing was a joke.

"If you tell Sana," Pete said, "I'll be fired. And I don't know if they'll give me a reference or not, so it could hurt my chances of getting another job, which could in turn keep me from paying my tuition. Do you understand?"

There was a tense pause.

Joshua looked down at his sneakers. "I don't want you to lose your job."

"Really?"

"Yeah." He nudged a crack in the linoleum with his shoe. "I know I give you a hard time, but I don't want anything *bad* to happen to you." He glanced up, saw Pete watching him, and immediately shifted his gaze back to the floor.

Pete stared at him for a second longer and then nodded. "That's a relief."

His pulse returned to a semblance of normalcy now that the immediate danger had passed. He could deal with Joshua knowing. Joshua was not someone who had authority over him. Of all the people who could have found out, it could have been worse. Though he did have a big mouth. What were the chances he'd actually keep this a secret?

He looked at Joshua askance. "That can't be it, though."

"Huh?"

"I mean you're being awfully open-minded about this. Aren't you disgusted? Scandalized? Something? You just found out your coworker is a porn star. I was expecting some judgment."

Joshua shrugged again. "Don't get me wrong, I'm really shocked, but I wouldn't say I *judge* you for it." He hesitated. "I was sort of hoping to hear some more about it, though. I'm curious."

Pete blinked. "Curious?"

"Yeah! Maybe that's how you can pay me back for not ratting you out. You can tell me all about it."

"All about . . . porn?" This was not going the way Pete had anticipated.

"Duh. Aren't you supposed to be smart? I wanna know *everything*. What's it like?" Joshua's energy was suddenly that of an excited kid. It was much more fitting than the serious man who'd been standing before him a moment ago. "Does it pay as well as they say? Are the guys hot? Do you get to have sex with whoever you want? Is that how you met your boyfriend?"

Pete's head spun from the deluge of questions. "This is not helping my anxiety." He shook himself off. "And he's not my boyfriend yet."

"Yeah, yeah." Joshua rolled his eyes. "I saw the way you two looked at each other. I'm expecting a Save the Date any day now."

Pete flushed. "Do you really think—"

"Answer my questions," Joshua whined. "It's the least you can do. You made me see you without a shirt on." He pointed to his phone in Pete's hand, which had long-since dimmed. "It was *traumatic*."

He rolled his eyes. "Your mature reaction sure was short-lived."

"Whatever. So tell me, do they make you—"

The door suddenly opened, and Pete jumped a solid foot in the air. Sana poked her colorful head in. "What the hell are you two doing in here?"

Pete darted a look at Joshua. He was staring at Pete, as if waiting to follow his lead.

"Um," Pete scrambled to say. "Nothing."

He winced. Wrong answer.

"*Nothing?*" Sana repeated. "Since when do you two goof off together? You don't even like each other."

"Oh, we've become very close recently." Joshua looped an arm over Pete's shoulders. "One might even say *intimate*. I discovered that Pete here isn't as boring as I thought."

He winked at Pete. It took everything Pete had not to roll his eyes until they popped out of his skull. It was more tact than he'd expected from Joshua, but still nowhere near the realm of subtlety. He was going to have to make one rule clear: no making jokes about this. Ever. Not that he expected Joshua to understand why they weren't funny.

Pete had just resolved to have a serious talk with him when Sana said the last thing he'd ever expected.

"Oh please, no one cares that Pete's in porn." She waved dismissively. "You need to keep your voice down, by the way. I could hear you through the door."

Pete felt his neutral expression morph into a rictus. Blood rushed into his ears, buzzing so loudly it drowned out thought. He took a step back and felt for the counter, using it to support him as he sucked in a breath that in no way made him less breathless. He stared at Sana, who appeared inexplicably calm despite the shock she'd just delivered.

Was he really going to have to go through this again? After he'd just dodged a goddamn minefield with Joshua?

"What the *fuck*?" Joshua squawked, almost perfectly echoing Pete's thoughts. "Could you really hear us?"

"Yeah, and you're lucky it was me standing out here." She glared at him. "Imagine if it had been someone who didn't already know. Now will you *please* keep your voice down? There are customers out here." She started to exit, but the complete silence that descended on the room must have stopped her. She turned back around and looked warily between them. "What?"

"You . . ." Pete's throat closed. He had to dry swallow several times before he could speak again. "You *know*?"

"Of course I know. And, for the record, I thought you were interesting way before I found out." She studied his face. "I'm sorry, I shouldn't have told you like that. I've just known for so long I forgot it was a big deal."

"How?" His voice was scratchy with panic.

It must have been apparent, because Sana slung an arm around him, steadying his shaking shoulders. "A friend of mine works for Murmur Inc. She turned me on to their LGBTQ section. I get the newsletter and everything. They featured you when you first started working for them, and I thought, 'Oh hey, that's Pete,' and then moved on with my life." She shrugged. "Seriously, I never gave it much thought. The Globe has antidiscrimination policies, and even if we didn't, I don't care. Frankly, no one should." She glared at Joshua.

"Hey, I don't *care*," he whined. "I was just surprised is all. At least I found out by accident. What were *you* doing watching gay porn?"

"Oh, well clearly I was getting my nails done." She arched a challenging brow at him. "What the fuck do you think I was doing?"

"But you're not gay!"

"Go tell that to all the straight men who watch lesbian porn. And, for the record, you have no idea what I am."

It seemed they were just about to settle in for a round of squabbling when Pete finally found his voice again. "Sana, you haven't . . . seen my work, have you?" He almost didn't want to know the answer. He prepared for his head to explode from the pressure of all his blood entering it at once.

"Of course not," she said. "I knew you wouldn't want me to."

"Really?" Joshua piped up. "You didn't even *try* to find his videos?"

A new horror occurred to Pete. "You're not going to, are you?"

"Of course I am." Joshua winked. "I'm only human."

Pete experienced something akin to an atomic blast inside his ribs. "You can't!"

"Why not?"

"Because it's . . ." he struggled with all the reasons he wanted to list before settling on, "totally unprofessional!"

Joshua opened his mouth to argue, but Sana cut in. "Joshua, if you watch *any* of Pete's body of work, you're fired."

"*What*? That's not fair! Besides, how will you know if I watched it?"

"Because there's no way in Jahannam you'd be able to keep quiet about it. You'd tell someone, and it would get back to me, and then believe me when I say I would take special pleasure in firing you. It would be involved. There might even be props."

Joshua looked like he'd bitten into a lemon. "Fine. I won't watch his videos. Even though he put them on the internet for the world to see, and I'm pretty sure this is a violation of my Constitutional right to freedom of speech. Or something." He glanced at Pete, and his expression mellowed a bit. "I meant what I said too. I won't tell anyone."

Pete almost couldn't believe his luck. "Thank you."

"*But*," he said, expression transforming to one of mischievous delight, "I want all the details later. Deal?"

Pete sighed. He should have known. "Deal."

Joshua opened his mouth, ostensibly to say more, but Sana cut him off. "Pete and I need to talk. You can go."

He stalked out of the room, muttering under his breath.

Sana turned to Pete. "You okay?"

"Yeah." He looked down at his shaking hands. "No."

"What do you need?

"Some air. I'm gonna take a break. Is that okay?"

"Sure." She patted him on the back. "This may not be what you want to hear right now, but if it helps, I never cared what you do in your free time. And if Joshua causes any problems for you, he's out."

"Is that really fair though?" Pete asked quietly. "I mean, I'm the one who . . . did what I did. Wouldn't it make more sense to get rid of the source? What if someone else stumbles upon my 'secret'?"

"Then we'll deal with it. You're not going to lose your job over this, end of story. You've always been great to work with, and you're not the one who brought your personal life into the shop. If anyone else chooses to, they do so at their own peril. Although, I honestly don't think it's going to be a problem. Try not to stress, okay?"

"Okay."

They walked out of the room together. Joshua was by the sink, scouring a plate with more force than necessary, but when he met Pete's gaze, he nodded at him.

Pete nodded back. He headed for the side door, already riffling in his pockets for his cigarettes. He stepped out into the brisk air and was grateful for once for its biting clarity. The sun was still high in a winter-blue sky, and the few people on the streets were buried in heavy jackets and earphones. No one was paying the slightest attention to him.

He stuck a cigarette in his mouth, made a little cave around it with his hand, and lit it. He had his phone out before he'd gotten through his first exhale. Evan's name was at the top of his recent calls.

It only rang once before he answered. "Hey! I thought you were at work?"

Anxiety descended on him like a swarm. He wet his dry lips and tried to speak but couldn't find the words.

"Pete? What's wrong? Are you all right?"

He took another drag on his cigarette, exhaled slowly, and ordered himself to calm down. He was fine. Everything was fine.

"I'm fine," he repeated out loud. "Sorry about that. I'm just kind of freaked out."

"What's wrong?"

"Nothing. That's the thing."

Evan laughed, and the sound was like a balm on Pete's frayed nerves. "I'm going to need you to be a touch less cryptic."

"Sorry." He took a breath, sans cigarette, and let it out sharply. "My coworker, Joshua, saw a promo for *Heat Wave*."

Evan gasped. "Let me guess. Something about it looked familiar."

"Yup."

"Wow, no wonder you sounded so freaked out. What happened?"

Pete filled him in. The recap took less than five minutes and helped put the situation in perspective for him. Really, very little had happened, and it had gone as well as it possibly could. By the end of it, his hands had stopped shaking.

"Your coworker is a jerk," was the first thing Evan said when he'd finished. "I can't believe he confronted you at your job. What if Sana hadn't been cool? What if a customer had overheard, or another employee?"

"I agree, though I think Joshua honestly didn't think it was me. And, in his weird way, he's already apologized."

"Good." Evan paused. "You could always quit, you know."

"Why would I do that?"

"You did just get outed. I don't think anyone would blame you."

Pete considered it for a moment. "It's going to take me a while to get used to the idea that they know, but no, I'm not going to quit. Though I'm still waiting for the other shoe to drop."

"You think it will? Sana made it pretty clear she's got your back."

"I don't know. I've had this apocalyptic fever dream in my head for over a year now where someone I know finds out I'm in porn, and it ruins my life. Like, snubbed by my loved ones, exiled from my home, barred from all future jobs. That sort of thing. It's really hard for me to believe that people know—have known all along even—and completely don't care."

"It's not hard for me to believe, if it's any consolation."

"Well, yeah, you're out. Obviously you're fine with it."

Evan chuckled. "I meant it's not hard for me to believe your friends stuck by you. People can be surprisingly tolerant, especially when faced with a real person. It's one thing to judge faceless sex workers you'll never meet, but when it's someone you love, it's different. Especially when that someone happens to be a smart, caring, funny, and totally gorgeous man named Pete."

Pete ducked his head down, even though Evan couldn't see him. "That's sweet." He paused for a beat while he gathered his thoughts. "Maybe . . . maybe I've been doing this to myself all these years."

"What do you mean?"

"What if you're right? And everyone I know would love me anyway if they found out? What if this whole persecution complex is just something I made up in my head? It's dawning on me that I might have been building this up into a much bigger thing, and if I'd just had faith in the people I claim to love the most, I could have saved myself a lot of angst."

Pete took a breath. Just saying that out loud gave him a strange sense of relief.

"I think that's partially true," Evan said evenly, "but I also think there are a lot of people out there who are small-minded bigots. I deal with them every day because of my choice to be out, and sometimes, it's downright ugly. I don't think the consequences you've been imagining are totally made up, but I do think that one day, if you were to tell your loved ones, you'd be surprised by how many allies you have."

"You're amazing." Pete smiled broadly. "What would I do without you?"

"You'll never find out."

He nearly choked on his cigarette at that and let it drop to the sidewalk, then crushed it beneath his shoe. "I . . . I should go back in."

He liked to think he'd come a long way in the short time he'd known Evan, but his replies still needed some work.

"Sure you're all right?"

"Yeah. The way I see it, I just have to rework my hypothesis."

"Come again?"

"Sorry, nerd talk. I was operating under the theory that if people found out about what I do, they'd reject me. Well, people found out, and that didn't happen, so that means I have to go back and rework my hypothesis and start again."

"Maybe your mom can be your next test subject."

Pete's anxiety returned in near full force. "I don't know if I'll *ever* be ready to tell her."

"Maybe not right now, but think about this: pretty soon, I'm going to meet her, and she's bound to ask how we know each other. What are we going to say?"

Pete stopped with his hand inches from the door handle. "I don't know."

"There are only a few options. Are we going to lie to her face? Make up some bullshit story? That's a question all couples get. Are we going to lie for the rest of our lives? Or what if it's years from now, and we're married or something, and people ask what your husband does for a living. What are you going to say? I have no intention of spending the rest of my life pretending to be someone I'm not."

Pete's brain had stopped somewhere around *married* and was now desperately trying to reboot. Bits and pieces of what Evan had said managed to seep in through the white noise. He was right: they couldn't lie forever, and considering how important it was to Evan that he be upfront about himself, Pete doubted he'd deal with lies for long.

Pete had to pose an important question to himself: was being with Evan more important than his privacy? Could he trust the people in his life to accept Evan? And perhaps accept Pete as well?

The answer was shockingly simple: yes.

Evan was precisely the man he could see himself being brave for. It might not be today, but if they could really have the future together that Evan saw for them, Pete could do anything. A sensation akin to lightning shot through Pete and made his limbs tingle. It was as if some sort of knotted-up energy inside him had been released.

"I want to see you tonight," Pete said suddenly. "There's something I want to tell you."

CHAPTER 16

Pete had never been one for grand gestures, but the moment he resolved to tell Evan he loved him, he knew he wanted to do something special.

But how would Evan want to be told?

There was a park near his house that had a beautiful lake surrounded by old-fashioned streetlamps. They could go for a walk, and he could tell him by the water, with the lights glittering off the surface. But it was freezing outside, and the lights were off as often as they were on. Professing his love while shivering in the dark sounded more creepy than romantic.

He could take him to a bookstore. Pete shook his head to himself as he finished cleaning up the Globe and got ready to go home. That was where *he* would want to be taken. Were there any comic book shops around? Probably, but there were sure to be other people there, and as accustomed as Pete was to performing in front of an audience, he'd rather this be more private. Dinner? It was nearly nine, and by the time he got home, it'd be even later. The chances that Evan hadn't eaten already were slim to none.

Pete riffled through a mental catalog of possibilities, but nothing seemed quite right for both of them. He was still trying to come up with something when he got home. He'd thought he'd ask his mom for ideas, but as soon as he walked through the door, he found a note on the counter saying she was at the movies with her girlfriends.

He crumpled it up and shot it at the kitchen trash, missing by about a foot. As he bent to retrieve it, he thought that he was glad she'd gotten a night off, almost as glad as he was to have the house to himself. He could ask Evan if he wanted to stay in tonight. Was that too boring?

Pete mulled it over as he darted upstairs. He'd texted Evan his address earlier and told him to come over right at nine thirty. He'd arrive any minute, which meant Pete didn't have much time to get dressed and make a decision. He threw on the outfit he'd been planning in his head since that afternoon: jeans and a black sweater. It wasn't much, but he hoped Evan would appreciate his attempt.

He was just jamming impatient fingers through his unruly hair when the doorbell rang. It was time. He raced downstairs to the beat of his fluttering heart and flung the front door open. Evan was on the other side, looking delectable as always with his tousled hair and cheeks nibbled pink by the chill.

"Hey," Pete greeted him. "How are—"

Evan crossed the threshold and kissed the words from his lips. Pete closed his eyes and melded into him, sliding his arms around his neck. Evan shuffled them inside and kicked the door shut behind them. He leaned back against it and pulled Pete tightly to him. Any desire Pete had to go anywhere that night evaporated.

Evan gave Pete one more deep, lingering kiss before he pressed their foreheads together and breathed, "Hey."

"Wow," Pete murmured, dazed. "You're lucky my mom isn't home."

"Would she kick me out?"

"No, but I might spontaneously combust from embarrassment."

"Huh. Well, having a fire would be more romantic."

Chuckling, Pete wriggled out of his grasp. "Come on. I'll show you my room."

"Taking a boy upstairs while your mom's not home?" Evan purred. "What will the neighbors think?"

"They'll think I'm really gay, which is what they thought before. Hurry up."

Evan took his shoes off by the door, and Pete led the way upstairs. They only made it halfway up before Evan declared that Pete was moving his ass like that on purpose and pounced on him. Several minutes later, Pete asked Evan if he had any theories as to what Pete's room was like. As predicted, curiosity was the only thing that could distract Evan from sex.

Pete opened his door and led Evan in by the hand. Evan whistled as he entered the room, eyes shooting straight to Pete's bookshelf. "This isn't what I pictured, and yet it's exactly what I pictured."

"How so?" Pete tried not to fidget.

Evan laughed. "I don't know. I think I almost expected an actual library. I knew there would be books. Lots and lots of books, both text and fictional. And I expected it to be messy, because smart people are always messy."

"Are they?"

"Oh yeah. Everyone who's truly brilliant knows there's no point to making your bed if you're just going to get in it again."

Pete snorted. "That's *exactly* what I tell my mom. Like, verbatim."

Evan laced their fingers together. "I knew it. So, where are we going tonight?"

"I came up with a few ideas, but nothing solid. Do you have a preference?"

"Just one." He sat on Pete's bed and used their joined hands to tug him over. "We could stay in. I'm sure we can find some way to entertain ourselves." He waggled his eyebrows.

Pete smiled. "Sounds good to me."

Evan reached up and touched his chin, silently asking for another kiss. Pete stood between his legs and leaned down to give it to him. The first brush of Evan's skin against his gave him a familiar rush. He wondered if that would ever stop, or if he'd spend the rest of his life being slightly out of breath whenever Evan was near.

It was amazing to think how quickly their relationship had developed. Just weeks ago, Pete had wondered if Evan even wanted to kiss him. Now he took the opportunity to do so whenever possible. Thinking about it strengthened his resolve: it was time to tell Evan how he felt.

Before the kiss could deepen, Pete pulled away. "There's something I want to talk to you about."

"Oh?" Evan leaned back on the mattress, propping himself up on his elbows. "What's that?"

Pete's eyes slid down his body, and for a moment, he completely forgot what he was going to say. He had to look away before he remembered. "I've been thinking a lot lately. About us."

Evan sat up, concern tightening his brow. "Because of what happened at your job?"

"No, not at all. Well, I mean, kind of because of that, but not really. I just, uh . . ." He trailed off, uncertain of how he wanted to begin. He should have rehearsed this ahead of time. Or would it be worse if he sounded rehearsed? God, he sucked at this.

"You seem nervous." Evan eyed him. "You're not breaking up with me, are you?"

"What?" Pete screeched. "No!"

"Then what? Are you going to propose?"

For a full five seconds, Pete lost the ability to speak English. He had to rely on his one year of high school Spanish in order to reply, "No."

"Good." Evan laughed. "Just making sure. It's a bit early for that."

A bit early. Pete filed that away to fret about on some night when he really needed to sleep. "Just bear with me while I try to get this out without falling all over myself. I've been thinking about how far we've come in these past few weeks. We got off to a bit of a bumpy start, mostly thanks to me, and I think that you've, um—" He struggled to think of the right word. *Inspired*? Too cheesy. *Influenced*? That sounded kinda sinister. He settled on, "Changed me."

That was apparently the wrong choice, because Evan looked mildly alarmed. "That wasn't my intention. I like you just how you are. I don't want you to change at all."

"Not in a bad way," Pete clarified. "And I don't even necessarily mean that *you* changed me. It's more like you encouraged me to make changes I've been wanting to make."

"Like what?"

"Actually leaving my room, and being more gregarious."

"I suppose that's true. You're certainly not the same tentative man I vetted on Joyce's porch." He winked. "Though the vocabulary hasn't changed."

Pete knew he had a whole speech to get through, but he couldn't stop himself from arguing, "Hey, I had reasons for being tentative."

"Really now?" He smirked. "Please share with the class."

Pete opened his mouth only to shut it again. This was not the conversation he wanted to have right now. "I don't want to get into it. It's in the past."

"Oh come on, you can't leave me hanging like that. When we first met, I thought you were just shy, but now it sounds like there's a reason you were so skittish around me. What is it?"

Pete sighed. "You're not going to let this go are you?"

"Nope. Spill."

"Fine. This is really embarrassing, but"—Pete looked at his shoes—"when we first met, I, um, was so attracted to you, it actually freaked me out. I thought I had to be imagining the chemistry between us, and when you were all over me, that freaked me out even more. I assumed you were just doing your job, you know? Acting like you were into me. I was determined not to fall for it. Which, of course, I did."

"Aw," Evan cooed, "you liked me so much it scared you. That's charming."

Pete turned red and grumbled, "I knew I shouldn't have told you."

"I'm glad you did. I felt the same way."

Pete peeked at him. "You did?"

"Oh yeah. And for the record, there was never a time, not even a moment, when I had to pretend to be into you."

Pete's chest swelled with emotion. He cupped Evan's face and was about to segue back into his speech, when Evan leaned back and asked, "Is that really all it was, though? I remember you being more resistant than lovestruck in the beginning."

Pete thought about it. "Oh yeah. There was the ex thing too, but that was only in the very beginning. I got over it."

Evan cocked his head to the side. "Ex thing?"

"Yeah, you kinda look like this ex-boyfriend of mine. Or at least, I used to think so. On the day of the audition, Colette texted me a photo of you."

Evan chuckled. "Do you have a picture of him? I wanna see."

Pete shook his head. "I blocked him on Facebook."

"Ouch. He must've done a number on you."

"That's putting it lightly."

"You don't have a physical photo of him?"

"Um." For a second, Pete's mind was blank. Then a lightbulb went off above his head. "Actually, I do. It's one of those wallet ones from high school. He gave it to me forever ago, and I stuck it in my desk. I think it's still there."

Evan held out a hand. "Fork it over."

Pete hesitated. It seemed like a bad omen to talk about Christopher when he was supposed to be telling Evan he loved him. He crinkled his nose. "You really want to see a photo of my ex-boyfriend? There are more fun things we could be doing." He lidded his eyes and leaned in for another kiss.

Evan turned his cheek. "Don't you use your porn-star face on me. I'm withholding sex until you show me the picture."

"If I took my pants off right now, you'd crack in under a minute."

Evan frowned. "Probably. Just get the damn picture, okay?"

Grumbling under his breath, Pete opened the top drawer of his desk. He riffled through it and extracted a wallet-sized photo stuck in a corner beneath a pile of old essays. He placed it in Evan's outstretched hand.

"There now. Was that so hard?" Evan teased. He glanced at it. His smile froze on his face. Then it shifted into a grimace. "Pete . . . what the hell?"

"What?" Pete studied the photo. An olive-skinned man with dark brown eyes and shiny black hair looked up at them. As far as senior photos went, it wasn't the worst, but his smile was forced, and he'd gotten one of those horrible cloud backgrounds. The photo was the only keepsake that had survived Pete's postbreakup bonfire, which had also cost him part of his left eyebrow and a good chunk of his dignity.

When Evan failed to speak, Pete nudged him with his elbow. "What is it?"

"This guy looks a lot like me," Evan said slowly. His voice sounded strange.

"Eh, not really," he replied. "There's a resemblance, no denying it, but just at first glance. You're nothing like him." He tried to take the photo back, but Evan had a death grip on it.

Pete craned his head down until he could see Evan's face. He looked a little pale. Pete frowned. "What's wrong?"

Evan stood up, forcing Pete to back away from him. "What do you mean 'There's a resemblance'? This guy could be one of my brothers!"

Icy panic crept into Pete's veins. "Are you mad at me?"

"No!" Evan yelled. He flinched. "Pretend I said that at a normal volume. I'm just trying to process. It'd be one thing if he had my eyes or smiled like me or something, but this is more than that. When I'm famous, this guy should enter my celebrity-lookalike contest. He'd win hands down."

"Okay," Pete said, unsure of how to approach this. "I'm sorry I upset you. I didn't mean to." In fact, that was the opposite of what he was trying to do.

"I'm not *upset*. I'm . . . I don't even know." Evan rubbed his temples. "Obviously this isn't your fault, and I swear I'm not the jealous type, but now I'm thinking back on the night we met—which was a really significant event for me—and I keep remembering how you *looked* at me. At the time, I thought . . ." He trailed off and glanced at the photograph again. "And now I realize you were looking at me like that because you were seeing *him*."

"It's not like that," Pete argued. "I mean, it sort of is, but I swear, I haven't thought about him around you in forever. I don't *want* to think about him. You're completely different people."

"Yeah, you keep saying that, and that you don't see the similarities anymore, but I don't know how I'm supposed to believe you when *I* see it." He sat back down on the bed. "You didn't . . . you didn't try out for *Heat Wave* because of him, did you? Like, was that why you wanted to fuck me?"

"Of course not!" Annoyance made Pete's skin prickle. "Seriously? After all the times *you* tried to fuck *me*, and I said no, that's what you think I was doing?"

Evan's agitation cleared a bit. "Hmm, that's a good point."

"It certainly is!" Pete made an exasperated noise and wiped his mouth with a hand. "I can't believe you think I would do that. What about me screams evil mastermind to you? Is it my imposing figure or the way I hyperventilate when I have to call to schedule a doctor's appointment?"

Evan held up his hands in surrender. "Okay, okay, I'm sorry. Look, you said me and him are different, right?"

"He and I," Pete corrected just to be contrary.

"Right, that. Maybe if you explain to me what happened between you guys, it'll help me understand. You said he burned you, right?"

Pete stared at him. He hadn't told anyone about that night, not even his mom. "I don't want to talk about Christopher."

Evan favored him with a small smile. "If it's any consolation, I'm sure I'll take your side."

Pete didn't share his mirth. "It was ugly, okay? And really painful. I've been doing my best to block it out."

"I don't want to force you to talk about it, but it really sounds like you haven't moved on, and that doesn't make it easy for me to believe you when you say you have. Burying it and getting over it are different things."

Pete sighed. He was right. "Okay, but it's really upsetting. Be prepared."

Evan patted the bed next to him. "Just call me Scar."

Pete took the seat, fiddling with the photo in his hands. "Christopher and I dated for a semester."

"That's all? You made it sound like you guys were serious."

"How long have we known each other again?"

Evan shut his mouth with an audible click.

"Anyway, it was an intense semester. We were both freshman, and we thought we were *so* adult. We went to museums together and drank fancy coffee and talked about books, the whole pretentious college kid experience. He was on a full scholarship, and he was living it up. I was paying my own way, however, and had just started doing porn. I thought about quitting when I met him, but I really needed the money, and I thought he'd understand."

"Let me guess," Evan said, "he didn't understand."

Pete shook his head. "One night, we were sharing a bottle of wine in his dorm room, and it became clear he wanted to have sex for the first time. I get tested regularly, and I'd only been in a handful of films at that point, but in the interest of full disclosure, I decided to tell him about my side job. I thought . . . I don't even know. I thought maybe he'd feel special. I was trusting him with my big, shameful secret, after all. I thought maybe he'd think it was cool that he was dating a porn star. Back then, I had actual fans, and I was riding this self-esteem high." He laughed bitterly. "That didn't last."

Evan put an arm loosely around his waist, not holding, but showing that he was there. "What'd he do when you told him?"

"He threw the wine bottle at me."

Evan gasped, but Pete continued before he could comment. "It missed, but it scared the shit out of me. There was glass everywhere. He started yelling that I was disgusting, and he couldn't believe he'd touched me, and how he probably had all these diseases now. He called me a whore."

Pete's throat tightened. His voice came out tinny. "And you know what? As he was screaming, I wasn't even thinking about losing him. I was thinking about his neighbors, worrying that they would overhear him. It was only after the fight that I thought 'my boyfriend just dumped me.' I guess that shows where my priorities were."

Pete took a shallow breath. "Needless to say, that was the end of that. I was certain he'd tell the whole school, but I guess he was too mortified, because I never heard anything. I also never saw him again."

"Would you have wanted to?"

"Back then? Maybe. He was more or less my first love. I tried to call and explain myself a couple of times, but he'd reject my calls and then text horrible things to me. I mean, *really* nasty, degrading stuff. Eventually I realized he was a judgmental asshole, and I blocked him on everything. Good riddance."

Pete sighed, expecting to feel terrible, but he oddly felt better. Lighter. He glanced at Evan. "Well, that's the whole sordid tale. Thoughts?"

"You're right about him being an asshole." Evan kissed his shoulder. "I'm glad you told me about him."

"Does that mean you believe me when I say you're nothing alike?"

"Yeah, but that's not why I'm glad. Did that make you feel any better?"

"Yeah, actually. I should have talked about it sooner, I guess, but I couldn't have given anyone else the full story. So, thanks for that."

"It's my pleasure, believe me. I feel like I understand a lot of your complexes way better now. After being rejected like that, I can see why the idea of coming out is terrifying."

"Yeah, to say the least. I had nightmares for a month afterward where instead of Christopher, it was my mom screaming at me."

"Yikes." Evan brushed his side with his thumb soothingly. "If you don't mind my asking, why'd you keep doing porn? I would think that would totally turn you off of it."

"I still needed the money, and I have a stubborn streak. I knew I didn't deserve what he'd said to me, so I started to get angry. By continuing to be in porn, I was proving a point to both myself and to him. He was small-minded and wrong, and I wasn't going to let him control me, whether we were together or not."

"That's a relief." Evan pivoted toward him on the bed and took his hand. "Tell me again, and this time I'll believe you. You don't see him when you look at me?"

"No," Pete said. "There was a tiny part of me that wondered in the beginning if my attraction to you was so strong because of him, but it only took meeting you twice for me to realize that wasn't the case. My feelings are for *you*, not for him. If you'd been anything like him, I never would have given you the time of day."

Evan nodded. "Okay, I'm convinced. Sorry I overreacted."

"You didn't really. I should have told you forever ago."

"Maybe, but there's never really a right time to bring up evil exes." He held out his arms. "We good?"

Pete tucked himself into them and snuggled up to his chest. "We're very good."

Evan kissed his hair. "I'm proud of us! As far as first fights go, that was a breeze."

Pete laughed. "Especially given my track record."

"Definitely. I say this one wipes your record clean. Though I have to say, I'm a little surprised. I wasn't expecting this to go so smoothly."

"Really? Why?"

"Nothing in particular." He seemed to consider it. "I guess because you've always been a bit of a flight risk, so I thought our first fight would involve more drama."

Pete sat straight up and twisted around to look at him. "Why would you think that?"

"Just like you said before: we had a bumpy start. But you came around, and that's what matters." He smiled, probably to show he was joking, but Pete found it not the tiniest bit funny.

If you wanted drama, you're about to get it. "Maybe I was a flight risk in the beginning, but you were just as bad."

Evan looked affronted. "How the hell did you come to that conclusion?"

Pete struggled to keep his irritation in check. "You did this whole confusing back-and-forth dance with me. You were so hot and cold, I couldn't even tell if you liked me or not."

"What?" Evan asked, incredulous. "You're accusing *me* of dancing around? I even told Colette I felt like you were gonna bolt at any second. We had to have a backup on standby."

"You weren't exactly upfront either. The day we met, you laid the seduction on thick and then disappeared back into Joyce's house. You literally left me out in the cold."

Evan sniffed. "That was different. I didn't know you back then. I thought I was auditioning potential coworkers."

"And *then*," Pete continued, as if he hadn't spoken, "the first time we kissed, you ran off like you couldn't get away from me fast enough. Joyce told me later you looked terrified. What the fuck was that all about? I spent the next week thinking I'd hurt you somehow."

Evan pressed his lips into a thin line and didn't respond.

Sensing victory, Pete went in for the kill. "And to top it all off, when we finally got past that and had our first date, you said all these things about how you'd liked me from the start, but then you *didn't* ask me to go home with you. In fact, you left me out in the cold *again*. You've done this over and over: you get close to me only to pull away, and then you wonder why I'm too anxious to make a move."

Pete folded his arms over his chest. A vein stood out by Evan's jaw, like he was grinding his teeth. Pete waited for a snappy comeback.

Instead, Evan sighed. "Yeah, you're right."

"What?" Pete's arms dropped to his side. "Really?"

"Yup. I admit it. I jerked you around a bit in the beginning. I had my reasons too, but I won't ruin my apology by trying to justify myself. You have every right to be mad at me."

"I'm not *mad*," Pete clarified, "and I accept your apology. I only brought it up because you called me dramatic. *You* are dramatic, Evan Darko, and if you hadn't done your whole dancing-around thing, I might have realized sooner that I'm in love with y—"

Pete cut himself off with a gasp and clapped his hands over his mouth. He stared at Evan in horrified, postapocalyptic silence and mentally begged the words to crawl back into his mouth.

Evan's dark eyes got huge. "You . . . you what?"

"Nothing," Pete mumbled through his fingers, knowing it was to no avail.

Evan grabbed him by the shoulders and pulled him closer. "You love me?"

Pete considered not answering. There had to be some way he could melt into the floor instead. But judging by Evan's stricken facial expression, escape was futile.

Hands still covering his mouth, he nodded his head up and down.

Evan stared at him for a moment longer before taking hold of Pete's wrists. Gently, he pulled his hands away from his mouth. "You mean it?"

"Yes," Pete whispered miserably. "That's why I invited you over tonight. I wanted to tell you, but then we started fighting, and . . ."

"How long have you known? Since we had sex?"

"Since the bathroom at the Globe. I woke up in the middle of the night and just . . . knew."

Evan fell silent again.

Pete wished he would say something. He didn't necessarily need to say it back, but the intermittent silence was making his skin crawl.

He got his wish a second later.

Evan brushed a finger down his cheek and looked him square in the eye. "I've been in love with you since almost the day we met."

Pete's stomach fell out through the soles of his feet. "What? You're not just saying that, right? Because I said it?"

Evan shook his head. "I realized it the first time we kissed, corny as that sounds. That was why I freaked out and ran away at Joyce's house. I realized I was *dizzy* for you—a man I barely knew—and it freaked me out."

A memory came to Pete, as vivid as if he were watching it play out in front of him: Evan, standing outside of the Globe the first time they met there, just days after the shoot in question. He'd told Pete that he'd realized something, that it had scared him. Then he'd told him his real name.

God, Pete was dense.

Evan ran a thumb over Pete's bottom lip. "You believe me, right?"

Pete did. He really did. "Yes."

Thinking back on every interaction he'd had with Evan, he had no idea how he'd missed it. Christ, now that he thought about it, Evan was a *romantic*. Sending him song recs and goofy selfies, calling him in the middle of the night, and always saying, *I miss you*.

Much as Pete still thought his flair for the dramatic had led to undue anxiety, he realized now Evan had told him in a hundred different ways that he loved him, and Pete had been too insecure to see it.

"I'm so sorry," Pete said. "I've been oblivious."

Evan smiled. "Yeah, but I like you that way. And hey, we managed to get both our first and second fights out of the way."

Pete snorted. "Yeah, and we survived both. Compared to the last fight I had with a boyfriend, that was downright congenial."

Pete waited for him to say something. When he didn't, he looked at him.

Evan's eyes had gotten big again.

Pete watched him warily. "What?"

"Did you just say *boyfriend*?"

Pete rolled his eyes. "Dude, we're in love. I think it's safe to say we're officially dating now."

"I know," Evan chuckled. "I just wanna hear you say it."

"You're my boyfriend," Pete said with feigned exasperation. "I guess that means I'll be dealing with these sorts of demands all the time now, huh?"

"Oh yeah, and all the dramatic exits I can dish out. Sound good?"

"Sounds *excellent*." Pete moved closer, forcing Evan to crane his neck up to look at him. "So, boyfriend, about staying in tonight . . ."

A smile slid across Evan's face and settled there. "You read my mind."

CHAPTER  17

After a vigorous and frankly imaginative round of make-up sex, they hung out in bed, talking and laughing, until 10 p.m. rolled around. Pete suggested they either call it a night or migrate to Evan's place. His mom would be home soon, and while he'd love for Evan to meet her, he'd rather not do it when they both reeked of sex.

Evan proceeded to wrap himself around Pete like a four-armed octopus and demand that they stay together. Pete relented under fear of being squashed to death by someone who loved him, though he supposed there were worst fates.

They got dressed, which inspired another round of demands from Evan—"You have to get naked the *second* we get home"—and this time Pete remembered to leave a note for his Mom. He tossed the hastily scrawled message onto the counter and left without looking back: *With the Boyfriend™. Can't wait for you meet him. Love you.*

Evan drove them to his place, and when they arrived at the apartment, they made it all of three steps in before they were undressing again, Scout and Sentry batting at their ankles. Somehow, they ended up in the cramped kitchen. It was Evan's turn to get crowded against the sink while Pete wrapped long fingers around them both and got them off in record time.

"Fuck," Evan panted after, bleary with postorgasm hormones, "I love your hands. And your eyes. And *you.*"

Pete couldn't remember ever smiling so much.

Their domestic bliss lasted all through the night and halfway through Evan making pancakes the next morning. Then, Evan's phone vibrated on the tiny breakfast table shoved into the corner. They ignored it, busy as they were shoving food into their mouths. Until Pete's phone buzzed next.

They shared a look across the table. Only one person would be trying to reach them both.

"Maybe she'll give up," Evan suggested.

"Oh yeah," Pete said, "and maybe Thelma and Louise were just really good friends."

Sure enough, when Pete's phone stopped ringing, Evan's started again.

He snatched it up and cradled it between his shoulder and ear. "Morning, Colette." He continued eating, but after a moment, he swallowed hastily and asked, "Why?"

Pete mouthed, *What's she saying?* But Evan waved him off.

More silence followed. Whatever Colette was talking about, it must have been involved. Pete tried to edge close enough to hear, but Evan casually leaned away from him.

He glared at him and fidgeted in his seat. Worst-case scenarios flashed through his brain: someone had died. Murmur Inc. had burned down. *Heat Wave* had received horrible reviews before it was even released. Or most likely, she'd found out about them somehow.

By the time Evan hung up, Pete had worked himself into a dry-mouthed panic.

He watched as Evan set his phone back down on the table, squirted some more syrup onto his stack, and took another bite, all without so much as glancing at Pete.

"Well?" Pete demanded.

Evan chewed, swallowed, and said, "That was Colette."

"Evan, darling," Pete said sweetly, "will you pass me a butter knife so I can *stab you with it.*"

"Sorry. She wants us to come down to Murmur Inc. as soon as possible."

"Why?"

"I don't know."

"How can you not know? She talked a *lot.*"

"She said she has something to show us. And as much as I hate to tell you this, because I know you're gonna freak out—" he fiddled with his fork, rolling it between his fingers "—she knew we were together."

Pete went rigid. "How?"

"I don't know, but when I answered the phone, the first thing she said was 'Tell Jaden that if he ever ignores my calls again, I will upload an outtakes reel of all his most embarrassing bloopers onto the homepage of Murmur Inc.'s website.'"

Pete blanched. "Jesus."

"Yeah, and then she said to get our perky butts—her words, not mine—down to the studio. I asked why, and she sort of rambled on about production this and marketing that, and . . . I admittedly zoned out a little."

"Right." Pete rubbed his temples. "So, we got called into the principal's office, is what you're telling me."

"Yeah. It obviously has something to do with *Heat Wave*." Evan looked at him sideways. "It could be nothing, you know."

"Or it could be something."

"What could she do to us now? Filming has pretty much wrapped."

"She could fire us. She told us from day one that *Heat Wave* was her baby. If she knows we started dating during production, even though that could jeopardize our on-screen chemistry, she could be furious. She might never work with us again."

Evan set his fork down and reached across the table, covering Pete's hand with his own. "It's going to be okay."

"I'm more worried about you than me. I never planned to be in porn forever anyway, but this is your dream, and you're new to the industry. Losing Murmur Inc. as a client this early in the game could be a career killer for you."

"I think you're overreacting a tiny bit. Remember: Murmur Inc. doesn't have any policies against office romances. And heartless business executive or not, Colette cares about the well-being of her people. She wants us to be happy and healthy. We didn't do anything wrong, and we *didn't* ruin her film. I don't think she'll screw us over just because."

"Okay." Pete glanced at him. "You're really not worried at all?"

"Nah. I try not to stress about hypotheticals. Maybe she'll fire us; maybe she won't. Maybe we'll get hit by a bus. Maybe you'll end up becoming the next Steve Jobs, and I'll be your trophy husband. Who knows? The point is"—he squeezed Pete's hand—"we're in this *together*."

Pete laced their fingers together. "Of course."

They finished eating breakfast, and after a brief interlude in which they petted Evan's cats into submission, they headed out. When they pulled into Murmur Inc.'s parking lot, it was surprisingly busy. Colette must've been recruiting, because a dozen twentysomethings were smoking by the side entrance. The way they huddled together and looked over their shoulders every five seconds said it all: nervous and new. It made Pete a little nostalgic. He smiled at them, took Evan's hand, and sailed past them to the side door.

They made their way up to the third floor, pulling apart just before they entered the main room. The office was as busy as ever. Pete almost took comfort in the familiarity of the moaning voices and the business-casual dress mixed with people in lingerie and latex. He was about to head for the recording booths—where Colette was waiting for them—when he spotted a familiar figure perching on a desk.

"J-Joyce?" he stammered, eyes wide.

Miraculously, she heard him over the din and looked up. Sure enough, it was Joyce, decked out from head to toe in pink lace. Six-inch black heels peeked out from beneath her long, folded legs. Her blonde hair had been stacked on top of her head, and her makeup seemed like it had been professionally done. She looked completely glamorous.

"Jaden!" she chirped, beaming. "What a lovely surprise. And Kyle too."

"Hey, Joyce," Evan said with a nod. He didn't look half as surprised as Pete felt.

"It's Kitten now," she said with a smile.

"Kitten," Pete repeated. "Nice choice. What are you doing here?"

"Can't you tell? I decided to give porn a try after all."

He shrugged. "I didn't want to assume anything. What made up your mind?"

"Colette finally talked me into it. Or at least, that's my story. In truth, I was the one who called her." She picked up a black riding crop from the desk and pointed it at Pete's chest. "You had a hand in my decision as well, actually."

"I always suspected I was a bad influence."

She laughed, and there was such genuine joy on her face, Pete smiled back.

"I'm serious. If it hadn't been for that talk we had when I first let Colette use my house, I don't know if I would have been brave enough to go through with it."

"Really? I feel like I made porn sound like a rough gig."

"You did, but I needed someone to be honest with me. If I'd walked in here expecting a fantasy, I would have been disillusioned within minutes. Now, I know to look at this as an opportunity to explore a part of myself I'd been holding back, and to share it with my fans. Which I already have quite a few of." She winked.

"I'm glad to hear that. I'm sure you'll be enormously successful. We have a meeting with Colette right now, but maybe we can chat more when we're finished?"

"I'm walking into a shoot in a couple of minutes, but don't worry, you'll be seeing a lot of me." She climbed to her feet, waved good-bye, and sashayed off toward the stairwell.

Pete watched her go, a strange emotion filling his chest.

Evan nudged him with his elbow. "What is it?"

"I'm not sure. I think . . . I guess I see some of myself in Joyce—Kitten. Only I think she's getting into porn for the right reasons, whereas I didn't."

"What do you mean?"

"Well, lots of us are in it for the money, right? I am too, but I also took this job because I thought porn would fix something about me that I didn't like."

"What?"

He grimaced. "Not to get all psychological or whatever, but I thought porn would help me be more confident, and it did for a while, but it was a temporary solution. I needed to push myself and not rely on porn or Colette or even you. I think Joyce is doing this for reasons that are sort of like mine only way healthier, and she'll be a lot more successful. You know?"

Evan nodded solemnly. "I do. Now, tell me about your mother, Freud."

"Hilarious. Does that make sense, though?"

Evan looked around and then gave Pete a quick peck. "It does. I'm glad for whatever part I had in your breakthrough."

"Me too. Come on. If we keep Colette waiting, she'll fire us regardless."

They made their way to Booth One and walked into a scene that was in full swing. A man and a woman were writhing together on a chaise staged in the center of a fake bedroom. Cameras hovered all around them like shiny black bugs. The man was sucking on the woman's nipples while she moaned rapturously, her curled hair spread out like a halo and her legs wrapped around him, each foot ending in a pointed toe.

"She's good," Evan murmured to Pete. "He needs to watch how he angles his face, though. You can barely see him."

Pete nodded. "Amateurs. Am I right?"

Someone tapped Pete on the shoulder. "It's about time you showed up." Colette.

He spun around. "I was wondering where you were. Not directing this one?"

"Of course not," she said smugly. "If I were, it wouldn't look like Jake is giving Brandy a mammogram."

"It's so hard to find good help these days," Evan lamented.

"Enough chitchat. I called you both here today for a reason. Care to venture a guess?"

Pete only half registered what she said, busy as he was watching Jake bury his face deeply between Brandy's legs. There was something weirdly enrapturing about it. "Um, sorry, what?"

"Just follow me." She led them across the room, carefully avoiding getting caught in the camera angles. She opened a wooden door and ushered them into an office. It wasn't her office; Pete had been there once before on the day he'd signed up to work for Murmur Inc., and it was both bigger and much more intimidating.

"This is Yolanda's," Colette explained without prompting. "She wanted to be here for this, but I needed her elsewhere. Have a seat." She gestured at two chairs across from the desk. They took them without a word.

There was an impressive desktop computer in the corner, sleek and no thicker than Pete's little finger. Colette touched the wireless mouse to wake it and then swiveled the screen to face them.

"It's not *totally* finished yet," she began, tapping a key on the keyboard, "but I can share the highlights with you now that the footage has been processed, and the music accompaniments have been added."

She clicked on a video file on the desktop, and a black screen popped up. A film Pete would have recognized anywhere began playing.

"*Heat Wave*," Evan said needlessly. "I didn't think it would be ready so soon."

"Like I said, there's still work to be done, but I wanted you both to see the fruits of your labor." She skipped the requisite adult content disclaimer in the beginning and jumped to the first scene: Pete and Evan standing together in Joyce's living room. It was bizarre. Pete knew the footage had only been taken a couple of weeks ago, but he thought he looked completely different. Younger. And visibly unnerved by the beautiful man standing next to him.

Evan experienced a sudden coughing fit. Pete would have bet money he was covering a chuckle.

Colette skipped to the kiss—which was as intoxicating as Pete remembered—and then to the handjob scene. Pete tried not to squirm in his seat. The film was *hot*. The raw footage they'd seen previously had been good, but now that the lighting and saturation had been adjusted, it looked like a real movie. It was vivid and spine-chilling. And the soft music in the background added just the right atmosphere.

It was more than that, though. As Colette skipped through more of the film to the final scene at the end—the afternoon date in the park—Pete realized there were definite aspects of art imitating life. He could see himself growing more relaxed around Evan with every scene change. In some places, he even swore he could see himself falling in love with him.

And Evan . . . Evan was mesmerizing. Now that Pete knew what to look for, he saw again that Evan had told the truth about loving him from the start. It was evident in the softness of his eyes when he looked at him, at the carefulness of his touch. Even when they were having sex, there was something deeper there, something that all the good acting in the world couldn't replicate.

"Wow," Pete breathed. "Ev—Kyle, you look amazing."

"I know his real name," Colette said calmly. "No need to hide it from me. Though I wasn't sure if *you* knew it until just now."

Whoops.

Evan chimed in. "You look pretty phenomenal yourself, Jaden. And your performance was spectacular."

Pete played it modest to compensate for his blunder. "Not at all. I was just trying to keep up with you."

Evan had a tender smile on his face. One of his hands flexed on his knee, and Pete suspected he was resisting the urge to reach out and touch him. "I thought you were unforgettable."

"Oh God," Colette interrupted, groaning, "you two are totally dating."

Pete's head snapped toward her. Fuck, were they that obvious? "Uh."

"Well . . ." Evan began, dragging the word out.

"That wasn't a question," Colette snapped. She pinched the bridge of her nose, took a deep breath, and then slumped in her chair like a marionette whose strings had been cut.

Oh shit, Pete thought. *Here it comes.*

"It's really not that big of a deal." Evan's tone was more than a little impertinent.

Pete shushed him. "Don't make her mad."

He shrugged. "Well, it's not."

"Porn stars," Colette groused, covering her face with her hands. "You'd think people who have sex all day would be better at keeping it in their pants. I've said it once, and I'll say it again: I lose my best actors to love."

"You haven't lost us," Pete piped up. "We're not quitting or anything."

Colette's fingers parted, and one long-lashed eye peeked at them. "You're not?"

"Of course not. Why would you think that?"

"Happens all the time. It's common enough for porn stars to date each other, or date people in the industry, and when things get serious, usually someone demands that someone else quit. Or they both demand it. Or they decide together that they don't want to sleep with anyone else. Whatever the case, it's bad for business."

"Is that why you tried to scare Jaden straight in the beginning?" Evan asked. He cocked his head. "Well, I suppose 'straight' isn't the right word."

Colette rubbed her temples. "I wasn't trying to *scare* him. Please believe me when I say I'm not mothering anyone. But if I see a crush forming on set, and I think it'll create problems, I discourage it. I'm not ashamed to admit it."

"Why would you think that, though?" Pete asked. "I mean, obviously if we'd broken up, things might have been awkward, but why were you so worried about that happening?"

"I will admit it wasn't strictly business. There was an element of concern to my threats."

Pete smiled. "You were worried about me?"

She eyed him. "Not in so many words. I know Darko's a good guy. I just saw the way you two were around each other and thought, 'This is going to be one of those ill-advised, on-screen romances that burns hot at first but ends with the actors hating each other.' I've been in this business a long time, and I've seen it happen." She looked thoughtfully at them. "I think I might have been wrong, though. Clearly I don't know you two as well as I thought. Especially you, Jaden."

Pete thought he understood what she was getting at. "Thank you. Does that mean I was never in any danger of being fired?"

"Oh no, you absolutely were. If things had gone sour between you two in the beginning, I would have replaced you." She sat up in her seat and folded her hands on the surface of the desk, once more the no-nonsense business executive. "I need to cut this therapy session short and get to business. Bear in mind, for being considered 'low budget,' porn is still expensive to produce. You two are going to have to do promos and events together, whether you break up tomorrow or not. Understand?"

"Understood," Pete confirmed.

"If it's any consolation," Evan added, "we've been getting along splendidly. All night, in fact."

Pete turned red.

Colette rolled her eyes. "I didn't start this project so I could cast you two in your own personal love story. Although"—her expression went from irritated to contemplative in a flash—"that would be an interesting marketing avenue. 'Watch this on-screen flame transform into a real-life romance.' It's so meta. I dunno if it's ever been done before."

"Don't turn our love into a marketing campaign," Pete chastised. "Actually, you don't need to. I have it on good authority that your ads are working just fine."

Colette raised an immaculate eyebrow. "Oh?"

"Yeah, a friend of mine saw one the other day and showed it to me."

"Did they now?" Colette asked, perking up. "Did they happen to say which site it was on? Because if we know where our targeted marketing is most effective, we can allocate a larger portion of our marketing budget to—" She stopped, eyes widening. "Wait, you're not out, right? Not like Darko is anyway."

"Nope," Pete said emphatically. "It finally happened. Someone I know in real life found me out there in cyberspace."

"Oof. That's rough, buddy. You okay?"

"Yeah, but I'd appreciate it if you wouldn't make this anymore personal by plastering our love lives all over your ads."

"Fine. I'll table that idea. For now. Which brings me to my next question." She folded her hands on the surface of the desk. "What am I going to do with you both?"

They looked at each other. Evan shrugged. Pete turned back to Colette. "What do you mean?"

"You're not under contract." Her eyes moved between them. "You're free to work or not work as many jobs as you want. That means if you don't want to work with anyone but each other, you can make that happen. But understand, eventually your job opportunities will dry up. Your audience is always craving new faces, new positions, new highs. And as much as I like you both, when you stop making me money, it's over."

"We understand that," Pete said.

"Then what are you going to do?"

"We're still figuring that out," Evan said. "I want to be a director ultimately, and Pete's only doing this until he graduates, so starring in porn forever was never the plan for either of us."

"Have you considered cam work?"

Evan gave her an odd look. "Why would we go from big screen to small? Isn't that like a step backward?"

"Actually, no," Pete interjected. "Cam work might not have the same production value as studio porn, but it's more interactive, and you can make your own schedule. It has pros and cons like any other job."

Evan looked impressed. "And here I thought I was the industry expert."

"Jaden is right. Cam work would give you more flexibility, and you'd be allowed to work solo, or exclusively with each other. One of my PSOs just started a channel with her girlfriend, actually. Jaden, you may remember Alexa from your early days. Her channel, Poster Girls, is one of our most popular."

"Oh yeah. Glad to hear she's doing well." He turned to Evan. "That's something to think about. We could have our own channel too. I hear they're the new hot thing."

"Really?"

"Yeah, it's like reality TV, only with lots of sex. Real couples letting people peek inside their bedrooms."

Evan glanced at Colette. "You think that's something we could do?"

"Sure," she said. "I just filmed a whole movie about you. That's pretty solid proof right there that I think people are gonna tune in."

He looked back to Pete. "You really like the idea?"

"Yeah. I wouldn't have to worry about working around school, and we wouldn't have to have sex with other people, which would be safer. What do you think?"

"I dunno." He rubbed his chin. "It seems pretty radical."

"Does it?"

"Yeah. I mean, you want us to have sex? On camera? *For money*? Perish the thought!"

Pete rolled his eyes so far heavenward, he thought he spotted a cherub.

Evan slung an arm around him. "No, but seriously, I think that sounds great. We're going to be having a lot of sex anyway. Might as well profit from it. The only question is, what would we call our channel?"

Pete thought about it. "How about 'StarX,' pronounced 'Star Cross'? Like star-crossed lovers. You know, because of our fateful meeting. Plus we're porn stars, and you're into astronomy, and I'm religious. It'd be like an inside joke with a little bit of both of us."

Evan's smile was scintillating. "I love it."

Colette nodded. "Very well. I'm sure we can work something out. I'd normally make new cam stars audition, but considering my familiarity with your work, I think we can find a spot for your channel."

Pete almost couldn't believe it. "You're being awfully accommodating."

Colette sighed. "I know. I hate it. But if *Heat Wave* is as big of a hit as I anticipate, you two are going to be in demand. I need you happy and ready to promo the shit out of it. And if that means catering to a few demands, so be it. Actually, that brings up another point I wanted to discuss with you."

She hit Enter on the keyboard again, and their final sex scene began to play in the middle of a particularly provocative part. Pete willed himself not to get hard as he watched Evan fuck him with a vengeance while he gripped the picnic blanket for dear life.

"This scene," she said, pointing to it, "is hot, but like I told you before, it doesn't seem like a first time. Even with the additional footage we shot, it sort of throws off the whole vibe of the earlier storyline. I think the film would benefit from filming another 'first' time. Something intimate. Something we can splice in before the park scene. Make sense?"

"I'm down for that," Evan said, grinning and folding his arms behind his head.

"*Quelle surprise*," Colette intoned. She looked to Pete. "What about you?"

"Yeah. I mean, if it'll help the film, I'll let you talk me into it." He tried to look innocent, but it must not have worked, because Evan snickered.

Colette sighed wearily and said again, "Porn stars."

CHAPTER  18

The day of Pete's birthday party dawned sunny and unseasonably warm. And since they lived in California, that was truly saying something. It almost felt like summer outside. Pete was able to wear the costume he'd planned on ever since Sana had talked him into a nineties theme: Quailman from *Doug*. He already owned a green sweater vest, and the underwear over the pants was self-explanatory. Getting the belt around his head to stand up, however, had taken a lot of patience and bendy wire.

Pete had tried to talk Evan into being Patti Mayonnaise, but Evan had assured him that he already had something in mind. When probed, he refused to give any hints. Whatever it was, Pete was certain it would make an impression.

Mom was a huge help, assisting with cleaning the house even when he begged her to let him do it. She also bought themed snacks: Nerds, Gushers, Pixy Stix, and Hi-C. And of course, there was plenty of booze.

"Mom," Pete said, as he nudged a bottle of Jameson closer to a bottle of Bombay Sapphire, "did you get some sort of discount for buying the entire liquor store?"

"Did I go a little overboard?" she called from the kitchen, where she was pulling Jell-O shots out of their fridge. She was dressed as Smee from *Hook*, complete with round glasses and a fetching fake gray beard.

"I'm expecting them to declare you lost at sea any minute now."

"You only turn twenty-one once, and if you remember it, you did it wrong." She emerged from the kitchen bearing three trays of little cups stacked on top of each other. She went to place them on the dining room table but couldn't find room between the craft beer and the various bottles of wine. "Hmm. Maybe I did overdo it a bit."

"I should say so. I'm not even a drinker."

"But you could be! Never sell yourself short, kiddo. You can be anything you set your mind to."

"Thanks, Mom. Your faith in me is . . . distressing."

There was a knock on the door, and Pete went to answer it. Raj was on the other side, dressed in white platform boots, bell-bottom jeans, and a shirt with the Union Jack on it. His dark hair was in twin pigtails on the sides of his head.

"Um," Pete said, "Cindy Brady?"

"I'm Baby Spice, you uncultured swine. Besides, *The Brady Bunch* first aired in the sixties." He jostled his way into the house. "Hey, Momma Griflow! Or should I say *captain*?"

"First mate, actually." She wrapped Raj in a hug. "Good to see you again. How's school going?"

Raj grabbed the Jameson off the table, unscrewed the cap, and took a swig straight from the bottle.

Mom nodded. "Sounds about right."

Raj launched into a detailed explanation of how he would murder half of their professors and make it look like an accident while Mom listened rapturously. Pete went to close the front door, but a purple heel blocked him.

"Rude," Sana said mildly, poking her head through the door. "And here I brought you the good stuff." She brandished a bottle of expensive whiskey in each hand.

"Hey!" Pete greeted. "You made it. I'm so happy to see—"

Joshua's blond head appeared above hers. "Hey, flamer."

". . . Sana, what did I ever do to you?"

"Sorry, but he overheard me talking about your party and insisted on coming." She pushed the door open and walked in. "I could have trussed him up and left him in the back of the Globe, but Mr. Hamm says I'm not allowed to do that anymore."

"Why ever not?" Pete teased.

"Something about 'fostering a positive work environment built on trust and mutual respect.' I knew I shouldn't have let him read those HR pamphlets."

Her hijab was bright orange today, and she had a green scarf tied around her neck. A purple, ankle-length dress and matching heels completed the look. It took Pete a moment to place her, but then it dawned on him: Daphne, from Scooby-Doo.

"Jinkies." Pete kissed her cheek. "You look great."

"So do you, but now I'm craving pork chops."

Joshua shuffled in after her. "Happy birthday." He handed Pete a bottle of wine.

"Uh, thanks." Pete eyed Joshua suspiciously. "Who are you supposed to be? You look just like you did that night at the club."

"I'm a raver. Doesn't get more nineties than that."

"Touché."

He put Joshua's bottle of wine on the table with the others and then helped Sana find a spot for her whiskey. "I think it's safe to say we have enough alcohol."

"I'll be the judge of that," said a voice that Pete instantly recognized.

"Evan," he said, turning around, "I guess I forgot to shut the do—" He stopped short, his mouth watering.

Evan was standing in the doorway in head-to-toe, form-fitting, green and white spandex. A motorcycle helmet that had been spray-painted green and gold was tucked under his arm. Gold bands decorated his wrists, and his white boots had a noticeable heel.

"A Power Ranger," Pete said. "You're the Green Ranger, right? I thought you were into comic book heroes?"

Evan clicked his way across the wood floors. Thanks to his shoes, they were nearly eye level. "My interests are diverse, thank you very much." He revolved in place. "What do you think?"

Skintight was not a bad look for Evan at all. The spandex clung to his ass in a way that made Pete want to ditch his own party. Even the heels were weirdly hot. Pete was going to have to examine that later. "I think you look great, but just to be sure, is this really how you want to meet my mother for the first time?"

"Trust me, it's best she knows what she's getting into from the start."

Pete glanced nervously at Mom. His worries were unfounded; a smile had overtaken her face at the sight of Evan. "Great costume!

I assume you're the boyfriend I've heard so much about. I think Pete said your name is Evan? Or shall I call you Dr. Tommy Oliver?"

"Dude," Evan said, nudging Pete, "you didn't tell me your mom is *awesome*."

"Yeah, she knows a lot about Power Rangers. I actually had a crush on the Green Ranger when I was a kid."

"Did you now?" Evan grinned. "Then I chose my costume well." He approached Mom and stuck out his hand. "Evan Darko. A pleasure."

"Mom," she replied, taking his hand. "Charmed. How did you and Pete meet?"

"It's a fascinating story," Joshua piped up.

Pete mustered his best venomous look and lobbed it at him. Joshua recoiled behind Sana, who promptly stamped on his foot with her purple heels.

As his sobs reverberated in the background, Evan replied, "We met through mutual friends."

It wasn't a complete lie. Colette was sort of a friend.

"Are you in school?"

"No, I work."

"What do you do?"

Evan glanced at Pete, asking a silent question with his eyes.

Pete sighed. Here came the moment of truth. Evan had made it clear from day one that he had no intention of lying about what he did for a living. Before the party, they'd reached a compromise: Evan didn't have to lie, but he also didn't need to go into detail.

All Pete could do now was pray his mom was as open-minded as he thought. "Go ahead, Evan. Tell her what you do."

Evan's relieved smile almost made the impending embarrassment worth it. Almost.

"I will tell you all about it," Evan said. "But first, will you show me where I can get some ice?"

"Sure thing. The kitchen's right over here."

She led him away. Evan looked over his shoulder and gave Pete a thumbs-up. Pete itched to follow them. Actually, if it were an option, he'd perch on Evan's shoulder like a gargoyle and listen to every word. But he supposed he'd just have to trust Evan to break the news gently.

It was a good sign that he'd thought to take her aside. Sana and Joshua already knew, but Raj didn't.

Pete supposed now was as good a time as any to tell him. Raj was standing over by the dining room table, examining the label on a bottle of champagne. Sana and Joshua were busy arguing about something he couldn't quite hear—coffee? Or car keys? Possibly anarchy—and so he was able to sidle up to Raj without feeling like he was neglecting them.

"How much alcohol is in champagne?" Raj asked without looking up.

"I dunno. I think it's not that much, but the bubbles make it seem like more."

"Excellent. Want some of this?"

"Sure, but first I want to talk to you about something."

Raj finally looked up. "Is it your hot boyfriend? He is hot, by the way. From a totally objective, straight-guy perspective, you hit the jackpot."

"Yeah, I did." Pete smiled. "And he's sweet and smart and funny too."

"Does he have a sister?"

"Um, yeah, actually. Like three of them."

"Score!" He glanced around the room. "Where's your mom? I promised her some of this."

"She's with Evan in the kitchen. He's breaking the news of what he does for a living to her."

"Oh God," Raj said. "Does he sell knives door to door? Is he a ukelelist in a folk band? Does he model for those weird stock images of attractive people eating salads?"

"Not nearly that bad," Pete assured him. "You know how I had all those misgivings about him in the beginning?"

"Of course. Was his job a part of that?"

"Sort of. See, he—"

Raj held up a hand. "Pete, I'm going to stop you right there. As someone who has watched you bumble your way through this romance from the beginning, it's my expert opinion that you're focusing way too much on things that don't matter."

"Okay, yeah. That's probably true, but I still need to tell you. He—"

"Nuh-uh. I don't care what your boyfriend does. You know what I care about?"

"What?"

"Does he love you?"

Pete answered without hesitation. "Yes."

"Do you love him?"

"Yes," he said just as quickly, but with a lot more blushing.

"Then fuck literally everything else," Raj said cheerfully. "As long as you're happy, I'm happy. And if he's good to you and treats you right, he can be one of those creepy party clowns for all I care. Now let's drink some champagne."

"Raj, you're the best."

Pete's happiness was temporary, however, because a second later his mom walked back into the room, looking dazed. Evan trailed behind her. Pete caught his eye. He shrugged and then shook his head.

Uh-oh.

Mom stopped a few feet away from him and jerked her head toward the other side of the room. "Pete, may I speak to you for a moment?"

"Okay." He followed her to the window.

Raj, bless him, appeared by her side long enough to press a glass of champagne into her hand before disappearing again.

Mom took a sip and then fixed him in her steady brown gaze. "Do you know what your boyfriend just told me in the kitchen?"

"Yes." He shifted his weight from foot to foot. "I've known what he does from the start."

"And you're all right with it?"

"Yes."

She looked hard at him. "You don't think there's anything morally wrong with it? You don't think he's cheating on you every time he's in one of those—" she made a sour face "—movies?"

Pete took a deep breath. As many times as he'd rehearsed his answer in his head, it didn't make it any easier to say out loud. His tongue felt like it was glued to the roof of his mouth. It was the truth, however, and it needed to be said.

"Honestly, no, I don't think it's wrong, and I don't think it's cheating." Pete was shocked by how steady his voice sounded.

Mom started to interrupt, but he stopped her. "Evan's job is just a job. It's how he earns a living. He knows how to separate work from his personal life. I trust him, which is way more important than what he does. And what's moral or immoral is completely subjective. When I was a kid, being gay was considered immoral. It still is in a lot of places. Hell, being a single parent like you used to be a big scandal." He shrugged. "Seems silly to cling to an idea of what a relationship should be like instead of enjoying the one I have."

He fell silent, scouring his mom's face for clues as to her reaction. Unfortunately, she had a poker face like no other. Why couldn't he have inherited that from her?

If it came down to it, he knew what he had to do. He hoped he'd never have to tell her, but he couldn't let her judge Evan in front of him. If she rejected Evan, he'd come clean. It might change their relationship forever, but it had to be done. Letting her condemn Evan for the same work he did would make him the worst sort of hypocrite. This was his chance to prove to Evan that he could be strong. And, more importantly, to prove it to himself.

Mom was excruciatingly silent. At one point, she lifted her glass and took a long drink from it. She wiped her mouth with the back of her hand, and still she didn't speak.

Pete cracked like a weak password. "Well?"

"Well," she said simply, "I guess that's that." She waved to Evan, who had been hovering ten feet away the whole time as if he were attached to an invisible tether. "You can come over now."

Evan inched closer. "Am I still invited to the party?" His tone was simultaneously playful and serious.

"Of course you are. You're my son's boyfriend. And your job sounds . . . um, very fascinating. And, uh, lucrative, I imagine."

Pete had to hand it to her, she was putting on a good show.

"It is," Evan said. He arranged a thousand-watt smile on his face, and Mom instantly smiled back. He was hard to resist when he turned on the charm. "It's a solid career. There's very little chance that I'll ever be out of a job."

"That's true. And with Pete here studying computer science, it sounds like you're both heading into in-demand fields."

Pete looked her up and down. "You're taking this well."

Mom let out a tight breath. "I suppose I can't cast stones. Not in this glass house. Besides, I raised you to do what you think is right, and it sounds like you've done exactly that. You're an adult. I trust your judgment."

"That's great," Pete said, relieved. "I was worried you would—" He stopped and replayed her words in his head. "Wait, what about glass houses?"

She stared at him again, brow scrunched in concentration, like she was trying to read something on his face. Then she sighed. "I suppose you're old enough now to know. Remember when I told you we didn't have much growing up? Me and your grandparents and your aunt Caren?"

"Yeah," Pete answered. He had the strangest urge to brace himself. Or take a seat. Or both.

"Well, your grandparents could barely put food on the table, let alone save for college. They managed to set some money aside for Caren, since she was older, but if I wanted to go, I had to pay my own way."

Horrific realization dawned on Pete. "Oh God. Are you going to say what I think you're going to say?"

She shrugged. "I paid for nursing school by stripping. A couple of the girls I had class with were putting themselves through college that way, and they always had so much cash, I decided to give it a try. It was very empowering."

Pete stared blankly into space. "Oh my God, my mom was a stripper."

"Hey, I'm not the one who's dating a porn star." She clapped him on the back. "Although, now that I think about it, I met your father at the club I worked at. He was a regular. Looks like the apple doesn't fall far from the tree."

You have no idea.

Pete wrestled with his feelings. "I guess I'm glad you understand, although finding out your mom was a stripper on your birthday in front of all your friends and your new boyfriend seems like one of those things that could traumatize a child."

"Don't worry," Raj called from across the room. "We totally didn't hear that. In fact, we couldn't hear a word you guys said."

"This party is off to an interesting start," Sana said.

"I am so *glad* I decided to come!" Joshua squealed, clapping his hands together.

Sana "accidentally" elbowed him in the ribs.

Pete would have to remember to get her a World's Best Boss mug or something. Speaking of which.

"Someone give me one of my presents," Pete said. "I've just been through an ordeal, and I need alcohol."

Sana helpfully supplied him with a plastic cup filled to the brim with whiskey and then raised her water glass. "To Pete!"

"To Pete!"

Everyone touched glasses.

Pete took a big gulp and coughed so hard he had to set it down. "I get the feeling turning twenty-one is going to be my first step toward never drinking."

Evan snaked an arm around his waist. "You're not missing out on much. Though I'd like to take you out drinking sometime. I owe you a legal beer."

"I think I can manage that," Pete agreed, taking another sip from his cup.

Evan laughed and, after setting his helmet down, took Pete by the hands and tugged him a few feet away from the others. "I got you a present."

"Is it more booze?" Pete was already feeling light on his feet. "Because we have a *lot* of that."

"It probably should have been, in keeping with the true spirit of a twenty-first birthday, but—" he pulled a thin package out from behind his back "—I actually got you something else."

Pete eyed his skintight outfit. "Where were you keeping that?"

"Just open it."

Pete took the package from him. It had been carefully but somewhat clumsily wrapped in blue paper with a pattern of yellow balloons. It was so adorable and obviously homemade, Pete had to bite his cheek to keep from smiling.

He ripped the paper off, revealing a simple black and silver picture frame. Inside was the photo of Evan and him from their "date" at Griffith Park. It was as bright and summery as he remembered. He and Evan stood out in sharp relief against the green grass. Evan's eyes were closed, his lips pressed to Pete's cheek and his eyelashes a dark, thick smudge. Pete had never seen himself look so happy: giant-eyed, toothy-grinned, seeping-from-his-pores happy.

"Wow," Pete breathed. "This is wonderful."

"You like it?" Evan edged closer, craning his neck over Pete's shoulder.

"I *love* it. Although, I don't know how appropriate it is, considering what we'd just finished doing when this photo was taken."

"That's what I like best about it." Evan pecked him on the cheek. "Everyone else will look at it and think it's a normal couple photo. The truth can be our inside joke."

"You know, that's kind of perfect for us. And this is a perfect gift. What made you think of it?"

"Well . . ." For the first time since Pete met him, Evan turned pink. "I was thinking about that photo of your ex, and I thought, you know, this one could replace that one. And you could keep it on your desk instead of tucked in a drawer. That way, when you're studying or reading or whatever, I'll be right there." He cleared his throat. "Or you know, you can put it wherever you want. That's just a suggestion."

"Why, Mr. Darko, I do believe you're flustered."

Evan pouted. "No, I'm not."

"No?"

". . . Maybe a little."

Pete set the picture down, took Evan's face in both of his hands, and kissed him. "I love you."

Evan's pout instantly became a smile. "Yeah?"

"Yeah."

"I love you too. Have for a long time."

Pete slipped his fingers into the hair on the nape Evan's neck. "You know, I think your hair was the first thing about you that I loved."

"That's funny, because I remember very distinctly the first time I looked into your eyes and thought, 'Damn, I want to get to know this guy.'"

"And *I* have a similar memory of seeing your eyes in morning light for the first time."

"I don't want to alarm you," Evan said, edging closer and lowering his voice, "but judging by this conversation, I think there's a chance that we are *really* gay for each other."

Pete burst out laughing. Evan threw an arm around his shoulders and laughed with him until they were both shaking. The others looked over at them, smiling even though they had no idea what was so funny. Pete wasn't even embarrassed. Happiness like this was bound to be contagious.

"So," Evan said when they'd both recovered, "we have an official couple photo, and I've met your mom, and your friends. That pretty much fulfills the traditional aspects of the relationship you said we were missing."

"Screw tradition," Pete said vehemently. "Let's do this all out of order. Backward and upside down and in whatever way we want. As long as we're doing it together. Right, Evan Darko?"

A smile swept over Evan's handsome face, and Pete thought that he'd never seen anything so beautiful. "It would be my pleasure, Pete Griflow."

Explore more of the *Murmur Inc.* universe at:
www.riptidepublishing.com/titles/universe/murmur-inc

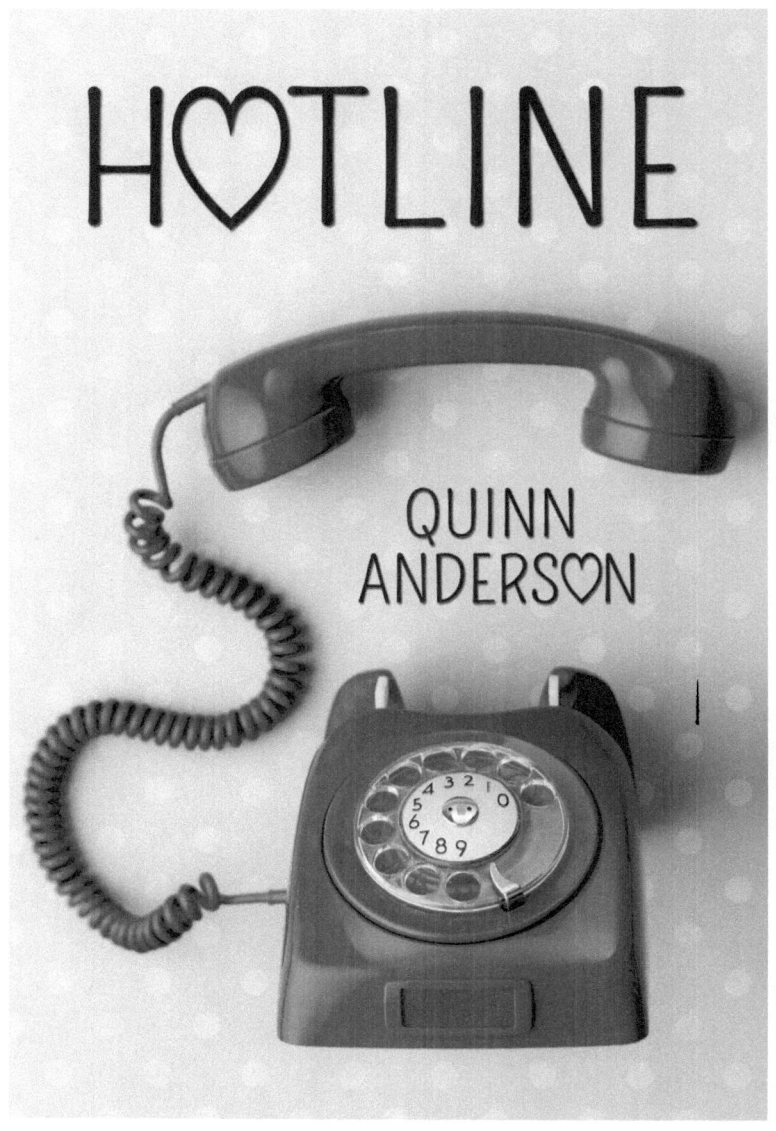

Dear Reader,

Thank you for reading Quinn Anderson's *Action*!

We know your time is precious and you have many, many entertainment options, so it means a lot that you've chosen to spend your time reading. We really hope you enjoyed it.

We'd be honored if you'd consider posting a review—good or bad—on sites like **Amazon, Barnes & Noble, Kobo, Goodreads, Twitter, Facebook, Tumblr,** and your blog or website. We'd also be honored if you told your friends and family about this book. Word of mouth is a book's lifeblood!

For more information on upcoming releases, author interviews, blog tours, contests, giveaways, and more, please sign up for our weekly, spam-free newsletter and visit us around the web:

    Newsletter: tinyurl.com/RiptideSignup
    Twitter: twitter.com/RiptideBooks
    Facebook: facebook.com/RiptidePublishing
    Goodreads: tinyurl.com/RiptideOnGoodreads
    Tumblr: riptidepublishing.tumblr.com

Thank you so much for Reading the Rainbow!

RiptidePublishing.com

ALSO BY QUINN ANDERSON

In Excess

Murmur Inc. series
Hotline

THE AUTHOR

Quinn Anderson is an alumna of the University of Dublin in Ireland and has a master's degree in psychology. She wrote her dissertation on sexuality in popular literature and continues to explore evolving themes in erotica in her professional life.

A nerd extraordinaire, she was raised on an unhealthy diet of video games, anime, pop culture, and comics from infancy. She stays true to her nerd roots in writing and in life, and frequently draws inspiration from her many fandoms, which include *Sherlock*, Harry Potter, *Supernatural, Lord of the Rings*, Star Wars, *Buffy*, Marvel, and more. You will often find her interacting with fellow fans online and offline via conventions and Tumblr, and she is happy to talk about anything from nerd life to writing tips. She has attended conventions on three separate continents and now considers herself a career geek. She advises anyone who attends pop culture events in the UK to watch out for Weeping Angels, as they are everywhere.

Her favorite television show is *Avatar: the Last Airbender*, her favorite film is *Tangled*, and her favorite book is *Ella Enchanted*. She can often be spotted at conventions, comic shops, and midnight book releases. If you're at an event, and you see a 6'2" redhead wandering around with a vague look on her face, that's probably her. Her favorite authors include J.K. Rowling, Gail Carson Levine, Libba Bray, and Tamora Pierce. When she's not writing, she enjoys traveling, cooking, spending too much time on the internet, screwing the rules, finding the Master Sword, guided falling, consulting for the NYPD, guarding the galaxy, boldly going, and catching 'em all.

Facebook: facebook.com/AuthorQuinnAnderson

Tumblr: quinnandersonwrites.tumblr.com

Email: quinnandersonwrites@gmail.com

Enjoy more stories like
Action
at RiptidePublishing.com!

Apple Polisher
ISBN: 978-1-62649-035-2

Dead Ringer
ISBN: 978-1-62649-338-4

Earn Bonus Bucks!

Earn 1 Bonus Buck for each dollar you spend. Find out how at
RiptidePublishing.com/news/bonus-bucks.

Win Free Ebooks for a Year!

Pre-order coming soon titles directly through our site and you'll
receive one entry into a drawing for a chance to win free books for
a year! Get the details at RiptidePublishing.com/contests.

www.ingramcontent.com/pod-product-compliance
Lightning Source LLC
Chambersburg PA
CBHW030646020726
47493CB00006B/1899